The End of Innocence

The End of Innocence

MONI MOHSIN

PENGUIN
FIG TREE

FIG TREE

Published by the Penguin Group
Penguin Books Ltd, 80 Strand, London WC2R ORL, England
Penguin Group (USA) Inc., 375 Hudson Street, New York, New York 10014, USA
Penguin Group (Canada), 90 Eglinton Avenue East, Suite 700, Toronto, Ontario, Canada M4P 2Y3
(a division of Pearson Penguin Canada Inc.)
Penguin Ireland, 25 St Stephen's Green, Dublin 2, Ireland (a division of Penguin Books Ltd)
Penguin Group (Australia), 250 Camberwell Road,
Camberwell, Victoria 3124, Australia (a division of Pearson Australia Group Pty Ltd)
Penguin Books India Pvt Ltd, 11 Community Centre,
Panchsheel Park, New Delhi – 110 017, India
Penguin Group (NZ), cnr Airborne and Rosedale Roads, Albany,
Auckland 1310, New Zealand (a division of Pearson New Zealand Ltd)
Penguin Books (South Africa) (Pty) Ltd, 24 Sturdee Avenue,
Rosebank, Johannesburg 2196, South Africa

Penguin Books Ltd, Registered Offices: 80 Strand, London WC2R ORL, England

www.penguin.com

First published 2006
1

Copyright © Moni Mohsin, 2006

The moral right of the author has been asserted

Set in 12/14.75 pt Monotype Dante
Typeset by Rowland Phototypesetting Ltd, Bury St Edmunds, Suffolk
Printed in Great Britain by Clays Ltd, St Ives plc

A CIP catalogue record for this book is available from the British Library

HARDBACK
ISBN-13: 978–0–670–91626–9
ISBN-10: 0–670–91626–9

TRADE PAPERBACK
ISBN-13: 978–1–905–49011–0
ISBN-10: 1–905–49011–9

For Mian and Bibi

Ik roi si dhi Punjab di, tu likh likh maaray vaen
Uj lakhaan dhiyaan rondiaan, kiss Varis Shah noon kaen?

Once a daughter of the Punjab did weep, and you poured out
    songs of lamentation
Today a thousand daughters weep, oh Varis, but who is there
    to listen?

Amrita Pritam (1947)

Prologue

Lahore. New Year's Eve, 2001

The first bar of Gloria Gaynor's 'I Will Survive' ripples through the marquee and everyone at my table abandons the cardamom ice cream and surges on to the dance floor. I, too, down my spoon and allow myself to be dragged to it by my elder sister, Sara. The floor is thronged with the well-heeled, well-soused members of the Imperial Club. But, to me, there seems a frantic edge to their merriment, as if they were all doing their utmost to forget what lurks outside.

Sara has grabbed her jovial husband and plunged into the crowd. She is now lost to me. The air is thick with the fumes of cigar smoke, Gucci's Envy and sweat. Music pounds from four speakers placed at each corner of the floor. I catch a brief glimpse of Sara's flushed, laughing face. She is watching me over her husband's shoulder. I see the familiar concern hovering behind the smile. I grin back dutifully. When she disappears from view again, I slip away. Just as I reach my empty table, I feel a tap on my shoulder. I turn around and groan inwardly. It's an aunt, an inveterate matchmaker, to whom I – unmarried at thirty-eight – am a personal affront. As usual, she has a single man in tow.

'Darling, I'd like you to meet Asif Khan.' She leans towards me with the pretext of smoothing my hair behind my ear, and hisses, 'His father is Climax Concrete. He's the only son!'

She flashes me a tight smile and bustles off, her velvet-upholstered buttocks gambolling behind her like a pair of playful puppies.

'Hiya!' bellows my suitor. I grimace as a spiral of smoke from his Marlboro drifts under my nose.

'Oh, you don't like smoke?' He exhales over his other shoulder, away from me. 'When I was at college in Illinois I once roomed with a guy who was allergic to cigarette smoke. But you know what I told him? I said, "Man, you gotta . . ."'

While he drones on about his allergic roommate, I watch a group standing not far from me. The men are encased in Italian wool suits. They talk in strident voices of 'profit margins' and 'bottom lines'. Their women pat their lacquered hair and murmur about all the other parties at which they will simply *have* to show their faces before the night ends. In the background, the dancers heave like the sea. A scantily clad model sways by the edge of the floor. A small appreciative crowd has gathered around her and is clapping and whistling her on. Two white-coated, turbaned bearers watch with expressionless faces.

I pluck at my suitor's sleeve, interrupting his monologue.

'Listen, I'm sure you're a very nice man, but if you'll excuse me . . .' I grab my shawl and hurry towards the exit, leaving the heir apparent to Climax Concrete staring after me. I steal a glance over my shoulder at my parents' table at the far end of the marquee. My mother, elegant in a midnight-blue sari, is deep in conversation with an old friend. My silver-haired father stares at the ceiling. I walk out.

My face tingles in the cold night air. Before me looms the Club building. I have spent many happy days here as a child, wolfing chicken cutlets and banana splits on the long terrace at the back. By the parking lot I see the glow of an electric fire. A crescent of shivering drivers huddles around it. Many of them will wait there till dawn.

I turn towards the dim garden. My high heels sink into the grass. As I walk, the noise from the marquee recedes. Goose bumps prickle my arms. I pull my shawl closer and look up at a granite sky. It is as dark as my past.

A loud whoop from the marquee reaches me across the silent garden. There is the sound of cheering and clapping. But it does not lure me back. For the truth is that I am no longer at ease in these cheerful, boisterous gatherings. I am far happier in my quiet office with my biddable computer for company.

Sensing someone close behind me, I swivel around. It is my father. The grass has muffled his approach.

'Sorry, I didn't mean to startle you. Mind if I join you?'

'Not at all.'

We stroll in silence. Presently, we reach a wrought-iron gate, now locked against possible gatecrashers. The security guards carry Kalashnikovs.

Through the elaborate metal curls of the gate, we have a clear view of the street. One moment the road is empty, and the next it's full of open army trucks. Filled with rows of greatcoated soldiers seated facing each other, the trucks roll past, one after another, on their way to the border. The soldiers hold their guns propped upright between their legs, their faces blank beneath their helmets. Their bayonets glint in the street lights. At last the convoy ends, and the street falls silent again.

'How long before India invades us?' I ask my father.

'There isn't going to be a war.'

'That's what you said the last time also.'

'Yes,' he sighs. 'I was wrong in '71. Do you remember that war, Laila? You were only a child then. I expect you've forgotten.'

No, I haven't forgotten that war. I remember everything. And everybody.

I

October 1971

Perched on the edge of a car seat, Rani and Laila hurtled towards a love story. Or as close to hurtling as anyone had come in Sardar Begum's ancient Lincoln. Sardar Begum sat in her habitual seat in the front, her beady eyes fixed on the speedometer, lest, in a fit of dementia, her geriatric driver should exceed her oft-repeated injunction of thirty miles an hour. A white muslin dupatta was lashed around her head, and her dove-grey kurta was buttoned up to the throat. Sardar Begum had not worn bright colours since her husband's 'departure' thirty odd years ago. The white muslin, in particular, was the flag of her widowhood. As always, her meaty hands gripped the sides of the seat, as if expecting any second to be catapulted from it.

Behind her sat Kaneez, her elderly maid. She was hunched over a thermos flask containing her mistress's afternoon tea. Her shawl was pulled low over her wrinkled forehead to conceal her disapproval. She scowled at her granddaughter, Rani, sitting by her. Straight and radiant as a sunflower in her yellow shalwar kameez, the fifteen-year-old was impervious to her grandmother's displeasure. Her honey-coloured eyes were alight with the excitement of her first visit to the cinema. Laila, Sardar Begum's eight-year-old granddaughter, bounced beside Rani. Spruce in a smocked dress and patent-leather shoes, she was flushed with her success at pulling off this improbable outing.

Of all the people in the car, Bua, Laila's middle-aged ayah, was the most relaxed. She lounged beside Laila, her fingers laced over her ample stomach, humming a tune from the recently released film, *Heer Ranjha*. The silver cross at her neck glittered in the afternoon sun, and the breeze from the window tugged at the handkerchief pinned to her chest. She was looking forward to watching a film and having a good weep. It cleared the head and lightened the heart, she believed. And *Heer Ranjha* was the biggest weepie of them all. 'Their love conquered everything but their fate,' she had sighed when relating the famous legend of the star-crossed lovers to Laila. Bua patted her handkerchief. It would come in useful at the cinema.

But Kaneez knew in her bones and blood that this trip to the cinema did not augur well. 'The cinema is no place for good girls,' she muttered.

Sardar Begum had made the announcement that had led to this unusual journey the week before. Laila was over for lunch at her grandmother's house in the village of Kalanpur. They were seated on Sardar Begum's daybed, in the courtyard under a shady neem tree. The daybed was a beautiful object, carved with peacocks and inlaid with mother-of-pearl. It was part of the elaborate dowry Sardar Begum had brought with her when she had come to this haveli as a bride over four decades ago. The haveli had been built by her late husband's forefathers and had wide verandas, high-ceilinged rooms and walls three feet thick. It was not an elegant abode, nor was it, with its unreliable plumbing and gloomy interior, a comfortable one, but it had a certain solidity, a presence as uncompromising as its current mistress, who was now trundling towards the washbasin.

They had just finished a lunch of ghee-soaked parathas and partridge curry. The servants had cleared away the detritus of the meal. Laila watched her grandmother wash her hands in the china basin over which Rani poured warm water from a jug. Rani was not Sardar Begum's servant, she was her servant's granddaughter, but she was expected to pitch in whenever she was summoned, cheerfully disregarding the fact that she was not paid.

While soaping her hands, Sardar Begum mentioned casually that the new Deputy Commissioner of Colewallah district had invited her and any guests of her choosing to a screening of *Heer Ranjha* at Colewallah town's cinema. But she had, she said, already declined the invitation. She had sent a note to the Commissioner thanking him for his kind remembrance of an old lady. The note had informed him, however, that being sixty-two years old, she was no longer of an age where such worldly diversions held any attraction for her, particularly at venues frequented by the sort of people of whose company her late, revered husband would not have approved.

Sardar Begum whooshed a handful of water around her mouth and spat it out in the basin.

'Humph! As if I'd sit alongside cobblers, truck drivers and barbers. My shoe even wouldn't grace them with its presence!' She dried her hands on the towel hanging off Rani's forearm. 'Koonj,' she ordered, 'throw away this water and fetch my digestive salts.'

Though Sardar Begum seldom wasted endearments on servants, she called Rani 'Koonj', the crane, in acknowledgement of her long neck and elegant gait. But Rani appeared not to have heard Sardar Begum's instructions. She stood with the empty jug dangling in one hand and the towel in the other, looking stricken.

Making her way back to the bed, Sardar Begum kicked off her shoes. She tucked a cushion under her neck and lay down on her side on the daybed. Her flabby stomach flopped beside her like a beanbag. She sucked on her teeth impatiently.

'Didn't you hear what I said, girl?' she snapped. 'Get my

salts and some toothpicks also.' Coming to with a start, Rani lifted the china basin and tottered off.

'Now, my dove, have you eaten enough?' Sardar Begum gazed with some concern at her granddaughter's skinny arms and knobbly knees. Never a plump child, Laila seemed particularly frail after her recent attack of typhoid. Her mother was obviously not feeding her enough.

Sardar Begum seldom agreed with her daughter-in-law, Fareeda. Hailing from the city, Fareeda was prone to some very odd notions. She had elected, for instance, to send her girls to a convent school run by Irish nuns in Lahore. It was a choice of which Sardar Begum disapproved heartily. She was also sceptical of her granddaughters' living arrangements. During termtime, the girls lived with Fareeda's widowed mother in Lahore, a big bustling city some seventy miles to the west, where no doubt they were being infected with all manner of sinful things like dance and boys. The rest of the year they spent with their parents at their home in the village of Sabzbagh, five miles from Sardar Begum's home.

Whatever their differences, Sardar Begum concurred wholeheartedly with Fareeda's decision to pluck Laila from school and bring her home to Sabzbagh, with its clean air and wholesome food, to nurse her back to health. She only wished she'd bring Laila's elder sister, Sara, too. What need had they of exams and books? It was hardly as if they would be required to earn a living, Allah forbid.

'One chapatti is not enough for a growing girl.' Sardar Begum stroked Laila's cheek. 'You should be eating three or four. When I was your age I could eat a whole lamb. You should eat properly now that you are here. None of those factory eggs and watery milk that you are fed in Lahore.'

Laila listened absently while she watched Rani empty the basin in a drain. Attuned to every gesture and expression of the older girl, Laila wondered why she had looked so put out just then. Why, only a moment before, she had winked at Laila when Sardar Begum had produced one of her thunderous postprandial belches. When Rani returned with the bottle of salts and toothpicks, she signalled to Laila to follow her into the haveli.

'Dadi, I need to do bathroom.' Laila slid off the bed and followed Rani into the house.

Her eyes shut to savour the exquisite pleasure of excavating her molars, Sardar Begum grunted in assent. As soon as Laila stepped into Sardar Begum's chilly room, Rani grabbed her wrist.

'She mustn't refuse,' she whispered urgently. 'Please, tell her she must go and take her with us. Only you can make her change her mind.' Her arrow-straight eyebrows drew together in an anxious line.

'Make her change her mind about what?' blinked Laila.

'The film. *Heer Ranjha*. I really, really want to see it. Everyone says it's the best, with such sad songs and the prettiest Heer ever. Everyone from Kalanpur has been to see it in the new cinema. The cinema, they say, is so big, with hundreds of seats, and so many lights that it is like a night sky thick with stars. Please. I've never been, and if we don't go now, I never will.'

'You want to go to the cinema?' Laila queried.

Rani nodded.

'Then why don't you?'

'You *know* my grandmother won't let me,' cried Rani. 'She thinks the cinema is a lewd place. I've never been, Laila,' she pleaded. 'This is my only chance. If *your* grandmother said she was taking us, *my* grandmother wouldn't dare object.'

Laila knew that Rani didn't have much fun living alone with the dour Kaneez. Rani's mother, Fatima, had remarried after Rani's father's death and lived in another village with her new husband. Kaneez kept Rani on a tight leash in Kalanpur, refusing to let her go to the bazaar on her own or even to visit her own mother. Laila knew how frustrating it was to be shadowed. Bua, her ayah, was her constant chaperone. Even in Lahore, where people were more modern, her other grandmother insisted that Bua accompany Laila to the birthday parties of her school friends.

But, unlike Rani, who never went anywhere, Laila went to plenty of birthday parties. *And* she got to see films. She and Sara had seen lots of films in Lahore – *The Swiss Family Robinson, Sinbad's Golden Voyage, King Kong, My Fair Lady*. They were familiar with all the cinemas where English 'family films' were shown. Her favourites were the Crown, which had a big golden crown poised on the roof like a hovering spaceship, and the candy-pink Plaza. Laila had never been to a cinema with an Urdu name. She'd heard of Naz and Sanobar, but they were in the part of town the girls did not frequent. And, anyway, those cinemas only screened Urdu and Punjabi films of which Fareeda did not approve. ('Too many vulgar dances with heaving, panting heroines. No thank you!')

'You want me to tell my grandmother that I want to see *Heer Ranjha* so she will take us all then?' asked Laila.

'Yes. Yes, please.'

'But I don't see Urdu films. Ammi says they're not good for me.'

'*Heer Ranjha* is not an Urdu film,' protested Rani. 'It is Punjabi, and it's very, very nice. You can ask anyone. It's got Ijaz and Firdaus in it. And Ijaz is married to that famous singer who has a big house in the best bit of Lahore, where your Lahore grandmother lives also? He's not like the other heroes who can only grunt and go dishum dishum.' Rani pretended to throw a punch. 'He speaks English and wears jacket suits.'

'How do you know all this?'

'I overheard our neighbours talking. Please, Laila, please. Can we go? Just this once. I want to see for myself.'

Laila thought about the twilit world of the cinema: the dark, tiered hall, the leatherette seats that snapped shut with a thwack and the red velvet curtains which rose in tasselled scallops to reveal a screen as big as a swimming pool standing on its side. And the drinks-sellers with wooden crates hoisted on their shoulders who ran the metal bottle-opener along the ridged Fanta bottle just as you passed them. And the special smell of the cinema – a pungent cocktail of packed bodies, cigarette smoke and fried food. How could she let Rani miss all that?

There was little that Laila would not do for Rani. For Laila, Rani had no equal. Rani alone had the unique ability to make the everyday wondrous and the dull delightful. Unlike Laila, she was not good at her studies. She was in school at Laila's father, Tariq's, insistence, and each year she barely managed to pass into the next class. But Rani was clever in ways that Laila envied. She knew how to mend a parrot's broken wing and get a wild squirrel to eat off her hand. Rani could cut carrots to look like flowers. She could do cartwheels, climb to the top of the tallest tree and weave stories of flying horses, talking snakes and princesses who led armies and fought like tigresses. And there was her talent for mimicry. She could imitate Bua's waddle, Kaneez's toothless mumble and Sardar Begum's characteristic scowls and salty streams of abuse till Laila and Sara were convulsed with laughter.

Rani could, however, be whimsical. Whereas Laila would opt for Rani's company over almost anyone else's every time, Rani was less constant in her affiliation when it came to choosing between the two sisters. When they planned great adventures and the twelve-year-old Sara wanted Laila left out of the game ('Oh, she's useless, she can't even remember the rules'), Rani stood up for her. But there were times when Sara and Rani would go off arm in arm to whisper about 'grown-up things', and when Laila tried to follow they would giggle and run away. When that happened, Laila felt the misery of exclusion as a physical pain, like shards of glass wedged in her throat.

Now, with Sara at school, Laila had unrivalled access to Rani. In fact, so constant had been Rani's attention that Laila had begun to hope, albeit tentatively, that Rani regarded her as a friend now and not an acolyte, whom she could indulge or ignore. But Laila knew that her time alone with Rani was limited. Soon the winter holidays would start and Sara would be back in Sabzbagh, demanding and claiming everyone's attention. But if Laila could pull off this visit to the cinema, it would cement her relationship with Rani and place it, once and for all, beyond Sara's reach.

'We'll go,' Laila said. 'I'll make Dadi take us.'

But convincing Sardar Begum was not easy. Having already declined the invitation, how could she now humble herself by retracting? She, Sardar Begum, who had never, ever eaten her words? The DC would think she was a senile fool. No, she couldn't bear the thought. Yet how could she refuse her granddaughter, so thin, so wan, so keen?

Her dilemma was resolved by the DC himself, who sent another letter apologizing for any misunderstanding. It had never been his intention to invite a personage as august as Sardar Begum to a public venue when thronged by the hoi polloi. Had he not mentioned that the Rubina Cinema would be closed for that particular show to all except a few hand-picked ladies from the military cantonment and, much more importantly, Sardar Begum and her companions? As for the film itself, while fully appreciating Sardar Begum's concerns – one could not be too careful in these louche times – he could recommend it unreservedly. Otherwise, he would never have suggested it to the widow of a man he still held in the highest esteem and the greatest regard. He had taken his own good wife and two teenage daughters to see it and had not suffered a moment's regret. Indeed, had the film not been so sad, he could have said that a most enjoyable time was had by all. It would therefore afford him deep gratification if Sardar Begum would graciously reconsider her decision.

Sardar Begum smirked when she received the DC's letter. So great was her triumph that she had herself driven the five miles to her son's home in Sabzbagh.

Unlike many of the villages in the district, Sabzbagh had a prosperous, well-fed look about it. There were no stagnant pools of water, no piles of rubbish putrefying in the sun, no gaggles of half-naked, malnourished children loitering about. The houses looked sturdy, the small, well-stocked bazaar was busy and the pathways clean. Sardar Begum's face darkened as the car passed the double-storeyed garment factory her son had built in the village. 'Stupid,' she muttered under her breath, 'stupid nonsense. Waste of money.' She glared at a woman entering its gate. Winding down her glass window, she bellowed: 'Haven't you got enough to do in your own home?' Sardar Begum smiled contentedly as she noted the woman's startled expression. But the smug smile quickly changed to a disapproving frown as the car sailed past a neat, fenced compound housing a church and school. 'Heathens. Pig-eaters.'

The car swept past the village and up the tree-lined drive to Tariq's bungalow. Built in the heyday of the Raj, the house was of weathered brick, draped with deep-pink bougainvillea. The doors and windows looked freshly painted, and the smooth lawn in front of the house was emerald green. The large garden was studded with stately trees – peepul, silk-cotton, laburnum, jacaranda – and boasted wide beds of roses, stocks, gladioli and irises. Unlike Sardar Begum's austere home, where the curtains had not been changed for twenty-five years, Tariq's house was full of soft rugs, pretty drapes and flowers in sparkling vases, courtesy of the elegant, spend-thrift Fareeda. But as far as Sardar Begum was concerned, expenditure on comfort was a waste of money. Had Tariq listened to her and married a solid girl from a solid land-owning family, he'd have cash under the mattress instead of shameless paintings of half-dressed women on the walls.

She found Tariq sitting in the garden immersed in the *Pakistan Times*. On a table at his elbow sat a silver tray with a bowl of nuts and a glass of freshly squeezed orange juice. Sardar Begum noted with disapproval that the nuts were shelled, salted peanuts, twice as costly as peanuts roasted in their shells. She was about to make a disparaging comment when she saw the anxiety in his face.

'Do the papers say if we're going to war?' she asked instead.

'No, they don't. Not yet, anyway,' he replied, folding the papers.

Sardar Begum sighed. 'After '65 I thought there were going to be no more wars with India. But we're going to fight again, aren't we? Except this time, it won't be over Kashmir. It will be over East Pakistan.' Then, remembering why she was there, she fished out the DC's letter from her handbag and thrust it at him.

'See how much they still respect me?' she taunted. 'You may want to shut me up in my haveli, but people – and people who are running things, not just sitters-around – want me among them.'

'Who says I want to cloister you?' laughed Tariq. Unlike his compact, stout mother, Tariq was a tall man, with a lean build. In his late thirties, he had retained his trim physique through horse-riding and tennis. 'I'd be delighted if you went to the cinema instead of sitting at home poring over your dreary ledgers.'

'You speak as if I want to go for myself,' she sniffed.

'Don't tell me you're doing it for the DC?'

'Of course not,' growled Sardar Begum. 'I'm doing it for my granddaughter. *She's* the one who's been badgering me.'

'I wouldn't have thought it was Laila's type of thing. *Heer Ranjha*, eh? Since when has she been so interested in romantic folk-tales? But of course she can go.'

'You'd better check with your wife first, lest she objects later. Where is she, by the way?'

'She's gone to Lahore for the day. To see Sara.'

If Fareeda disapproved of Sardar Begum's choice of film, it was not conveyed to Sardar Begum. She was merely told that Laila would accompany her to the film and, should Bua's services be required, she was available.

'Yes, I suppose she'd better come along, heathen though she is,' said Sardar Begum. 'I'll need someone to carry my tea thermos and handbag.'

The following afternoon, Sardar Begum awaited her grand-daughter's arrival in the haveli. She sat on her daybed, ramrod straight, her hands resting on her elderly leather handbag. Except for three parallel lines on her forehead, her pale skin was butter-smooth. From her ears dangled her customary gold hoops, which, over the years, had elongated her lobes into pendulous pink sacks. Her hair – the colour of carrot halwa, thanks to monthly applications of henna – snaked down her back in a thin plait. In her youth, Sardar Begum's thick hair had been a lustrous black – 'long enough to sit on'. But, in its natural state, it was now sugar-white. Sardar Begum felt that the colour aged her. Hence the henna.

Kaneez stood by Sardar Begum, holding her thermos flask. Years of arthritis had curved her spine into a sickle. Rani, nervy and fidgety, watched the door as an angler watches his line. They did not have long to wait. A few minutes later, Laila bounded into the courtyard, with Bua following close behind. But when Sardar Begum rose to leave, Laila dropped her bombshell.

'I won't go without Rani.' She lifted her chin challengingly at her grandmother.

Sardar Begum was tempted to call Laila's bluff. But she was looking forward to the film herself and didn't want to ruin the mood by arguing. With a grimace, she flicked her fingers at Rani.

'Koonj, didn't you hear what Laila Bibi said? Hurry up and get ready. You're coming with us.'

Rani raced out of the courtyard, slamming the heavy door behind her.

Kaneez recoiled as if she had been struck. 'No, no,' she quavered. 'She can't go to the cinema. She's never been.'

'So?'

'The cinema is not a good place. She'll be corrupted.'

'She'll be corrupted while in *my* care? Have you lost your mind?' barked Sardar Begum.

Kaneez looked away, her toothless mouth slack.

'All right, all right. If you're that concerned, you shrivelled old misery, you'd better come along to guard her yourself,' said Sardar Begum.

Moments later, Rani burst into the courtyard, flushed and breathless, a sunbeam in her cheap yellow cotton. Kaneez pulled her shawl over her head and muttered that she was ready.

The Lincoln bowled along under an azure sky towards Colewallah town. On either side of the road lay fields of sugar cane and groves of oranges and guavas. Tractors laden with harvested cane plied the road. The air smelt of petrol, dust and rotting fruit.

Colewallah was a small market town, twelve miles from Kalanpur. It was a new settlement, having sprung up only fifty years previously around a train station built by the British on the Lahore–Karachi railway line. It now boasted a hospital, a cattle market, a bustling bazaar, a college and, at a discreet distance of three miles, a small military cantonment. It had, however, little to offer its citizens by way of entertainment. Until a fortnight ago, that was, when Rubina Cinema had thrown open its portals with much fanfare to Colewallah's grateful populace.

Laila was disappointed by her first glimpse of Rubina. An unimpressive concrete box, it had none of the ornamental flourishes of a Plaza or a Crown. Nor did it have a single hand-painted cutout of a film star, which adorned the façades of Lahori cinemas. Laila looked in vain for a billboard. All she saw was a modest Urdu sign proclaiming the cinema's name. There were no food-vendors, no rows of parked cars in the forecourt, no ranks of bicycles, no queues of jostling, staring men by the two-rupee ticket booth, past which middle-class mothers had to hurry their daughters. Save for a mangy dog lying on its side, the forecourt was deserted. It didn't look like a cinema at all.

The manager met them at the entrance. He was a rotund man with a handlebar moustache and was flanked by two flunkeys. Primed by the Deputy Commissioner, he was all bows and smiles. He addressed them in English, which he felt befitted the majesty of his guests.

'Wel-you-come,' he beamed, leading them up some stairs. 'This way, please. Straight away to the top.' He showed them into the main hall. It was vacant. 'Where would you like to sit?' he asked, switching to Urdu, now that he had exhausted his limited knowledge of English. 'You can choose anywhere, you know.' He waved at the empty rows.

'I know.' Sardar Begum stabbed him with a Look. She couldn't bear people rising above themselves. 'We'll sit there.'

Single file, they made their way to her chosen row. Their footsteps echoed on the uncarpeted floor. One of the under-lings darted in before them and gave a quick wipe to the first five seats with a duster. Sardar Begum signalled to Kaneez to go first. Kaneez gripped Rani's hand and pulled her along behind her. Laila made to follow, but Sardar Begum restrained her.

'No,' she pronounced. 'Bua will sit by Rani. We will sit in the row above the servants.'

But Laila wriggled free and, ignoring her grandmother's flared nostrils, dived in after Rani. Ensconced beside her friend, Laila smiled winningly at Sardar Begum.

'Please sit with me, Dadi.' Laila patted the seat beside her.

Sardar Begum complied, albeit with a scowl. When Bua lowered herself gingerly into the seat next to hers, Sardar Begum's mouth tightened, but she did not comment.

But Laila was too busy drinking in her surroundings to attend to her grandmother's discomfiture. The hall was small – smaller than her auditorium at school. The lights were bare bulbs screwed into the walls. There were no frescoes, no plaster rosettes, no cornices. Not even curtains to cover the naked screen. And it smelt of just-dried limewash. With a scornful smile, she turned to Rani to express her disdain. But before she could do so, Rani said, 'Isn't this wonderful? Look at all those lights. It's like a mela, a fairground.'

Laila stared at her in disbelief.

'And see how high it is.' Rani gazed up. 'I've never seen a roof this high before.'

Laila reluctantly conceded that the ceiling was indeed high.

'That white wall in front? What's that?'

'That's the screen where the film will be shown,' Laila replied.

'Heer and Ranjha will dance in front of it?'

'No. They'll be inside.'

'You mean, they will part it like a curtain and step inside?'

'Not exactly.' Laila did not understand the mysteries of projection in enough detail to attempt an explanation. 'Just wait and see.'

Just then, they heard voices. The manager hurried to the

door. Amid the sound of laughter and the tick-tick of high heels, four ladies dressed in flowered shalwar kameezes, sporting identical beehive hairdos and carrying bright handbags in the crooks of their arms entered the hall. Standing out like peacocks in a chicken coop, they looked around with bright-eyed curiosity. Their gaze alighted on Sardar Begum's group. They nodded politely at Sardar Begum and allowed the patron to bow them to their seats.

Sardar Begum did not acknowledge the greeting. 'Upstarters,' she muttered. 'Army wives, no doubt. Have we been kept waiting for *them?*'

'Don't they look lovely?' Rani whispered to Laila. 'Look at their hair. How do they get it to stand on top of their heads like that?'

The ladies' teased hair reminded Laila of her least favourite schoolteacher's hairstyle, which looked like a gleaming black helmet. Suddenly, the light bulbs were switched off with a loud *chock*, plunging the hall into darkness. Almost immediately, the credits began rolling across the screen. Laila settled back to watch.

She was familiar with the legend of Heer and Ranjha. Songs about the star-crossed lovers were played on the radio, and there was a long Punjabi poem about Heer, from which Sardar Begum would sometimes quote when in a mellow mood. But it had been only the evening before that Laila had heard the story in its entirety. Snug under her satin quilt, her head resting on a pillow stuffed with the silk cotton from her father's tree, she had listened to Bua's version of the ancient story.

'Heer was the most beautiful girl in all of Punjab. She belonged to the clans of the Sials. Very wealthy they were, with lots of land and big herds of cattle. And very proud also. Ranjha was also from a good family. But he was a dreamer and spent all day playing the flute. Very handsome he was, with big, big eyes and pale skin. Good families were wanting him to marry their girls, but he was not bothered.' Bua paused to inhale a pinch of snuff.

'One day, his sister-in-law scoffed: "If you think you are so much better than anyone else, go marry Heer Sialan."' Bua snapped shut the tiny box and stuffed it into her bra. 'Now, Ranjha was lazy, but he still had a man's pride. He said, "I'll show you," and set off dressed as a shepherd, carrying only his flute. Next day he reached an orchard. He was tired, so he lay down under a tree and fell asleep.

'Now this orchard belonged to the Sials, and it wasn't long before Ranjha was found there. Someone prodded him awake with their foot, and when he opened his eyes he found himself looking up at the most beautiful girl he'd ever seen. It was Heer, who had come to her father's orchard with her friends. Of course, he fell in love, there and then. As for Heer, as soon as Ranjha opened his eyes, she drowned in them. So big they were, with long, curling lashes, and the colour of almonds.'

'Like Bambi's?'

'Whose?' Bua frowned. 'Anyway, from then on, they were inseparable. Heer would pretend she was going to see her friends, but she'd sneak out to be with the shepherd. But there was a problem. Heer was already engaged to another man, a fellow Sial. As her wedding drew near, Heer suddenly announced to her family that she did not want to marry him. Her parents were shocked. What had got into their nice, obedient girl?

'One day, Heer's wicked uncle, Kaidu – he was lame in one leg, just like Kaneez's son-in-law, Mashooq – he decided to spy on Heer to find out what she was getting up to. He followed her to the orchard and saw her embracing a shepherd. Kaidu limped back as fast as he could and told Heer's father. He was furious. Naturally. She had refused the man he had chosen for her and gone out and found someone for herself. She had flouted his authority. When Heer came home, all

Limerick
CITY & COUNTY

Cappamore Library
Borrower Receipt

Customer name: Doyle Leanne

Title: The girl with all the gifts /
ID: 30012007070286
Due: 23/07/14

Title: End of innocence /
ID: 30012005067664
Due: 23/07/14

Total items: 2
09/07/2014 17:45
Checked out: 2
Overdue: 0
Hold requests: 0
Ready for pickup: 0

Thank you for using the self service system.
Check us out online at
www.limerick.ie

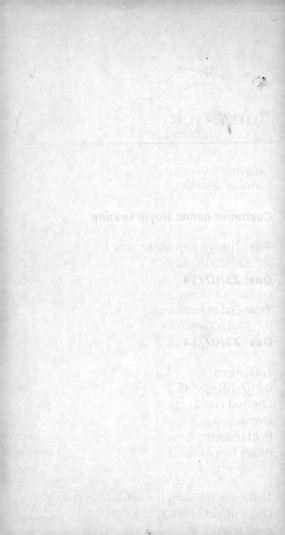

happy and giddy, he dragged her by her thick plait to her room and threw her in. "Next week you are getting married," he shouted through the locked door. Heer howled and hurled herself against the door, but no one came.

'Next day, Ranjha waited in the orchard, but when three days passed and still no Heer, he sought out her friends. "Heer?" they laughed. "Don't you know she's getting married next week? Her house is all lit up with candles, and every night there is singing and dancing." Ranjha asked whom she was marrying. Her cousin, they said, the one she'd been engaged to for years. Heer had never mentioned her engagement. So Ranjha decided he'd leave the world.'

'How? Kill himself?' asked Laila.

'No, Baba, there are other ways of leaving. He became a yogi. He gave up his home, his fine clothes, even his people. He wrapped a yellow sarong around him and wandered the world barefoot, homeless and broken. There was only one word on his lips, "Heer."'

'Did Heer marry her cousin then?'

'Marry?' Bua snorted. 'On the eve of her wedding, as the groom's party was approaching with blazing torches and prancing horses and dancing guests, Heer swallowed poison. If she couldn't marry Ranjha, she decided, she wouldn't marry at all. When they came to fetch her, she was dressed in her bridal clothes, covered in jewels and lying on her bed. She had never looked more beautiful, for her soul had gone to meet Ranjha.'

'What did her parents do?'

'Her mother cried, and her father hung his head in shame.'

'He felt guilty?'

'Oh, no, not guilty.' Bua shook her head. 'He wasn't ashamed of *his* behaviour but of hers. Good girls don't make up their own minds about whom they want to marry and who not. They have to bow to the wishes of their parents, who know best. Heer was naughty. She knew her father had promised her to his kinsman. But still she went her own way. Also, when she killed herself on the night of her wedding, it was a slap in her father's face, because with a house full of guests and each one eager to see the bride, he couldn't cover it up. So she made him lose face in front of everyone.'

'What became of Ranjha?'

'Now, I'm forgetting that bit of the story, but I think he came to Heer's house dressed as a yogi and tried to tell them that he was from good family, but would they listen? Anyway, it was too late. Heer was dead. After that, Ranjha was also heard of no more.' Bua yawned. 'So sad. You'll see for yourself when you see the film tomorrow.'

The Heer that Laila had imagined had been a slender girl, with elongated, gazelle eyes, dimples and rippling brown hair. But the Heer who appeared on the screen was a hefty woman with a thick neck and traces of a moustache. Her eyes were slathered with kohl, and crimson lipstick was smeared over her fat lips. When she ran through the orchard, she reminded Laila of a galumphing cow, her rope-like plait thudding against her bottom. Ranjha was not much better. True, he had big sleepy eyes. But his moustache drooped, and he had a double chin.

Bua hadn't said what they did when they became inseparable. Laila had not thought about it either. But, in the film, all they did was dance and sing and sigh and embrace. At the slightest excuse, they would burst into song. Heer would drape herself against a tree trunk or flop to the ground panting as if she'd done a hundred-yard sprint. Ranjha would come and loom over her with a slimy smile.

Bored, Laila looked sideways at Rani. Rani sat bolt upright, transfixed. Her hands gripped the armrests of her seat. Laila glanced at her grandmother. Sardar Begum was frowning at the screen and shaking her head slightly, like Laila sometimes did when she was watching a scary film and the heroine was about to open a door behind which lurked a terrible secret. Leaning out further, Laila saw that Bua had unpinned her handkerchief and was weeping copiously into it. Only Kaneez seemed unaffected. When Laila looked at her, she returned her gaze steadily.

The intermission was as unceremonious as the start of the film had been. All thirty of the 200-watt bulbs were switched on abruptly, almost blinding the nine occupants of the hall. The screen went white, and the door into the auditorium was flung open. The flunkeys reappeared, preceded by the manager, who sauntered in smiling like a groom at the head of a wedding party. The boys carried large trays weighed down with rattling crockery. Standing in the centre of the hall, the manager waved one boy towards Sardar Begum and the other towards the army wives. With his hands behind his back, he bowed first to Sardar Begum and then to the other party.

There was a bowl of hard-boiled eggs and a plate of Nice biscuits on Sardar Begum's tray. Spicy chickpeas were rolled up in newspaper cones. A steel teapot held milky tea. The boy was about to pour out the tea, when Sardar Begum stopped him.

'I've got my own,' she declared, holding aloft her flask. As an afterthought, she added: 'But you can give to *them* if you want.' She nodded towards her servants.

According to the rules governing Sardar Begum's household, it was not seemly for servants to eat in front of their employer. So when the tea boy handed Rani a steaming cup, she hesitated, glancing covertly at Sardar Begum. Was she meant to accept?

'Take it, Rani,' Laila urged. 'Here.' She thrust the cup into Rani's hand, spilling some tea into the saucer.

Rani sank deep into her seat before she took a sip from her tea. However, despite cajoling from Laila, she declined the food. Kaneez had nothing, not even the tea. But Bua, who was marinated in the more democratic atmosphere of Sabzbagh, readily accepted the tea and even took a biscuit. However, she took the precaution of politely turning her back on Sardar Begum before dunking her biscuit into the cup.

Sardar Begum handed an egg to Laila. 'Eat!' she ordered.

'I'd rather have the chickpeas.'

'Always eating wrong things,' complained Sardar Begum.

'Wasn't Heer horrid?' Laila asked Rani. 'So fat and old.'

'Heer?' Rani's eyebrows soared. 'She looked like a princess with her gold earrings and satin clothes. And her body was so full, so,' Rani lowered her voice, 'womanly.'

'Womanly?'

'Hmm. No wonder Ranjha fell in love with her. And as for him, if someone sang and played his flute to me as sweetly as he, I don't know *what* I'd do.'

'*Rani!*' squawked Laila. She'd expected to have a chuckle with Rani, to poke fun at that moon-eyed couple, at their quivering lips and their syrupy looks. Instead, Rani was taking their side.

'Do you know something?' Rani whispered into Laila's ear. 'The actor Ijaz, the one who is Ranjha – well, he's in love with Firdaus, the actress who is doing Heer's role. In real life. That's why they look at each other that way. Because they're not acting.'

'Who told you?'

'I know.'

'But you said he was married to the famous singer who lives near my Lahore grandmother.'

Rani glanced over her shoulder at Kaneez.

'Shh, keep your voice down,' she whispered to Laila. 'The

24

singer? He *is* married to her, but she's old, and he's in love with Firdaus. I've heard they've become like a couple.'

'That's not fair!' Laila tried to picture her father in a mango orchard, singing and dancing with a woman other than Fareeda. Actually, she couldn't even imagine him dancing with Fareeda. She pursed her lips.

'Why are you looking so cranky?' Rani nudged Laila.

'Because you're being silly. How can you be married to one person and in love with another?'

'I don't know. But people are. All the time.'

'How do *you* know all this?'

'It's something you find out when you get older.' She shrugged. 'Like I am.'

'What have you found out?' Kaneez's face appeared above Rani's shoulder. 'Tell me at once!'

'Oh, nothing, Amman.' Rani clicked her tongue in exasperation.

'Don't you click your tongue at me!' Kaneez jerked Rani's wrist. 'Just because you're at a cinema doesn't mean you can do whatever you want.'

Rani prised her wrist out of her grasp. Kaneez glared at her and withdrew into her seat.

'Why's she like that today?' Laila asked Rani.

'She's always like that,' grumbled Rani, rubbing her wrist.

'Laila baby, toilet?' Bua trilled across the seats.

The ladies with the high hairdos in the front tittered.

'I'm not a baby. If I want to go, I'll go myself,' Laila hissed back.

'No, you won't!' Sardar Begum wagged a finger at Laila. 'I won't have you running around this place by yourself.'

'I don't need to go,' Laila repeated sullenly.

'Don't frown. You'll get lines on your forehead.'

The boys cleared away the tea, and the film resumed where it had left off. If Laila had found the first half slow, the second half was interminable. Imprisoned in her house, Heer mooned about, singing mournful songs. There was a funny moment when Ranjha appeared in his saffron robes, one plump shoulder bare and a begging bowl slung around his neck. But soon even that diversion palled. Laila peered at Rani in the gloom. Tears streamed unchecked down her cheeks. Laila could hear Bua snuffling, and even Sardar Begum blew her nose twice. The backcombed ladies had been giggling in the first half. Now, they were silent. No doubt they too were weeping.

Laila tried to sympathize with the lovers, so she too could claim to have relished the film. She tried to put herself in Heer's place, to understand her distress. But it didn't seem right to kill yourself because you could no longer sing and dance with a shepherd. Laila tried to think of other sad things to make herself cry. She recalled the painful humiliation of exclusion from Rani and Sara's gossip sessions. How they turned their backs on her and dropped their voices, how they communicated with muffled laughs and twitching eyebrows, and how awful she felt. She felt a prickling sensation behind her lids and narrowed her eyes to squeeze out a tear. One slid out of her right eye just as the movie ended and the lights came on.

She turned eagerly to Rani, to exult in their shared tears. But Rani seemed sapped. When Laila pointed to her own tear, she smiled weakly. She ran her hands down her wet cheeks and pulled her dupatta over her head. With a loud sigh, Sardar Begum hoisted herself out of her seat. It was their signal to depart. At the exit, they met the women from the cantonment. Once again, they greeted Sardar Begum. To Laila's relief, this time, her grandmother acknowledged their salutation – albeit with a cool nod.

'I hope you enjoyed the film,' the manager beamed at them all. 'So sad it was.'

A cantonment lady fished out two ten-rupee notes from her orange handbag and handed them to the manager.

'Oh, please, no, no. There's no need for this.' He shook his head and took a step backwards.

'We insist.' The woman stepped forward with the money held out.

'Well, if it pleases you . . .' The manager smoothly palmed the money.

Sardar Begum immediately motioned to Kaneez to pass her her handbag. Counting out three ten-rupee notes, she held them out in a fan to the manager. He demurred again.

'It is our pleasure and you will accept.' Sardar Begum thrust the money at him and sailed out.

On the way home they were all quiet, mulling in their different ways on the film. Sardar Begum was the first to speak.

'Oh-ho, what a pity that Heer became wayward! What need had she? She had a pretty face, a good name, money, family. What a waste!'

'Waste of what?' queried Laila. Being menials, the other occupants of the car could not question Sardar Begum's opinions. Kaneez, due to her long years with Sardar Begum, could perhaps have voiced a view but, sunk in her own thoughts, she stared glassily out of her window.

'Waste of a life, what else?' replied Sardar Begum. 'She should have married her cousin, as her parents had arranged. Instead, she threw away her reputation and her life. For what?'

'For love?' Laila ventured doubtfully. That's what Bua had said, hadn't she?

'Love!' snorted Sardar Begum. 'This love-shove is also nonsense. It doesn't last two days. What lasts is duty. Obligation. Respect. Regard. I feel sorry for Heer. Don't think I have a stone for a heart. But if she had been dutiful, she wouldn't have had to poison herself. That's where love leads, see? To shame and disgrace. That's why good marriages are never built on love.'

'But my parents love each other,' protested Laila. 'Ammi told me they married because she was in love with Aba and he with her.'

'No, they didn't!' snapped Sardar Begum. 'Your Ammi married my son because she respected him. As she should. And as for Tariq,' she murmured, 'only Allah knows why he does what he does.'

'But *I* love my parents,' cried Laila. 'And Sara and Rani and Bua. There's nothing shameful in that.'

'And me?' Sardar Begum glared at Laila. 'Don't you love me?'

'Of course. But if I love you all, how can that be wrong?'

'I'm not talking about *that* love,' chuckled Sardar Begum, delighted with her granddaughter's innocence. 'That love is your duty. In the holy Koran it is written you must love your parents, your children, even your distant relatives. The love I meant is a different sort of love – the kind that Heer felt for Ranjha, the kind that tears you away from your family, that makes you forget your duty. That's a dangerous love. It's not allowed. No girl must love like that.'

'What's the point of telling them that now?' asked Kaneez. 'After you've shown them the film. It's too late.' Her words hung in the car, like a thick miasma.

Sardar Begum spun around to skewer her with a Look. But Kaneez was gazing out of the window. All she could see in the gathering darkness was her own furrowed face reflected in the glass.

2

The next day, Laila came down with fever. Fearing a relapse of typhoid, Fareeda confined her to bed. And there she stayed for five days, being fed chicken soup and medicines, until the fever subsided. It had been, it seemed, a passing cold, but Fareeda was not a woman who took such things lightly.

On the fifth day, Laila kicked aside her bed coverings. She glanced at the pile of books at her bedside. On top of the pile lay *The Castle of Adventure*. It was her favourite among Enid Blyton's books, but having read it for the third time recently, she did not pick it up. She wished Fareeda would let her get up. Far off, beyond the hedge that separated her house from the servants' quarters, she heard a dog bark.

That was another thing Fareeda wouldn't let her do – keep a dog. For years, Laila had yearned for a dog that would sleep at the foot of her bed as Timmy did with George in Enid Blyton's Famous Five series. Big and shaggy like Timmy, her dog would reach up to her waist. But while his powerful jaws and ferocious bark would terrorize strangers, he would adore her. He'd follow her everywhere and alert her to the slightest hint of danger with his protective growl. With Timmy beside her, she would be free to roam far beyond Sabzbagh, unencumbered by Bua.

'Oh, no need to worry about Laila,' her parents would say airily. 'She has Timmy to look after her.'

Together they'd have splendid adventures, eliciting high praise and heartfelt gratitude from grown-ups. They would solve mysteries, rescue people in trouble, warn unwary adults of looming danger. Laila could see herself tensed on the very edge of the huge canal that flowed past Sabzbagh, gripping one end of a rope while Timmy swam into the middle with the other end clenched between his teeth to the flailing adult floundering in the water. As soon as the drowning man got the rope in his hands, Laila would pull him in, tugging with all her might, while Timmy swam beside him, ensuring his safety.

Flopping at Laila's feet on the canal bank, the exhausted man would cough up all the water he'd swallowed. Then he'd take Laila's hand in a gesture of infinite gratitude. She'd tell nobody, but of course everyone would find out, and Timmy and she would be garlanded at a public ceremony with balloons, streamers and a loudspeaker – perhaps even a military band. There'd be a picture in the paper of the Fearless Girl Heroine and Her Courageous Dog. Sara would not feature in the picture or the accompanying article.

Laila had begged her parents repeatedly for a dog, but they always refused. It would be unfair on the dog, they said, to leave it behind for the seven months of the year she spent in Lahore attending school. 'No, darling, it would get lonely and pine.' End of discussion.

'I want to get up now,' Laila demanded, as Fareeda entered her bedroom, holding a thermometer. Fareeda's clothes were crisp, her hair glossy. As always, she reminded Laila of a freshly unwrapped mint, clean, smooth and dry. Feeling scruffy in her limp pyjamas, Laila said: 'I want to take off these silly pyjamas and go outside and play.'

'What, in your vest?' joked Fareeda, shaking the thermometer.

'You know what I mean. I'm bored of staying in bed with Bua and you fussing over me.'

'Open your mouth.' Fareeda inserted the thermometer in Laila's mouth. 'If you don't have a fever, you can get up, but no playing just yet.'

'I don't have a fever, do I?' challenged Laila, as Fareeda removed the thermometer.

Fareeda peered at the glass tube. 'Looks like it's gone.'

'See! Told you so.' Laila swung her bare feet to the floor.

'Put on your dressing gown and slippers and come out with me to the veranda.'

'And do what? Stare at the garden?'

When Laila pushed open the hallway door and stepped grudgingly on to the veranda, she whooped with joy. Perched on a stool was Rani. On seeing Fareeda, the girl jumped to her feet and raised a hand to her forehead in greeting.

'When did you come?' squealed Laila.

'Just now. Your mother sent for me in the car,' said Rani in a low, shy voice.

Fareeda rumpled Laila's hair. 'As a treat for you.'

As Fareeda turned to go, Rani lifted a basket lying by her feet and said, 'Umm, there's this. Big Begum Sahiba sent these for Laila Bibi. She said to give them to you.'

Fareeda looked inside the basket. A dozen eggs nestled on a folded towel. Suspicious that Fareeda fed her daughters on a diet of battery eggs, Sardar Begum had taken to sending them eggs from her own hens.

'Oh, desi eggs. Again!' remarked Fareeda dryly. 'Please thank Begum Sahiba for her generosity. But what's this?' Fareeda lifted out a damp handkerchief folded in on itself.

Rani reddened. 'It's something I made for Laila Bibi.'

'For me?' queried Laila. 'What is it?'

Peeling aside the damp folds of the cloth, she saw a circlet of yellow chambeli. She lifted the fragile bracelet and draped it around her wrist.

'It's lovely,' she said, inhaling the scent of the small, vivid flowers. 'Will you do it up for me?'

Rani deftly knotted the thread.

'It *is* lovely.' Fareeda raised Laila's arm and examined the bracelet. The flowers were woven together in a delicate plait. 'How did you do that? Not even the flower-sellers in Lahore can make bracelets like this.'

Rani flushed pink with pleasure. 'I don't know. I'll make one for you if you like.'

'I'd like that very much. Now I must go. But mind, no jumping about. Is that clear?'

Laila nodded and threw herself into a deckchair. She motioned to an upright chair beside her. Rani sauntered over, head erect, shoulders thrown back, her bright eyes alert. With Fareeda's departure, she changed from an awkward, tongue-tied adolescent to a poised young woman. Accustomed to Rani's shyness in front of her parents, Laila did not comment on her transformation. Rani smoothed her kameez over her thighs and sat down.

'Is this shalwar kameez new?' Laila eyed the blue tunic and matching drawstring trousers. They were made of coarse cotton, but the sky-blue complemented Rani's colouring, emphasizing the toffee tones in her hair and eyes. The cuffs and hem of her shirt were edged in white. Rani looked clean and cool.

'Want to see something special?' Rani drew aside the white shawl from her breast with a flourish. 'Tun-tana!' She stuck out her puny chest. The shirt was close fitting, and its neckline was lower than usual. Piped in white, it had a fussy scalloped pattern, like fan-shaped seashells laid side by side. 'Isn't it pretty?'

'Hmm.' Laila did not like frills and flounces and often clashed with Fareeda over the elaborate party dresses that she sometimes chose for her.

Rani draped the shawl over her front again, patting it into place. 'I asked a seamstress to copy one of Heer's kameezes from the film. Of course, hers was satin, but I like this. It makes me look like a girl, doesn't it? Not like those sack-like things my grandmother makes for me, like an old crone's.'

Rani hunched her back, folded her lips over her teeth and, with her neck stretched out like a tortoise, hobbled around Laila's chair. Laila laughed, delighted with Rani's imitation of Kaneez.

'And now this!' Rani announced. Pushing her shawl back to reveal her slender form, she pulled her shirt tight against her middle and thrust out one hip in a provocative pose. She threw Laila a simmering look over her shoulder. Laila pursed her mouth, unsure who Rani was mimicking now.

'Who's that supposed to be?' she asked. The pose was alien yet unsettlingly familiar. She had seen it struck before, but never by Rani.

'Guess,' Rani purred, wetting her lips.

'I can't.' Laila scowled. Rani looked grown-up. In a strange, alarming kind of way.

'Me,' Rani pouted, caressing her cocked hip with one hand while twirling a lock of hair with the other. 'I'm just being me.'

'No, you're not,' Laila snapped, piqued. 'You don't stand like that or do those stupid things with your lips. You look silly. Stop it!'

Rani's face fell. She swaddled herself in her shawl and sat down. 'I was trying to look like Heer,' she confessed in a small voice. 'The way she looked at Ranjha over her shoulder.'

'Well, you're not Heer, so you don't have to copy her.'

'I wish I was Heer. I wish I were beautiful like her so someone would fall in love with me as deeply as Ranjha did with her. I want to be adored and sung to and smiled at.' She cupped her face in her hands.

Laila sat up, anxious to reclaim her friend's attention, to haul her back to the familiar, to herself.

'But you heard what Dadi said, didn't you?' Laila shook

33

Rani's knee. 'Girls mustn't love like that. It's wrong and shameful. Don't you remember?'

'Hmm?' Rani was miles away.

'Heer had to kill herself. Have you forgotten?' Laila's voice was shrill. '*And* she shamed her family.'

'Everyone has to die some time,' Rani grinned. 'What do I care as long as I get to dance and sing and taste some real happiness before dying?' She jumped to her feet and twirled on her toes, her white shawl flapping at her back like an angel's wings. She laughed as she spun, her arms raised to the ceiling, laughter gushing like a waterfall out of her flung-back head.

Laila watched, bemused by her abrupt change of mood. Rani was happy, wasn't she? She laughed and played with them. They went on picnics together and stole raw mangoes and sang, with Rani beating the back of a spoon on an old biscuit tin to keep time. So what did she mean about tasting real happiness? The question nagged at Laila, but she was reluctant to voice it. She felt as if Rani had suddenly taken a flying leap across a deep, wide chasm. She had cleared to the other side, leaving Laila behind, alone and confused.

Laila reached out and grabbed a corner of Rani's shirt. Mid-twirl, Rani stopped. Her shawl subsided against her with a sigh. Breathless, she looked down at Laila's upturned face.

'You mustn't say silly things,' said Laila.

'What silly things?' Rani was flushed after her dance.

'About death and things.' Laila dropped her gaze to the hem of Rani's shirt. A single thread shaped like a comma hung loose.

'Why? Did I frighten you?' Rani looked amused.

'Of course not. I don't like it, that's all.'

'What's there not to like?'

'Why are you being like this?'

'Like what?'

'All funny and weird.'

Rani touched Laila lightly on the cheek. 'I'm sorry, I forgot you are just eight.'

'I'm not a child.' Laila brushed off Rani's hand.

'All right, all right, you're not,' Rani laughed. 'You're my friend. Would you like to play carom? Shall I fetch your board?'

Of course, she was miles better at carom than Laila. Where Laila had to take careful aim before shooting while also muttering a prayer under her breath and kissing the counter for luck, Rani hardly needed to look at the board. She flicked counters into the pockets as easily as popping grapes into her mouth. But still Rani managed to lose. She won the first two games easily, but she lost the last three with a series of hysterical errors.

Once, arms flailing and a look of mock alarm on her face, she fell over the board with a crash and had to forfeit all her winnings. Another time, she took aim with her eyes crossed, so the counters skittered all over the board without a single one entering any of the four pockets. She played the last game pretending to be Bua. She fingered an invisible cross at her neck, muttered invocations to the Holy Mother, and called her 'Lailu Baby'. Every so often, she would lunge across the board to place a hand on Laila's brow to check whether 'the big fever' was back. Laila laughed till tears ran down her face. And when, as if on cue, Bua waddled out on to the veranda and placed a hand on Laila's forehead, both girls howled with laughter.

Nobody was a patch on Rani when she was like this. But only as long as she stayed like this.

3

Rani stood wringing her hands under a massive banyan tree about a mile from Sardar Begum's haveli. The tree was famous in Kalanpur. Many years ago, the body of a beautiful young woman had been found propped up against its trunk. It appeared, from the marks on her throat, that she had been strangled. The girl had been a stranger to the village, and her identity was never established. Nor was it ever discovered why she was killed, or indeed by whom. But one hot, moonless night, when Dullah the blacksmith was walking past the tree, shrill peals of laughter rent the silence. He stopped, looked around, even called out. Again, silence. No one stepped forth. Moments later, the laughter rang out again, louder, higher, and he realized that it was coming from the tree. His blood turned to ice, for he knew then that this was no earthly sound.

The tree was sited on the edge of a sugar-cane field but separated from it by a wide water channel bordered by high stands of bullrushes. Since Dullah's experience, no one had ventured near the banyan, for Dullah's word was trusted in the village and, if he said the tree was cursed, then so it was.

Over the years, the tree's appearance had grown more ominous, as if it were trying to live up to its reputation. Its trunk had thickened; its foliage had grown more dense. Ariel roots, the size of a child's leg, hung from the canopy like a hangman's ropes. Nothing grew in the banyan's inky shade.

Rani tried not to think of the murdered woman as she paced beneath the tree. Her mouth was dry and her palms damp. A slight wind whispered in the sugar cane beyond. Her head jerked up. Was that he? She shrank behind the tree trunk, half thrilled, half fearful, her eyes fixed on the head-high cane. When nothing larger than a rabbit emerged, she let out a pent-up breath. Would he come? Their exchange had been so brief, so furtive. Had she understood him correctly? 'The borh tree,' he had whispered. 'Tomorrow at four.'

Why had he chosen this place for a meeting? Young and dashing, he didn't look the type to frequent such a god-forsaken spot. But then, what did she know about him, except the little she had gleaned from his appearance? He was well off, at least compared to herself. He wore sturdy leather sandals instead of rubber flip-flops and, unlike the faded, shabby cottons of the villagers, his clothes seemed new. He certainly wasn't as rich as Laila. Unlike Laila, he didn't ride in a car or wear western clothes. What else did she know about him? He didn't seem that much older than her. Although he was clean-shaven, his skin looked soft and smooth, as if it had first made acquaintance with a razor only recently.

Rani had noticed him three months back, an alien face amid the familiar crowd outside her school. That first day she had felt his gaze upon her, probing and insistent. She had not returned his look. She had hurried home, taking the shortcut that led past Tariq's tube well. Rani's school, Punjab Model Girls' School, lay beyond Kalanpur, and it took her half an hour's brisk walk to make the journey.

When Rani was younger, Sardar Begum had deputed her elderly driver to cycle her to and from school. Balanced side-saddle on the crossbar of his old bike, Rani had borne with the driver's asthmatic wheezing and odour of unwashed clothes. But when she turned twelve, Rani informed Kaneez that she was quite capable of walking there with the two other girls from Kalanpur who also attended the same school. But on the day that she had first seen him at the school gate, she had been so flustered that she had run home without waiting for her usual companions.

Rani guessed he was from a neighbouring village. He was certainly not from Kalanpur, most of whose inhabitants she knew by face if not by name. She took to watching out for him. On the days he was there, she would quickly avert her face, lest he think that she'd been looking for him. But try as she might to conceal her pleasure, she couldn't stop grinning as she walked home with her friends. On the days that he wasn't there, disappointment settled on her shoulders like a wet sack. And then, around the time she went to the cinema, he didn't come for six days in a row.

Rani was frantic. Each day, she'd pause in the midst of the jostling, chattering stream of schoolgirls pouring out of the school gates. Standing on tiptoe with neck outstretched, she searched the crowd in vain. Just as she had convinced herself that he had moved away, or worse, lost interest, she finally saw him again. He was standing behind the gatepost and, as she rounded the corner, she ran into him. His hand shot out to steady her. Close up, she saw that his front tooth was slightly chipped and a tiny scar sliced his right eyebrow into two. His teeth glistened white against his coppery skin. She looked him straight in the eye and gave him a smile of such radiance that he blinked and fell back a step. Swamped by embarrassment, Rani shook off his hand and ran all the way home.

The next day, he spoke to her. Having spotted him early, Rani was hurrying though the gates with her head down when he appeared beside her. He bent and, retrieving a pencil from near her feet, held it up to her.

'Is this yours?' he asked in a loud voice, blowing dust off the pencil.

Rani stopped. Clutching her books to her thudding chest, she peeped up at the unfamiliar pencil and shook her head mutely.

'Someone else must have dropped it then.' He spoke in the

same ringing tone. But before she could move away, he muttered, 'The borh tree. Tomorrow at four.' Then he disappeared into the crowd. It was done so quickly and quietly that even Rani's walking companions, who were just behind her, did not hear.

She was sure he'd said the banyan tree. She couldn't have misheard. Unless he meant some other banyan tree elsewhere. Rani had assumed that he meant this banyan tree just beyond her village. Did he know she was from Kalanpur? The school was a short walk from the main Sabzbagh–Kalanpur road. For all he knew, she could be from Sabzbagh, or indeed from Bridgebad or any of the villages in the area. Come to think of it, *he* could be from as far afield as Colewallah. But no further, for she could not imagine a place further than that.

The call for maghreb prayer carried over from the village mosque. He was already an hour late. Had Sardar Begum been in Kalanpur, she would be laying out her prayer mat on her divan in the courtyard. Soon, Kaneez would serve her mistress tea on a tray in her bedroom. Then she'd help Nazeer, the cook, carry the daybed on to the veranda. She'd collect the cushions, fold the sheets, roll up the mattress and take them indoors. She might stop to attend to the odd task but, failing that, she'd return to the quarter. And notice Rani's absence. Rani's heart plunged, but, no, wait, she mustn't panic needlessly. Her grandmother was away in Sargodha with Sardar Begum, who was visiting her daughter.

Kaneez had entrusted Sardar Begum's cook's wife to keep an eye on Rani, as she had on previous occasions. But this time, exactly two days after Kaneez's departure, the cook's wife had suffered a late miscarriage and taken to her bed. The next day, she had summoned Rani to her bedside and feebly enquired if she was all right. Did she have enough food in the house? Oil? Bread? Rani had assured her that she had everything she needed and was well able to look after herself. She mustn't worry about her. In fact, if there was anything that she, Rani, could do for her, she had only to ask. The cook's wife had smiled weakly and closed her eyes. With no one to keep tabs on her, it had been easy for Rani to slip out and make her way undetected to the borh tree.

Rani twisted her dupatta in her restless fingers. She was stupid and credulous to have believed him. She should leave. What was she doing in this ill-fated place, waiting for a man who had spoken to her for the first time only yesterday? Nervously, she turned back to look at the tree. Where, a moment ago, mynahs had been chattering, now all was quiet. Each green-black leaf hung still. The whorls and twists in the gnarled old bark looked like eyes – eyes that bored into her wayward soul. Rani felt the skin on her neck prickle as she heard a faint rustle behind her. Too frightened to turn around, she was poised for flight when someone touched her elbow. It was he. He had come.

He grinned at her, displaying his dazzling teeth. He was spruce in a donkey-grey shalwar kameez with a big, flowing collar. His hair was brushed forward in a quiff. Rani was glad she had changed into her new blue shalwar kameez. Did he like it? Shy at the thought, she stared at her flip-flops. He fingered his quiff and cleared his throat.

'Have you been waiting long?' His voice was thin.

Rani nodded, but then, nervous that he might take that as a reproach, shook her head.

'Were you scared to come here?' he queried.

'A little,' she mumbled, reluctant to dwell on this betrayal behind her grandmother's back.

'Don't worry,' he said smoothly, pulling on the points of his collar. 'It takes more than a tree to scare me. I come from a family of soldiers, you know. We don't scare easily. My elder brother is in East Pakistan, killing Hindus and smashing those scrawny Bengalis' faces for trying to break away from us.'

Rani nodded absently. How had the conversation come to scrawny Bengalis?

Suddenly, a parrot shot out from a branch above him. He flung his arms over his head and cowered in terror. At the sight of him crouching before her, Rani giggled. He stood up and scowled at her.

'That stupid bird took me by surprise,' he muttered. He pushed his dishevelled hair off his forehead. His hair was thick and inclined to curl. It reminded Rani of Ijaz's hair in the film. But he was much slimmer than Ijaz, and more handsome. Had Rani been less intoxicated by their encounter, she might have noticed his close-set eyes and pigeon chest.

'So! So you're from Kalanpur, are you? What does your father do?' he asked.

'My father's dead. I live with my grandmother.' Shy of looking him in the face, Rani kept her eyes on the second button of his shirt.

'And your mother? She dead too?' he asked.

'No, she lives in another village, called Dera, with my stepfather.'

'How come you don't live with them?'

'They have children of their own,' replied Rani.

'Strange.'

Rani felt a sudden surge of anger. Who was he to pronounce on her family set-up?

'What's strange about people having children?' she asked heatedly.

'Where does your grandmother live in Kalanpur?'

'At Sardar Begum's haveli.' Seeing his eyebrows shoot up, Rani added quickly, 'In her servants' quarters.'

He asked her if she got on with her grandmother. It was an odd sort of question. She had never really thought about her relationship with Kaneez. As far as she was concerned, it just was. So she nodded.

'Do you tell her most things?'

'I suppose so.'

'Have you told her about us?'

'Us?' she queried.

'You know, meeting here like this? Did you tell her you were coming to see me?'

Rani gasped. Was he mad?

'So you haven't,' he mocked.

'Of course not. She'd . . . she'd lock me up. Do your, er, people know?'

'I'm a man.' His lip curled. 'I don't need to ask anyone's permission. I'm seventeen. I make my own decisions.' There was a moment's silence. And then he asked: 'If you're so scared of your grandmother, why did you come?'

Put on the spot, Rani blushed. 'I don't know.' But she was lying. She *did* know. She was curious to meet the enigmatic stranger at the gate. He intrigued her with his silent scrutiny, his expensive clothes. Why did he come, day after day? Why did he single *her* out with that steady stare, the stare that made her feel hot all over one second and gave her goose bumps the next? Did he like her? Did he think she was pretty? A little like Heer, perhaps?

For the past few days – in fact, ever since she had been to see the film – Rani had been restless. The cinema had brought home to her all that she was missing. She had never been beyond Colewallah. The things that Laila and Sara spoke of – airports, swimming pools, circuses with Chinese acrobats – were as remote to her as the moon. And likely to remain so. A bleak future awaited her. She knew no young men she could marry. No one would come looking for her. Even her own mother had abandoned her. Guarded by her grandmother, she would die in the long shadow of Sardar Begum's haveli. She would never see Lahore. Never ride in a train or wear high heels or own a suitcase. Never be loved, like Heer.

That was why Rani had seized her chance. She hadn't known what this meeting would lead to, but if she had declined to meet him, she might never have another opportunity. Rani knew the risks. If her grandmother found out, her freedom would be slashed altogether. Her visits to Sabzbagh would be stopped. She would be removed from school. Locked up, flogged, even. But still she wanted to lift the curtain and glimpse the forbidden.

'I wanted to know, to see for myself,' she mumbled.

'What *I* would be like?' He smirked at her. 'And do you like what you see?'

Blushing, Rani looked away.

'It's good you are shy. Brazen women who look you in the eye are bad, shameless,' he observed approvingly.

'Is that . . . is that why you wanted to meet me? Because I am shy?'

'That and other things also,' he grinned. 'I liked the way you looked. Your hair, your eyes. That's why I came to your school for so many days. To see you. *Just* to see you.'

'Just to see *me*?' breathed Rani.

'You don't know, but I followed you almost all the way home that first day. I kept back and hid behind trees and bushes so the other two girls who were also coming that way wouldn't spot me. That's how I knew you were from Kalanpur. Myself, I'm from Sawan. That's the village across the canal close to Bridgebad, where that fat white woman lives. We are landowners. One field of rice and another of vegetables. We also have three cows and eight goats. My mother tends them. She also does embroidery and from the money she gets, she makes these special clothes for me. She says I look like a prince. You think so too? She gives me money to spend behind my father's back. My father is strict. He works in the milk plant near Sabzbagh. Your Sardar Begum's son lives there. Did you know?' Without waiting for her response, he continued: 'My elder brother's a soldier. This wide, and strong as a bull. I bet the Indians run like squawking chickens when they see him.

'I also want to join the army and go kill those bastard Bengalis, but my father says I'm too young and he can only spare one son at a time.' He kicked a stone, and for a minute he looked like a sulky child. 'But I can fight with my bare hands if need be.' He held up his slender, hairless hands, and Rani was glad that his father had intervened.

'So are you at school?' asked Rani.

'School?' he scoffed. 'School's for kids. I work. My father wants me to be an electrician. He says there's good money in that. He pays a man in Colewallah to teach me. But I hate it. Fiddling around with wires all day. That's no life for a man. A man should be out and about being strong and manly, not hunched over a table like a woman doing embroidery.'

'What do you do then?'

'My father gives me my bus fare every morning. With that and the little bit extra my mother gives me on the side I go to Bridgebad, Sabzbagh, Champa, even Colewallah, when I feel like it. I roam the bazaars, sit at tea stalls. Sometimes I just wander wherever the road takes me. That's how I came by your school.'

'And that electrician man doesn't tell your father?'

'He's not a man. I told you, he's a woman. Walks like one and talks like one. As long as he gets his money, he keeps quiet, the little sissy.' He spat on the ground in disgust.

Rani gazed at him admiringly. She didn't have the guts to play truant from school.

'Why didn't your father send your brother to the electrician instead of you?'

'Because my brother is a blockhead, only good for heavy work,' he sneered. 'It's just as well, though, that he's away, otherwise, he would have followed me and told on me. And then my father would have thrashed me. Can't stand anyone having fun, my father,' he grimaced. 'But worse than any thrashing, I wouldn't have met you.' He smiled and half lifted his hand to her face.

Rani watched, mesmerized, as his hand neared her cheek. She should turn away like a decent woman undoubtedly would. But at the same time, she yearned for him to stroke her face. She could not remember the last time an adult had shown her affection. When his hand dropped to his side, she almost cried out in disappointment. Had she displeased him? Was she supposed to have stepped closer to show her willingness? But hadn't he said bold women were not nice?

She wished she knew how to behave. In the film it had been so easy. Heer and Ranjha had looked into each other's eyes, music had struck up in the background and they had fallen into an embrace. Rani studied him covertly. She saw the quiff, the grey drip-dry shalwar kameez with its big, fashionable collar, the chunky watch on his slender wrist, the shiny leather sandals, and she was smitten. That such a sophisticated, affluent man should single her out in the entire school was beyond anything she could imagine for herself.

'What is your name?' There was an intent look on his face.

'Rani,' she whispered.

A cow lowed in the distance. The animals were being driven home for the evening. The sky was orange, and flights of mynahs, crows and parrots were returning home to roost.

'I m-must go,' she stammered. The afternoon had slipped by unnoticed. What if someone saw her? What if they told her grandmother? She had never lied to her before. She looked despairingly at the cane fields behind which lay her village. It seemed so remote in the fading light.

He came up close behind her.

'Stay a while,' he murmured. His breath was warm on the back of her neck. Rani shut her eyes and savoured the feathery caress of his voice. Every inch of her skin was aware of his presence. She had never felt more alive.

'Look what I've brought you.'

Rani opened her eyes. He was holding out glass bangles. A deep cyclamen pink, they were flecked with gold. Even in that dim light, they glowed translucently.

'They're beautiful,' breathed Rani.

'Here, give me your hand. Let me put them on for you.'

It was not within her at that moment to refuse him. He grasped her trembling hand and eased the fragile glass bangles over her wrist and on to her forearm. Her pulse throbbed visibly in her upturned wrist. Long after he'd slid the last of the dozen bangles home, he continued to hold her. With their heads bowed towards each other, they gazed at his fingers encircling her narrow wrist. The silence stretched between them like a thin, taut membrane.

4

Laila threw open the drawing-room door. Her parents were sitting by Tariq's Philips radio. The silver radio was the size of an overnight case, with a tuning dial as large as an Olympic medal. She could tell from Tariq and Fareeda's posture that they were listening to the BBC's World Service. Again. They leaned towards the radio, foreheads knitted in identical frowns, heads held at an angle like intelligent birds.

'I wanted to ask if I . . .?'

'Shush.' Tariq put a finger to his lips.

Fareeda didn't even look up. Of late, her parents had become obsessed with the news. Often, she caught them speaking to each other in hushed voices, with the same frowns and tight faces with which they listened to the radio. More than once, Laila had heard the word 'war', but they brushed aside her queries with false smiles and a swift change of subject.

But the servants spoke of the trouble in East Pakistan freely in her presence. In the kitchen the talk would often turn to Shareef, the driver's son, who was in the army and whose regiment had been sent four months ago to East Pakistan to quell the rebellion there. Barkat, the driver, was worried. He'd asked Bua to pray in her church for Shareef's safe return.

'It's not fair.' Laila stamped her foot. 'No one speaks to me!'

Slamming the door, she stomped out of the house. She wished she could visit Kalanpur and see Rani. Sardar Begum had taken off for Sargodha on one of her quarterly visits to her daughter. She had taken Kaneez with her, but Rani was still in Kalanpur. Laila knew, however, that it would be pointless to ask permission to visit Rani, for there was no question of going to Kalanpur in her grandmother's absence. And she didn't want to play with any of the servants' children closer to home. Compared to Rani, they were all boring and babyish.

Reaching into her pocket, Laila extracted a letter Sara had sent for her two days ago, when Fareeda had returned from a trip to Lahore. She had read it three times already, and its contents had driven home to her the necessity of establishing beyond any doubt Rani's undivided allegiance before Sara's arrival. She read the letter once again.

Dear Laila,

How are you? I am fine. Yesterday I went to Uzma's birthday party. There was a cake like a big heart. Inside it was choclate. Lots of girls had come. I won the prize in the treasure hunt. The prize was hidden in a watering can in the garden. Lots of girls passed by it but no one found it except me. My prize was a ping-pong set with two bats and three balls. The balls look like small round eggs and are very light. I have learnt to play it and got very good at it everyone says so. I will bring it with me when I come to Sabzbagh. Then Rani and I can play and you can watch. If you meet Rani please give her love from my side and tell her that I miss her too and I have lots of secret jokes to tell her when we meet. Two days ago Nani took me to Bookworm. She bought me a grown-up book called Little Women by Louisa May Allcott. I have read sixteen pages and will tell you the story when I see you. It is very nice. Nani wanted to get you a present also. So I chose Naughtiest Girl in School for you. I am sending it for you with Ammi. It is by Enid Blyton. Your favourite. I hope you like it.

Your loving sister,
Sara.
PS: I miss you.
PPS: Please give my love to Bua. And Dadi.

Laila was sitting on the swing in the garden when Tariq came looking for her.

'Sorry for snapping at you, darling, but I was listening to something important on the radio.'

'You're always listening to something important these days,' mumbled Laila.

'How would you like to go on a picnic?'

'A picnic? Where?' Laila jumped up from the swing.

'Near Kalanpur. We could ask your Dadi and Rani to join us if you like.'

'Is Dadi back?' enquired Laila.

'She got back the day before yesterday.'

'When can we go?' asked Laila, slipping her hand in her father's.

'Today. Now. I can also check on my saplings there. Yes, a picnic will be good. Let's see what your mother thinks.'

As Fareeda did nothing by halves, soon the entire household had been mobilized in the preparation of an elaborate picnic. Hampers were brought out of the storeroom, thermos flasks were filled with juice and tea, beakers were enfolded in newspaper, and plastic-handled cutlery was wrapped in cotton napkins and tied with string. In the kitchen, Rehmat, the cook, prepared cucumber and egg sandwiches, crumb-fried drumsticks and lamb cutlets. A basket of fruit was packed separately, and a tin was found for Rehmat's carrot cake. Cushions, rugs, a canteen of iced water and a towel and soap dish were added to the mound of stuff to be packed into the car. Laila contributed her ball, binoculars and magnifying glass to the pile. When Fareeda asked teasingly why she was taking along the binoculars and magnifying glass, Laila looked at her in astonishment.

'To solve a mystery, of course. The world is full of them, you know.'

Tariq had already despatched Amanat, the gardener, on a

bicycle to Kalanpur to request the presence of Sardar Begum and Rani by the tube well.

Sardar Begum's reply came as the Azeems were setting off in their white Zephyr. They encountered Amanat on the driveway. Barkat slowed the car down to a halt. Tariq wound down his window and mouthed, 'Well?'

Wiping the sweat off his forehead with the back of his hand, Amanat dismounted from his bike. He frowned as he tried to recall the exact words of Sardar Begum's crisp rejoinder to her son's invitation.

'Sahib, Big Begum Sahiba says – let me remember what she said, for she said I must repeat exactly – yes, she says that she does not appreciate such short notice for big journeys requiring early planning. She also said,' and here he flushed and his voice dropped, 'did you think she was sitting swatting flies that she could get up and come on a picnic just like that?'

Tariq nodded and wound up the window. Smiling wryly at his anxious daughter, he remarked, 'Don't worry, they're coming.'

But when they reached their destination, there was no sign of Sardar Begum. So Laila and Tariq went for a walk. Barkat and Bua unloaded the boot while Fareeda chose the picnic spot with her customary diligence.

'No, no, not there, Barkat,' she wagged a finger at the driver. 'Can't you see that anthill? Here, under the shade of this peepul. Yes, just here. Bua, place the cushions in the shade. You know how Big Begum Sahiba dislikes the sun on her face. Don't unpack the food just yet. It'll go off in the sun.'

Fareeda worried occasionally that her punctiliousness might be tiresome for others, but even if she had wanted to relax her standards, she couldn't. Such was the power of her mother's example that perfectionism was now a reflex with Fareeda. Fareeda's mother, Mrs Yasmeen Khan, wife of Ambassador

C. P. Khan, had run a model home. Ambassador Khan's diplomatic postings took his family to a new country every three years, but so smooth was the household's transition that it was like the flow of water. Mrs Khan's household was a sparkling stream – clean, clear and energetic. It seemed effortless, but behind the lavish hospitality and impeccable service lay the discipline and organizational skills of a field marshal. Yasmeen Khan took her duties as the ambassador's consort very seriously indeed. A soiled napkin, a single cobweb reflected badly not just on her husband but on her country. And when it was a country they had fought so hard to liberate, the slightest slip was intolerable.

As a teenager, Fareeda had found her mother's discipline irksome. But she had understood the necessity of vigilance when she had come to Sabzbagh. Here in the anarchic household of one of Tariq's cousins, she had seen servants gossiping in grimy kitchens, children screaming obscenities, dripping taps, ripped curtains and greasy doorknobs. At the heart of this unloved home she had found the obese lady of the house reclining on grimy cushions while a bored-looking maid kneaded her yellow feet.

Fareeda, with her prim, polite upbringing, had been appalled. She had concluded then that control was crucial, not only as a safeguard against her household's decline into disorder, but her own corruption. She need not maintain the stranglehold of her mother-in-law but, nonetheless, discipline – no, not even discipline, for that was far too harsh a word – *vigilance* was required in all things pertaining to her life in Sabzbagh. She would run a tight ship in her home. Bring up her children decently. And she would be productive, do things that fed her soul. She would not let herself go.

She had succeeded, she reckoned. Her household was efficient. Her children had good manners. Her life, what with the house and her good works, was reassuringly full. She was busy, she was in control. Her achievement was all the sweeter for the fact that nobody had thought it possible. Her society friends in Lahore had been astounded at her decision to wed Tariq and live in Sabzbagh.

'Sabz*where*?' they had shrieked. 'You won't last a month. No shops, no cinemas, not even a decent bakery for fifty miles. And his family lives in the Stone Age. If, by some miracle, you do end up staying, you'll become just like those women – fat, lazy and vacant.'

Even her parents, who knew her better, had voiced concern.

'You *do* know, darling, that Tariq's background is very different,' they had murmured. 'His female cousins still do purdah and they haven't been to college. You'll be a fish out of water.'

But what neither her family nor her friends knew was that Sabzbagh fulfilled Fareeda's deep need for repose. An only child, Fareeda had led a pampered if peripatetic life. She had spent her life trailing her parents from one temporary home to another in a succession of glamorous cities – Cairo, Moscow, Rome, Istanbul. Her childhood had been defined by the din of airports, the smell of packing straw, different schools and alien tongues. In her mind, she was forever the new girl, frozen in the doorway of the classroom of yet another school, with the speculative gaze of twenty unknown children trained upon her.

On the surface she seemed happy enough. She was sociable and charming. Among her small group of friends, she was even gregarious. But she nursed deep within her the longing to belong, to settle, to matter.

And then, on a visit to Lahore, she had a chance encounter with Tariq. It changed everything for Fareeda. While he talked of Sabzbagh, Fareeda watched his face grow animated and enthusiasm creep into his measured tones. So vivid was his account that she heard the bells as cows were driven home in the evening amid a gauzy cloud of golden dust. She closed her eyes and imagined his mother's haveli, in which generations of his family had lived and died. She let herself soak in the serene silence of the long, still evenings, punctured only by the whirr of cicadas and the velvety flap of a fruit bat's wing. She wanted to be part of it.

But the ease with which she had taken to Sabzbagh after their marriage had still astonished Tariq. She had settled in that village with the contentment of a mother hen settling on her eggs. She loved dispensing medicine, warm clothes, jobs and advice. If ever she missed the giddy whirl of her previous life, she never said.

She had proved all her doubters wrong.

When Tariq and Laila returned from their walk, the picnic rug was spread out beneath the peepul tree, cushions were scattered about invitingly and Fareeda sat with her back against the tree trunk, legs outstretched, sipping fresh orange juice. From behind her dark glasses, she admired the view.

The sky was a steady blue, washed paler near the horizon. On the left lay a guava orchard, the short, shaggy trees laden with pale green, unripe fruit. To her right stretched a long line of poplar trees, bordering an irrigation channel. Beyond the trees lay her husband's tube well and, further on, his acres of wheat and cane.

Laila flopped down beside her mother and accepted a glass of juice. Just then, she heard the sound of an approaching car and saw the Lincoln bump along the dirt track, trailing clouds of dust. It came to a halt beside their white Zephyr. Barkat sprang to open Sardar Begum's door and leapt back as he was met by a volley of invective audible to Laila from a distance of thirty yards.

'Let this dust settle, fool, before you open my door,' barked Sardar Begum. 'You want to suffocate me? Already my lungs are finished.' She reached out and slammed the door shut. The car remained sealed and stationary long after the dust had subsided.

It had been three whole weeks since Laila had last met Rani. Too impatient to wait any longer, Laila thumped her glass down and raced over to the Lincoln. She made for the front passenger window. Unmindful of its powdering of dust, she pressed her face to the glass and saw a distinctly sulky-looking Rani. Uncaring of her grandmother's ire, she wrenched open the door. But before she could even say hello, Sardar Begum cooed from the back seat, 'I'm at the back, my moon.' She held out her hand.

Laila grabbed her grandmother's hand and pressed a perfunctory kiss on it. Then she pelted Rani with a hail of questions.

'What took you so long? We've been waiting ages and ages. Why haven't you been to see me all these days? Where have you been? What have you been doing?'

Rani ignored her. Very deliberately, she turned her face to the windscreen.

'No use talking to her, Laila,' remarked Sardar Begum. 'She's in a huff because I forced her to come. When I told her she was coming to the picnic, she said she had to study, if you please. You'd think she was sitting an exam to become president from all the studying she's been doing recently. Kalay Khan, Rani, what are you waiting for? Get off and unpack.'

'But Begum Saab,' the driver demurred, 'you yourself said to wait till the dust settles.'

'Did I ask you to wait till the day of judgement?' she snapped.

It took half an hour to unload Sardar Begum's car. A succession of tiffin-carriers, baskets and cooking pots were ferried by the drivers to where Fareeda had spread out her rug. The drivers then withdrew to the cars, and Bua and Rani served the food. When Fareeda's baskets were unpacked, Sardar Begum eyed the dainty sandwiches and cutlets in disbelief. She lifted a drumstick between forefinger and thumb and held it aloft. Examining it from all sides, she asked in mock innocence, 'Is this doll's food?'

Tariq saw his wife's face tighten and leapt to her defence.

'No, Maanji, it's normal food for normal people,' he said, wishing yet again that after fourteen years of marriage, his mother would have the grace to accept his choice of wife.

But Sardar Begum was not the accepting type. She could not forget that Tariq had married Fareeda against her wishes. Ever the pragmatist, Sardar Begum had sought an alliance with a wealthy landed family in the adjoining district.

'You have no brothers,' she had reasoned with her son. 'You need to build support in the area – people who will be your eyes and ears and arms. Tomorrow you might want to fight elections; you'll need a network. Also, a girl from the landed gentry will have good habits. She'll be obedient, sober, economical.'

But Tariq had other ideas. He wanted a partner, an equal with whom he could share his interests. When he chose Fareeda, Sardar Begum was horrified. Had Tariq lost his mind?

'And what will a party-going, piano-playing, car-driving memsahib do in Sabzbagh?' demanded Sardar Begum. Exactly the same question was being pondered by Sardar Begum's sisters-in-law, who were delighted to hear of this reversal in the fortunes of their haughty relative. Sardar Begum's in-laws had still not forgiven her for her unilateral declaration of independence upon her husband's death thirty-three years ago. While nibbling on tiny curried quail's legs, they gossiped gleefully about Tariq Azeem's fiancée.

'I hear she wears skirts and invites strange men to comb her hair.'

'No! In her home?'

'Worse, much worse. In shops, in full view of the world.'

'Shameless!' they had clapped in delight. 'Wait and see. She will bury them in shame. Heaps and heaps of shame.'

Fareeda hadn't yet heaped shame on the house of Azeem, much to the disappointment of Tariq's aunts. Nor had she thrown decadent parties or galloped a stallion through Sabzbagh bazaar. Fareeda had, in fact, confounded Sardar Begum and dismayed her aunts-in-law by giving every semblance of quiet contentment.

But Tariq knew that Fareeda's happiness was based on living independently. Knowing his mother's autocratic nature only too well, Tariq had chosen to live away from her. Sardar Begum had bought the farm at Sabzbagh from a colonial family soon after the subcontinent gained independence and the British sailed for home. For years, the bungalow had lain unoccupied and derelict. Sardar Begum had toyed with the idea of demolishing the house, but Tariq had prevailed upon her to let it be. The year he got married, Tariq had it repaired and refurbished and, much to Sardar Begum's chagrin, it was to the bungalow and not the haveli that he brought Fareeda. The arrangement suited Tariq's purpose perfectly. In Sabzbagh Fareeda was beyond the range of Sardar Begum's interfering arm and critical gaze. Tariq, meanwhile, was close enough to his mother to provide support, yet far enough to ensure privacy. In choosing to live separately, Tariq had flouted custom.

'Look at that!' his relatives had clucked in false sympathy. 'He the only son and she an elderly widow, and still he is refusing to do his duty and live with her. His mother should never have sent him to study in England. If a boy stays away so long from his own kith and kin, his blood turns white, he forgets his obligations. Allah knows we tried our best to dissuade her, but would she listen?'

Others blamed his wife. She must be a practitioner of the black arts. How else could you explain a devoted son's abandonment of his own mother? This is what came of marrying sly city types. They turned you against your own flesh and blood.

Too proud to admit that she had been thwarted by her son, Sardar Begum pretended that the new arrangement was her idea. She gave short shrift to anyone who dared probe.

'Of course it was my decision,' she snapped. 'This house is Tariq's, but as long as I am alive I will remain its mistress. And why live on top of each other when we can afford to have two, two, no four, four houses each?'

Though she put on a brave face in public, Sardar Begum saw no reason to hide her real feelings in private. Hence, although her disapproval of Fareeda had blunted over the years, Sardar Begum didn't see why she should abstain from all criticism of her daughter-in-law. If Fareeda's food was foolish, she would say so. Sitting upright on the picnic rug, Sardar Begum ordered Rani to display the offerings from Kalanpur.

'Rani, pass around our food. Give a paratha to Laila Bibi. No wonder the child is skin and bone if these chicken bones are all she gets to eat.'

In sullen silence, Rani unscrewed the tiffin carrier. There was omelette with fresh coriander and chopped scallions; lamb chops in yoghurt; seekh kebabs; karahi chicken; and minced lamb with whole chillies. Rani opened a separate box, lifted out a pile of parathas wrapped in greasy brown paper and slapped it down on a plate.

Surveying the spread with a beatific smile, Sardar Begum spread out her arms.

'*Now* eat.'

Despite herself, Fareeda laughed. Tariq shook his head.

'You'll kill us with all this rich food, Maanji,' he said to his mother.

'Better to die on a full stomach than an empty one.'

Despite Sardar Begum's barbed comments, lunch was an amicable affair. She found, much to her evident surprise, that Fareeda's reviled drumsticks were rather good after all. Not only did she scoff three in rapid succession, but she also had the grace to compliment her daughter-in-law between mouthfuls. ('These are not so bad. Soaked like this in chutney they are good, even.') Tariq tucked into the kebabs and chops and, thus, good humour was restored to the party.

Sardar Begum regaled them with anecdotes about her visit to Sargodha. Apparently, Tariq's sister was doing well but was heartily sick of her overbearing mother-in-law.

'Constantly sticking her leg in your sister's home she is. Always wanting to know how much this cost, where she got that, and Allah knows what else. Why can't the old witch mind her own business?'

Fareeda and Tariq exchanged a wry smile over her bent head. But although Laila listened to the conversation with half an ear and made a heroic attempt to taste the food her grandmother piled on her plate, she was miserably aware of Rani's closed face.

Rani stood above them, swishing a towel to and fro to keep the flies off the food. Although Laila tried several times to catch her eye, she did not acknowledge her with so much as a flicker of an eyelid. Fareeda, who had the urban liberal's dislike of child servants, whispered to Bua to take over from Rani, but despite the ayah's good-natured offer, Rani refused to relinquish the towel. Sardar Begum noticed the exchange.

'If she wants to be a martyr, Bua, let her. Fareeda, you enjoy your food. No use draping grapevines over thorn trees.'

A tide of crimson swept over Rani's neck. It seemed to Laila that she was on the verge of tears. Despite Rani's frostiness, Laila wanted to jump up and throw her arms around her.

'Don't be mean to Rani, Dadi,' Laila mumbled, colouring at her own audacity at admonishing her grandmother. She plucked at the grass by her knee, waiting for the storm to break over her head.

'Laila!' rebuked Fareeda, ever mindful of her duty. 'How can you speak to your Dadi like that? Apologize at once.'

But Sardar Begum shushed her with a wave of her hand.

'Mean? *Me?*' She turned the full beam of her glare on Laila. 'You are calling me mean because of *memsahib's*,' she tossed her head at Rani, 'mood? Well, let me tell you why she's so moody. Because I made her come. And why? Because *you* asked for her and I didn't want to disappoint you. That's why.'

'Sorry.' Laila responded mechanically, keen not to prolong the friction.

'Humph!' snorted Sardar Begum, picking up an abandoned cutlet.

'Come on, Maanji. Laila's apologized,' said Tariq, who hated conflict as much as Laila. 'She didn't mean to be rude. She was just defending her friend, which, you will agree, is an honourable thing to do.'

'And you, Tariq Sahib,' Sardar Begum rounded on her son, 'can stop lecturing me about honourable things to do. Who do you think you are? A schoolmaster? Your sermons may be applauded in your factory, but I'm not one of your two-paisa babus, understand? Lecturing me about honour as if I was yesterday's child! Humph!' Sardar Begum tossed her head. 'I know more about honour than you, even if you live to be a hundred.'

Tariq raised his hands in surrender.

'I know, I know, neither Laila nor I should have spoken to you like that. Our deepest, profoundest apologies. Laila, please go and kiss your grandmother.'

'All right then,' muttered the old lady and opened her arms to receive Laila's embrace.

Laila did so and, when she straightened, she caught Rani's eye and was rewarded with a watery smile. It was worth the scolding.

'Now, Rani, I insist you stop this fanning nonsense and eat something,' said Fareeda briskly, stacking up the dirty plates. 'We've finished, so why don't you and Bua and the drivers help yourselves to whatever you want, hmm? There's plenty of food left.'

'Wait!' Sardar Begum held up her hand like a traffic warden. 'Give me their plates and I'll put in their food. No, no, *those* plates.' She pointed at the quarter plates. She pulled the plates out of Fareeda's hands and reached for the omelette. Meat was too good to waste on staff. Slicing the omelette into slivers, Sardar Begum looked up and caught her son's reproving eye. Her hand stilled.

'What?' she bristled.

'Just let them help themselves, Maanji.'

Sardar Begum's eyes flickered from Tariq's face to Fareeda's deliberately expressionless one. She then glanced at Bua and Rani. After a moment's indecision, she replaced the plates quietly on the rug and waved at the servants to take it all away. However, she couldn't help shouting after them, 'Don't you dare finish the cake!'

'What exams are you preparing for?' Laila asked Rani. They were sitting on the grass, their bare feet dangling in the stream. The servants had eaten and packed the picnic paraphernalia into the cars. Far from her employers' gaze, Bua leaned against the Zephyr's bonnet and smoked companionably with the drivers. Tariq, Fareeda and Sardar Begum had gone for a walk to inspect the new saplings. Sardar Begum was armed with a notebook to count up and note the exact number of plants to ascertain that her son was not being cheated.

'Oh, just normal exams,' Rani replied, without looking at Laila. She was pulling the leaves off a thin poplar branch she had found lying on the ground.

'But I thought you'd just had them. Didn't you tell me when we went to see the film that you'd failed in arithmetic?'

'So? These are new ones.' Rani inspected the leafless branch. From one end, she ripped off a tiny bit of the soft bark with her teeth.

'So soon?'

Rani spat out the bark. 'Why are *you* so bothered about my exams?'

Hurt by Rani's tone, Laila fell silent. The water felt cold on her bare feet. She lifted them out of the stream and anxiously probed the soft wrinkled skin between her toes for evidence of killer worms. Fareeda had often warned her about the millions of invisible worms that swam about in dirty water and buried themselves into the skin of the 'careless people' who dipped their feet in it. The worms swam through the streams of blood that flowed up careless people's legs into their tummies and gave them all sorts of horrid diseases.

The warning had echoed in Laila's head when she had seen Rani fling off her flip-flops and plunge her nut-brown feet into the stream. Rani was being careless. Laila had been about to stop her, but she had looked so merry with her feet splashing in the water that Laila had been tempted to join her. Carefully removing her white socks and brown T-bar shoes, she had lowered her own pale feet into the stream.

Now, she shivered, as she imagined hundreds, no, millions of worms swarming up her body. There would be traffic jams in her veins with all the millions of worms pushing, jostling and streaming up her calves. Her legs would ache unbearably as her veins bulged to bursting point. But not by so much as a sigh would she reveal her agony. Before she reached home today, the worms would already be in her stomach. By midnight, she would be bleeding. By dawn, she would be dead. When Bua came to wake her the next morning, she'd find her grinning skeleton stretched out on the bed. The worms would have devoured her overnight. And then Rani would be sorry. Sorry that she had snapped at her and hadn't treated her better.

Laila reached for her socks and tried to pull them over her wet feet. She felt like crying. She turned her back on Rani and, grunting and sobbing with frustration, she tried once again to pull up her wrinkled, stubborn socks. Then Rani came to kneel beside her. She took Laila's feet in her lap and gently wiped them dry with her shawl. Rani eased on the socks and did up her shoes for her. Socked and shod, Laila felt less vulnerable. Rani sat on her haunches and wrapped her arms around her knees.

'You're right. I don't have any exams,' she admitted in a low voice.

'Then why did you lie?'

'Because . . .' Rani coloured under Laila's frank gaze, 'because instead of coming here today I wanted to do something else.'

'What?'

Rani's gaze dropped.

'Do what?' Laila repeated.

'I wanted to meet a friend of mine,' Rani whispered.

'A friend? But you could have brought her with you.' Though she was not pleased to have a rival for Rani's attention, Laila was prepared to be magnanimous in the abstract. 'No one would have minded, you know.'

'I couldn't.'

'Why not?'

'Because my friend is a boy.' Rani said it so softly that Laila almost didn't hear.

'A *boy*?' She didn't know Rani knew any boys. She and Sara certainly didn't. Their convent school was for girls only. All their friends, even outside school, were girls. Admittedly, their parent's friends had two sons whom they met occasionally, but they were not their *friends*. Samir, the younger one, always spat in her Coke and tripped her up in races. And Saqib, the elder one, had yellow pimples on his forehead and a clump of scraggly hairs on his chin. He marched around with an air gun, with which he shot frogs in his mother's ornamental pond. No, they were definitely not friends, even though Sara sometimes became all coy and simpering when Saqib was sauntering around with his air gun. But, still, he wasn't a *friend*. In fact, both brothers were equally disgusting.

'What's your friend like?' asked Laila suspiciously.

Rani's face bloomed. Her lips lifted in a wide, slow smile.

'He's kind and strong and brave and,' she giggled, 'handsome.'

Laila could not think of a single boy who answered that description. In her limited experience, boys just weren't like that. Even her school friends who had brothers agreed. Boys were messy and smelly and greedy and loud. How could girls possibly befriend them?

Laila didn't know any girls who had boys for friends. Except, perhaps, seven-year-old Bets in Enid Blyton's Five Find-Outers, who was friends with Fatty and Larry. And then there was Nora from the adventure series, who got on well with Paul. Perhaps Rani's friendship with this boy was like that of Nora and Paul. It could well be that they solved mysteries together.

'What do you do together?' asked Laila.

Rani blushed and looked away.

'Do you solve mysteries?'

'Mysteries?' queried Rani, nonplussed. 'What do you mean?'

'Finding out things. Like why a mysterious red light flashes on top of a hill at night. Or who stole your neighbour's cat.'

'Nobody stole my neighbour's cat.'

Laila sighed. Sometimes Rani just didn't understand.

'So, if you don't solve mysteries, then what do you do?'

'We talk.' Rani smiled self-consciously.

'About what?'

'Oh, lots of things. About what we want to do. He wants to be a soldier. And I tell him about the haveli and Sabzbagh and your house and how one day I want to see Lahore and wander around its bazaars and see a film at that cinema with the crown on the top. He's promised to take me. He said he'd show me the big mosque with domes of solid gold and the airport with huge planes that make so much wind that they can whip off your plait if you don't hold on tight to it. I'm going to see your Lahore.'

'You think your grandmother will let you go?' Laila felt a twinge of jealousy.

A couple of years back, Sara had wanted Rani to come to Lahore with them for a visit. The girls had planned the trip for days. They had told Rani all about the adventures they would have. They would go to the zoo and show her crocodiles and lions, and take her boating on the Ravi, which was even wider than the Sabzbagh canal. They would visit Anarkali bazaar and buy her new clothes and take her to Shezan restaurant and order tutti-frutti ice cream in tall, cold glasses with hot chocolate sauce dripping down the sides. But Kaneez had vetoed the visit. Despite much pleading from Fareeda as well as the girls, she had not relented.

'My grandmother doesn't know. Promise you won't tell her,' said Rani. 'Her, or anyone else. Promise!'

'I promise. But how have you managed to make friends with him without your grandmother knowing?'

'I meet him in secret. Like Heer and Ranjha.'

'Do you sing and dance like them?' Laila wrinkled her nose.

'No, silly!' Rani laughed. 'I told you, we talk.'

Rani lowered her eyes. Her lashes rested on her cheeks like the thick fringes on Fareeda's velvet cushions. She looked different to Laila, and yet nothing about her appeared to have changed. Rani wore her chestnut-brown hair, as usual, in a thick plait down her back. She had not filled out. Her collarbones still jutted out like china shelves, and the little hollow at the base of her throat was as deep as ever. Nor had she pierced her nose or plucked her thick, straight eyebrows. And yet she seemed different. She seemed alight, as though a spotlight was trained exclusively on her. Everything about her glowed – her eyes, her hair, her golden skin.

'You don't solve mysteries,' complained Laila. 'You don't even dance. I bet you don't play. Your friend sounds really boring.'

'He's not. He's not boring at all. I feel so happy when I am with him. It's like . . . like the monsoon.'

'The monsoon?'

'Yes. It just happens and, when it does, it sweeps away everything before it. Do you understand? Do you know what I mean?'

Laila nodded. She did not know what Rani meant, but she appreciated the urgency of Rani's desire to make her understand. Laila knew instinctively that this was important to Rani, perhaps more important than anything she had ever divulged to her before. Perhaps these were the sorts of things that she told Sara. It was vital, if she was to raise their friendship to a higher level, to at least pretend to understand. So, Laila nodded again, more vigorously this time.

'He makes me feel important and beautiful. When I'm with him, it doesn't matter any more that my mother never sends for me or that no one cares if I am happy as long as I am good. None of that matters when I'm with him. Because he and I together, we become something new. Can you understand?' Rani gripped Laila's shoulders. 'When I'm with him, I'm not Rani, the servant girl. I become someone else. Someone who matters. Like you or Sara.'

'But you *do* matter,' Laila protested. 'You matter to *me*.'

'I matter to you as Rani who lives in Kalanpur. I don't matter to you in school with all your friends who come in cars, or when you go to the cinema in Lahore, or when you're sitting in a hotel eating ice cream. Do I?' She gave Laila a little shake and turned away. 'You don't understand. I wish you were older.'

Laila's eyes widened in alarm. Had she said something wrong? Had she been found wanting? Was Rani wishing that she could speak to Sara instead of her? She wanted to grab Rani's hands, to shout that she was her friend, that she mattered to her, mattered more than anyone else, that she *did* wish she could come to Lahore with her, but she didn't know how. Whatever she said, it seemed, came out wrong.

Rani turned back to her. Laila was relieved to see that she was smiling.

'He says I'm a real rani, a princess. And you know something,' she giggled, 'with him, I feel like one. I've never felt like that with anyone before.'

A crimson bud of jealousy unfurled in Laila's stomach. At least when Rani ran off with Sara, she knew who her rival was and what she was up against. But this shadowy figure, this hateful boy who had usurped her friend, was an alien threat.

'Who is he?' Laila demanded. 'What's his name?'

'I can't tell you. He made me promise I wouldn't. If his father finds out, he'll thrash him, because he's not supposed to be with me. He's supposed to be somewhere else.'

Laila wished that his father *would* thrash him to death. 'I tell you everything,' she said, 'everything that ever happens to me, and you won't even tell me his name.'

'If I could, I would, really. You know that.' Rani took a step towards Laila and held out the poplar cane. 'See, I made a switch for you. You can pretend it's a sword.'

Laila looked scornfully at Rani's offering. 'It's not a sword. It's a silly stick. You give it to your friend. Anyway, you like him more than me.' Laila knew she sounded petulant. She was possibly even endangering her friendship with Rani, but she was past caring. She wanted to hurt Rani.

'I *don't* like him more than you. I like him differently, that's all.' Rani reached for Laila's hand, but Laila brushed her off.

'Then go to him. That's what you wanted, didn't you? Rather than come here on this picnic with me you wanted to go and meet him, secretly. Didn't you?'

'Shh! Lower your voice. It's not like that. I don't get many chances to meet him. I thought if I said I had to study then big Begum Sahiba would take my grandmother to the picnic and I could go to meet him. I didn't say I'd rather see him than you.'

'But you wanted to, didn't you?' accused Laila.

'Lailu, why are you being so angry and unkind?'

'*You're* the one who's being mean.'

'I'm not,' whispered Rani. 'You have so many people to love you. So many things to do, so many places to go to. I have only him.'

'What about me? You have me, don't you?'

'You don't understand. Maybe when you grow up . . .'

'Don't tell me to grow up,' Laila yelled. 'I *am* grown up.' She turned and raced back to the car. She felt hot tears welling up in her throat as she ran, but she swallowed hard to push them down into her stomach. She didn't want to have to answer awkward questions from Bua or her mother. However mean Rani had been to her, she had made a promise she couldn't break.

5

The sun was climbing in the sky as Laila and Bua hurried towards the church. Indian coral trees lining the canal road blazed with scarlet, talon-like blossoms. Parakeet shrieked in the bald blue sky. Across the canal, they were burning stubble in the fields. The scent of wood smoke and cattle dung drifted over. From the mosque on the far bank of the canal, a mullah called his congregation to prayer. The mud-coloured canal slid past, silent, swift, sleek as a snake. Visitors from Lahore who came to stay with the Azeems often mistook it for a river. ('Hai, look how fast it flows. Must be very deep also.')

Laila's parents had forbidden her to come to the canal by herself. Every year it claimed at least one life, often of unwary visitors who underestimated its furious current and depth. Unlike the canal near Laila's grandmother's house in Lahore in which boys in dripping loincloths cavorted all summer, no one swam in this canal, no matter how hot the sun.

Even now, although Bua gripped Laila's hand firmly, there was something illicit about being on this deserted dust road. Traffic was always thin here – the occasional jeep, trailing a parachute of dust; the odd herd of goats chewing on the elephant grass that grew in thick clumps on the canal bank; but, mostly, the few men who worked in the powdered-milk factory beyond the village and used the canal road as a shortcut.

Normally, Bua took the road that led past the guava orchard, but because they were late, she'd taken this shorter route. Fareeda had delayed them unknowingly. They had planned to creep out by the side veranda at nine-thirty while she was still in the dining room having her third cup of coffee. That would have allowed them to get to mass comfortably by ten. But a telephone call had spoilt everything. Fareeda had come upon them as Bua was drawing the bolt on the door into the veranda.

'Where are you going?' she asked, flying past in her flowered dressing gown to answer the telephone.

'To visit my niece, Marium, the nurse,' replied Bua quickly. 'She's just returned from Dipalpur and . . .' But Fareeda wasn't listening. She'd already lifted the receiver, and motioned them to wait. Laila sighed.

'Now, you let me do the talking. Understand?' Bua whispered to Laila.

Laila nodded. She knew she mustn't mention the church. While it was perfectly all right for Bua to go to church, it wasn't so for Laila. Her mother was funny like that. It was fine for Sara and Laila to attend a convent in Lahore, but she didn't like them going to the church in Sabzbagh. Especially not to pray.

'Darling, you're a Muslim,' she sighed, whenever Laila brought up the subject.

'But I *like* the church.'

Fareeda didn't see the statue of Mary in her sky-blue plaster shawl through Laila's eyes, nor did she understand the lure of those big tinsel stars hanging from the ceiling or the scent of melting wax and incense and polished wood. It was a special place for Laila, warm, welcoming, forbidden. Feminine.

The village mosque, on the other hand, had a resolutely masculine atmosphere. It was stark and stern with bare white walls enclosing a brick-paved courtyard that got so hot in the summer, it seemed to shimmer in the afternoon sun. The mullah there had a long bushy beard and a bad temper. Once, when Laila had dragged Bua in, just to have a look, he had chased them out.

'Out! Out! Females not allowed in the mosque,' he had

yelled, brown flecks of tobacco-stained spittle landing on his beard. 'And heathens like you,' he poked Bua with a bony forefinger, 'who believe in three gods, will go straight to hell.'

Unlike the mullah, the nuns were kind. They let Laila thump on their piano, gave her gooey fudge at Christmas and went into ecstasies over her smocked dresses.

'Look, Sister, how pretty these pink roses are on Laila Baby's dress. So real they look. Just like the rose she is herself.'

But Fareeda didn't share Laila's fondness for the sisters. She did not think they were kind. 'They're quacks,' she had snapped just the day before. 'Cutting up young women in that clinic of theirs. They should be shut down immediately.'

Now, Fareeda replaced the receiver on its cradle and smiled at her daughter.

'Hello, darling. You're looking sweet,' she said, taking in Laila's pink going-out dress and long white socks. 'Where are you off to? Anywhere special?'

Bua's words came out in a rush. 'To meet my niece, Bibi. The one who got married last month?'

'So early in the day?'

'If we leave it any later, it will be Laila's resting time, so instead of tiring her . . .'

The phone rang again. Fareeda picked it up and waved them away.

On the canal road, Laila skipped along by Bua's side. She reached almost up to Bua's ear now. Last year, she could only see past Bua's shoulder if she stood on the tips of her toes.

Bua panted as she hurried along on her short, fat legs. But despite her fifty-odd years, her dark, burnished skin was still smooth, stretched tight over her podgy face. When she laughed, her cheeks rode up her face, almost squeezing shut her eyes.

She was dressed, as usual, in a plain cambric shalwar kameez. A pristine white handkerchief folded into a square was pinned to her bosom. She was particular about this hand-kerchief and changed it twice a day so that it never looked creased or grimy. The handkerchief, Bua had been assured by the French nun who had pinned it to her chest before her interview with Fareeda all those years ago, was the sign of a good ayah.

And, indeed, it was the handkerchief that had impressed Fareeda. Bua had come to the Azeems from the convent, sent over by the nun who had heard Fareeda was looking for an ayah for her firstborn. Bua had just been widowed and was desperate for a job. Fareeda, meanwhile, had already 'inter-viewed' eleven women from Sabzbagh and concluded that peasant women were not cut out to be ayahs. They were sluggish and careless, unable to appreciate the importance of boiling, scrubbing, timing and smiling. Fareeda had been on the verge of appointing a sour-faced but efficient nurse from Lahore when Bua had walked in, crackling in her starched clothes, with a broad smile and a frosty handkerchief pinned to her chest.

'Oh, Mary, Mother of God,' she panted now. 'Such pains in my side I get when I walk fast. Your Bua is getting old, little baba. Remember to give her a nice funeral in the church when she dies. With tears and sad songs. I wonder if anyone will ever visit my poor grave?' She gave Laila a pointed look.

'You won't die, Bua, not for ages and ages,' replied Laila, producing her stock answer to Bua's stock question.

'Everyone has to go one day, Lailu, but it's nice to know you don't want me to die tomorrow.'

A man cycled past. A fat-bellied dog chained to his handle-bars trotted beside him. Laila tugged Bua's hand.

'Look, Bua, that dog is going to have babies.'

'How do you know?'

'See its tummy, it's fat – full of babies.' Laila beamed at the dog. In her mind, she was already among a litter of fluffy brown puppies licking her sandalled feet with their warm pink tongues.

'Hush! Who tells you these dirty things?'

'What dirty things?'

'About tummies full of babies.'

'Oh, that! Ammi told me. She said everyone – dogs, cats, you, even – came out of their mothers' tummies. She told me she went to the hospital and a doctor pulled me out of her tummy.'

'No, he didn't,' snapped Bua. 'I've told you so many times I found you behind a jasmine bush in the back garden.' Bua's crisp tone softened as she warmed to her story. 'It had rained at night. When I went out what did I see? A tiny baby wrapped in your green blanket lying behind the bush. With apricot cheeks and eyes big as frying pans. I brought you in and showed you to Bibi. "Oh, what a sweet little baby, Bua," she said. "Let's keep her. She'll be Sara's little sister." Have you forgotten all that?'

'No,' mumbled Laila, bored by the reiteration of a story she had come to mistrust. 'So how was Sara born?' She knew the answer to this question too, but she asked simply to goad Bua.

'Same way. Only, she was behind the cactus.'

'And who left us there?'

'Uff, Baba, what questions you ask! I told you it had rained. You must have dropped from the sky.'

'I didn't break into little, little bits falling from the sky? Rehmat's son broke both legs when he fell from a tree. And it wasn't very high even.'

'God laid you down gently, like a feather on a breeze.'

'So Ammi was lying, was she, when she said I came out of her tummy?'

'It's not for me to say who's lying and who's not,' Bua sniffed.

Laila straddled a divided world. On one side stood her

mother, and on the other, Bua. Laila knew Bua's account was unreliable. Three years ago, when Bua had first told her the story of her origins, Laila had spent an entire monsoon rushing out after every downpour to search for a baby. With her skirt bunched up above her knees in one hand and Tariq's walking stick in the other, she had pounded every rain-soaked bush in the garden in quest of a blanket-wrapped bundle. But her only noteworthy encounter had been with a mongoose, which had leapt out with bared teeth and spiky, sodden fur, an enraged loo-brush on legs. Laila had dropped the stick and fled, bawling. That day, a crack had appeared in her faith in the world according to Bua.

'Now hurry or we'll miss church.' Bua pulled Laila's hand.

'Bua, tell me the story about the church and the Irish sister.'

'Again, Baba?'

Laila nodded. That story was a particular favourite of hers. It had a fairy-tale quality about it, with a golden-haired princess, a separation, a promise and, finally, a happy union. And unlike most fairy tales she knew, it wasn't set 'long, long ago, in a faraway land' but right here in Sabzbagh.

'All right, then. The Irish man, Mr O'Brian, who owned the farm before your family, had a daughter, an only daughter. She was a good, God-fearing girl. When she was twenty, she told her father she wanted to become a nun. She could have got married hundred, hundred times, if she'd wanted. So pretty she was with golden hair, milky skin and eyes the colour of Mary's shawl. And her papa so rich. But, no, she loved Jesus, only Jesus.' Bua kissed the cross suspended from her neck.

'Her papa tried to stop her, but she wouldn't listen. She sold off the jewellery her dead mother had left her and went off to Rome. Her father asked her to return . . .'

'No, he wrote to her every day begging her to return. You're not telling it properly . . .'

'All right, Baba,' Bua chuckled. 'He wrote her many, many letters begging her to return. He didn't get a reply. Not a single one. Where had she the time? So busy praying she was, the holy girl. So he followed and begged her to come home. She turned her face to the wall and prayed. But he also didn't give up. He agreed to let her become a nun but promised that, if she came back, he'd build her a convent in Sabzbagh, where she could do God's work.'

'And she made Christians out of your family and lots of other families, too, and sisters came from India and Ireland and France and Sri Lanka to help in God's work. And they started a school and clinic.' Laila finished the story for her. 'So when your mother died when you were a girl, your father brought you to live with the nuns here. And the sisters were like mummies to you. Weren't they?'

'Yes, Baba, so good they were to me. Mutton two times a week and a set of new clothes every winters and every summers.'

'And the Irish sister? Was she also good to you?'

'Only for a little while, because she died two years after I came. Cholera. The angels carried her up to heaven on their own wings.'

'Didn't they get tired?' Laila gave Bua a wry look.

'Angels are not fat little people like your Bua.'

'What are they then?'

'They're made of light, very strong like the lights at the airport in Lahore, except that we can't see it. Now, we're here.' Bua pushed open the wooden gate and ushered Laila through. 'Here, let me wipe your dusty shoes. Otherwise, what will the sister think, eh, Lailu? Now, remember to greet them nicely.'

The path to the church had been sprinkled with water to settle the dust. The moist earth smelt of rain. The nuns were proud gardeners. The path was lined with dahlias and hot-red hibiscus with their tongues hanging out. The church itself was a brick building mounted on a concrete plinth. There was a big golden bell on the roof. The windows and doors were painted emerald green and covered in mosquito netting. Behind the church were two low buildings. The nuns lived in one and the other was a school for Christian girls. Amanat's daughters attended this school. They sat on the floor and wrote on wooden slates with reed pens dipped in ink.

Beyond the nuns' residential block lay the maternity clinic. It was a two-roomed structure crouching behind a hedge. Laila had been in the front room of the clinic. It had white-washed walls lined with wooden shelves. Rows of bottles full of liquids, some milky, some clear, filled the shelves. A bench ran below the shelves. A desk and a chair were placed in the centre. Both wobbled on the uneven brick floor. The room smelt of medicines. The back room lay beyond a door that was always kept shut. Laila had never been inside that room.

The nuns who worked in the clinic were Sri Lankans. Their predecessor had left in a hurry after the glucose incident. The village seamstress, a hefty woman, had strode into the clinic complaining of 'weakness'. She suffered from low blood pressure. So the nun on duty had laid her down and administered a glucose drip. But the seamstress was diabetic. She was found dead by the hedge behind the clinic, where she fell on her way home. The seamstress was not the first casualty of the nuns' patchy medical knowledge.

Over the years, Fareeda had kept a grim tally of the botched cases at the convent clinic. She had held her tongue because she knew that the local midwife was no better. But with the seamstress's death, Fareeda's enmity with the sisters – a long-smouldering ember – burst into flames. She threatened to have the clinic shut down and the guilty nun jailed.

The Mother Superior, a Canadian whose mild manner concealed a sharp mind, acted quickly. The nun whom Fareeda had threatened with jail was packed off to Lahore that same evening. The next day, Mother Superior visited Fareeda with a bunch of dahlias. Sitting on the lawn sipping Earl Grey tea and nibbling the ginger biscuits her hostess had grudgingly offered, the nun admired Fareeda's double gladioli and murmured how sorry she was that the Lord had summoned the poor seamstress so hastily.

She also gently reminded Fareeda that the land on which the convent and indeed the clinic stood had been gifted them by the Irish family who had planted orchards on this barren land. Hence, the nuns were within their rights to offer solace to the poor ladies of this area. But humans were human, and didn't it also say in the holy Koran that they were fallible? Mistakes were made by all, and what could one do but beg the Lord's forgiveness?

Of course, as Tariq Azeem's wife, Fareeda had a right to feel protective about the people of this village, for Mr Azeem was widely regarded as a generous benefactor. But when the villagers chose not to consult them, did the Azeems have a right to intervene? But all this was very complex and really shouldn't be discussed on such a lovely spring day. How *did* Fareeda keep the squirrels off her glads?

Fareeda was stunned by the woman's gall. Here was this nun, this visitor, this *foreigner*, not only brushing aside a fatal error as an everyday event, but also warning Fareeda not to pry into the goings on at the convent. Who did she think she was? How dare she remind Fareeda about the O'Brian legacy? Was she trying to pull rank by reminding her who was here first?

'Indeed, Sister, we all make mistakes,' said Fareeda, stirring her tea. 'But some mistakes are so grave that even God, all forgiving though He is, would expect us to account for them. Those who have suffered from these "mistakes" would also find it hard to turn the other cheek. And even if they were to do so, the law of this land would not be lenient. Not when the same mistake was made over and over again. For we must remind ourselves that, though the land may have been granted in colonial times, it is now a part of Pakistan. More tea?'

Two Sri Lankan nuns arrived in Sabzbagh a month after the seamstress was buried. Though they'd been in Sabzbagh now for two years, they could only manage very broken Urdu. Their patients thought this very strange. As Bua remarked, 'It's all right for white people like Mother Superior not to speak Urdu, but why should someone as black as your Bua not know, hmm?' Despite the language barrier, the nuns were kept busy in the clinic.

Today, they hovered by the church door, greeting the villagers who had come to attend the service. Mother Superior was away in the hills of Abbotabad, where the sisters ran a small boarding school. In her absence, her second-in-command, Sister Clementine, was in charge of the convent.

Sister Clementine was an Indian from Kerala. She had round, rubbery features and skin the colour of bitter chocolate. Frizzy hairs escaped from the sides of her wimple, and there were damp patches under her bolster-like arms. As always, Laila's eyes were drawn to her feet. Wide and splayed, they reminded Laila of Fareeda's Japanese fan opened to its fullest. Today, they were wedged into black sandals with broad straps that strained to control her yellow-nailed toes.

Sister Clementine had a modest background. Her father was a plumber by profession and a moaner by inclination. He had spent most of his underemployed life in a singlet and shorts, lying on a string bed and bemoaning his singular misfortune.

'Five girls I have. Not one, not two, but five. To feed, to clothe, to wed. Why He upstairs hates me, I don't know.'

Though loath by nature to count his advantages, secretly,

he did not think himself all that unlucky, for his daughters were, with one exception, extraordinarily pretty. He had high hopes of his girls, whom he trusted would ensnare sufficiently good matches for him to abandon his fitful work altogether. Already the simpering smiles and doe-like eyes of his two eldest girls, Sharmila and Sushila, had elicited discreet enquiries from interested parties. As for Shirley, the youngest, the plainest, nicknamed Cowpat, he had found a solution for her too.

When Shirley was seven, she asked her mother if she could wear pink on her wedding day. Her father raised himself from his string bed on one bony elbow and cackled, 'Oh no, Cowpat, you're not getting married. You're pledged to the church. As soon as I saw your poor fat face, I said to myself: "No hope of getting this Cowpat a husband." Even if I were to find you a halfwit or a widower, so much dowry he will ask for, to make up for what God left out. Poor men like me can't afford ugly daughters. No, child. You're going to be a nun. No husband-marriage for you. You'll get church and prayer in this world, and heaven in the next. Think of that! Stop blinking like an owl and scratch my back, in the middle where your poor father can't reach. Aah, that's my Cowpat.'

And so, Shirley entered the church on leaden feet and became Sister Clementine. And she found that once she donned a nun's habit, she was viewed differently. The very face that was pitied for its homeliness now, framed by a wimple, became a beacon of virtue. It seemed to Sister Clementine that a simple change of costume had transformed her from pariah to paragon. Even her family came to regard her as an asset, now that she had access to influence. Particularly when Sharmila's husband abandoned her after the birth of their second daughter, Clementine's lot rose still higher with her family. Now, Sharmila was the burden, while Clementine was the dutiful daughter, the possible saviour.

'Ask your nun sisters to help a bit, eh?' her father would wheedle, rubbing forefinger and thumb at Clementine. 'So many mouths to feed I have, with these brats of Sharmila's on top. Please, eh?'

Clementine relished this unexpected reversal. She grew into her role.

'You think the Church is there just to feed the litters of runaway scoundrels?' she scolded. 'I saw that carpenter boy with his shifty eyes and rat-teeth, and at once I knew he was going to rub your faces in the dirt. I warned you all, but too busy listening to his big talk and jingling pockets you were.'

Clementine's triumph was short-lived. The next year, in 1957, her church sent her across the border to Pakistan. There was some talk of her returning home after the '65 war with India, but to Sister Clementine's intense disappointment, it never happened. She remained stranded in Sabzbagh as relations between the two countries tautened once again.

Now, she stood on the steps rubbing her aching stomach. Bua scurried up to Sister Clementine and kissed her hand.

'Sister Clema-tee, I hope you won't mind, but this baby here was eating my head – "I want to come, I want to come" – so I thought, who am I to refuse if the child wants to be holy? Let Sister jee decide . . .' Bua nudged Laila. This was her cue to throw her arms around Sister Clementine and press her face to the nun's middle. But Laila hung back, overcome by shyness.

Sister Clementine held out a hand.

'Child, you want to come to our church, no?'

Laila took her hand. Sister Clementine wheezed as she heaved herself up the three steps to the entrance of the church.

'Oh my, these wheat chapattis will kill me,' she groaned. 'From mother's milk I went straight to rice like everyone at home and, even after so many years, this wheat is so hard for me to digest – hard as rocks, crashing together and giving me too much of stomach-ache. These Punjabis must be having stone-crushers in their bellies. How else they are eating chapattis three, three times a day, eh?

'Tell me, child, what is your daddy saying about this bad fighting in East Pakistan, eh? BBC radio says there's sure to be war, what with the army doing what it's doing in Bengal. But Radio Pakistan is saying everything is going nicely there. Bengalis are saying sorry, and Mujib is also doing "yes sir" to General Yahya. What does your daddy say? He must be knowing, him having all his big friends in Lahore. They must be telling him. Will there be war with India? Will I get to go home?'

Laila did not know what to say. These names, Mujib and Yahya, were mentioned often in her home, but all she knew was that General Yahya, who lived a car journey away in Rawalpindi and wore a khaki uniform and a peaked cap, was Pakistan's ruler, and the bare-headed, bespectacled Mujib was a Bengali who wore kurta-pyjama and lived far away in a watery place called Dhaka. Mujib had done something bad, and General Yahya was now punishing him. In fact, Barkat's son had been sent to Dhaka to punish Mujib and anyone else who took his side. Laila had gleaned this from the servants' talk.

'So, child, you ask your daddy and let me know, yes?' said Sister Clementine.

'Yes, Sister.'

Laila spotted Amanat and his family as they filed in to the church. She counted five of his seven children. She also saw the village tonga-driver. He was unshaven and bleary-eyed. His wife had a black eye she was trying to conceal with the edge of her shawl.

'Hello, Miss Laila.'

Laila released her hand from Sister Clementine's damp clasp and turned to see her father's secretary, Mr Jacob. Aside from the nuns, he was the only member of the congregation in western clothes.

Mr Jacob was an Anglo-Indian. He was different to the local Christians, for he had white blood in his veins. Mr Jacob was very particular about his white ancestry – even though the said ancestor had died a hundred years ago. It proved that he was not a low-caste convert like the other Christians of Sabzbagh. He was, he insisted, part English. Once, Sara had asked him why he was so black if he was really part white.

'Oh that's the subcontinental sun for you,' Mr Jacob had replied cheerily. 'Plays havoc with white skin.'

His dark complexion notwithstanding, Mr Jacob took every care to live up to his white credentials. He never wore a shalwar kameez or what he referred to as 'native dress'. He always wore socks, even in the blistering heat of June. And he ate his curry with a spoon.

Today, he was dressed in a polycotton safari suit. A thin strand of hair was pulled up from above his right ear, combed carefully across the top of his gleaming scalp and glued down with Brylcreem into a curl behind his left ear. Once, Laila had seen him riding pillion on his son's motorbike. As they roared past, she had caught a glimpse of Mr Jacob's face. His head was completely bald, and a long ribbon of hair streamed behind his right ear. He looked as if he would give anything to plaster that strand down over his scalp, but his hands were full of folders.

'Hello, Mr Jacob,' said Laila.

'Does your mother know you're here?' He stooped to whisper in her ear.

Laila breathed in a great waft of Fair and Lovely skin-bleach cream and shook her head.

'Then we won't tell anyone, either. You're here with Bua?'

Bua nodded at Mr Jacob. 'Come on, Lailu. Prayers are starting.'

It was dim inside the church. A Sri Lankan nun sat at the upright piano by the altar. Another stood by to turn the pages of the music book. A vase with three blooms of wine-red hibiscus was placed on the altar. The altar cloth was embroidered with red-roofed chalets with smoke curling from their chimneys. Fareeda had an identical cloth at home, which she kept folded in a cupboard. It was a present from a long-departed French nun who had started a small sewing room at the convent.

Most of the narrow benches were already full, with people shuffling and sliding down to make room for each other. Bua led Laila to the last empty bench, at the back. Only a few people had picked up copies of the Urdu hymnbook. Like Bua, the rest, Laila guessed, could not read. Across the aisle, Laila noticed that the tonga-driver held his open copy upside-down.

A beam of sunlight streamed in from a skylight, spotlighting the small but dramatic figure on the cross above the altar. Laila had never noticed him before. But for a ragged cloth around his middle, he was naked. Even from where she sat, Laila could count his ribs. His eyes were closed, his head drooped, and his palms, with their long, loosely curled fingers, dripped blood. Blood also trickled down his feet and his forehead, which was encircled by a spiky Alice band. He looked sad but beautiful, with magnolia skin, long caramel locks and a slim, straight nose like a sharpened pencil. Laila peered at Bua's blunt profile and, gazing past her, at Amanat's bulging eyes and sloping forehead. The man on the cross didn't look like anyone in the church.

'Bua, is that your prophet on the cross?' Laila whispered.

'Yes, that's Jesus.'

'Why does he look so different to everyone here?'

'Because he is Irish.'

'Shush, everybody.' Facing the congregation, Sister Clementine raised a finger to her lips. 'Shush. Now. We will start with "I Cannot Come". For those who can read, it's on page fourteen. The rest, sing by heart. Ready, Sister?'

Her fingers poised above the keys like the talons of a hawk about to swoop on its hapless prey, the nun at the piano nodded. But in that still second, as her hands began their descent towards the keys and the congregation took a deep breath to dive into the music, there was a loud crash behind them. Sister Clementine dropped her hymnbook. Fifty heads swivelled around in unison. Someone was pounding on the net door, kept closed to keep out the flies.

Bua pushed Laila behind her. 'Quick, hide. It's your mother. She's found us.'

Recovering her composure, Sister Clementine waddled towards the door.

'Who is it? What do you want?' she called.

Leaning out into the aisle, Laila saw a girl silhouetted against the sun. Her arms were flung out, and her face was pressed against the netting, flattening her features and making them unrecognizable. Sister Clementine pulled open the door, and the girl stumbled in. Laila knew her instantly.

'Rani!' she called, and pushing past Bua, she ran towards the girl. But Sister Clementine got to her first. She called over her shoulder at the congregation.

'You, all! Stop staring and sing. Play, Sister. Play!' With that, Sister Clementine dragged Rani out into the sun.

The nun's fingers crashed into the keys, and the congregation burst into song. Bua called out to Laila. But Laila ignored her and slipped out of the church. She saw them at once. They were under the mango tree by the gate. Sister Clementine had Rani by her heaving shoulders and, though

Laila couldn't hear what was being said, she could see that the nun was speaking firmly. Rani was crying. Her hands fluttered like poplar leaves in a gale. Laila crept up behind.

'You've got to help me,' Rani sobbed. 'No one else will help me.'

Sister Clementine changed tack. She spoke soothingly, as if calming a startled horse. 'Child, I've told you, I can't help you. It is against my religion. I will burn in hell for it. You must tell your mother. She . . .'

'I can't!' Rani shrieked. 'She'll die. And I'll be killed too.'

'Shush!' Sister Clementine shook her. 'You want the whole world to hear of your shame? You tell your mother, she'll get you married, and you will be fine. You'll see.'

'You don't understand.' Tears coursed down Rani's face. 'You just don't understand.'

'Rani?' called Laila.

Rani's head jerked up. Laila had never seen her like this. Her bloodshot eyes were swollen, and the glossy hair she normally parted in the middle and wore in a neat plait clung to her blotchy face in wisps. Her sweat-drenched shirt was plastered to her slender frame.

'What are you doing here, Laila?' Sister Clementine spun round. 'Go inside at once. Where's Bua?'

'Here, Sister,' Bua puffed as she reached the mango tree 'Here only.'

'Take the child in.'

'No,' Laila shouted. 'I want to stay here. Rani, why are you crying? Has anyone hurt you?'

Rani shook her head, her eyes darting from side to side. 'You didn't see me here,' she said in a hoarse voice, backing away from Laila. She turned and fled, banging the wooden gate behind her.

Laila wanted to run after her, but Bua had a firm grip on her arm.

'What's happened to Rani?' demanded Laila.

Sister Clementine pursed her lips and exchanged a look with Bua.

'Shush, Lailu,' admonished Bua. 'Small mouth, big talk. It's rude for children to question grown-ups.'

6

Laila watched her mother apply make-up at her dressing table. She liked the sounds and smells of this ritual. There was a grown-up allure about the snap of her compact, the discreet cloudburst of hair spray, the whispering squirt of perfume. Dressed in her flannel pyjamas, Laila sat cross-legged on her parent's bed. She rubbed her bare foot against the jade-green brocade of the bedspread. Laila liked this coverlet much more than the cream jacquard one Fareeda used in the summer. Whereas that was a blank sheet, this was a rich tapestry of stories.

It was woven in a repeated pattern of pagodas with smiley roofs. A river meandered by the pagoda and a bridge curved over it. A willow tree leaned its shaggy head toward the river and, in the foreground, two tiny figures clad in baggy pyjamas and mandarin jackets flew a kite. Laila had always thought the figures were girls and had once rashly confided in Sara that in her mind the smaller one was herself and the bigger one flying the kite was Sara. The pagoda behind them was their house, to which all grown-ups were barred entry.

'Those are not girls, stupid, they are boys,' Sara had snorted.

'No, they're not. They're girls. They've got pigtails. See?' Laila had jabbed a finger at the fine curving line of a plait just discernible on the bigger figure. 'They're girls.'

'No, they're not. In China, boys wore pigtails. Like Red Indians. You don't even know that.'

'I do,' Laila had quavered.

'Oh, no, you don't.' Scenting blood, Sara had chanted, 'You're a stupid little cry-baby. Cry-baby, cry-baby.'

'I'm not a cry-baby,' Laila had howled, furious with herself for her ignorance and her tears. Laila's torture had continued for weeks, during which all Sara had to do was whisper 'pigtail' to reduce Laila to a writhing mass of embarrassment. It had been a cruel lesson, and Laila had resolved never again to confide her more fanciful thoughts to Sara.

Laila covered the pigtailed figures with her foot and said, 'I saw Rani today.'

'Rani?' Fareeda's chin was tilted towards her chest, her raised hands inserting a pin into her chignon. 'Kaneez's Rani?'

Laila nodded, her face blank. She did not want Fareeda to glimpse her inner agitation. Since sighting Rani at the church earlier that day, Laila's insides had churned with guilt, fear and shame. When she had first seen Rani sobbing under the mango tree, she had been too confused to understand what was happening. Later, after Rani's abrupt departure when had tried to question Sister Clementine and been rebuffed, Laila had begun to suspect that she was to blame.

During the service, her suspicion had grown and solidified into an awful conviction that she was the cause of Rani's distress. Why else would Rani have ignored her, no, dismissed her, before fleeing? What had she said? *'You* didn't see me here.' She hadn't said it to Bua or even Sister Clementine but to *her*, to Laila. That could only mean one thing. Rani didn't want to be her friend any more. She had been too hurt by Laila's jealous outburst at the picnic. But, even so, why had she come to the church? Surely not to report her to Sister Clementine? Rani knew she could get Laila into much greater trouble by telling Fareeda. So why come to the church? Perhaps Rani had come to the house too, but Fareeda wasn't telling her.

Laila watched her mother carefully in the mirror, alert to the slightest hint of subterfuge.

'Where did you see her?' Three Fareedas lowered their

arms and gazed at Laila from the triptych of the dressing-table mirror.

'I saw her when I went out with Bua today,' Laila mumbled, reluctant to mention the church.

'Here in Sabzbagh? What was she doing so far from home?' Fareeda turned her face this way and that to examine her round bun of hair in the mirror.

'I don't know. She looked . . . sad. She was crying.'

'Did she tell you why?'

Laila shook her head.

'What was she doing here?' repeated Fareeda. 'Was she alone? Where exactly did you bump into her?'

So Rani hadn't come to the house. Had Fareeda wanted to keep Rani's visit secret, she would have changed the subject. Or told Laila off smartly for sticking her nose into issues that did not concern her. To pretend ignorance like this was not her way.

Laila changed the subject. 'Is Mrs Bullock going to have a big dinner party tonight?'

'I shouldn't think so. She's inviting the new colonel who's arrived at Colewallah Cantonment in place of Colonel Jamshed.'

Hester Bullock, one of a handful of the British who had elected to stay on after Independence, lived across the canal from the Azeems. Though divided by a twenty-year age gap and a profound difference in sensibility – Hester was an unapologetic Raj relic, while Fareeda's parents had struggled for national independence – an unlikely friendship had sprung up between the two women. Initially, Fareeda had been wary of the Englishwoman's brusque manner and frequent rants against 'these bumbling fools', as she called all Pakistani politicians. But, despite herself, Fareeda had grown to appreciate Hester's gruff sincerity and unexpected acts of generosity – an invitation to stay after a bad storm snapped the electricity cables in Sabzbagh; pony rides for the girls during their holidays; Christmas dinner with turkey and the trimmings. And, if truth be told, the social isolation of Sabzbagh had forced Fareeda to reconsider some of the prejudices she could afford to indulge in cosmopolitan Lahore.

Fareeda dabbed Diorella at her throat and replaced the bottle on the dressing table, exactly in line with the can of hairspray and the jar of night cream. She liked her things to be just so. She caught Laila's eye in the mirror and winked at her.

Laila had heard it said by the older ladies in her family that Fareeda had salt in her face. Laila didn't know what that meant, but she thought Fareeda very pretty. Her eyes were large and expressive. In repose, they were clear, tranquil pools, but Laila had seen them freeze into ice cubes. Her face was defined by jutting cheekbones and a square chin, but its angularity was offset by a cushiony mouth and a rounded forehead. Fareeda's face looked softer when framed by her wavy, shoulder-length hair. But she found the swing of her wayward locks irksome and preferred to have it out of the way, if not swept up in a chignon, then pulled back with a tortoiseshell clasp.

Fareeda raised her bare arms to push back a stray lock of hair. Not for the first time, Laila wished she had her mother's apricot skin and rounded, creamy limbs. But of the two sisters, it was Sara who took after Fareeda. Laila had inherited Tariq's height and slender build. Laila pulled back the sleeve of her pyjama jacket and examined her gravy-brown arm. Her upper arms were scarcely wider than her wrists, which made her jagged elbows seem huge. There was a scab on her elbow. Laila prodded it, testing to see if it was ripe enough to be pulled.

'Don't, darling.' Fareeda was standing above her. 'It'll scar.'

Laila straightened her sleeve. She'd wait till she was in the privacy of her room to plunder the scab properly. She watched as Fareeda shook out the pleats of her pale-green sari.

'You look pretty.' Laila flung out her arms.

'Thank you, little squirrel.' Fareeda dropped a kiss on top of Laila's head. Her emerald pendant brushed against Laila's face.

'I like your sari.' Laila fingered the trailing pallu of Fareeda's sari.

'It's a jamdani. It's a bit chilly for jamdani, but I thought I'd wear it one last time before packing it away for the winter.'

'Did you buy it in Lahore?'

'No, I got it on our last visit to East Pakistan,' said Fareeda.

'When did you go?'

'Oh, about five years ago. Yes, I think it was 1966, the year you got measles.'

'Why didn't you take me?'

'Because you'd just started school.'

'Is it nice?'

'What, Chittagong? It's lovely. All lush and green. That juicy green we get after the monsoon? All day long a soft, salty breeze blows in from the sea. When you run your tongue over your lips, you can taste the sea.'

'Will you take me one day so I can also taste the sea?' asked Laila.

'I hope so. Now, you must go to bed. Shall I take you to your room?'

Laila's bed was turned down. An Enid Blyton paperback lay face down on a pink satin quilt.

'Which one is this?' Fareeda removed the book from the bed.

'*The Adventures of the Wishing Chair*. Can I have new curtains?'

'Why? What's wrong with these?'

'They have teddy bears on them. They're for babies.'

'What sort do you want?'

'Flowered ones like Sara's.' Laila scrambled on to the bed. 'I also want you to put away all these dolls. I'll keep Monopoly and Ludo and the carom board, as well as my paint box and my books and my treasure box. But the rest you can put away.'

'Why?'

'I want to be grown-up. Like everyone else.' Laila slid down under the quilt, pulled it up to her chest and folded her arms over it.

'You know, you should enjoy your childhood as long as you can. When you are older, you'll realize how precious it was.'

'Does that mean I can't have new curtains?'

Fareeda's lips twitched. 'We'll see.' She kissed Laila's cheek and moved to the door. But at the door, she turned back, a thoughtful expression on her face. 'Why are you, all of a sudden, in such a hurry to grow up? Has something happened?'

Laila hesitated for a moment but then shook her head.

'You know, darling, that if something bothers you, you can always tell me, don't you?'

Laila nodded. 'Could you please send Bua to me?'

'Of course. Good night.' Fareeda turned the handle and made a moue of distaste. It was greasy. She made a mental note to tell Bua off.

'The Empress sent her servants to search for the girl. They scrambled over high mountains and waded across rushing rivers, but the girl had vanished, like breath on a mirror. She'd jumped on to her magic horse . . .'

'Bua, why did Rani come to the church today?' Laila lay on her stomach across the bed. Her chin was cupped in her palm.

'Baba, I'm telling you such a nice story.'

'I want to know about Rani.'

'Know what about Rani?' Bua yawned and stretched out on

the rug. She tucked a cushion under her head, clasped her arms over her dome-like stomach and shut her eyes.

'Don't pretend to be asleep, because I know you're not. Why was Rani there?'

'Uff, baba, it's so late.' Bua's eyes were still closed. 'Soon your parents will be home from memsahib's dinner. Shut your eyes and go to sleep.'

'I'm not sleepy. Why did she come?'

'Why did *who* come?'

'Stop acting stupid,' Laila shouted.

Bua's eyes flew open, and she reared up in indignation.

'Is that any way to speak to your old, sick ayah? Hain? After everything I've done for you, washing your nappies when you were a baby, feeding you, bathing you, getting up ten, ten times a night to see that the jinns hadn't taken you . . .'

'I'm sorry.' Laila slid off the bed and snuggled into Bua's lap. Bua smelt comfortingly of snuff and starch. 'Can I have a pinch of your snuff?'

'Look at you!' Bua cuffed Laila gently on the side of her head. 'Next you'll want a drag of my hookah. And Bibi will say, "Bua, you've taught my little girl bad things like smoke and snuff." And she'll kick me out with a big kick on my bottoms.'

'No one will kick you out. I won't let them.' Laila rested her back against Bua's stomach and toyed with the cross around her neck. 'Why won't you tell me about Rani?'

'Because I don't know anything to tell.'

'When Rani left, you and Sister Clementine stood whispering together.'

'So? We were whispering about other things.' Bua shrugged.

'Ammi also wanted to know why Rani was crying.'

Bua spun Laila around to face her. 'How did she know Rani was there? You told her?'

'I didn't say *where* I saw her,' said Laila.

'What did you say then?'

'I saw Rani when I was out with you and she looked sad,' explained Laila.

'And what did Bibi say?'

'I told you. She wanted to know why Rani had been crying.'

'Oh, Lailu. I wish you hadn't. Now we'll all get into trouble.'

'Why?'

'Because Bibi will find out that I took you to the church and she'll get angry with me and she'll find out about Rani and . . .'

'Find out *what* about Rani?'

'Tchah! You're like a puppy with a bone. Going on gnawing, gnawing. All right then. Rani has been a bad girl.'

'But Rani's *not* a bad girl.' Rising to her knees, Laila brought her face close to Bua's and enunciated deliberately, threateningly, 'Don't call Rani a bad girl, Bua. She's a good girl.'

Taken aback, Bua retracted. 'You're right, baba. She's not a bad girl.'

Mollified, Laila rested her back against Bua's stomach again. 'Bua,' she asked casually, 'could Rani be upset because someone had been mean to her?'

'Could be.'

'And could that person who'd been mean – could it by any chance have been a girl?'

'A girl?'

'Mmm, say, around eight years old? Could Rani have come to the church to tell on that other girl who'd been mean to her?'

Bua's arms reached out on either side of Laila to enfold her in a plump embrace.

'No, my baba. All eight-year-old girls should rest easy, because they have nothing to do with Rani's . . . er . . . problem.'

'What's her problem?'

'Her situation . . . Her problem is something she's done herself.'

'Done herself?' Laila tried to imagine an action peculiar enough to land Rani in church. As far as Laila knew, Rani had no truck with the nuns. Unlike Sabzbagh, Kalanpur had never been a focus of missionary activity. It had barely any Christians at all. The few girls who attended school in Kalanpur went to the Kalanpur Model School. No one came to the convent, where it was feared they would be made to sing hymns about three gods.

'But what has she done that she needed to tell *Sister Clementine* about? She doesn't even know Sister Clementine.'

'Some things you can't tell children.'

'If you don't tell me, I'll tell Ammi you took me to the church.'

Bua gave Laila a hard stare. 'All right then. I'll tell you what she did. But only if you promise not to tell your mother or Rani.'

Hester Bullock's dining room was lit by a chandelier. It was the only chandelier in Colewallah district. It had been brought out from Waterford in 1934 by Gerald O'Brian, at the special request of his neighbour, Thomas Rambridge. Tonight, with only seven of its sixteen bulbs working, it still managed to cast a mellow glow on the dining room, which had changed little since Thomas Rambridge had assembled that tinkling crystal bouquet.

The Turkish rug on the dark wooden floor was more than a little frayed from successive generations of pointers and retrievers cutting their teeth on its tassels. Above a stucco fireplace was the stuffed head of a leopard, minus one of its yellowed canines. A carriage clock ticked on the mantelpiece. A shisham sideboard stretched along one wall. Displayed on it was an assortment of silver objects – a punch bowl the size of a bird bath, a Kashmiri samovar with a matching tray, a Victorian tea service and a jumble of silver trophies won at horsy conclaves all over the subcontinent.

The wall above the sideboard was hung with black-and-white photographs. They were mostly taken at the racecourses of Bombay, Delhi, Lahore and Karachi, and featured Thomas Rambridge, a barrel-chested, bow-legged man in a pith helmet and jodhpurs, holding the reins of handsome thoroughbreds. In one photograph, Mrs Rambridge also made an appearance. She clutched a crocodile handbag and looked out at the world with the small, wary eyes she had bequeathed to Hester.

The November evening was chilly, and a log fire crackled in the grate. Even through the closed windows, guests could hear the distant yowl of jackals. Bridgebad House sat in the middle of Hester Bullock's estate of some nine thousand acres. As the crow flew, it was four miles from Sabzbagh but, embalmed in a different age, it was a world away.

When guests drove down the avenue of jamun trees leading up to the house, they felt as if they were travelling back to the heyday of the Raj. Rose-covered pergolas, grass tennis courts, the elegant, columned portico, the massive presence of the house itself – all hinted at a life of affluence and certainty.

Yet the plaster on the portico was falling away in chunks. The tennis court was overgrown with weeds, and the bedrooms on the first floor of the house were shuttered and shrouded in dustsheets. Once the focus of many a jolly party – tennis weekends, race dances and duck shoots, for which Lahore's gymkhana crowd would motor down in open-topped cars – the house now echoed only to Hester's imperious 'koi hais.'

Around a dining table that could seat eighteen, tonight six people were gathered for dinner. Two silver candlesticks stood on either side of a murky crystal bowl of narcissi. A bearer in a limp turban and a white brass-buttoned Nehru jacket shuffled barefoot around the table serving the guests thick beige soup from a silver tureen.

'Ah, mulligatawny soup,' boomed Colonel Butt. He was in his mid-forties and had black patent-leather hair and an imposing chin. Dressed in a blazer, with a silk cravat tucked into the collar of his cream shirt, he looked urbane and at ease. It had taken him at least twenty minutes of fiddling in front of his mirror to get the folds of the cravat just so. But Colonel Butt was a dogged man. It had given him great pleasure eventually to impose his will on the slippery silk. He'd checked himself in the flyblown mirror in Hester's entrance hall and been gratified to see that the cravat looked just right – not too rigid, not too contrived, in fact, almost effortless in its fluid grace. Effortlessness was a virtue the colonel coveted, since almost everything in his life had come to him with great effort.

He poured himself a third ladle of soup. 'I haven't had decent mulligatawny soup since my posting to Karachi four years ago. Still, mustn't complain. Colewallah cantt is not without its charms.'

'Such as?' Hester raised her peppery eyebrows. Hester was a tall, thickset woman in her early sixties with no neck and several chins. She had short grey hair, cut with little regard for fashion or fancy, small, shrewd eyes and pink cheeks mapped by a fine network of thread veins. Her only concessions to vanity were a smear of orange lipstick and a diamond brooch pinned to her prow-like bosom.

'Oh, fresh air, fireflies, buffalo milk by the bucketful, peas, tomatoes and whatnots from the garden. You should ask my wife. This is her department.'

Mrs Butt, a sparrow-like woman with sharp features and a shrill voice, looked up from her soup.

'Yes, yes, lots of vegetables. Peas and cabbages and carrots, and snakes and bats also, but schooling is the real problem, isn't it, Mrs Azeem?'

'For children, vegetables or bats?' asked Fareeda, smiling.

'What? Oh no, I meant the children. Hamad is thirteen and Huma baby ten, and I don't know what to do. I've left them in Pindi with my mother-in-law – my own mother passed away seven years ago – but it's so far. I've been here only three weeks, and already I'm missing them too much. We were lucky before with postings in Pindi, Kharian and Karachi – all towns with schools.'

Fareeda nodded. 'During term time our girls stay with my mother in Lahore, which, luckily, is a bit nearer than Pindi.'

'How often do you visit them?'

'Whenever I want. In fact, I may go tomorrow for the day to see my elder daughter.'

'Hai, see, so lucky! I can only go twice a month. So, where in Lahore does your mother live?'

'Gulberg.'

'Where in Gulberg?'

Fareeda raised her eyebrows. Noticing the gesture from across the table, the colonel cut in. 'I hardly think it's appropriate to grill Mrs Azeem.'

'She doesn't mind. Anyways, what's to mind?' shrugged Mrs Butt. 'I'm only asking, and that also because my mother's family's from Lahore. Otherwise, I have no interest.'

Fareeda gave Mrs Butt her mother's address.

'Is that the house with tall, tall mango trees in the back garden?' squealed Mrs Butt. 'Hai, Allah, my auntie's house is just on its backside. As children we'd climb up the common wall and eye your green mangoes. Imagine! Your mother and my auntie have adjoining backsides.'

'Who'd have thought that, eh?' Hester guffawed. 'Adjoining backsides, indeed.'

The colonel scowled at his wife. Mrs Butt looked puzzled. With a shrug, she applied herself to her soup.

Edward Seaton was the sixth guest at dinner. He was a

mild-mannered elderly Englishman with thinning grey hair, pale blue eyes and a bow tie. He served Hester as a farm manager-cum-vet.

'How is your project doing?' he asked Tariq. 'I believe you've received a grant from the British Development Association?'

'Where did you hear that?'

'Oh, the good old Imperial Club grapevine,' said Mr Seaton. 'Last week in Lahore, I ran into Davies, the BDA chap, at the Club. He was all praise for your project. He didn't see why you shouldn't get your grant.'

'They hinted the same to me when they came to have a look, but I don't want to count on it until I have the money in hand.'

'Wise, but unnecessarily modest, if I may say so. That's a fine programme you run, and it deserves every bit of help it can get.'

'Excuse my ignorance, but what is your project, Tariq Sahib?' enquired the colonel.

'Oh, our Tariq here is a bit of a visionary,' laughed Hester. 'He's set up a nice little garment factory in Sabzbagh. They stitch children's clothes on electric machines. At first, Fareeda used to oversee the finish, but now your people more or less run it themselves, don't they?'

'That's right, Hester,' said Tariq. 'With any luck we'll be branching into knitwear soon.'

'Is it very profitable?' the colonel asked Tariq.

'We run it as a cooperative. Everyone's fully trained now, and they set and meet their own targets. I helped them find markets in Lahore, but now they've got their own contacts. It's a small cottage industry, really, but they can go on to bigger things.'

'And these young men, having acquired all this know-how, will be content to stay in their villages, or will they head for the towns?' queried the colonel.

'Young women. We train women. Our entire centre is run by and for women.'

'Women? Why?'

'Because it's time they got to run something too. Don't you think?'

'They run their homes, don't they?' asked the colonel.

'And what a thankless task that is!' harrumphed Hester.

'*And* unpaid,' pointed out Fareeda.

'Yes, but they have the satisfaction of raising their children,' persisted the colonel.

'And since it is women who raise children, isn't it important to educate them too?' asked Tariq.

'Already it's so hard to find good ayahs,' Mrs Butt chipped in. 'You educate these village girls, and they'll turn up their noses at working in our homes.'

'I hope so,' said Tariq.

'You hope so?' shrieked Mrs Butt. 'Then you are your own worst enemy.'

'What Tariq means, I think, Mrs Butt,' Mr Seaton explained, 'is that village girls should also have some freedom in deciding their future.'

'They have too much freedom already, if you ask me,' sniffed Mrs Butt. 'The way they run around the fields and mix-up with men, I've never seen such fast behaviour in Karachi even. Why, only yesterday, I caught the girl who does our ironing . . .'

'Youngsters will be youngsters,' the colonel chided his wife. Turning to Tariq, he continued, 'I'm all for idealism, Mr Azeem. God knows, I'm as idealistic and liberal as the next johnnie. It's all very well to educate these simple girls and put fine ideas in their heads, but where are you going to find jobs for them in Sabzbagh? How many garment factories can you subsidize?'

'Oh, come on, Colonel.' Hester waved an impatient hand.

'Those who can't work in factories can become seamstresses and take in work. They're not training rocket-scientists, you know.'

A flash of irritation crossed the colonel's face. But, schooling his features into a bland smile, he said to Hester, 'I hear your family has had a long association with Bridgebad, Mrs Bullock. How did they come to settle here?'

'None of this "Mrs Bullock" nonsense. I'm Hester.'

The colonel inclined his head as if acknowledging a salute from a captain.

'Well, Daddy came out here in the early twenties after the Great War.' Hester dabbed her mouth with a napkin, smudging orange lipstick over the corners of her lips. 'The government had just laid out this irrigation network – the canal dividing my land from Tariq's here is part of it, as I'm sure you know. Edgar Cole, a senior officer in the administration, was the brain behind the irrigation scheme. He named this particular district after himself. "Old King Cole", Daddy used to call him. But there was one small problem. There was nobody to farm it.'

Tariq cleared his throat. 'Correction, Hester . . .'

'Sorry. There were a few people, like Tariq's family, who've lived in these parts, for what, a few hundred years now? But the ordinary man in the field, the kammi, didn't know how to farm.'

'It wasn't as if they didn't *know*, Hester . . .'

'Oh, all right. There hadn't been the opportunity, with water so scarce. So the government invited white families to settle, farm and kick – or shall we say *mould*? – the kammis into shape. Is that better, Tariq?' She threw him a mischievous smile.

'Daddy took nine thousand acres on lease – oh, yes, it's leased – and was given a charter to breed mules for the army. He built this house, named the estate Bridgebad, imported bloodstock from Ireland and got on with breeding horses. Of course, he also reared mules, but it was for its racers that Bridgebad became famous. By the mid thirties he was selling to maharajas all over India.

'By then, other white settlers had also arrived in the area. There were the Hays of Haypore, near Colewallah town, and James Russell had a nice little holding fifteen miles from here. Of course the O'Brians were across the canal, and there was that odd bird, Ferguson, who went native and wore dhotis. But, apart from Ferguson, who died last year, the others went off in dribs and drabs after Independence.'

'What happened to the rest of your family?'

'Poor old Toby got mixed up with a money-grubbing Eurasian girl in Srinagar. Daddy hit the roof and threw him out. So he went off to live in Goa with his chee-chee girl. Within a year he'd died of dysentery. My parents died in a car crash in '45. Henry was killed in the war in Burma.'

Hester drained her glass and replaced it with a thud on the table.

'I inherited Bridgebad. My late husband's family had been in and out of India for a hundred years. He felt at home here. Horses were still selling. Farm was making a tidy profit. Even when the others started packing up after '47, we thought we'd take our chances here. My husband, as Tariq will tell you, passed away ten years ago, while shooting duck on Bridgebad Lake. As for me, well, I'm the last of the Mohicans. No children. When I drop, you can plant me under the narcissi in the front lawn.' Hester picked up a silver bell and rang it furiously.

'Koi hai? Hayat? There you are. We've finished the soup.'

'Yes, memsahib.' The bearer removed the soup plates.

Hayat returned bearing aloft a steaming silver platter. It was piled high with lamb chops, lamb kidneys, calves' liver, a quail or two, and chicken legs covered with a muddy brown sauce. The meat was hemmed in by a continuous ridge of stiff mashed potatoes, pinched into little peaks by thick fingers that had left their imprints on the mash.

'Meex grill,' Hayat announced solemnly.

'How is Laila doing? I hope fully recovered from the typhoid?' Mr Seaton enquired of Fareeda.

'Oh, yes, thank you.' Fareeda helped herself to a chicken breast. 'She's fine now, but she tires quite easily. I haven't sent her back to school yet, because the winter holidays are almost here. In fact, what with all this sabre-rattling with India, I thought I ought to bring Sara here as well. I can't help thinking she'll be safer here than in Lahore.'

'Hurry, man, hurry. We haven't got all night.' Hester clapped her hands at Hayat. 'What's this about sabre-rattling? You think there's going to be war with India, Tariq?'

The possibility of a third war with India had grown ever more real as political events had unfolded disastrously over the previous year in East Pakistan, or Bengal, as it had been known before Independence. A national election almost a year ago had yielded an East Pakistani majority. Tired of being treated as a colony of its physically larger but less populous western wing, the Bengalis had voted as one for a fellow Bengali, Sheikh Mujeeb-ur-Rehman. West Pakistan had not accepted the results.

The Bengalis had rebelled. In retaliation, General Yahya Khan, the army chief and martial-law administrator, had launched a ferocious military crackdown. Mujib was arrested and taken to West Pakistan. His close associates had escaped to India, where they had formed a government in exile. A bitter civil war had raged for eight months now. Though the government imposed almost total censorship on news from Bengal, rumours of rape camps, of pillage and slaughter, had leaked out. Millions of East Pakistani refugees streamed into India.

Still smarting from the inconclusive war with Pakistan of

1965, India had been covertly training Bengali militants, the mukti bahini, to fight West Pakistani soldiers. Now it did so openly.

Separated from East Pakistan by a thousand miles of hostile Indian territory, West Pakistani lines of communication were stretched to the limit. The Eastern Command was isolated in Bengal, and the Bengalis and Indians were closing in. Morale in the Pakistani army had plummeted. Sceptics like Tariq, who did not believe the government's propaganda of a successful military campaign, watched with concern.

'I hope there isn't going to be a war, Hester,' said Tariq. 'But I fear there will be. With all due respect to Colonel Butt, army action is not a panacea . . .'

'Ours is a highly disciplined army, Tariq Sahib,' the colonel cut in. 'We are not some motley crew of irregulars that is going to run amok . . .'

'But isn't that what the soldiers *are* doing?' Fareeda interrupted. 'Running amok? What else would you call rape camps and torture chambers?'

'You mustn't believe everything you hear, madam.' The colonel's thin smile did not slip. 'Particularly when it is reported by biased outsiders. You should have faith in your own people.'

'Oh, but I do. I have complete faith in the Bengalis.'

'Haw, you are Bengali?' Mrs Butt yelped. 'I was thinking you were Punjabi, like us.'

Fareeda ignored Mrs Butt's outburst. The woman was clearly an idiot.

'Touching though it is,' scoffed the colonel, 'your faith in the Bengalis is not reciprocated.' The colonel addressed himself to Fareeda. 'You let a mukti bahini thug in here tonight and he'll slit your throat as you sleep. Our boys are risking their lives so that . . .'

'Hester's question was about the likelihood of war with India, Colonel,' Mr Seaton reminded him softly. 'What is the possibility of that?'

'Zero, absolutely zero.' The colonel jabbed the air with his knife. 'Unless the Indians want a bloody nose. Oh, they'll carry on aiding these wretched Bingos through the back door. But they won't come out and fight like men. You needn't worry about a war.' He turned his sleek Brylcreemed head from Fareeda to Hester. 'Life will continue here in Bridgebad just as it always has. That, I guarantee you.'

'That's the pity of it,' said Hester. 'Half the country plunged into a civil war, and here we are, carrying on as if nothing were amiss.'

'Believe me, you wouldn't want to be in the thick of it,' muttered the colonel, fingering his cravat.

Fareeda decided she did not like the colonel's cravat. The colours – crimson swirls on a sulphurous yellow background – were gaudy, and it was tied all wrong. Instead of lying unobtrusively against his throat, it thrust out of his collar like the bristling ruff of an enraged cockerel. And the blazer with those ghastly brassy buttons. So flashy.

Gazing at her husband across the table, Fareeda smiled. He was understated in a pale-blue sea-island cotton shirt and grey wool trousers. At his wrists gleamed the simple platinum cufflinks her parents had given him at their wedding. It occurred to her that Tariq had changed little since she had spotted him at a garden party fourteen years ago.

He'd been standing to one side, a tall, lanky man, with thick hair flopping over one eyebrow. Though he had laughed and chatted readily enough, she noticed that he was quite content to observe as well. Fareeda sensed that, like her, he was in the crowd though not of it. There were no loud brays of laughter, no backslapping, no elaborate display of bonhomie. He did not flit from person to person. He spoke to few people but concentrated fully on them when he did so. Fareeda strained to hear his quiet conversation.

His looks, Fareeda reflected now, had worn well. His thick hair was threaded with silver at the temples but still flopped boyishly over his right eye. While many of the lean, lithe youths she had known in Lahore were now portly figures, Tariq could fit comfortably into the cricketing whites he'd had at college. She observed his heaped plate. It was quite unfair how he never seemed to gain any weight. And he ate silently, unlike the colonel, who sawed and chomped his meat as if he were squatting by a fire in a neolithic cave.

'So you admit, then, that there are atrocious things going on in East Pakistan?' Tariq asked the colonel.

'Civil war is not a polite, sanitary affair. It's like war within a household. Between husband and wife, if you will.'

Hester cleared her throat. '*Que sera, sera*, as they say. What will be, will be. Now where's that bread pudding? Hurry up, Hayat, or we'll be here till tiffin tomorrow.'

7

A few days later, in Fareeda's kitchen at Sabzbagh, Rehmat dropped a pinch of saffron into an empty teacup. He poured a teaspoon of warm water over the crimson threads and, cradling the cup in both hands, swirled the tangerine liquid. Bringing the cup up to his cauliflower nose, he inhaled deeply.

'Ah, Lailu, smell that.' The cook brought the cup over to the kitchen bench where Laila sat next to Bua. He held it under Laila's nose. 'Isn't that the best scent in the world?'

Laila pushed it away. 'I prefer the smell of petrol.'

'Petrol? Petrol? How can you compare the smell of petrol to zafraan? Bua, what do we make of this girl?'

Busy lighting her hookah, Bua grunted.

'All right, then, try these.' Rehmat offered slivers of almonds to Laila. He had the hands of a surgeon, long of finger and slender of palm. When he sliced vegetables, his hands moved so fast that they seemed to blur. Though he was an inspired cook, Rehmat looked as if he'd never had a square meal himself. He lived on gallons of stewed tea and an endless chain of unfiltered K-2. Rehmat was in his sixties, but with his sparse white hair and thin turkey neck, he seemed ancient to Laila. Ancient and pious. There was a navy-blue smudge in the middle of his forehead. He had got it from touching his head to his straw prayer-mat five times a day, every day for all his adult life.

The smudge was a special sign of holiness, Barkat, the driver, had told Laila. On the day of judgement, when a stormy darkness would engulf the world and shrieking people would run helter-skelter, a piercing light would beam out from his forehead, and he'd be able to guide people to safety. Laila had seen pictures of coal-miners going down shafts with head-lamps. She imagined Rehmat would look much the same on the day of judgement.

'I was going to put these on the rice pudding I'm making for your grandmother, but you can have some.' He held out the almonds to Laila.

'Uh-uh. Don't like nuts.'

'Don't like nuts, don't like zafraan? What *do* you teach this little girl, Bua?'

'She likes nuts. Laila, eat!' Bua ordered. 'They're good for the brain. Brain gets used up with studies. Almonds put it back.'

'Only if Rehmat lets me help make the pudding first,' bargained Laila.

'I've already cooked it, but you can help decorate it.' He led Laila to the stone-topped table on which he rolled the dough for his paper-thin chappatis. He let her scatter the nuts over the pudding. Then he wiped the edges of the glass bowl with a dishcloth and pursed his lips.

'What a waste of zafraan and almonds.'

'Isn't this the kheer we're taking to Dadi's house this evening?' Laila asked.

'Same, same. But who will eat? Your grandmother will take one bite only. Your parents will have two spoonfuls. You will have your ant's share, and the rest that greedy Kaneez will polish off. Waste, such waste.'

'Kaneez isn't greedy. She's so thin she'd look like a toothpick if she didn't have a hunched back. She's nice. She lets me shell peas,' said Laila.

Rehmat snorted. 'Making a child do all her work!'

Kaneez was not popular among the servants at Sabzbagh. They thought her aloof and haughty, as if the length of her service with Sardar Begum gave her licence to put on airs.

Laila was looking forward to this visit to Sardar Begum's

haveli with an equal mix of eagerness and dread. She was desperate to see Rani so she could apologize for her peevishness at the picnic and also find out why she had come to the church in such a state last Sunday. Though Bua had given her an explanation, Laila was not satisfied with it. Having been protected much of her life from unsavoury facts through evasive half-lies, Laila had developed finely tuned sensors when it came to detecting explanations from adults that did not ring true. Bua's explanation seemed too pallid to justify such tumult in Rani. The only thing was to ask Rani herself, even if it meant receiving an earful first.

Laila joined Bua on the green bench. Over the years, the bench had served her as a grocery shop, a restaurant and a train. But now Laila thought of it mainly as a bench. She snuggled up to Bua and let her gaze roam over the large kitchen.

It was the nicest kitchen in the world. In Lahore, the cooking was done on a gas stove, but Rehmat cooked with big lumps of coal, lustrous as a crow's breast, which gave off a warm, smoky aroma. A fridge hummed in one corner of the room, and an enamel sink with a brass tap was in the other. Whenever Laila turned the tap, the cool, metallic smell of brass would linger on her hands. No other tap in the world made her hands smell golden.

A battered swivel-chair stood by the bench. Rehmat had appropriated it when Tariq retired it from his study. It was reserved exclusively for Rehmat's use. The only picture in the room was a gold-framed photograph of the Kaaba. It hung above the door to keep out evil influences. Rehmat's son-in-law had brought it for him when he returned from a pilgrimage to Mecca.

'Baba Rehmat, when will you go to Mecca for Haj?' asked Laila.

'When He summons me.' Rehmat pointed upwards. 'You

can't just get up and go; you have to be called. And He only calls those He wants.'

'Dadi went.'

'She was called.'

'My other grandmother's also been.'

'She must have been called also.'

'How come you've not been called even though you are so holy? Nor Barkat, nor Fazal, nor Kaneez? Does Allah only invite rich people?'

'We-ell.' Rehmat scratched his head. 'Maybe the rich can accept his invitation more readily.'

'And if you go without being called?' asked Laila.

'People try. But either they fall ill, or they can't get on a plane, or when they land there is a letter already waiting calling them back because a dear one has died at home,' explained Rehmat. 'That happens to rich people also. You can't go uninvited to Allah's house.'

'How will Allah call you?'

'Maybe I'll hear a voice. Or have a dream. Maybe someone will insist I go with him. He can act through agents, you know.'

'Like secret agents in wars?'

'Don't talk about the war.' Barkat's weary voice sounded from the door.

'Barkat!' Laila ran to greet her parents' driver. Barkat dropped a lump of raw sugar studded with almonds into Laila's palm.

'All the way from Simbal for you,' said the driver, patting Laila's head. 'Made from my brother's sugar cane. The sweetest, the purest, once eaten, never forgotten.'

'Welcome back, Barkat. When did you return?' asked Bua.

'Our bus got in at midday.'

'And not a moment too soon,' muttered Rehmat. 'My hands were about to fall off, cooking ten chapattis every meal time for that replacement driver. Man eats like a jinn. How's your family?'

Barkat lowered himself on the bench beside Bua. Bua sat in her habitual pose, with one foot resting on the ground and the other drawn up on to the bench. From time to time, she dipped her head to draw on the hookah's spout. Laila sat down between them.

Barkat removed his white, crocheted cap and ran a hand over his close-cropped grey hair. Although well over fifty, he was a burly man with big shoulders and strong arms. Usually, when he returned from a month's stay in his village in far-off Potohar, his ruddy face glowed. He often boasted that the spring water in his village was the best in the world: 'My Simbal is full of hundred-year-old men who can open walnuts with their teeth. Every second man in my Simbal is a soldier.'

But this time, he looked tired and drawn, as if he hadn't slept for days. There were dark circles under his eyes.

'Rehmat, make Barkat some tea,' said Bua. 'Is everything in your village all right, Barkat?'

'Have they been making you slave in the fields? These Potoharis have no pity for anyone, not even old men like you.' Rehmat chuckled as he handed Barkat a steaming mug of tea.

But Barkat did not rise to the jest. He placed the mug quietly between his feet.

'Barkat, may my tongue drop off before it comes to pass, but there isn't any bad news about Shareef from East Pakistan, is there?' asked Rehmat.

Barkat's head drooped. 'Shareef is still alive,' he replied. 'As far as I know, he's not wounded either.'

'May the Holy Mother encase him in an invisible shield,' said Bua. 'May bullets bounce off him.'

'But that is good news, Barkat,' said Rehmat. 'The boy is alive and well.'

'Yes, but for how long? While we were in Simbal, news came that two boys from the village had been killed in action. They were younger than Shareef. I know their parents, I grew up with them. They are broken, broken.' He shook his head.

Laila touched Barkat's arm. 'But Shareef will be fine. You'll see, he'll be fine.'

Barkat stroked her head and murmured, 'Honey and sugar in your mouth, little one.'

'When did you last hear from him?' asked Bua.

'Just before I left, I got this letter.' Carefully, he removed a folded piece of paper from his breast pocket. 'Here, Rehmat, you read. I've read it so many times that the letters look like ants to me.'

Rehmat unfolded the paper, fished out a pair of glasses from his breast pocket and placed them on the tip of his nose. He cleared his throat and began reading in a loud, formal voice.

'My revered Abu, after asalam-elekum, I ask after your health. I hope, that with the grace of Almighty Allah, you, my mother, my brother and my sisters are happy. My platoon has been moved to the district of Joydepur. It is hot and muggy here. We seem always to be trudging through rice fields with water swirling around our ankles. Many boys have malaria; some have been bitten by snakes. I dream at night of the cool breeze that ripples through the orchards of Sabzbagh. In the months that I have been here we have done too much fighting. The Bengalis are small, thin people, but they are sly and quick and fight like scorpions. They neither look like us, nor speak our language, nor eat the same food. I have begun to hate them and am proud to say that I have already killed four. But now at night I sleep with my eyes open. I know a ghazi should not speak like this, but I am frightened. I don't want to become a shaheed. Already sixteen jawans I knew here have been killed. Please ask my mother to pray for me. Allah listens to a mother's prayers. Also, if I have done you any wrong, please forgive me today, for I don't know what will happen tomorrow. Your loving and obedient son, Mohammed Shareef.'

Rehmat finished the letter and handed it back to Barkat. A pot of boiling water bubbled unheeded on the stove. Rehmat removed his glasses and replaced them in his pocket. Laila stole a look at Barkat. His eyes were fixed unseeingly on the floor. Bua was muttering a prayer under her breath. Laila could tell she was praying from the way she fingered her cross.

'What is a ghazi, Barkat?' Laila asked.

'Uh?' Barkat roused himself from his stupor. 'A ghazi is a Muslim who goes to fight a jehad and comes back alive.'

'And a shaheed?'

'A shaheed is one who is martyred in jehad.'

'A ghazi when he finally dies, even as an old man in his bed, goes straight to paradise, no questions asked,' added Rehmat. 'Both ghazis and shaheeds have very high standing in heaven. On judgement day, while sinners like us trudge past in rags, they will sit up high on golden thrones gazing down at us.'

'And a jehad is a battle, isn't it?'

'Jehad is a fight against unbelievers, kaffirs,' said Rehmat fiercely. 'It's a Muslim's duty.'

'But my mother says the Bengalis are our brothers. They are Muslims too, aren't they?'

Rehmat snorted. 'Then why do they fight us?' He handed the letter back to Barkat. 'Have you met Bibi and Sahib yet?'

Barkat pocketed the letter. 'Yes. They told me we're going to Kalanpur this evening. How have things been there?'

'The same. Sardar Begum is Sardar Begum. Kaneez is still alive,' Rehmat said dryly. 'And that son-of-a-dog . . .'

'Um-hm, no bad language in front of the child,' Bua warned. 'Otherwise, the Owners will pull *my* ears.'

Though Bua's veiled reference was for Laila's benefit, Laila knew that Bua was talking about her parents. When not wishing to name them, the servants often spoke of them as 'the Owners', or else, 'the Others'. When Bua used either of these codes, Laila understood that an implicit criticism of her parents was to follow. Laila was used to hearing Bua carp about Fareeda's pernickety nature or Sardar Begum's tight-fistedness. Young as she was, she knew that Bua was letting off steam. And Bua, for her part, appreciated that her complaints must never cross that fine line into open rebellion which would divide Laila's loyalties.

'Let me guess,' Barkat said with a sardonic smile. 'You mean Mashooq, Kaneez's son-in-law?'

'Who else? I met him in the bazaar, and he was whining about how hard it was to feed five mouths on a labourer's salary at the milk plant. As if I earn ten thousand rupees a month and my children live on cream and honey! How, if Tariq Sahib wanted, he could speak to his employer at the factory and have his salary doubled in the blinking of an eye. How his children were starving to death. "Oye!" I wanted to say. "Your children wouldn't starve if you spent your money buying food for them instead of pouring it down the gutters of that liquor shop." But, I thought, I say one thing, and this lunatic will say a hundred. So I waited, with still the groceries to buy and lunch to prepare and that leech leaning on my cycle handlebars. Had he kept me another ten minutes, I'd never have been able to prepare lunch in time. And what an earful I would have got from the Others then, hain? The Others are not caring why or how you became late. They want their work done on time. They are not caring about your problems.'

'Mashooq did the same to me the day before I left for my holiday,' said Barkat. 'He lurched up to me in the bazaar, breathing filthy fumes in my face. "If it isn't the trusted slave from the great house," he sneered. "What do you do when your master snaps his fingers at you? Lie down at his feet like an obedient dog?" I knew he was drunk, so I didn't bother to break his face, as I would have if he'd been sober. I've seen him with these sinful eyes only – Allah silence my tongue this instant if I'm lying – outside the houses of bazaar women . . .'

'Hush, Barkat,' said Bua. 'Child is listening. If it repeats to the Owners and says it heard from you, they will pull out all our tongues.'

'Why did he accost you like that?' Rehmat peered at Barkat through a haze of cigarette smoke.

'Who knows what goes on inside the head of a crazy man? All I know is that Mashooq is a pervert. Look at the way he treats his wife.'

'He beats her, doesn't he?' asked Laila.

'Beats her?' snorted Barkat. 'If he wasn't afraid of your parents and Sardar Begum, he'd have killed Fatima by now. You know well enough, Bua, that last year he broke her jaw, an arm and two ribs. If their neighbours hadn't alerted us in time, Allah alone knows what he'd have done to her. As it was, she had to spend a week in hospital.

'I'm not saying a man shouldn't lift a hand against his wife. If the wife is disobedient, it's his right – no, duty – to set her straight. When I got married, my wife wouldn't show my mother proper respect. She refused to make hot chappatis for her, and sometimes she'd even answer me back. I used to hit her, across the cheek with the back of my hand. Tharrap! Like that. And then I'd make her apologize to me. But I only did it when she misbehaved. And why only then? Because I'm a man. Not a dog.'

'Quite right, Barkat,' Rehmat agreed, fishing in his pocket for a match to relight his cigarette. 'A man has to be a man. Not a mouse and not a dog. But a man.'

'Can a wife beat her husband?' asked Laila.

'No,' said Barkat. 'Women are weaker.'

'Even if she picked up an axe or a knife?' Laila made a slicing motion with her hand.

'Lailu! Little girls don't talk like that.' Bua seized Laila's hand and placed it in her lap. 'All husbands beat their wives. It's their right. My late husband – may Jesus Christ bless his soul – he'd never use a stick on a donkey even, so good he was. But he used to hurl his shoe at me whenever I put too much salt in the food.'

'My Abu doesn't beat my Ammi,' declared Laila.

'That's different,' said Barkat. 'Rich men can command obedience.'

'But if a man beats his wife needlessly, and she's too weak to beat him back, then what can she do?'

'She must tell her brother or her father, and they will help her,' Barkat replied.

'And if they don't?'

'They will. The holy Koran says men must take pity on those weaker than themselves. Our religion is very good to women. Before Islam came, do you know what they did to newborn girls in the holy city of Mecca? They used to bury them alive. Yes. Ask Rehmat if you don't believe me.'

'That was the age of ignorance.' Rehmat nodded. 'Our holy prophet, may peace be upon him, put a stop to all that. And now women go to schools, go out to work, even sing and dance inside the TV – but only shameless women do that.'

They were all agreed, however, that Kaneez's daughter Fatima was not a shameless woman. In fact, they were unanimous in their opinion of her as a virtuous woman, singularly unfortunate in being shackled to Mashooq. As Barkat had observed when Fatima went back to Mashooq after the last beating, 'It wouldn't surprise me if tomorrow we heard he'd killed her.'

'May Allah bring Mashooq on the right path.' Rehmat brushed his clothes, showering the floor with cigarette ash.

'What I don't understand is why he has so much anger inside him. He has a job, a wife, children, a roof over his head. What more does he want?'

'Some men, no matter how much they have, are never happy. He's one of those.' Barkat got up and stretched. 'Laila, baby, are you ready to go to your grandmother's?'

'No, she has to brush her hair and wash her hands,' Bua said. 'Look how much crumpled your dress is, Lailu. Come, you have to change also.'

Sardar Begum sat cross-legged on the daybed in her courtyard poring over a tattered register. She had needed glasses for the last twenty years but had refused to wear them. 'There's nothing wrong with my eyes,' she insisted.

'But, Maanji,' Fareeda had sighed, 'you are long-sighted. You need . . .'

'They are my eyes or yours?'

'Yours.'

'Then?'

She held the register at arm's length and craned her neck back. Her thin red plait curled down her back like a gecko's tail. The lines on her brow were deeper than usual as she scrutinized the register.

'This doesn't add up,' she muttered. 'Sixty rupees for meat, fifty for chicken, don't add up to one hundred and twenty. It's written a hundred and twenty, isn't it, Kaneez?' She jabbed a finger at the entry in the register.

Kaneez raised herself with some difficulty from her squatting position on the ground by her mistress's bed. 'I can't see without my glasses.'

'Then get your glasses, fool,' snapped Sardar Begum. 'Why do you have to pretend you can do without them?'

Kaneez fumbled in the pocket of her shapeless sludge-coloured tunic and produced a pair of spectacles held together with string. Placing them on her hooked nose, she squinted at the register.

'Looks like a hundred and ten to me.'

'Can't be. You're blind. Fetch Nazeer.'

Kaneez was about to shuffle off when Sardar Begum looked up and saw her son's family enter the courtyard. Quickly, she shoved the register under a sheet.

Sardar Begum's registers were a constant source of tension with her son. In these well-thumbed books she kept account of every single paisa that went from her hands. It was a habit she had acquired on the death of her husband and clung to ever since.

Her husband, a placid, bookish man some twelve years her senior, had passed away with little fuss early on in their marriage. He had left his young widow with two small children, the haveli and five thousand acres of land. He had also left behind a fine library of Persian literature and Arabic philosophy that seldom found mention in Sardar Begum's account of her struggles.

'What had I? Nothing. Nothing except this house and some land,' she'd say with a careless wave encompassing the haveli and the fields beyond. 'And most of that also left barren. Tariq's father was a good man but a not-so-good farmer.'

Sardar Begum, however, had the makings of a very good farmer. Though reared for a life of secluded indolence by a wealthy landowning father, she chafed at the bonds imposed on her by purdah. She yearned for the big, masculine world outside; for news of local elections won and lost; innovations in farming; roads extended; tube wells dug; fluctuations in the market, anything except the narrow, smothering world of purdah.

Her husband was a sympathetic man who tried to channel her lively intelligence and unquenchable curiosity into reading and writing. But hers was too literal a mind, too earthy a sensibility, to appreciate the effete verse of Hafiz or the complex philosophy of Ibn Khaldun. The books that she yearned for were the registers and ledgers in which the farm accounts were kept. So he indulged her, bringing the books along with him to the women's section of the haveli when he retired for the night.

Sardar Begum soon grew familiar with the tables of income and expenditure written in the manager's neat hand. She questioned her husband closely on expenses incurred too early, crops sold too cheap. Whenever she barked a question, he would look up from his book with a distracted frown. It was on one such evening, while she sat cross-legged on the floor with the open register in her lap and he was in an armchair, slowly turning the pages of a book, that he lurched forward, clutching at his chest. Sardar Begum leapt to his side. But there was little she could do.

'The doctors said it was heart,' Sardar Begum told the multitudes of mourners who came to his funeral. 'And I think so they were right. His heart was very big. Always he was giving, giving. Food, clothes, money. The poor around here were so fat and spoiled. He'd always say, "If you give to others, Allah will give to you." So innocent he was, bless him. If you ask me, his heart had grown so big that it burst.'

The house was still seething with mourners when Sardar Begum announced her decision to take charge of her children's patrimony. Her husband's family was aghast. A woman, and that, too, a widow who flouted the laws of purdah was a public disgrace. Besides, what need had she to dirty her soft hands when they were there to do it for her? But, for Sardar Begum, this was an opportunity, and she wasn't about to let it pass. And so, Sardar Begum became a farmer of distinction. She was a quick learner and, unlike her late husband, ruthless. She had a low tolerance for 'lying-cheating lazy tenants'. If they did not produce results in two seasons, they were flung off her land.

But her ambitions were not limited to farming. She had plans for her son. When, upon his return from Oxford, Tariq rejected the civil service for Sabzbagh, Sardar Begum was pleased, for it was here that his destiny lay. Nonetheless, Sardar Begum found it difficult to relinquish her beloved ledgers – even to her son. It was only when Tariq threatened to leave for the city that she acquiesced grudgingly.

But still she found her 'register habit' hard to break. Now she gripped Kaneez's hand and muttered, 'Don't call Nazeer just yet. And don't mention the accounts in front of Tariq Sahib.' Then with arms outstretched and face garlanded with smiles, she called out: 'Light of my eyes, beat of my heart, flow of my blood. Welcome, welcome.'

'Salaam, Maanji.'

'Salaam, salaam, may you live a thousand years. Come here, my little dove.'

Laila sidled up to her grandmother and was enfolded in a cushiony embrace redolent of Imperial Leather soap, Touch Me talcum powder and the cloves and neem leaves that Sardar Begum scattered in her wardrobe.

'Ah, my own flesh and blood. Sit here.' Sardar Begum drew Laila down beside her.

A white sheet covered the bed, and matching bolster cushions lay like bookends on either side. Three rattan-backed chairs faced the daybed in a semicircle.

'How are you, Kaneez?' asked Tariq, taking a chair.

'I'm all right, Tariq Sahib. Just getting on.'

'You're looking quite frail to me.'

'Don't you believe it,' Sardar Begum snapped. 'She eats like a horse.'

'Do I have the teeth to eat like a horse?' Kaneez's tone was indignant. Having served Sardar Begum for the best part of her life, she could take liberties the other servants dared not. She was the only one in her household, for instance, who could contradict her mistress. And though Sardar Begum ranted and raged at Kaneez, she often followed her advice.

'Here, Maanji,' said Fareeda to Sardar Begum, 'I brought you some kheer.' She handed the pudding to Kaneez.

'Bring it here, Kaneez, let me see.' Sardar Begum crooked her finger.

'What's this hard thing under me?' Laila tugged the ledger out from under the sheet.

'Oh, no,' Tariq groaned. 'It's her damned register. Are you still accounting for every anna and every paisa? Why can't you use your time to do something more enjoyable and useful?'

Sardar Begum plucked the ledger from Laila's hands.

'What's more useful than accounts? You want these fat, greedy servants to eat me up?'

'Nazeer's been with you for twenty years. Even if he were to pilfer the odd ten rupees, what difference would it make?' said Tariq. 'You won't starve.'

'Every flood starts with a droplet. Look at this kheer. At least two bags of nuts in it and enough zafraan to scent a garden. Your cook thinks money grows on trees? I know how hard it is to earn . . .'

'Can I go to see Rani?' Laila jumped up from the bed.

'No, you stay with your grandmother.' Sardar Begum pulled Laila down by her wrist.

'But . . .'

'Perhaps Kaneez will fetch Rani later,' Fareeda suggested.

'Now? Please?'

'All right,' said Sardar Begum, relenting. 'Go, Kaneez. Take the kheer to the kitchen and bring some sherbet for everyone. And get Rani.'

A breeze rustled the leaves of the neem tree, releasing their astringent scent. Sardar Begum's pet peacock, Haseen, strutted along the encircling wall of the haveli. The setting sun picked out the blaze of turquoise in Haseen's breast and bathed the haveli's worn bricks in a honey glow. The house seemed to be in repose at that hour, its verandas in shadow, its thick-walled rooms silent.

'It's so peaceful here,' murmured Fareeda.

'Then why can't you come and live here?' Sardar Begum tucked the register under her knee. 'This house is too big for an old woman by herself.'

'For the hundredth time, Maanji,' said Tariq wearily, 'it's best we live separately. Anyway, if I was to live here, we both know it wouldn't be peaceful any more.'

Sardar Begum knew there was little chance that Tariq would ever move to Kalanpur but, in her idle moments, she diverted herself with the thought of how different his life would have been had he lived with her. Under her guidance he would not have grown so engrossed in his charitable work. It was fine, she felt, occasionally to help the poor. After all, it ran in his blood. His father had been equally foolish. But doing so at the expense of pursuing his destiny was the height of stupidity.

It was Sardar Begum's unwavering belief that Tariq was meant for higher things. He had all the right credentials. He was landed, had an impeccable bloodline and was connected through his parents to some powerful families in Punjab. His link to Fareeda's family, she acknowledged grudgingly, was also not harmful. Moreover, he'd received a fine education, had a good brain, integrity and, Allah alone knew why, but he seemed to command respect from those around him. Who could hold a candle to Tariq Azeem in the whole of Colewallah? Forget Colewallah, in the whole of the Punjab?

He could have contested the last election from Sabzbagh and romped home. All those lazy peasants who'd been fattening themselves on the Azeems' largesse for generations would have cast tens of thousands of votes for him. But, instead of being a minister or a governor and making speeches, cutting ribbons and shaking hands with presidents and kings, Tariq was running a tailoring shop. Her heart wept tears of blood at the waste, the loss.

Tariq, however, had no intention of realizing his mother's ambitions for him. He knew that he did not have the stomach for politics. He had neither the requisite ruthlessness nor the hunger for public approbation. He was much happier doing his bit out of the limelight. He knew Sabzbagh was a small pond, but it was *his* pond. Tariq also did not like the idea of public probes and inquiry committees. He was too much his mother's son, too conscious, despite his education, of his social standing, to feel the need to justify his decisions.

Sardar Begum's sole comfort was the thought that Tariq hadn't allowed his farming to slip. In fact, in introducing better seeds, experimenting with new crops and mechanizing some of the ancient methods his forebears had practised, he had raised his yields significantly.

'Talking of peaceful, is there going to be war?' asked Sardar Begum.

'We're already at war,' replied Tariq.

'I don't mean the Bengalis. I mean the Indians. As long as it's just the Bengalis, the fighting will take place there. But once the Indians get into it, it will spill out here as well.'

'It may well come to that.'

'In that case, you'd better move in here. You live too close to that canal. If a bomb fell on it, you'd all drown. Allah forbid. Dust and ashes in my mouth. Also, with that big industry there, you'll be targets. Best is if you come here.' Sardar Begum's voice quickened, and a pair of heavy gold bangles clunked on her creamy wrists as she outlined her plans. 'Fareeda, you hire some trucks, pack them with everything you've collected for the girls' dowries – jewellery, silver, linen, clothes, everything – and all *your* good things also, and put your car behind them and follow them here. Call Sara immediately from Lahore and all of you shift here tomorrow. There! I've spoken.'

'But, Maanji, we're not at war with India yet,' Fareeda protested.

'They'll ask your permission before attacking you?'

'Let's not get carried away.' Tariq spoke firmly. 'First, war hasn't started yet. Second, even if the Indians were to attack us tomorrow, won't they go for the military installations in Lahore and Pindi rather than a measly little powdered-milk factory near Sabzbagh?'

'Don't listen to me. What do I know? I'm only your mother after all.'

'Don't be upset.' Fareeda patted Sardar Begum's hand. 'Allah willing, there won't be a war. He will protect us all.'

'Doubtless, but even Allah says, "Trust in me but tether your camel first." ' Sardar Begum clutched Fareeda's hand. 'Promise me, if there is war, you'll send the girls to me.'

Fareeda leaned out of her chair awkwardly, her hand imprisoned in Sardar Begum's grip.

'Sister Clementine also wanted to know if we were going to fight with India.' Laila's voice dropped like a stone into a pool of silence.

'Whose sister?' Sardar Begum's head swivelled round to Laila.

Laila reddened but was saved from replying by Rani and Kaneez's timely approach. Rani carried a large brass tray with freshly squeezed lemonade and a dish of sticky gulab jamans. Beside her granddaughter's tall, lissom frame, Kaneez's hunched body looked like a hook. A tablecloth was folded over her bent arm. Carrying a table on his head, Nazeer, the cook, brought up the rear.

Rani looked much more like herself since Laila had seen

her a week ago in the church. Her hair was smooth and her muslin dupatta was draped modestly across her bosom. She looked calm and self-possessed. True, her face was sallow and her cheeks a little hollow, but when she smiled, it was as if an electric light had been switched on in a cellar.

Laila hopped from foot to foot while the servants salaamed her parents and laid out the food and drink. Then she launched herself at Rani and hugged her tight. Inhibited by Tariq and Fareeda's presence, Rani grinned awkwardly at Laila's upturned face.

'Enough!' ordered Sardar Begum in an indulgent voice that belied the command. 'Why haven't you been to see me, Koonj? You know no one massages my feet the way you do. Your grandmother mangles them with her pincers. Where have you been?'

'Nowhere, Begum Sahiba.'

'Then why have you been hiding yourself?'

'She's not well.' Kaneez spoke up. 'Complains of headache and dizziness. So I told her to rest.'

'What's the matter, Rani?' Fareeda asked. 'Have you had fever?'

'No.' Rani hung her head.

'Why are you standing there with that foolish face?' Sardar Begum demanded of Nazeer. 'Go! Work!'

'How old are you now, Rani?' Fareeda questioned.

Rani looked at her grandmother enquiringly.

'She was three when Fatima married again,' replied Kaneez. 'That was twelve years ago last monsoon.'

'So you're fifteen. You should be doing your Matric exams soon, shouldn't you? I hope you haven't dropped out of school?'

'She still goes,' said Kaneez. 'But I'm thinking of removing her.'

'Why?' Fareeda frowned.

'People will say I'm trying to rise above myself. Also, what will she do with so much education? In the end, she has to marry and have children like everyone else.'

'While I'm alive, no one dare say a word about you or your Koonj,' Sardar Begum said firmly. 'But, I agree, too much education for girls is not good. It confuses them.'

'Matric is not too much education,' protested Tariq. 'Is there a problem with school fees?'

'What you give more than covers her fees and books,' replied Kaneez.

'Then what?' Fareeda asked. 'Has Mashooq been bothering you?'

'He hasn't come here since that time you warned him,' said Kaneez.

'Rani, don't *you* want to complete your Matric?' asked Fareeda.

Rani glanced up at Fareeda but did not reply.

'Well? Do you or don't you?'

'I want to, but I don't know if I can,' she mumbled.

'Why ever not?' enquired Tariq.

'Don't know.'

'What's the matter with you?' Sardar Begum barked. 'Answer properly when Sahib speaks to you.'

'Do you like children, Rani?' Fareeda asked gently.

Rani's face paled.

'You don't have to look so frightened. All I want to know is if you'd like to join our centre at the village. The woman who used to mind the children while their mothers worked has to go. You could take her place. You'd be good with small children.'

'No, no, Bibi,' Kaneez quavered. 'I beg you, no. I'm a poor widow, all by myself. If Rani starts working in a factory, people will say she's up to no good. As it is, with school only, they are constantly whispering that I want to sell her . . .'

'Sell Rani?' laughed Laila incredulously. 'How can you sell Rani? She's not a potato or a, a . . . table.'

'Now look what you've done, you stupid woman,' Sardar Begum scolded. 'You girls run off and play. And *you* go as well.' She shooed Kaneez away.

As soon as they were out of earshot, Fareeda spoke to her mother-in-law.

'What's wrong with Rani? I've never seen her so listless.'

'I don't know. It's the first time I've seen her in days.'

'Are you sure Mashooq is not bothering them?'

'Better not be. I'll make enquiries,' said Sardar Begum. 'And this factory job for Rani? Don't speak of it again.'

'Why?' asked Tariq.

'It's fine for the daughters of your Christian babus to become tailors or nurses or whatever, but it's not suitable for Rani.'

'Why?'

'Kaneez's right. She's vulnerable,' explained Sardar Begum. 'There'll be talk and no one will marry her.'

'A better man will marry her,' Tariq insisted.

'Kaneez came to work for me before you were born. She's passed through fire in her life. She deserves some peace now.' Sardar Begum lowered her feet to the ground.

'I don't want to see Rani suffer either. I want her to have a job so she's not dependent on a hopeless lout like her mother is,' said Tariq.

Sardar Begum snorted. 'A woman is always dependent.'

'*You* weren't.'

'My circumstances were different. In any case, this whole factory thing is rubbish. You are like a child playing make-believe games. You think you can change people's lives, their thinking, with a mere factory? You're wrong. And you'll see for yourself soon enough.' Sardar Begum rose to her feet. 'Where are all these lazy, useless servants? Nazeer? Kaneez?

Switch on the lights. Can't you see how dark it's got? And carry my bed in. What do I pay you for? Sitting around all day, breaking my chairs under your fat backsides?'

Rani and Laila stood in a corner of the veranda where Sardar Begum's cane-backed folding chairs were stacked in rickety towers. All around them was the smell of mouldy wood and bird droppings. Laila had guessed from the older girl's tight grip on her wrist, her quick strides and her set expression, that she was being led off on some urgent errand.

'What is it?' Laila asked. 'Tell me.'

'Shh! Keep your voice down,' scolded Rani. She peered back at the group in the courtyard. Deep in conversation, they appeared not to have heard Laila. Rani turned back to Laila.

'What is it?' Laila repeated more softly. 'Are you angry with me?'

'Angry? What for?'

'For the bad things I said about you and your, er, friend at the picnic,' Laila said in a small voice.

'Oh, that!' Rani regarded Laila with pursed lips. 'No, I'm not angry about that. But I *was* sad then.'

'I didn't mean it.' Laila reached for Rani's hand. 'I'm sorry if I made you sad. Please be my friend again.'

Rani paused with her head on one side, as if considering Laila's request. 'All right then. But you haven't told anyone about my friend, have you?'

'Of course not,' Laila replied with some asperity. 'I promised you, didn't I?'

'Yes, you did. Now can I trust you with another secret?'

Laila nodded vigorously.

Rani placed both hands on Laila's shoulders and crouched down until she was at her eye level. 'It's going to be a very special secret between you and me. Just you and me.'

'You're not even going to tell Sara?' asked Laila breathlessly.

'No, not even Sara. It's just between us. Do you understand?'
Laila nodded again.

'But before I tell you the secret, I have to ask you something. Have you told anyone that you saw me at the church?'

'I told Ammi.'

'What did you tell her?' Rani's fingers dug into her shoulders.

'I . . . I think I said you looked . . . upset,' faltered Laila. 'But I didn't say you were at the church,' she added hurriedly. 'I just said I saw you in Sabzbagh.'

'What did she say?'

'Nothing.'

'Are you sure?'

'She asked why you were upset, and I said I didn't know. That's all,' said Laila.

'You promise?'

'I promise.'

'And Bua? Did she say anything?' asked Rani.

'To Ammi? No. She even got annoyed with me for telling Ammi that we saw you, because she wasn't meant to take me to the church. I'm not allowed, you see.'

'Now, listen to me carefully.' Rani's eyes bore into Laila's. 'You know my visit to the church? That's to remain a secret between us. You are not to tell *anyone*, not your parents, not Sara, not *anyone*. Promise me.'

'Cross my heart and hope to die,' declared Laila, slashing her chest with her hands. She had heard Sara and her friends use the expression at school. Though she did not quite understand what it meant to cross one's heart, it seemed apt for the solemnity of the occasion.

Rani shook her head. 'Promise on the holy Koran,' she insisted. 'No, promise on your parents' lives and on Sara's also, that you will never ever tell anyone. Promise? Good. Now you and I are partners. Here, place your right hand on my left and lace your fingers through mine like this. There, that seals our partnership.'

'What should we call ourselves?' asked Laila.

'Call ourselves? What do you mean?'

'We must give our partnership a name. Everyone does. We can be the Two Detectives.' Her mind raced, telescoping all the Enid Blyton mysteries she had read. Dressed in mackintoshes and wellies, she was striding across rain-lashed moors with Julian and George; she was crouched over a tin drum helping Larry and Pip write secret letters in invisible ink in the shed at the bottom of Fatty's garden; and then she was rowing with all her might with Peggy and Jack across a choppy lake to their hideout on the secret island. Somehow, she could not picture Rani in her flapping shawl and flip-flops alongside them.

'We can't be exactly like them,' she murmured. 'But our name must start with the same letter, like the Secret Seven or the Famous Five. We must also think of a password. I know! We can be the Troublesome Two. Or how about the Terrific Two? Do you like that?' She beamed at Rani.

'No,' said Rani. 'I don't. You're Laila and I'm Rani, and that's all. Now, listen to me. You have to do something for me. I'm going to set you a task, but only if you stop all this rubbish about names and words and stupid, babyish things. Or else I'm going to find another partner.' She turned on her heel as if about to flounce off, but waited in that pose, peering expectantly over her shoulder at Laila.

'Oh, no, please,' pleaded Laila. They weren't going to be like the Famous Five after all. But all was not lost. If she couldn't be George or Peggy, at least she could still be Laila, Rani's special friend. She grabbed Rani's arm. 'I won't mention names again. I promise. Let me be your partner.'

'All right then.' Rani relented. 'I'm going to set you a task you have to carry out very carefully. Without telling a single person. Come closer so I can whisper in your ear. Your task is to spy on Bua. You have to find out what she says about me to your mother. That's the most important. Second, you have to report to me if you hear anything about me in your home. Even if it is your parents who say it, or the servants, or anyone. Anyone at all. You are to come and tell me at once. Understand?'

Deeply flattered to be entrusted with such a serious responsibility, Laila did not think to ask Rani why she should spy on Bua till she was in bed that night. As she drifted off to sleep, it occurred to her vaguely that Rani had not really confided in her at all. She hadn't even explained why she'd been at the church. Or why she had looked so distraught. So Laila had no way of verifying whether what Bua had told her had been the truth or not. Rani had concluded their secret meeting abruptly when Sardar Begum had called for the lights to be switched on. Giving Laila a perfunctory pat on the head, she had mouthed the words, 'Remember your promise,' and run off to switch on the lights. Rani hadn't mentioned her new friend either. Did she still see him secretly? But Laila was not perturbed by these omissions. Rani must have forgotten in the excitement of the moment. Soon, she would reveal all. Laila smiled contentedly into her pillow. After all, they were partners now. The Terrific Two.

8

The forty-five minutes after breakfast were Fareeda's favourite time of day. By then, Tariq had left, either for the factory or the farm. She had watched Laila wolf down her breakfast and sent her out to the garden to play. She had examined Rehmat's accounts and given him the menu for the day. She had overseen the handing over of the dirty laundry to the washerman who called every morning at eight. She had also sorted through the myriad chores which Fazal, the bearer, presented to her each day. The leaking pipe in the guest bathroom; the smoking electric iron; the need for new dusters, silver polish and electric bulbs, had all been dealt with.

Now, for the next three-quarters of an hour, before the usual flood of villagers washed up at her door with petitions and requests, she could do as she liked. She spent that time in the dining room sipping coffee, reading the papers and sorting through her mail. It was understood in the household that this was her time to herself and she was not to be bothered unnecessarily. Fareeda had just poured herself a fresh cup of coffee when she was disturbed by Fazal, the bearer.

'Bibi?'

'Yes, Fazal.' Fareeda answered from behind the papers.

'Bibi, Babu Jacob is here to see you. Says it's urgent.'

'Tell him Sahib is away in Colewallah for the day.' Her hand emerged from behind the newspaper screen to reach for her cup. 'He'll be back by this evening. If this urgent business can't wait till tomorrow morning, he can drop in after eight this evening.'

'He knows Sahib is away. He wants to speak to you.'

Fareeda lowered a corner of the paper and frowned at Fazal. 'What about?'

'He's brought a fat file and says he needs some signings from you.'

'My signature? Whatever for? All right,' she sighed, folding the paper. 'Show him in.'

A minute later, Mr Jacob bustled in. He was dressed in a half-sleeved fawn safari suit. Three fountain pens were hooked by their caps into his breast pocket. A pair of bifocals hung on a thin silver chain from his neck. He carried a thick manila folder under his arm.

'Good morning, Bibi. I'm very sorry to be a botheration and that too so unobligingly early in the morning, but an unexpected development has developed which I thought to bring to your kind notice without any further loss of valuable time. And seeing that Mian Sahib is temporarily unavailable on a mission of, no doubt, utmost importance in Colewallah, I thought it the very best to act speedily so as not to imperil . . .'

'What is it, Jacob?' Fareeda put the paper down and pushed her coffee to one side. 'What can't wait till this evening? Will you have a cup of tea?'

'Thank you kindly, no. I have already partaken of the one cup I permit myself in the morning. I think we should hasten with all due speed to attend to the business at hand, which really is of a most urgent nature.'

'Yes, but what is it?'

'I shall divulge it to you now.' He placed the folder on the dining table and looked pointedly at a chair.

'Please have a seat.' Fareeda respected Mr Jacob for his diligence. She also knew that he was devoted to Tariq and as fiercely committed to the project as he. Yet, all too often, she wished Mr Jacob could bring himself to be brief.

'Thank you kindly.' Mr Jacob sat down. Placing his hands on the file, he paused for effect.

'Mr Jacob, please.'

'Yes, Bibi.' He took a deep breath and began. 'As you will no doubt recall, earlier this year, on the twentieth of February 1971 to be precise, Tariq Sahib had approached the British Development Association for some financial assistance in the running of his worthy garment project, from which, along with so many other young girls of this and neighbouring villages, my daughters, Farhana and Rehana, have benefited immeasurably.'

'Please get to the point.'

'Of course. Well, since I have ascertained that you are well and truly in the picture, I shall now proceed. In order to entertain our Sahib's request, Mr Davies of the Association had requested us to furnish him with certain documentations. One was a short proposal outlining what we hoped to achieve at the centre and so on and so forth.'

'Yes, I know the proposal. Tariq and I drafted it together.'

'Next was the full audited accounts of the same since its inception.'

'But all that's been taken care of.'

'Indeed it has. Tariq Sahib has been meticulous in the proper maintenance of accounts. No, it is not that.'

'Then, Mr Jacob, *what* is it?' Fareeda reached out to remove the single wilted bloom from the crystal rose-bowl placed in the centre of the table. 'And, really, I don't mean to be rude, but could you please say what you need to say?'

'Of course, no offence meant and none taken,' he beamed. 'This morning I received not one but two letters from Mr Davies in Lahore to say that he was in full possession of all the documents that we had sent them. However, since the original application was made in February and some time has elapsed between now and then, this being November, of course, could they please have a progress report bringing them up to the date? That is it. The urgent business.'

'Why can't Tariq deal with it tomorrow?' Fareeda dropped the flower on to her side plate.

'Oh, because it's got to be done today.' Mr Jacob looked surprised. 'Didn't I tell you? They have to have it in Lahore tomorrow.'

'No, you didn't tell me, Mr Jacob. Why the urgency?'

'Our proposal is in the final stage of consideration. Decision will be taken in the coming week.'

'Why didn't they tell us so earlier?'

'Apparently they had sent a letter, with three subsequent copies over the last two months, but they failed to be delivered due to their having an error in the address. They said Sabzwal instead of Sabzbagh, and hence the letters went to the village on the other side of the Ravi. It is only now they have been forwarded on to us.'

'That's not very clever of them.'

Mr Jacob turned his palms up. 'What is one to say, except that these are not the British who ruled over us? *My* ancestors never made such careless blunders, such, to borrow if I may an expression from sport, unforced errors. Perhaps that is why their nation is in decline now.'

'I don't even know whether I can reach Tariq.' Fareeda ran a hand across her forehead. 'He was to see the Deputy Commissioner and then look at some milk cows for the farm, and he also had to attend the funeral of an old friend of his father's. But, right now, he must still be on the road. What are we to do, Mr Jacob? I suppose we could ask for an extension. After all, the fault was theirs, not ours.'

'We could ask for an extension but, begging your pardon in advance for any transgression, I don't think we should. It will not create a good enough impression. We should submit the report on the dot of time. Regardless of discomfort endured.'

'But how?'

'Excuse my impertinence, but my humbled suggestion is that you should do it, Bibi. You made the original proposal with Sahib. And first class it was. This is easy as compared to that. I would do it myself, but my English is not so good, owing to the fact that I did not have a chance to complete my BA due to my father's sudden and unexpected demise thirty-five years previously, while I was in year one of BA. Hence, I am self-taught. But, although my English may be weak, my organization is strong. I don't mean to blow my own horn, but what I mean to say is that what God takes with one hand, He gives with the other.'

Fareeda blanked out Mr Jacob's oration. Her mind was on the report. She was familiar with its content. It shouldn't be too complicated to update it. Tariq would be pleased and surprised.

'So, I have all the facts and configurations here.' Babu Jacob patted his papers. 'I shall furnish you with whatsoever you should require. It should take no more than three, top most, four hours. If we have a neat copy typed and ready by three o'clock this afternoon, I myself could take the bus into Lahore and straight away go to BDA's office, delivering it person-ally and individually so that it is on Mr Davies' desk when he arrives tomorrow morning. When he realizes what a superhuman effort we have made to remain in the time allotted, no doubt he will be more than kindly disposed towards our work.'

Fareeda looked at his file. 'Show me the letter. But first, let me call Fazal and tell him not to disturb us for the next couple of hours.'

Two and half hours later, Fareeda tossed a biro on the dining table and flexed her fingers.

'Well, Mr Jacob, it's beginning to take shape.'

'Yes, Bibi, it's becoming shipshape.' Mr Jacob smiled at her over his bifocals. 'Now all we have to do is to add on the last quarter's accounts as an appendix, and then go through the summary once more, before committing ourselves to the final copy, which I will then type out for your final-most perusal.'

'Let's take a fifteen-minute break first.'

'Of course.'

Fareeda called out for Fazal.

'Fazal, will you bring Mr Jacob some squash? Coffee for me, please. Where's Laila?'

'With Bua and Sister Clementine on the front lawn.'

'Why's Sister Clementine here?' Fareeda wrinkled her nose.

'She's been waiting to see you for the last hour, Bibi. Said it was very, very important. I told her you'd asked not to be disturbed. She said she'd wait, but she had to see you today.'

'Oh, God, why has everyone got urgent work today? Tell her to come back another day. No, wait. I'm taking fifteen minutes off anyway. Send her in.'

This was the first time that Sister Clementine had been invited into the Azeems' home. On her one previous visit to the house, before the unfortunate affair of the seamstress, she had accompanied Mother Superior to wish Mrs Azeem a happy new year. Then, they had sat in the garden with Fareeda. The servants had brought out big trays bearing samosas, fruit cake and egg sandwiches. The teacups had had gold edges, and the forks they'd been offered with the fruitcake had been the smallest that Sister Clementine had ever seen. Not knowing whether she could use such a dainty object correctly, Sister Clementine had regretfully refused the cake. She had consoled herself with two samosas and two sandwiches. The garden had also looked pretty, with neat beds of gladioli and phlox and sweet peas. But what Sister Clementine had really wanted to see was the inside of the house, the fine furnishings, the rugs, the silver.

Now, as she entered the dining room behind Fazal, her eyes

darted about, taking in the apple-green drapes, the polished dining table littered with papers and the thin-legged console table with a silver bowl piled high with fruit. There was a strange blue and white painting above the fireplace. It looked either like a woman lying on her side with a bird in her hand or a sailing ship tossing on the sea, Sister Clementine wasn't quite sure which.

The delicious aroma of coffee hung in the air. That rich, intense scent was unmistakable. Coffee was one of the things Sister Clementine had missed most, even more than her sisters, when she first arrived in Sabzbagh. She had been shocked to discover that a small bottle of instant coffee in Lahore cost thirty-five rupees – far more than the kitchen budget at the convent would allow. And so, Sister Clementine had resigned herself to Yellow Label Lipton Tea like everyone else.

But today that tantalizing scent brought back a vivid memory. She was home in Kerala, waking in the morning to the drum of raindrops on the tin roof. Banana leaves moved languidly on the smoothest of breezes outside. Her mother hummed a song under her breath as she poured out the dark steaming liquid into enamel mugs. In Kerala, coffee had been the everyday scent of morning, as common as dew on grass, but here, elusive and expensive, it was the perfume of wealth, of privilege.

'Sister Clementine, I'm speaking to you. Sister?'

Sister Clementine blinked. She dragged her mind back to the present.

'Oh, hello, Mrs Azeem.'

'What can I do for you, Sister?' Fareeda did not invite her to sit down. 'Could you hurry? I'm very busy today.'

Sister Clementine's mind went blank. It had seemed so simple when she'd thought about it at home. Fareeda would welcome her warmly, take her to the sitting room, ply her with tea, perhaps even lunch. They would chat amiably while the servants hovered around, pressing cold drinks and delicate little sweets on her. Having graciously accepted a couple of sweets, she would indicate to Fareeda with a little look that she needed to speak to her alone. Without a moment's hesitation, Fareeda would dismiss the servants with a single clap of her hands. Only when the door clicked shut behind the last servant would she gently tell Fareeda about Rani.

At first, Fareeda would be speechless. Embarrassed, dismayed, she would hang her head. But Sister Clementine would pat her on the knee, tell her that we were all fallible and advise her to get the girl married. Her eyes shining with gratitude, Fareeda would thank her profusely for showing her the way.

But she, Clementine, would brush aside her gratitude and rise to leave. Fareeda would insist that there was no question of her walking. The driver would run her home in the car. Fareeda would walk down the front steps with her and hand her into the car, leaning down to give her one last grateful smile from the open window.

But now that she was here, Sister Clementine didn't know quite how to start. Fareeda looked so cool, so unapproachable, across the table with that big silver fruit-bowl behind her. She wished Bua had come in with her. Bua had assured her that all would be well. All she had to do was to tell her. But how?

Even Laila's presence would be welcome now. She had been so sweet to her just now in the garden. Asking her why she'd come and what she was going to tell her mother. Quizzing her ever so politely. So concerned, she'd been, so interested. Laila had even offered to bring her in and sit with her while she talked to Fareeda, but Bua had pulled Laila down with a glare. Fareeda, Bua had said, would be most annoyed if Laila accompanied her inside and would send her straight out again. Clementine wished Bua had allowed the girl to come in with her. She looked around desperately to find some way into the conversation she had planned at the convent. Sister Clementine's gaze alighted on Mr Jacob.

'Hello, Babu Jacob,' she trilled. Momentary relief at spotting a possible ally lent her voice added enthusiasm. 'How are you? What are you doing here?'

'Er, good morning, Sister. I'm very fine, thank you kindly, very fine,' Mr Jacob mumbled. Like most people on the farm, he was well aware of Fareeda's hostility towards the nuns. Unwilling to annoy either woman, he kept his eyes on his files.

Sister Clementine sensed his discomfort, and it added to her own. She realized that she could not expect any help from him. She should have waited till Mother Superior got back from Abbotabad. *She* would have known what to say. But what if it was too late by then? What if the girl did something foolish, or, worse, did nothing at all and was found out? Then everyone would blame her. Besides, the girl was almost part of the Azeem family. They *had* to be told. But how to tell without annoying Fareeda? She seemed in a bad mood already.

'Sister, you'd better hurry up and tell me what you want. I'm very busy today,' Fareeda said again, looking pointedly at the papers scattered on the table.

'It's not that I'm wanting something from you, exactly.' Sister Clementine gripped the back of a dining chair for support. 'At least not for myself. It's just that, I am wanting to tell you something.'

'Tell me what?'

'Umm, about girls and things.'

'Sister, you're not making sense.'

Sister Clementine glowered at Mr Jacob's bent head. Pretending as if he didn't even know her name. Why couldn't he help her? Everyone knew he could talk to the Azeems about whatever he wanted. Look at him now, sitting there as if he was about to tuck into a dish of fish and rice. He'd probably been offered coffee as well. Well, he could forget about his daughters coming to the convent and wanting to learn the piano. Ever.

Fareeda misinterpreted Sister Clementine's frown.

'Mr Jacob, would you leave us for a while? But do come back in ten minutes sharp. I want to finish this work.'

Mr Jacob scraped back his chair and departed with unfeigned relief.

'Sister Clementine, you have ten minutes.'

Sister Clementine pulled out a chair and sank into it. She knew she hadn't been invited to sit, but if she had to break the news about Rani, she was going to do it sitting down.

'Please give me one second, only.' She dabbed at her forehead with a handkerchief, on which a little red 'C' was embroidered in one corner. The nun mopped her brow and then began folding the handkerchief into smaller and smaller squares, until it could be compressed no further. Sister Clementine replaced the hanky in her sleeve and said a silent 'Hail Mary' before embarking on her task.

'Mrs Azeem, I know you are always trying to help people,' she began. 'Finding them jobs, putting them in schools, getting them out of jail and into hospitals and whatnot. We are like you, only. With helping people, I mean.'

'If you say so.'

'But sometimes we are not being able to help.'

'I'm glad you acknowledge your limitations, Sister.'

'Oh? Yes, yes. We are all humans, no? Making mistakes and all.' Sister Clementine looked appealingly at Fareeda.

'If you're telling me that you've made another fatal mistake . . .' Fareeda let the sentence dangle, unfinished.

'No, no, no one's died. Not yet.' Sister Clementine was alarmed at the turn the conversation had taken. The last thing she wanted to do was to remind Fareeda about the seamstress. Mother Superior would be furious. Goodness, what had she let herself in for?

'What do you mean, "not yet"? I forbid you to touch another woman from Sabzbagh.' Fareeda's voice was harsh.

'No, no, no. You are not understanding,' Sister Clementine moaned, burying her face in her hands. 'We are not touching young girls.' Her voice was muffled by her hands. 'I'm only saying that when they come to us, we are sending them away. But still I'm worrying, what's to become of them?'

'You just leave them alone. Whoever needs help can come to me. I'm like an umbrella over the women of this village. They all know that I protect and support and help. They don't need you when they have *me*. Now, please leave. I'm very busy and you've already made me waste enough time.'

Sister Clementine nodded. Slowly, she rose from her chair. Her shoulders sagged, and her feet felt heavy as she trudged towards the door. She felt old, deflated, dismissed. The nun paused at the pantry door and turned around.

'Can I ask you a question, Mrs Azeem?'

'If you must.'

'Is that a woman or a ship?' Sister Clementine nodded at the painting above the mantelpiece.

'A woman.'

'Ah. Well, goodbye, then.'

'Goodbye, Sister.'

Laila brought her face close to the window and blew on the glass. The small cloud of condensation that appeared was an almost perfect circle. With her forefinger, she wrote a capital 'T' in its middle and then another 'T'. She looped the two letters together. The Terrific Two. Best friends, detectives and adventurers. For ever and ever and ever after. She studied the letters, pleased by the flamboyance of their loops. They looked assured, grown-up, like Sara's joined-up writing. Would she lose her special place in Rani's affections once Sara arrived? Rani had promised her she wouldn't, but that was before Laila had let her down. Laila rubbed out what was left of the evaporating circle and slouched back to her mother's desk.

Everything was in perfect order on it. The silver-framed photograph of herself and Sara was in line with the desk calendar. Fareeda's gold fountain pen and three Deer pencils, their tips sharpened to a point, stood bolt upright in a polished silver beaker. There wasn't a speck of dust on the desk's surface.

Laila stared at her arithmetic exercise book. Fareeda had given her some division sums to solve. They didn't look difficult, but Laila was too distracted by the letter and the events of the day before to pay attention. She wished she had been able to sit in on the meeting between Sister Clementine and her mother. Laila had guessed the nun's call was connected to Rani's visit to the church. It had to be. Why else would she come? The pointed glances she had intercepted between Bua and Sister Clementine on the lawn had confirmed her suspicion. No, this was by no means a casual call.

Laila had tried her best to discover the purpose of the nun's visit. Sister Clementine, Laila felt, would have divulged something, had her ayah not been present. But under Bua's watchful eye, the nun had clammed up. 'So good you are to ask, but I'm here for nothing special,' she'd repeated. When her offer to accompany Sister Clementine indoors had been declined, Laila had even considered the possibility of creeping up to the dining-room window to eavesdrop. But she could tell from the determined set of Bua's jaw that she was not going to let Laila anywhere near the dining room. Frustrated, Laila had given up. But yesterday's frustration had given way to today's unease.

What would she tell Rani? That she had failed in her very first test as her partner? Worse, she had failed as a detective. George would have found some way of giving Bua the slip. Rani would have every right to be cross with her.

Because of her incompetence, the mystery might slip from their fingers. And when Sara returned to Sabzbagh, she would saunter straight back into her old place at the centre of Rani's heart.

Laila was gazing moodily out of the window when Fareeda returned.

'Finished?' she asked.

'Er, no, not yet.' Laila covered her book with her arms.

'Hurry up, then.' Fareeda sat down opposite Laila and removed a sheet of writing paper from a drawer in the desk. 'I'll write a letter while you finish those sums.'

'Who are you writing to?' Laila peered across the desk.

'Dr Hameed in Lahore. I'm sending him two patients. Please do your sums.'

Laila looked down at her book. A minute later, she peeked furtively at her mother's head bent over the paper. She watched Fareeda's blue and gold fountain pen flow across the page and considered how best to tackle Sister Clementine's visit without arousing her suspicions.

'Ammi . . .'

'Hmm?' Fareeda did not look up.

'You know yesterday?' Laila toyed with her pencil.

'Hmm.'

'Well, yesterday, when Sister Clementine came, I asked her if she would like me to take her in to see you. You remember you said we should always be polite to guests? Well, I was.'

'Good.' Fareeda looked up and smiled.

'But she said, no, she'd go in alone.'

Fareeda had turned her attention back to the letter. Laila waited for her to take the bait, but when she didn't, Laila took a deep breath and ploughed on.

'It wasn't nice of her to refuse me, was it? I wonder why she did that?'

'Oh, I suppose she wanted to see me alone,' Fareeda said

absently, tilting her head to one side to ascertain that the lines of her handwriting were straight.

'What about?' Laila tried to keep her tone as casual as possible.

'I honestly don't know.' Fareeda picked up the page and slowly wafted it about to dry the ink. 'I couldn't make head nor tail of what she said.'

'Oh? She didn't say why she'd come?' Sister Clementine couldn't have left without saying why she had come. Or could she?

Fareeda's lips moved silently as she scanned the letter, checking it for errors. Curbing her impatience, Laila rephrased her question as an exclamation.

'How odd!'

Fareeda looked up. 'What's odd?'

'That Sister Clementine should come and go without saying anything to you.'

'I suppose she did say something, but it was so garbled I couldn't understand a thing.' Fareeda reached into the drawer for an envelope.

'She didn't mention anyone's name, did she?' Laila held her breath.

Fareeda put the envelope on the desk and locked eyes with Laila.

'Why are *you* so interested in Sister Clementine's visit?' she probed.

'No reason.' Laila dropped her gaze.

'Has Bua put you up to this? Because if she has, I'll have to have a word with her. If she wants to know chapter and verse of Sister Clementine's visit, she can ask me herself. I won't have you meddling in the affairs of grown-ups. And nor are you to act as a snoop for anyone. Is that clear?'

Fareeda was always on guard for any signs of unhealthy precocity in her daughters. She feared that, here in Sabzbagh, with mostly servants for company, they might be drawn into the affairs of adults. Laila retreated in alarm.

'Oh, no. I was just wondering, that's all. Because she doesn't come here that often. Sister Clementine, I mean,' she babbled. 'That's why. I mean that's why I wondered why she'd come. Nothing to do with Bua. Promise.'

Anxious to allay her mother's doubts, Laila cast about frantically for a credible story. 'I was just, er, just wondering about Christmas. Whether she'd come to talk to you about Christmas. And whether she'd come to ask us to go and see the church done up with stars and streamers and things on Christmas Day.'

To Laila's intense relief, the story seemed to work, for Fareeda shrugged and went back to the letter. With a thumping heart, she watched Fareeda fold the letter into a precise rectangle and slide it into the waiting envelope. She licked and sealed it. Laila marvelled at how she could do that without ever messing up her pink lipstick. Fareeda picked up her fountain pen once again and wrote the address on the envelope in her strong, upright hand. Laila liked Fareeda's handwriting. It was bold, elegant and yet legible. She sometimes had difficulty reading other people's joined-up writing, but never her mother's. She wished she could also read her mind with equal facility.

Fareeda replaced the pen in the silver cup and folded her arms across her middle.

'I don't see why you can't go to the church for Christmas. I suppose you could even take the nuns a cake or something.' The offer was by way of apology for her earlier harshness.

'Could I, could I really?' Laila jumped up.

'Well, you can't go empty-handed at Christmas. Now, show me your work.'

Laila didn't mind being chided for not finishing her sums. She was going to church at Christmas. But, more importantly, *much* more importantly, she hadn't let Rani down or, for that matter, the Terrific Two. Sara would have to take a back seat.

Later that day, two visitors dropped in. The first was Sardar Begum, who ambled in unannounced, and the second was Rani, tagging behind her shyly, carrying Sardar Begum's shawl and handbag over her arm. Sardar Begum rarely visited Sabzbagh. She was inhibited by two considerations, one born of pride, the other propriety. In her hide-bound book of rules, it was the duty of the young to call upon the elderly. It would be unseemly for her to go chasing after company – particularly her own family's. And, second, though she always referred to it as '*Tariq's* residence', she thought of Sabzbagh as Fareeda's home. As such, she did not wish to impose on her daughter-in-law's hospitality too often.

Of course, she broke her own rules whenever the situation warranted. During Laila's illness, she had been a frequent visitor, dropping in every other day with some talisman or the other to ensure her granddaughter's speedy recovery – ten-rupee notes wrapped in scraps of brocade to be distributed among the poor, a glass of milk blessed with health-giving prayers, a turquoise brought from the shrine of a saint in Iran. On the rare occasion when loneliness got the better of her, she came with an excuse – a small matter to be discussed with Tariq urgently, or a present for the family needing immediate delivery – and stressed as soon as she arrived her need to be off to attend to the myriad tasks which awaited her.

Fareeda bore up stoically to Sardar Begum's rare visits. While keenly aware of the older woman's fierce resistance to their marriage, she knew that, since then, Sardar Begum had become her staunch defender to the world. Any criticism of her 'memsahib daughter-in-law' from Tariq's aunts was met with a crushing retort: 'She's worth ten, ten of you.' But

Fareeda often wondered whether she defended her out of a sense of duty rather than any genuine affection.

'I've brought you some rice,' declared Sardar Begum, collapsing into an armchair. 'I didn't know whether you had enough to last out the war.'

Fareeda blushed. Just the day before, she had instructed Rehmat to buy in twice their usual monthly ration of flour and sugar. If Tariq found out, he'd rebuke her for panicking. 'Are we preparing for a siege?' he'd ask. She, too, had suffered a pang of conscience, but then she'd told herself firmly that a single sack of flour and three bags of sugar hardly amounted to stock-piling.

Sardar Begum was dressed in her 'visiting' clothes – a shalwar kurta in sage green teamed with a man's sleeveless cardigan buttoned all the way up and, as always, her white muslin dupatta. She wore flat black slip-ons and white socks on her size-three feet. Once, Fareeda had bought her court shoes in oxblood leather with a sensible stacked heel. Having examined them from all sides – she was searching for the price ticket – Sardar Begum returned them with a cool comment about the heel being unbecomingly high for a widow. Thereafter, Fareeda restricted her presents to woollen shawls in sober shades of dust, rust and sludge.

Sardar Begum folded her hands in her lap and gave the room a quick once-over to check whether her son's hard-earned money had been squandered on yet more expensive gewgaws from Lahore. Her hawk eyes scoured the room, taking in the familiar Persian rug underfoot; a cluster of Kangra miniatures on the far wall; the gilt mirror above the fireplace; the rows of silver-framed photographs; and the shelves of leather-bound books Tariq had inherited from his father. Satisfied that no new acquisitions had appeared since her last visit, she enquired after Tariq and Laila.

'Tariq is in Colewallah town,' said Fareeda. 'Laila is in the

community. Its branches were home to a colony of grey-and-white-striped squirrels and an army of mynahs, hoopoes, warblers and parrots. There were beehives, too, velvety dewlaps suspended from the higher boughs. Once a year, a man with a very tall ladder and a net over his face came to remove the honey. The girls watched from a distance as the enraged bees swarmed around his head.

Laila loved the scarlet flowers the tree sprouted in spring. They were bulbous, robust blooms, which fell to the ground with a satisfying thud. Their thick red petals were like ox tongues. And at the beginning of summer the tree produced the very substance after which it was named. As soft as down, as delicate as cobwebs, the silk cotton drifted down from the tree all month long and draped itself around the garden like candyfloss. The girls gathered the cotton and stuffed their pillows with it. Sara had two silk cotton pillows and Laila one.

Two swings hung side by side from the same branch. Laila offered Rani Sara's swing and hopped on to her own.

'I've got news for you,' Laila announced.

'What?'

'Sister Clementine came to see Ammi yesterday.'

Rani stiffened. 'What, here?' Even she, who did not live in Sabzbagh, had heard of the frosty relations between the nuns and Fareeda. That was why she had chosen to go to the convent. The nuns, she had thought, would not speak to Fareeda of her visit.

'Yes, here. In the dining room.'

'Were you there?'

'No. Bua wouldn't let me go.'

'Then?'

'First, I asked Sister Clementine why she had come. But she wouldn't say. She might have if Bua hadn't been there, but

Bua kept giving her funny, frowny looks.' Laila stopped to see whether her account had met with satisfaction.

'Go on,' encouraged Rani.

'So then I asked Ammi. This morning.'

'You didn't!'

'I did!' Laila grinned, pleased at Rani's reaction to her courage.

'Did she tell you anything?'

'Not a lot. But only because Sister Clementine didn't say anything.'

'What do you mean, she didn't say anything?' Rani frowned. 'Why did she come then?'

'Ammi said Sister Clementine was so muddled that she couldn't understand anything. Also, she didn't mention any names. Not yours, not Bua's, not mine, nobody's.' Laila felt a small twinge of guilt about this last claim. When she had asked Fareeda if Sister Clementine had mentioned any names, her mother had neither confirmed nor denied it. Which meant, probably, that no names were mentioned.

'Your mother didn't seem angry?'

'Er, no. Not about Sister Clementine's visit.'

Rani took the news in silence.

'Rani? Are you all right?' asked Laila, worried that she might have said something inappropriate. It was hard to gauge Rani's moods these days.

'I'm fine, fine, fine,' she laughed. She jumped up, lifted Laila bodily from her swing and twirled her around. 'You are the best partner I could ever have.'

Dizzy from the twirl and Rani's praise, Laila flushed with delight.

'I've been a good detective, haven't I?'

'The best ever.' Rani thumped Laila on the back. But then she paused, and after a bit she asked, 'And Bua? Did she see

Sister Clementine when she came out after speaking to your mother?'

Laila shook her head. 'No. We'd gone indoors by then. I have my glass of milk at that time.'

'Very good!' Rani beamed.

Emboldened by Rani's praise, Laila asked, 'Why were you so worried about Sister Clementine coming here and speaking to Ammi? Was it to do with your visit to the church?'

'In a way,' she said, shrugging. 'I'll explain later. Now hop back on your swing and let me push you till your toes tickle the sky.'

Laila realized she was being rebuffed, but she was so relieved to see the return of the old, light-hearted Rani that she went along with it gamely. She tucked away her unanswered queries into a deep drawer of her mind and climbed back on to the swing.

Soon the swing was slicing through the air, climbing higher and higher. Laila shut her eyes and savoured the wind on her face. She was a good detective. She had solved the case of the nun's visit. She had done so without the benefit of any clues, disguises or dogs. She'd done it all on her own.

'On the way here, big Begum Sahiba was saying that Barkat's son is probably dead,' yelled Rani.

'Why?' Laila strained to hear above the rush of the wind.

'Because lots of soldiers have died already.'

'Who told you?'

'Everyone knows.'

'But Shareef isn't dead,' Laila insisted. 'I saw a letter from him with my own eyes.'

'Maybe he wrote it just before he died.'

Perhaps Shareef *had* died since writing the letter. But Laila couldn't imagine him dead. She had seen him less than six months ago, when he'd come to say goodbye to his parents before leaving for East Pakistan.

His hair was short and spiky and, instead of his usual shalwar kurta, he wore a stiff khaki uniform. Otherwise, he was unchanged. His large red ears stuck out from his head like car doors left open. The big potato in his scrawny neck bobbed up and down when he swallowed. Sara had nicknamed him Goofy after Goofy Goat in the Disney cartoon.

Unlike his elder brother, who was a stenographer in a government office in Lahore, Shareef was not bright. After he'd failed his Matric exams three years in a row, Barkat had reluctantly accepted his son's academic limitations and pulled him out of school. A few days later, Barkat had him enlisted in the army. Several young men from Simbal had enlisted and done well out of it. Though Barkat accepted that Shareef was never going to distinguish himself as a soldier, at least he'd receive a steady salary. Shareef hadn't had the courage to tell his father that he did not want to join the army. He dreamt, instead, of running his own poultry farm.

The first time Shareef came back to Sabzbagh after enlisting, a visibly proud Barkat had brought him to meet Tariq and Fareeda. Laila remembered how Shareef had stood beside his father, wordless, leaden-footed in his heavy new boots, a gawky grin plastered to his face. When Tariq had congratulated him and shaken him by the hand, Shareef's ears had turned such a deep crimson that Laila had thought they'd burst into flames. Laila couldn't imagine Goofy fighting, let alone killing. Or dying.

'Shareef can't be dead,' Laila murmured.

'What did you say?' asked Rani.

'Dadi *did* say that there was going to be a big war with India,' shouted Laila. 'And because we are so close to the milk factory, the Indians are going to come for us first.'

'But Nazeer says we're going to beat the Hindus because our soldiers eat meat and fight like lions, while theirs eat cabbage and run like rabbits.'

'But what if they win?' asked Laila anxiously.

'They won't. And even if they do, I'm ready for them,' Rani said.

'How?'

'I've hidden a bag of extra hot chilli powder by the door. If Indian soldiers come into our house, I'll hurl fistfuls of chilli into their eyes until they run away screaming.'

Laila wondered if her parents had any such defensive contingencies. There was always her father's shotgun, with which he sometimes shot partridge. But suppose the Indians came when her parents were out walking, or at Hester's or something? Then what? Laila mentally ran through the things in her bedroom, rejecting most of them as possible weapons. If it came to the worst, she could always slam her wooden carom board on a soldier's head. She'd seen heroes in films do that with tables and chairs, to villains who always passed out with a loud crash. Yes, she could do that.

'Push me higher,' she shouted at Rani. 'I haven't touched the sky yet.'

9

Mist draped the orange trees in the distance like a mosquito net. The sky was swollen with slate-coloured clouds. The last few leaves of the shisham trees shivered in a chilly breeze. A single stork perched on the canal bank, its snowy feathers standing out starkly against the milky brown of the water. It was a raw morning, and Tariq was thankful for his thick sweater and quilted jacket. But the dreary day did not lower his spirits, for, as a farmer, he knew winter showers were invaluable for his crops. As a child, he had often heard his mother refer to winter rains as 'gold from the sky'.

He touched his heel to the mare's side and, ever responsive to his smallest signal, she sprang forward. The cold wind stung Tariq's face and numbed his hands, but with the rhythmic drum of the mare's hooves in his ears and the scent of frosted grass in his nose, he did not mind. He gave the mare her head, relishing her effortless speed on the packed earth.

To his right, the canal gleamed dully between the trees, and on his left, stretched his land – mango and citrus orchards, fields of sugar cane and wheat and acid-green mustard. His heart lifted at the sight of those neat rectangular fields, punctuated here and there with the dwellings of his employees. Smoke spiralled from their chimneys and lights glimmered in the windows. He was proud of those houses. Though small, they were built of solid bricks and mortar. They were all connected to electricity and had the use of running water. Soon, he hoped to lay down sewage pipes.

When he had first moved to Sabzbagh, nearly all the villagers lived in mud huts. They fetched water from communal taps and lit their huts at night with hurricane lamps. Driving out in the evening, he could go for miles without seeing an electric light. It was picturesque but archaic. Now, he believed, one or two houses even had televisions.

He had been right not to have become a civil servant or a box wallah. His efforts in those labyrinthine bureaucracies would have made not a jot of difference to anyone, but here, he could see at first hand what a change he had wrought. No other village in the district could hold a candle to Sabzbagh.

But in his zeal to forge on, was he becoming a little overbearing, perhaps? What had his mother called him at the picnic that day? A school master? She'd accused him of lecturing her. As if he were some pompous, sanctimonious bore. Was she also implying that he was authoritarian? God knew, he did his best to be democratic, consensual. But was it a crime to put his superior education at the disposal of his villagers? Besides, his mother was a fine one to talk. She who didn't allow a chick to cheep in her house without her permission.

She just couldn't stand opposition, that was the truth of it. Just because he had chosen to follow a different path, she was determined to undermine his efforts. Well, she would just have to lump it. He knew he was on the right track. He had only to look around him to see that. All this prosperity, this progress, it was his doing. And the villagers', of course. And also Fareeda's. He mustn't forget Fareeda. In fact, it could be said that hers had been the greatest contribution. After all, he belonged here. This was his home, his place. The same went for the villagers. Whatever their achievement, it was for themselves. But Fareeda was an outsider. She didn't have to live in this alien place, amongst an alien people. She'd had to make a huge adjustment to fit into this milieu. And she *had* fitted in – by and large.

True, she could be a little punctilious at times. It was a quality that perplexed the villagers. What was the need for all that hair-splitting? They were also baffled by her polite reserve and her halting, city Punjabi. Tariq knew she tried her best to sympathize. She didn't shout at them for not vaccinating their babies or marrying off their adolescent girls to old men. Instead, she expressed her disapproval in prolonged, chilly silences, which the villagers found discomfiting. In fact, they were far more comfortable with Sardar Begum's rants and forthright rudeness. They were accustomed to such outbursts from their superiors and bore them with the same stoicism as they did thunderstorms, certain in the knowledge that they would soon roll away and, with some luck, leave behind a windfall. Tariq knew if Fareeda were ever to discover this, she would be hurt. She thought of herself as the evolved patron, the kinder, gentler face of old martinets like Sardar Begum. What she lacked in instinctive understanding, she made up for in reformist zeal.

On the whole, though, Tariq did not dwell too much on Fareeda's compulsions. It was enough for him that she lived in Sabzbagh gracefully. She was a good, if sometimes unnecessarily firm mother, a loving, supportive wife and a great organizer. Her clockwork home was very comfortable indeed.

When he rode into his backyard, Tariq saw Fazal emerge from the pantry. Dressed in his customary fez, white shalwar kameez and black wool Nehru jacket, the bearer cut an imposing figure. Of all Tariq's staff, Sardar Begum disliked Fazal the most, even more than the heathen Bua and the profligate Rehmat. Fazal, to her mind, had airs that ill became a servant. It was a view that was shared to some extent by Rehmat and Barkat.

The silver-haired Fazal had the carriage of a viceroy. Having once served briefly in C. P. Khan's household, he had never recovered from the distinction. On his arrival in the Azeem household, he had tried to establish his superiority over the other servants by dint of his travels and undoubted sophistication. But he had received short shrift from Barkat and Rehmat. Fazal had, in the end, contented himself with splicing his conversations with the odd sarky one-liner. With his masters, however, he was all quiet efficiency and discreet coughs.

'How did you know I'd be back early?' asked Tariq, dismounting and handing the reins to the bearer.

'I had a feeling, Sahib,' replied Fazal with a glimmer of a smile.

'Is the groom here to collect the horse?'

'No, Sahib. I'll ask Amanat to walk it back. Can I help with your boots?'

Tariq eyed the bearer's pristine uniform and then his muddy boots. 'I'll manage. Are Bibi and Laila at breakfast yet?'

'No, Sahib, not yet. But the breakfast table is laid.'

'Good. Wait ten minutes till I shower, and then get my eggs ready. I want to make an early start at the factory.'

At four-thirty that afternoon, an elderly green Austin drove up to the house. A uniformed driver jumped out and held the back door open. A pink-stockinged leg ending in a plump foot wedged into a golden-buckled court shoe swung out of the car door. The Austin rocked as Hester gripped the open door and hoisted her bulk out. She straightened her navy-blue crimplene dress over her dimpled knees, grasped her alligator handbag by its strap and lumbered towards the house. Fazal showed her into the sitting room and hurried off to fetch Fareeda.

Fareeda had spent most of the day at the garment factory, trawling, under Tariq's critical gaze, through the project report she had drafted with Mr Jacob. The donors in Lahore had written back with minute, tiresome queries, and Tariq had sent for her to provide clarification. He had been curt with

her when she had not been able to supply the answers immediately. He'd clicked his tongue and tapped his foot and looked
heavenward as she leafed through the pages slowly and
frowned over the questions. She'd been tempted, then, to fling
the papers at him and tell him to do it himself. But Jacob's
embarrassed presence had inhibited her.

Fareeda had returned to the house seething. She had
just drawn the curtains and stretched out on her bed for a
rest when there was a light tap on her bedroom door, punctuated by a discreet cough. She was not pleased when Fazal
informed her of Hester's presence in the sitting room. Yet few
could have guessed that from her effusive welcome minutes
later.

'Ah, Hester,' she gushed, entering the drawing room with
arms outstretched. 'What a wonderful surprise.' Having
planted a kiss on Hester's bristly cheek, Fareeda sat down.

'Sorry to barge in without warning,' said Hester. 'But I had
a favour to ask.'

'Anything at all. But first tell me whether you'd like coffee
or tea so I can tell Fazal.'

'A cuppa cha would do nicely. I wondered whether you
could send over your electrician chappie to my house for a
quick dekko? Awful nuisance, but the lights in my house aren't
working. Some problem with my transformer, I'm told. Our
bijli wallah's a bit of a nincompoop and couldn't sort it out.
So thought I'd ask you, since your house is always bright as a
lighthouse.'

Fareeda laughed away the compliment and promised to
send her electrician over the next day.

'I'm leaving for Lahore now,' said Hester. 'But Hayat's
around. Can I get you anything from Lahore?'

'Some vitamin C tablets for Laila, if it's not too much
trouble. She likes the ones that fizz in water. I've run out.'

'No problem. I'll pop into Johnson's. Won't take two ticks.

Ah, tea. And chicken patties with tomato chutney. What a treat.' Hester helped herself to one. 'What's your news here at the farm?'

'All well. Tariq's quite close to getting the funds for his project. We're keeping our fingers crossed.'

'Excellent, excellent. And how are your nuns doing?'

'Hardly *my* nuns,' Fareeda grimaced. 'Fine, I suppose. Why do you ask?'

'On my way here I saw a couple of them going towards the bazaar in a tonga. Waved rather cheerily. Wonder if they'd wave half as cheerily if they knew I was a lapsed Christian?'

Fareeda snorted. 'I was visited by one of them last week. I didn't quite grasp what she wanted. There was some nonsense about treating girls at that clinic of theirs.'

'Do you think our pious, God-fearing sisters perform abortions?' Hester asked.

'I sincerely hope not. There are enough murdering midwives around for *that*! Why do these village women still insist on going to them and those ghastly midwives when they can come to me and I would send them to a good doctor at a decent hospital? *Why?*'

'Habit,' pronounced Hester. 'One can't change people overnight with a wave of a wand, much as one would like to. Talking of change, what did you think of our new colonel?'

'I thought he was a bit bumptious,' Fareeda sniffed. 'Who's he to tell us what we ought or ought not to be doing for our villagers? Isn't that a bit presumptuous for an outsider?'

'An outsider,' echoed Hester softly, gazing into her tea cup. 'I wonder if the good folk of Bridgebad still think of me as an outsider?'

'Oh, but, Hester, you've spent an entire lifetime here.'

'Is that enough?' reflected Hester. Then, in a bright voice, she said: 'Oh, look who's here.'

Fareeda turned to see Laila leaning against the door jamb. 'Come in, darling,' Fareeda beckoned to her. 'Come and say hello to Mrs Bullock.'

'Hello.' Laila sidled up to her mother.

'How's our little patient? Recovered from her fever?' Hester snapped open her handbag and pulled out an object wrapped loosely in a linen handkerchief. 'I almost forgot, tiddlywink. I brought you something.'

Laila craned her neck for a closer look. 'What is it?' she asked.

'Laila!' Fareeda's tone was sharp. 'What's come over you? Say thank you first.'

'But I haven't even seen it, yet,' Laila protested. 'What if I don't like it?'

'How many times have I told you, it's the thought that counts?' Fareeda shook her head.

'Of course it's not,' Hester said briskly. 'Thoughts don't matter. The road to hell being paved with good intentions and all that. Actions – or in this case – presents matter. You're quite right to have a look first. Here, open it yourself, but careful, it's quite fragile.'

Probing through the handkerchief, Laila could tell that the thing inside was smooth and knobbly at the same time. It also felt cool, like stone, but lighter. She unfolded the hanky and saw a carved mustard-coloured horse no bigger than her palm. Its nostrils were flared, its neck taut. The tail streamed out behind it as if it was galloping away from a hungry lion. Laila ran her fingers over the delicate legs, the finely carved sinews straining in immobile flight. Cradling the horse in her palm, Laila murmured, 'It looks like it's carved out of honey.'

'It's amber,' Hester told her. 'My father gave it to me when I was your age. I'd just won my first show-jumping contest.'

'Hester, it's too much,' Fareeda protested.

'Thank you, Mrs Bullock,' said Laila. She got her thanks in quickly, before Fareeda could ask her to return the present.

'Entirely my pleasure, my dear,' said Hester. 'I hope you'll get as much joy from it as I have.'

'I still think it's excessive,' Fareeda objected.

'Oh, stuff and nonsense. I'm happy and Laila's happy. So what's the fuss about, eh?' Hester placed her hands on either side of her thighs and hauled herself out of the depths of the sofa. She pulled her dress out from between the cheeks of her bottom. 'Righty-ho, I must be off. Thanks awfully for the tea. Do remember to send the electrician, and I won't forget the vitamins.'

'Of course.' Fareeda followed Hester out into the entrance hall. Fazal held open the door with the impassivity of an Easter Island monolith. Both women stepped out into the portico.

It was late afternoon. Sunlight filtered through a row of cypress trees and lay in broad tiger-stripes across the front lawn. The village milkman was clanking down the drive-way on a bicycle that needed oiling. A pair of kites wheeled and turned in a cloudless sky. Hester heard the birds' thin, mournful cry and shivered.

'Are you cold?' asked Fareeda. 'Can I get you a shawl?'

'Just someone walking over my grave.' Hester patted Fareeda's arm. 'Cheerio.'

The driver slammed the door shut, and Hester waved a handkerchief out of the window. Fareeda watched the car disappear around the bend in the driveway. As she stood there, an arm crept around her waist. Fareeda smiled and pulled Laila into her side.

'What did Mrs Bullock mean when she said someone was walking over her grave?' Laila asked.

'It's an expression which means you're feeling uneasy. Anxious.'

'What about?'

'Usually people say it when they feel something nasty is going to happen but don't know what.'

'Is something nasty going to happen?'

'Of course not,' Fareeda squeezed Laila's shoulder. 'Why should it?'

10

The wind rushed in through the car's open window and lashed Laila's hair against her cheek. Pushing it back, Laila turned in the front seat to look at her ayah. Bua lay in the back, a length of cloth, part bandanna, part bandage, wound tightly around her forehead. Her eyes were shut, but from time to time she moaned.

'Oh, Holy Mother, please take pity on this orphan, this widow. Take her wretched headache away. Still these hammers pounding her poor skull. What have I done to deserve this, hain, Mother?'

'Bua, you orphan, you widow, wind your window down and get some fresh air.' Barkat took his eyes off the road briefly to address her reflection in the rear-view mirror. 'It will blow the pain away.'

'No, no, no,' she groaned. 'It will whip my head off my neck. Leave me to my misfortune. Ooh, Mother, hear me.'

Bua's headaches were a regular occurrence, and Laila was accustomed to their bizarre manifestations. Bua described a pain that leapt up from her shoulders and entered through her ears, raced all around her head, galloping from one ear to the other, from the back of her throat to the crown of her head, like the devil riding a maddened bull. The headache usually came after a reprimand from Fareeda or an altercation with another servant. It stayed till Bua had broadcast her suffering and received some mollifying overtures from the other party. This particular headache had come upon her after lunch, following an argument with Fazal, and looked set to stay at least till dinner. Hence, when Laila had asked Fareeda if she could visit her grandmother in Kalanpur, Fareeda had taken one look at Bua's martyred face and told Laila to take her ayah with her.

As they drove towards Kalanpur, Barkat looked sideways at Laila and grinned. 'So, Lailu, who in Kalanpur are you going to see? Your grandmother or Rani?'

'Both,' Laila replied primly, and turned to look out of the window. She was acutely aware of her grandmother's dislike of competition. And that, too, from a servant.

They were on the narrow metalled road that ran from Sabzbagh to the bustling town of Hisar in the next district, thirty miles away. Except for a huddle of huts midway, the five miles of road between Kalanpur and Sabzbagh were mostly bordered by cane and wheat fields dotted with the occasional brick kiln. As they passed the huts, children and dogs rushed out and gave chase to the car, screaming and barking with delight.

'May the devil take them,' muttered Barkat. 'Haven't they seen a car before?'

A group of straight-backed women balancing brass water pots on their heads turned in slow motion to stare at the passing vehicle. Further down the road, Laila saw two buffaloes lower themselves into a pool of stagnant water. They seemed unperturbed by its thick skin of green slime. Barkat swerved to avoid a dead dog lying in the middle of the road. It lay on its side, its belly unzipped. A cloud of crows pecked at its bloody entrails. They rose cawing in the air as the car bore down on them.

Barkat switched on the radio. A high-pitched whine, backed by wailing violins alternated with crackling static.

'What's that?'

'*Who's* that?' Barkat corrected Laila. 'That's the Queen of Melody, Madame Noor Jehan. Wah! What a voice she has. Sweeter than a garden full of bulbuls. No, Bua?'

Bua grunted.

'Allah has given her a special gift, Lailu. God has blessed her with the unique ability to rouse men's honour, so that they are ready to shed their blood at the sound of her voice. When she sings about our homeland, even old men stagger to their feet to do jehad. There is something in her voice that turns men into lions. Haven't you heard her song "My Darling Soldier Boy"?'

Laila shook her head.

'What about "My Country's Handsome Braves"?'

'No.'

'Uff, even now, when I hear that song, the hairs on my arms stand up to salute her. See.' Barkat pushed his sinewy arm under Laila's nose. 'She recorded that song during the '65 war. You were a baby then, too small to remember. She came into the radio station, removed her shoes – she always does that before singing, because she says singing is like praying for her . . .'

'Like taking off your shoes outside a mosque?'

'Exactly. She removed her shoes, told the recording people to get ready – "What are you looking at? Tune up, ji," she said. Then she poured out the song straight from her liver, right to the end, without stopping even once to draw breath. When she finished, all the studio wallahs' faces were wet with tears. As long as we have Allah and Madame Noor Jehan on our side, we cannot lose. May Allah give her eternal life. Amen.'

When they arrived at Sardar Begum's haveli, the courtyard was deserted. The daybed was under the neem tree but, though the cushions were in place and the Urdu newspapers she favoured were folded into a neat pile, there was no sign of Sardar Begum. Bua and Laila were debating whether to look for Kaneez in the kitchen or to brave Sardar Begum's bedroom, when Kaneez shuffled out from the veranda.

'Salaam, Kaneez,' said Laila. 'Where's my grandmother?'

'Asleep,' said Kaneez, brushing Laila's cheek with her wrinkled, callused hand. 'You look so much like your father when he was your age.'

'If Dadi's asleep, I'll go and see Rani,' said Laila.

'She's at home. Bua, come to the kitchen, I'll give you some tea.' Kaneez nodded at Bua's bandanna. 'Make your headache better.'

Tempted, Bua asked Laila, 'You'll be all right?' But Laila was already out of the door.

'Come. No need to worry. You know Rani will take care of her.'

Sardar Begum's kitchen had a nodding acquaintance with the twentieth century, thanks to the single tube-light on the ceiling. The cooking was done on a wood-fired hearth, which had left traces of its smoky breath on the whitewashed chimneybreast. Sardar Begum's haveli did have a fridge but, because she feared that Nazeer would pilfer cream off the milk, she kept it in her bedroom. Water was brought into the kitchen from a hand pump outside, and drinking water was stored in three round-bottomed earthenware pots balanced on a wooden stand. Since Sardar Begum seldom lingered in the kitchen, she had not equipped it with any chairs or benches. The servants were expected to squat on the rush mats placed on the floor.

Bua squatted on one of them while Kaneez boiled the water.

'How have you been, Kaneez?'

'As well as can be expected at my age. Would you like some cardamom in your tea? It will do you good.'

'If your mistress doesn't begrudge it,' sniffed Bua.

'Oh, she's not as bad as all that. She has a kind heart and gives quite freely. What she can't bear is for people to help themselves. But she won't mind me giving you two pods of cardamom.'

'If you say so.' Bua asked in a casual tone, 'How is Rani?' She had not seen the girl when she had visited recently with Sardar Begum. Bua had been at the church that Sunday and had missed Sardar Begum's visit.

'Rani's better. She was quite sick before.' Kaneez handed the tea to Bua. 'Must have caught something at school.'

Bua dipped her head and took a sip of tea. 'And Fatima? What news of her?' asked Bua.

'None. I get to hear from her little and see her even less.'

'Because Mashooq won't let her visit?'

Kaneez sat down beside Bua. After a long silence, she said, 'Tell me, Bua, why is it that Allah punishes the same people over and over again, even if they are blameless?'

'What do you mean?' Bua peered at her warily over the rim of her cup.

'I am munhoos, ill starred. All my life I have been dogged by misfortune. When my husband died, I was still a girl. With a baby.'

'Kaneez.' Bua lowered her cup. 'You are not the only one. My mother died when I was a child, and I was also widowed after just fifteen years of marriage.'

'Still, you had fifteen years of married life, fifteen years of living in your own home.'

Bua nodded. 'My mother's body hadn't even cooled when my father dragged me off to the convent. Seven years old I was. I pleaded with him to let me stay with my brothers and him. Our home was small, but we had a pigeon coop on the roof, and I was up there all day with the birds. You should have seen how much they loved me. As soon as they heard my footsteps on the stairs, they'd start cooing and billing and fluttering. But my father wouldn't listen. Instead of letting even one person whisper even one word of gossip, he threw me in there with the nuns, whom I'd never even met. Every night I was wetting my pillow with too many tears.'

Though Bua had known Kaneez for all the years she had worked for Fareeda, she could not claim to be her confidante. Bua was too daunted by Kaneez's reserve to risk familiarity. But, today, Bua sensed that Kaneez was inclined to talk. Pressing home the advantage, she asked, 'What plans do you have for Rani? Have you got a nice man in mind? One can't wait too long with girls.'

Kaneez laughed. It was a harsh sound, like a rusty gate being pushed open. 'Plans? What good has it ever done me to make plans? Allah has foiled each one.'

'I've always wondered, Kaneez, why you didn't remarry? You were young. Not like me. I was already thirty-five when my husband died.'

'I was still in my teens. But I didn't remarry because I didn't want a stepfather to soil my daughter. There's no knowing with men.'

'That's true,' Bua nodded. 'Men can do anything. They are animals at heart.' Encouraged by this rare intimacy, Bua nudged Kaneez's shoulder and asked, 'So why did you marry your lovely girl to that beast Mashooq, eh?'

A shutter slammed down over Kaneez's face. She rose and said in a bleak voice, 'I see you've finished your tea. Go and see if Begum Sahiba has woken up. If she finds out Laila is here but hasn't been to see her, there will be trouble for you.'

Realizing that she had blundered, Bua rose awkwardly to her feet. She took a conciliatory step towards Kaneez, but the old woman turned her back on the ayah.

'Don't keep my mistress waiting. Go.'

Kaneez's manner did not brook any argument. With a helpless shrug, Bua slunk off to look for Laila. Watching Bua from the kitchen window, Kaneez felt the anger drain out of her. She hadn't intended to be so sharp with Bua. She knew that the ayah hadn't meant badly. In fact, it was probably just a clumsy attempt at sympathy. But a lifetime's habit of discouraging pity had left Kaneez unable to accept compassion. It seemed to Kaneez that the only two emotions she had permitted herself since her husband's death all those years ago were sorrow and pride.

Kaneez had been proud when she had thwarted all those gossipmongers in Kalanpur who had predicted that the nineteen-year-old widow would soon stray and bring shame on herself. She had also been proud of the fact that she had never accepted charity. Instead, she had provided for herself and her daughter through her own toil. She had worn her independence and virtue like a medal until her daughter had grown up. And then, with her head held high, she had gone looking for a suitable match for her. She had soon found one. And why not? Fatima was as lovely as a firefly, and Kaneez had lived an exemplary life, on that there could be no two opinions. Fatima's husband was a distant kinsman, an electrician by trade. Her daughter's marriage was happy and, watching them together, Kaneez felt vindicated. A child was born to them within the year. A girl, admittedly, but Kaneez was confident boys would soon follow. Her self-sacrifice had been worth it. Her work was now done.

But three years into their marriage, Fatima's husband had died of cobra bite. Fatima was devastated, but Kaneez felt betrayed. She refused to believe that this could happen to her again. Then, summoning up her last vestiges of resolve, she went looking again for another match for her bereaved daughter. For a year she searched and waited. Then she discovered why no one had offered for Fatima's hand. Since the same fate had befallen both mother and daughter, people thought they were cursed. It was being whispered in the village that whoever married Fatima would die in three years.

A distraught Kaneez appealed to Sardar Begum, who advised her to wait a while. In due course, Mashooq presented himself at the haveli. He had seen Fatima in the Sabzbagh bazaar. He had made enquiries, discovered who she was and begun his pursuit. A clever, cynical man, he was not prey to the same superstitions as the villagers. Nor was he blind to her connections with the haveli. He later said he had been struck by her beauty and her sweet temperament, which, he declared, 'shone from her face like goodness from the face of angels'.

'How many angels has he seen, I'd like to know?' snorted Sardar Begum, when Kaneez repeated his remark to her. Gradually, Sardar Begum was won over by Mashooq's exquisite respectfulness – he bowed low when salaaming, kept his eyes cast down and called her huzoor, majesty. She liked a man who knew his place. She was also aware of his prospects.

'He has a house and a job,' she advised Kaneez. 'If nothing else, at least Fatima will be comfortable.' There were, however, two serious shortcomings in the new suitor. One was his appearance – Sardar Begum found his pitted skin and limp regrettable. But she was prepared to overlook these flaws if she knew more about his background. On those details, he was annoyingly vague.

Mashooq was a newcomer to Colewallah district. He claimed to be an orphan with no family. Kaneez made some discreet enquiries, but no one could shed any light on his past, his people or his home. When another month passed without the appearance of a better suitor, Sardar Begum was prepared to ignore that flaw too.

Kaneez accepted reluctantly. She consulted Fatima but, as she well knew, Fatima would have married a tree if she had asked her to.

Even now, Kaneez shivered at the memory of the day when Fatima first saw Mashooq. He had come to see Sardar Begum – he came every week to plead his case. Fatima was helping Kaneez in the kitchen when Sardar Begum called out for her tea. Kaneez was busy, so she sent Fatima. As Fatima crossed the courtyard with the tray in her hands, Kaneez saw from the kitchen window that Mashooq had stepped out from behind a pillar and blocked her path. He lifted a hand and stroked her cheek. She could see Fatima's face clearly. After twelve years, she could still recall the look of pure revulsion that flickered over her daughter's face before she quashed it for ever.

Kaneez knew that she should have put a stop to it then. But she lacked the courage to visualize a different future for Fatima. Fatima, for her part, went off meekly with her new husband. Her only request to her mother was that she keep Rani and bring her up in the haveli. 'Look after her,' she whispered to Kaneez, when she was embracing her mother for the last time. 'She's all I have left of my husband.'

Bua was right. How could she have married off her daughter to that monstrous brute? But Kaneez had one consolation. She had looked after Rani. At least in that she had not failed Fatima.

Rani sat on a low stool in her tiny yard, bent over an embroidery frame. Laila quietly opened the door of the quarter and crept on tiptoe towards her. When she was within lunging distance, she roared and sprang on Rani, knocking her backwards. Startled, the older girl screamed. When she saw it was Laila, Rani grinned and pulled her leg from under her. Laila thumped down beside Rani on the smooth dirt floor.

'Scared you, scared you,' Laila chanted, sticking her tongue out at Rani.

'You did. You nearly frightened me to death,' gasped Rani, helping Laila to her feet. 'When did you come?'

'Just now.'

'You didn't stop with your grandmother?'

'She's asleep. What are you making?' Laila picked up the frame. A purple rose was embroidered in neat satin stitch on white cotton.

'A pillow case.' Rani looked at the frame over Laila's shoulder. 'Do you like it?'

'It's pretty.'

'Come, I'll show you the matching sheets.'

Rani led Laila towards the room she shared with her grandmother. Like the rest of the servants' quarters that crouched behind Sardar Begum's haveli, Rani and Kaneez's home was built on a tiny piece of land. It was enclosed by a mud wall with a single door. The door opened into the handkerchief-sized yard, a covered corner of which served as a kitchen. The opposite corner was curtained off by a sheet of corrugated metal grating, dug upright into the ground. It was the height of a tall man and concealed the privy and tap that served them as a bathroom.

The room smelt of cold bricks. Washed with white distemper, the walls were bare, save for a row of clothes pegs and a two-year-old calendar. It hung open on the month of December, illustrated by a picture of a fat blond baby, clutching a pink teddy bear. Two string beds stood at right angles, leaving just enough room for a chair and a deep tin trunk. The trunk was covered with a starched cotton cloth and, arranged neatly on it, were a plastic comb, a mirror, a bottle of hair oil, a small tin of talcum powder and an empty bottle of Diorella. The perfume bottle held a single yellow rose, plucked from Sardar Begum's garden, and a spray of neem leaves.

'You still have this? I gave it to you ages ago,' asked Laila, fingering the bottle.

Rani nodded. 'At first, when it was new, I'd fill it with water and dab it on my neck, it smelt so nice. But now the water has no scent, so I use the bottle as a vase. It reminds me of your home, of soft rugs, of bright, airy rooms and of your mother. She taught me how to put flowers in vases.'

Actually, as Fareeda would readily admit, Rani had not

needed teaching. Accompanying Sardar Begum on an unannounced visit to Sabzbagh, Rani had come upon Fareeda arranging flowers in the pantry. Since the girls were away at school in Lahore, Fareeda had invited Rani to stay and help. The girl had watched with interest as Fareeda selected blooms from a basket of cut flowers, snipped off excess leaves, trimmed the stems, and arranged them in the vase. Fareeda had offered to let her do the next vase.

She had been hesitant at first, soliciting Fareeda's approval every time her hand alighted on a cut flower. But Fareeda had waved her on. After completing one arrangement, Rani grew more confident, making bolder choices, mixing yellow chrysanthemums with orange gerbera, and white stocks with mauve roses. She seemed to know instinctively that a glass bowl required a different sort of arrangement to a silver flute. Gradually, she'd forgotten about Fareeda and hummed as she worked, totally absorbed in her task. Fareeda noted that her decisions were swift, her eye sure, her hands deft. When she had finished, Rani had cleared up the debris of the fallen petals, clipped stems and discarded leaves, wiped clean the work surface and lined up all the vases for Fareeda's inspection. Delighted with her handiwork, Fareeda had praised Rani unreservedly. Rani had flushed with pleasure.

Now, putting her toiletries and the bottle to one side, Rani opened the trunk. Delving past the layers of clothes, towels and blankets, she lifted out a folded white bed sheet and pointed out the same purple rose.

Laila ran her hand over the cloth. It felt much rougher than her sheets at home.

'Do you like it?'

Laila nodded.

Rani replaced the sheet in the trunk. 'I have to put it right at the bottom, underneath these towels, so my grandmother doesn't find it. Now all I have to do is to finish the pillow cases and get some cooking pots,' she counted the list on her fingers, 'six glasses and a jug and four sets of new clothes. Oh, and shoes, golden and shiny, with heels – like brides wear – and maybe even some lipstick. Then it will be ready.'

'What will?' asked Laila, puzzled.

'My dowry,' Rani blushed.

'Why are you making your dowry now?'

'Just like that.' Rani giggled and tugged at Laila's hand. 'Let's go outside.'

She led Laila out into the yard, where a small wooden crate had been upended. Raising a side of the crate with one hand, she reached in with the other and scooped out a tiny black chick.

'Ooh, it's so cute. Can I hold it?' Laila held out her cupped palms.

'Yes, but gently. Its leg is injured. See?' Rani touched one of its toothpick legs, to which she had tied a match-sized splint with a string.' I rescued him from the rubbish heap. He'd been left for dead.' Lit by the afternoon sun, Rani's skin was the colour of toasted peanuts. Her eyes were flecked with gold, and fudge-coloured streaks gleamed in her dark hair.

'What does he eat?' Laila cradled the chick in her palm.

'Grain. Want to see?'

Rani turned towards the kitchen, but stopped suddenly, as if she had remembered something urgent. She gulped, clamped a hand to her mouth and dashed behind the metal screen. There was the sound of gasping and retching, and then silence. A moment later, Laila heard the splash of running water. Presently, Rani emerged, looking pale and sheepish.

'Are you ill?' Laila asked, peering at Rani's face for signs of illness.

Rani wiped her face with her shawl.

'Have you got cholera?

'No. I'm all right.'

'My mother can take you to the doctor, you know.'

'No!' Rani shouted. 'You mention it to your mother and I'll never speak to you again.'

Laila recoiled, dropping the chick. She felt a surge of anger. She wanted to shout at Rani, to ask what had come over her these days, but she held back, lest it jeopardize their relationship again. Rani swept the bird under the crate. Then she cupped the younger girl's face in her hands and said softly, 'I'm fine, not ill at all. I ate too many guavas. That's all. Forgive me?'

'Was it because you were ill that you came to see the sisters at the convent that day? Did you want medicines?'

'I've told you, I'm not ill.' Rani looked cross again.

'But if you're not ill, then why are you crying?'

'I'm not.'

'You are. See?' Laila flicked a teardrop from the corner of Rani's eye.

'I'm crying because I'm both happy and sad. Sad that I upset you and happy . . . happy because . . . it's a secret. Can I trust you not to tell?'

'A secret? *Of course* you can trust me. I've kept all your other secrets, you know. Haven't told anyone. But I'll promise again if you like.'

'Like before. On the Koran, your parents, Sara, Bua, everyone. OK then.' Rani lowered her voice to a whisper. 'I'm getting married.'

'M-married?' Laila stammered. 'When?'

'Soon.'

'Next week?'

'Not next week. But maybe next month.'

'Why? Why so soon?' Laila was trying hard not to cry.

'Because he's promised me we will,' said Rani. 'He's told me I mustn't worry. Everything will be all right. His parents will come and ask my grandmother. Properly, like it's done for good girls. At first I thought he was going to run away and leave me all alone. He had begun to shout at me and avoid me, making excuses not to meet. Once, he even told me he hated me, and that I'd ruined his life.' Rani's chin quivered momentarily, but then she rushed on. 'But now he is being so nice with me all the time, stroking my hair and buying me salted peanuts and telling me how pretty I look. The only thing is, he's said I must wait for a bit and I mustn't tell anyone. Until he comes with his parents and proposes. So, you see, that's why you must keep it to yourself. Because if you don't, and he finds out, he'll be so angry again that he might not even come.' The prospect seemed to alarm her, and a look akin to panic crossed her face. 'No, he won't do that. He can't. He's promised.' Brightening visibly, she asked, 'Do you think I'll look nice in high heels?'

'But what about our partnership and the Terrific Two and the mystery which we haven't even solved yet?' Laila cried. 'You promised we'd solve it together. *You promised!*'

Rani cocked her head to one side. 'What are you talking about? What mystery?'

'The mystery of the church. Why you came crying to the church that day and talked to Sister Clementine,' Laila shouted. 'Why you asked me to spy on Bua and report on Sister Clementine.'

Rani clamped a hand over Laila's mouth. 'You'll get me into trouble if you shout like that.' She scowled at Laila, but when she saw the younger girl's genuine distress, she put her arms around her. 'Listen to me now,' she soothed. 'What happened at the church that day is not important any more. It's all in the past, like a bad dream that is now over. Or a mystery, even, that's been solved. You must forget about it. But that doesn't mean we're no longer partners. We will always be partners, you and I. We are special friends, remember? And so we will stay, for ever and always. The only difference is that I am going to get married. But,' she added quickly, seeing Laila's face crumple, 'he won't take your place in my heart.'

'Who's *he*?' demanded Laila in a furious whisper.

'He? Oh you mean *him*. My . . . the man I'm going to marry?'

'It's your friend, isn't it? What's his name?'

Rani coloured. 'If I tell, you promise not to tell even your own shadow?'

Laila nodded, desperate to know, despite herself.

'Come here, I'll whisper it in your ear.'

Just as Rani brought her mouth to Laila's ear, Bua stumped into the yard. Rani's hand fell to her side. She edged away from Laila.

'Come on, Lailu, your grandmother's woken up.' Bua's voice was loud, almost strident. 'She's asking for you.'

'Can I stay a little bit longer? Please? Oh, please?' Laila begged. 'Can't you go and tell her I'll come in two minutes?'

'What? And get my plait yanked out from the roots?' snorted Bua. 'It's not enough that I'm going grey without going bald also? You know how she gets if she's made to wait. You are coming with me now.'

Still smarting from Kaneez's rebuke, Bua was not in an indulgent mood. It was because of Rani, really, that she had been insulted by Kaneez. Well, from now on, she wasn't going to bother to ask about her. The girl had got herself into this mess, she could jolly well get herself out of it too.

Laila glanced at Rani for support, but her face was as blank as a rubbed-out blackboard. Laila wanted to cry with frustration, to stamp her foot and demand that Bua leave and Rani speak. But one look at their tight, stubborn faces told her that neither was about to oblige. Reluctantly, she took Bua's hand. Bua was about to stalk off with Laila when she paused, raked Rani with her gaze and asked, 'How are you feeling?' Her tone was brusque.

'Fine,' Rani mumbled.

'Still, I wouldn't like to be in your shoes, baba. Not for a haveli, not for a palace.'

'You haven't, you haven't . . .' Rani searched Bua's face anxiously.

'Told anyone? What for? To get a hundred shoes on my head for bringing such shameful news? You think a mad dog has bitten me?'

'Thank you,' Rani whispered.

'Be thankful when it's all over – one way or another. Come, Laila.' Pulling Laila by the arm, Bua made for the door.

As she was being dragged away behind Bua, Laila turned to look over her shoulder one last time. Rani stood framed in the doorway, a hand shielding her eyes from the sun. She pressed her forefinger to her lips to remind Laila of her promise. Laila was tempted to turn her back on Rani. Let her totter off on her golden high heels to her new husband. But the thought of never seeing her again was like a corkscrew in her heart. Laila nodded and crossed her heart. Rani waved. Then Bua pulled her round the corner and Laila lost Rani.

If there was one thing Sardar Begum hated more than being cheated, it was being made to wait. It was not that she was unusually impatient, for she could wait for the monsoons as the clouds gathered and dispersed week after sultry week; smile serenely for the full nine months of her pregnancy; and even face the prospect of waiting for a thousand years in her grave for the day of judgement with some equanimity. She could bear the delays decreed by Allah, for what was she but His lowly creature, placed on earth solely to submit to His will? But being made to wait for another person and that, too, someone younger or socially inferior, was a different matter.

It was not just a matter of simple discourtesy. To Sardar Begum, it smacked of gross insubordination, indeed of social anarchy, a sure sign that the end of the world was nigh. A strict social order, a rigid hierarchy, was an article of faith to her. People should adhere to their assigned space and be thankful for it. That was one of the main reasons for her fondness for the long-departed English – their unswerving commitment to a rigid pecking-order.

'They may have eaten pigs and not washed their backsides,' she was fond of saying to her granddaughters, 'but those farangis knew how to keep everyone in their place. When people forget their place, they step out of the bounds decided by Allah. That's when the devil begins his work. Now, what are the Bengalis doing but forgetting their place? Allah has decreed a place for everyone – one for me, one for the sweeper, and one for the Bengali. As long as we remember it and honour it, all will be well.'

So, when Laila reached the haveli, she found her grand-mother in a sour mood. It had been a full fifteen minutes since Sardar Begum had woken up, twelve since she'd learnt about Laila's whereabouts, and nine minutes since she had sent for her. She sat in her bedroom, on the hard wooden divan permanently positioned to face Mecca.

Hers was an austere room with little else beside her divan, a worn rug on the floor and two hard-backed sofas covered in faded green tapestry. Matching curtains hung in the windows flanking the fireplace. The windows were positioned so that they opened out into the shadowy veranda. Hence, Sardar Begum's room was always gloomy – until evening, when she switched on a pair of harsh fluorescent ceiling-lights. Despite her son's frequent entreaties to replace them with bulbs, she refused.

'There will be plenty of time for me to lie in the dark in my grave,' she would sniff. 'Also, they are cheaper to run than bulbs and, unlike you, I don't have money to scatter from rooftops.'

The fridge was housed in a specially constructed alcove off her room. It perched on a low wooden platform and, threaded around its door handle, was a small brass amulet to ward off the evil eye.

Sardar Begum received Laila's greeting with a snort. Her gimlet eyes were glued to a large steel clock on the wall. She sipped milky tea and nibbled on a soggy, tea-dunked rusk.

'Finally! You've decided to spare a moment of your precious time for me. Thank you, thank you kindly,' she sniffed.

'I came to see you first, Dadi. You were asleep.' Laila perched on the edge of the divan.

'Asleep? With so many worries, you think I can sleep? I haven't slept since he went.' Sardar Begum jerked her chin towards the picture of her late husband over the mantelpiece. It was a grainy, much enlarged copy of a sepia photograph. It showed a portly young man in jodhpurs and turban astride a stallion, with a falcon perched on his wrist. It was an atypical image, for he had been a quiet sort who much preferred reading to hunting. Nevertheless, Sardar Begum liked to remember him thus, and every day a fresh garland of marigolds was hung around the gilt frame. The only other photograph in the room was a picture of Tariq, dressed in the black robes, edged with white rabbit fur, of Wadham graduands.

'I wasn't asleep. I was simply lying here looking at the ceiling.' It was Sardar Begum's fond claim that she neither slept nor ate – she was too worried about Tariq to sleep and too ill to eat. These were the hallmarks of a delicate constitution such as hers. Laila did not argue.

'And you? Why were you skulking in the servants' quarters?' she asked Laila.

'I went to see Rani.'

'I might have guessed. And what did she give you? A grandmother's love?'

'Don't be like that, Dadi,' Laila pouted. 'I *did* come to see you first. I promise, I did. But Kaneez said –'

'Kaneez said, Kaneez said,' Sardar Begum mimicked in a high-pitched voice. 'Don't you know Kaneez lost her brains along with her teeth? Only I put up with a brainless, toothless, useless old thing like her. Anyone else would have thrown her out long since. I'm too kind, that's my flaw. Too kind and too soft. Now, give me a kiss, and next time don't go rushing off to hang around servants. You give them ideas above their station.'

Laila hugged her grandmother and was duly offered milky tea, which she disliked but accepted for fear of straining the fragile truce. But she drew the line at rusks, asking instead for carrot halwa. Kaneez was sent for and told to bring halwa for the little bibi.

Sardar Begum pinched Laila's spindly forearm. 'You're too thin. Too thin and too tall. How much more are you going to grow?'

'How do I know?' Laila shrugged.

'Better stop soon, understand? One inch more, two inches at most. Then stop. Otherwise, where will we find a husband for you?'

'I don't want a husband.'

Sardar Begum's hand flew to her mouth. 'Touch your ears at once. Bite your tongue. Tell Allah you didn't mean that. To be left, unmarried and unwanted . . . The shame, the misfortune. An unattached elderly girl is an abomination. God forbid that it should happen to you.'

'But I'm a child,' Laila protested.

'Oho, I'm not saying marry now, this minute. But one day. Every girl must.' Sardar Begum gave Laila a hard stare. 'Tell me, have you grown up yet?'

'Grown up? How?' Laila gazed, wide-eyed, at Sardar Begum.

'If you don't know, it hasn't happened yet,' she said. 'That means you're going to grow taller still. May your growing-up come quickly in that case.'

'Do girls grow up when they get married?'

'No, silly. They grow up much before then. Or should do. Sara must be near to it now if she's not so already. But who tells *me* anything? I'm always kept in the dark till the end.'

Kaneez entered with the tea and halwa.

'Why have you brought two plates?' Sardar Begum barked at Kaneez. 'Who do you think I'm entertaining? A wedding party?'

'I thought you might like to try some,' said Kaneez. 'I know how you like to nibble.'

'Me? Eat halwa? With my sugar so high? You want to kill me?'

'Sugar won't kill you, Dadi,' said Laila.

'I'm not talking of sugar, sugar. I'm talking of the sugar that comes in my small bathroom. What does your mother call it? "Die" something.'

'Oh, diabetes. My other grandmother has it too.'

'But you have three spoonfuls of sugar in your tea,' Kaneez reminded Sardar Begum.

'Who asked you?' her employer bristled. 'Are you a doctor to tell me what I should or shouldn't have? Take this extra plate and go. Vanish!

'Drink your tea.' Sardar Begum offered the steaming cup to Laila. 'It's made with buffalo milk. If I were your mother, I'd put a stop to all this going about in the sun, running around like the boy who used to keep the parrots off our mango trees. I'd keep you indoors until evening and make sure you drink eight glasses of milk a day, till you were white as a jasmine bud.'

'I don't want to be a jasmine bud.' Large circles of grease floated on the thick, creamy tea. Laila replaced it on the tray with a shudder.

'Then what do you want? To be black as a crow? Silly girl. I don't know what they teach you in your Christian school, but let me tell you, men from good families like dainty, white girls, not rough, black giants. Talking of men, are there any Masters in your school?' The intent look reappeared in Sardar Begum's eyes.

Laila shook her head. 'Only Miss teachers.'

'Thank God. Never know with your mother. She might have put the two of you in a boys' school. And what about your mullah? Does he still come to teach you the Koran?'

Her mouth full of halwa, Laila nodded.

'And you study from him alone?'

'I do, but Ammi gets Bua to sit in the room.'

'She sees some sense sometimes. Never be alone with him, do you hear? The longer their beards, the dirtier their minds. And if once a girl loses her character, she loses everything.'

'What's a girl's character?' Laila asked.

'Her pride, her value.'

'Do boys also have character?'

'They don't need character,' Sardar Begum chuckled. 'They have status instead.'

Dismissing her grandmother's cryptic comments, Laila thought of Rani. Why had she said that the mystery was solved? Who had solved it? She couldn't imagine Rani married, with children and things. What if she didn't like Rani's husband? What if he was boring and mean and wouldn't let Rani play hide and seek with her and Sara? Eat tart, green mangoes with salt and chilli under the neem tree? What if he wasn't even from Kalanpur?

'Dadi, will you tell me something?'

'Certainly, my moon.' Sardar Begum stroked Laila's arm.

'You know when a girl gets married? Does she always have to go and live in her husband's home?'

'Yes, my moon, always.'

'Even if he lives far away, say, in another village, or another city?'

'Yes, even then.'

'But what about all her friends that she leaves behind? When do they see her?'

'When she comes home to visit. But, usually, girls get so busy in their new homes that they seldom have time for friends and fun. They're not carefree like unmarried girls.'

'That's not fair!' cried Laila.

'It's not so bad. It's fun getting married, having lots of nice new clothes and jewellery and lipsticks and powders and being fussed over and, if you're lucky, as, Allah willing, you will be, having a husband who is nice to you, like your Aba is to your Ammi, and a saint for a mother-in-law like your Ammi has in me.'

'But what about the friends you leave behind? What happens to them?'

'Oh, they're soon forgotten.' Sardar Begum tossed her head. 'Hear that? That's the call for maghreb prayer. You'd better get going. I don't want you travelling in the dark. And don't look so glum. You're not getting married next month, you know.' Sardar Begum pinched Laila's cheek. 'One thing more. Don't tell your parents about our chat? Or your father will scream at me for even mentioning the word "marriage" to you. As if he can keep you a child for ever. Promise, you won't tell? That's my moon. Go with God.'

The sun was sliding behind the fields as Barkat sped towards Sabzbagh. Through a haze of dust and wood smoke, young boys were driving home their herds of goats and cattle. Bats swooped and rose in the headlights of the car. When they drove past the huts, only a couple of dogs gave half-hearted chase. Everyone else was gathered around the small fires that flickered in the open space between the huts. Shrouded in their shawls and huddled in a circle, the villagers looked like taut, full sacks waiting to be packed into a tractor.

Laila sat beside Bua. A storm of questions raged in her head. She was aching to ask Bua about Rani but knew that she mustn't. She'd promised on the Koran, on her sister's and her parents' lives, and Bua's also. If she broke her word, they might all drop dead suddenly, like statues being knocked over. Or die horrible slow deaths, writhing in agony like the snake that Amanat had once pounded to death with a bamboo staff. And it would be all her fault. Also, Rani might never speak to her again. But, wait – she could ask Rani herself. After all, she had been about to tell her the name of her friend when Bua had interrupted them. She'd also make Rani tell about the church and the mystery. Laila smiled in the dark, pleased with herself. Now, even more than usual, she couldn't wait to see Rani again.

II

The next day was a Sunday, and Tariq, Fareeda and Laila sat in the garden waiting for Hester. It had rained the evening before and winter had come overnight. But, for the moment, there was bright sunshine, and the thick scent of molasses floated across from the village, where cane was being crushed into crumbly brown sugar. Laila slipped her legs off the long, polished arms of her planter chair and reached for the dry fruit tray.

The emergence of the dry-fruit tray – for some reason it was never referred to as 'dried' fruit, but always 'dry' fruit – was an essential part of the many rituals that marked the departure of summer and the arrival of winter. Woollen clothes that had spent the summer months hibernating in iron trunks were unpacked and arranged in piles in the sweater cupboard. Rugs that had lain rolled up in the storeroom were sunned, beaten and spread on bare terrazzo floors. Oil-fired heaters were cleaned and repaired, and a special visit was made in the last week of October to Lahore's Beadon Road, where light-skinned, green-eyed Pathans sold big sacks of nuts and preserved fruit.

Considered too 'hot' for the summer months – 'rots the liver and thickens the blood' – dry fruit was consumed only after the shisham trees had lost their leaves. Every household had its own version of the tray. Sardar Begum had a copper platter with three enormous wooden bowls of roasted chickpeas sprinkled with salt and chilli, dates stuffed with slivers of almonds and chewy nuggets of dark cardamom-scented sohan halwa. Hester, who had never quite got the point, had a single china plate with broken bits of old, hard Cadbury's milk chocolate and musty peanuts.

Fareeda's tray, on the other hand, was a Kashmiri silver salver with matching bowls containing an assortment of Beadon Road's finest – crisp, salted pistachio nuts; bite-sized disks of white nougat rolled in sesame seed; long thin pine nuts, shelled and dry roasted to a pale gold; wrinkled honey-coloured raisins; 'paper shelled' almonds that you could crush in your palm; and sticky, sweet peanut crunch.

Laila helped herself to a handful of pistachio nuts. She licked the salt off the shells before prising them apart to reveal the vivid green flesh.

'Ammi, can I visit Dadi today?'

'Hmm?' Fareeda scanned the pages of the *Society Mirror* for the photographs of a wedding she had attended recently in Lahore. 'Go to Dadi's? But you went yesterday.'

'Can I go again?'

'Why?'

'Just like that.'

'No, you can't. It's Barkat's day off,' she replied, her eyes still on the magazine.

'Tomorrow, then? Can I go tomorrow?'

'Your grandmother is supposed to go to Sargodha to-morrow to stay with your aunt again. Why's she returning so soon again, Tariq?' asked Fareeda. 'I thought she didn't like imposing on your brother-in-law's hospitality.'

'Hmm?' Tariq looked up from the papers. 'Apparently my sister's mother-in-law hasn't been too well. Even though she can't stand the sight of her, my mother's got to be seen to be doing the right thing, and so she's going to ask after her health. Shouldn't take her more than two or three days. I don't think she's even taking Kaneez this time. Why do you ask?'

'No reason,' shrugged Fareeda. 'Just wondered, that's all.'

'But can I still go to Kalanpur?' persisted Laila.

'To do what?' Fareeda asked. 'Dadi won't be there.'

'But Rani will.'

'So it's not Dadi at all that you want to see.' Fareeda returned her attention to the magazine. 'I'm sorry, but you can't travel five miles by car just to go and play when you have plenty of children right here.'

'Please?'

'I said no. With a war looming, we can't be wasteful with petrol.'

'Not that you'd guess it from the papers.' Tariq spoke from behind a paper wall of the *Pakistan News*.

'Guess what?' asked Laila and Fareeda in unison.

'That there was a war looming.' Tariq turned the pages of the newspaper. As usual, there was no news on East Pakistan. Instead, the papers were stuffed with reports of robberies and coach accidents, unimportant court cases and tedious speeches by minor dignitaries.

Tariq turned the page to find two columns on the news of a forthcoming holiday. 'Capital Wears Deserted Looks,' he read.

'"Capital city, Islamabad, has assumed deserted looks owing to large outflow of government employees to other stations because of twin holidays on eve of the birthday of the Holy Prophet (May Peace be upon Him). The government employees have left for their native towns and cities for three days including two holidays of the Holy Prophet's birthday, weekly off and one casual leave they have taken to add to the strength of their duration of enjoyment among their near and dear ones who are always considering them some super creatures. Islamabad which stands distinguished due to its specific cultural milieu can be seen dejected like hollow-eyed virgin, who is disappointingly staring at the vast expanses before her to search for the dearest one who has lost into bottoms of unknown destination."'

He laughed aloud as he read the last line.

'What's funny?' asked Fareeda.

'These inane newspapers.'

'Hester is bound to have some news,' Fareeda suggested. 'She returned yesterday from Lahore. She'll give us all the juicy morsels over lunch.'

Tariq folded the paper and dropped it on the lawn.

'Why so glum, darling?' he asked Laila.

'Because Ammi won't let me go to Kalanpur.'

'You went only yesterday. Why the urgency to return?'

'I want to see Rani,' replied Laila.

'Didn't you see her yesterday?'

'I want to see her again. I need to ask her something.'

'Too bad. You should've done your asking yesterday. Your mother's right, you can't be driven back and forth, asking questions like Hercule Poirot.'

'But I only want . . .'

Laila's words were drowned out by the horn of Hester's Austin. Dressed in a purple belted dress with white spots the size of tennis balls, she alighted from her car and made her way towards them. She clutched a bunch of narcissi.

'Hello, all. I brought these for you.' She thrust the dripping flowers at Fareeda.

'Thank you, Hester, they're lovely.' Fareeda grasped the wet stalks gingerly and held them at arm's length.

Still sulking over her parents' refusal to let her go to Kalanpur, Laila mumbled a hello to Hester. Tariq pulled up a sturdy planter chair for their guest.

'Oh, no, not that one.' Hester opted for a straight-backed chair instead. 'Once I subside into that planter, you'll need a crane to lift me out.'

Laila giggled at the image of Hester dangling high above from the claws of a crane, clutching her handbag and scissoring her fat pink legs in the air. Fareeda shot her a warning look.

She handed Laila the narcissi and instructed her to go indoors and find a vase.

'Good trip, Hester?' asked Tariq.

'Oh, yes, sold a filly to a moustachioed landowner from Sargodha. Probably some relative of yours.'

'Not everyone in Sargodha is related to me,' laughed Tariq.

Fareeda served Hester chilled pomegranate juice from a crystal jug. Hester's gaze moved from the sparkling glass to the immaculate flowerbeds, the smooth lawn and the trimmed hedges of Fareeda's garden.

'Must say, Fareeda, you do keep everything looking tip-top,' she murmured appreciatively.

'So, what's the news, Hester?' asked Tariq. 'What's the chit-chat at the Imperial?'

Hester's husband had been one of the first members of the Imperial Club in Lahore. The Club's rules did not allow women to become members – 'lady members disallowed', it said in discreet gold lettering by the receptionist's desk. But the rules had been bent to accommodate Hester, who had thrown a volcanic tantrum when she had discovered that, as a widow, she was no longer allowed to use the Club's facilities. When in Lahore, Hester always stayed, as a point of principle, in one of the musty rooms at the Club, where she never failed to remind the hapless secretary that Geoffrey Bullock had been the third Englishman to join the Club after the then Governor and Commissioner of Lahore.

'The usual.' Hester waved her glass in the air. 'Who's diddled whom. Who is setting up what mill.'

'What about Dhaka?' asked Tariq.

'What about it?'

'Is no one talking about it?'

'A few. In passing. Mostly about how the Bingos had it coming and how the army's going to sort them out. The common consensus, as far as I can make out, is that Mujeeb is an Indian agent who's been put up to this by Indira Gandhi. Her father, Nehru, couldn't bear the sight of an independent, sovereign Pakistan, and nor can she. So, it's a plot hatched by Mujeeb and Indira. Simple as that!'

'I see,' said Tariq. 'And what about the millions of Bengalis who voted for Mujeeb? Are they also in Indira's pay?'

'Oh, no, they are just bolshy babus, really, who've swallowed Mujeeb's propaganda hook, line and sinker. He's whipped them all up into a right old frenzy, and now they're all leaping about demanding freedom. But the army's going to sort them out sharpish.'

'Aren't they the least bit worried that it might not be so easy?' asked Fareeda.

'Goodness, no,' said Hester. 'Sitting out here one tends to worry more. I suppose the isolation does it to you. Up in Lahore, they couldn't give a damn. But here's the odd thing. While the civvies are gung-ho, the army, I hear, is in a panic. Privately, of course. General Niazi's blubbing like a child in his bunker in Dhaka. Apparently, he's petrified now that the Bengalis and Indians are closing in.'

'Who told you?' questioned Tariq.

Hester tapped her nose conspiratorially. 'I have my sources.'

'Those idiots in Lahore are so cheerful because they believe the army's propaganda. Even though the army itself no longer believes it,' said Fareeda scornfully.

'Quite so,' said Hester.

'And General Yahya? What does he think?' probed Tariq.

'I must confess, I have a sneaking regard for the old general,' said Hester. 'He said he'd have a proper election, and he's done it. Pity he miscalculated the results so grossly. Well, one hears, he's holed up in GHQ sloshing back the whiskey and stringing along General Niazi in Dhaka with assurances that help is on its way from China, America, Timbuktu. Wherever. Meanwhile, he's said to be seeking solace in the company of a lady friend.'

'A lady friend?' breathed Fareeda. 'Oh, do tell. Who is she?'

'She goes by the name of General Rani,' chortled Hester.

'You're joking!'

'That's what they call her.'

'But what's her real name? Who is she?'

'Haven't the faintest,' said Hester. 'Apparently, it's all highly secretive, with the lady being smuggled in and out of curtained cars and being hustled through back doors to GHQ.'

'How delicious,' Fareeda laughed.

'Ammi, I've put Mrs Bullock's flowers in the yellow vase and placed it on your bedside table,' Laila announced, dropping into the chair she had recently vacated.

'Good girl.'

'By the way,' said Hester, 'thanks awfully for sending your electrician over. Hayat tells me he had the whole thing sorted out in two ticks. Such a relief to come back to light. And I brought you these.' She handed Fareeda a paper bag. 'Laila's vitamins, remember? Now, tell me, young lady, have you started riding yet?'

'No.' Laila threw an accusatory look at her father.

'What are you waiting for?'

'Aba says I'm too little to go on his horse.'

'I've been meaning to get a smaller pony for her, but I haven't got around to it,' explained Tariq, a trifle sheepishly.

'Bring Laila over to Bridgebad. I might have just the ticket for her.'

Bua was not a scheming woman. But in one area of her life, she did think strategically. And this was in the giving and receiving of favours. She was acutely aware of her own value in the village as a conduit to patronage through her connection with the Azeems. From time to time, therefore, she entertained requests in return for small considerations. But Bua was selective in the requests she promoted. While she did not want to be swamped with demands, she had no wish to be overlooked either. Her position as a woman of influence within the village hinged upon her ability to swing the odd favour. To protect her position, therefore, she only made promises she could deliver. It was pointless, for instance, to guarantee someone a job in Tariq's factory, for which he handpicked suitable candidates. Nor would it to do for Bua to bombard her employers with petitions, lest they tire of her demands. There were some pleas Bua rejected because she did not like the petitioner. And there were still others where the payoff was too small. But there were almost none that she refused out of fear.

Rani was therefore an exception. Though disapproving of Rani's conduct, Bua was sympathetic to her plight. Had she been any other girl in the village, Bua would have pleaded her case with Fareeda, whom she knew to be tolerant about such things.

But Rani's was a complicated case. While neither a servant nor a relative of the Azeems, the girl had a special place in the family. In many ways, she had a closer link with Tariq and Fareeda than Bua. And, if Rani herself had chosen not to appeal to Fareeda, then who was Bua to interfere? Bua could approach Sardar Begum. But she was too frightened of her wrath. It would be akin to putting her head in the maw of a wheat thresher. Her other option was to bypass both Sardar Begum and Fareeda and tell Tariq. But Bua was embarrassed to discuss pregnancies with a man. And then, if Sardar Begum found out that Bua had been carrying tales to Tariq of the shameless goings-on in her establishment, when all along she had predicted the same outcome from his project, what then?

She could, of course, tell Kaneez. But how? After her last visit to Kalanpur, Bua knew for certain that Kaneez would be devastated. She would also be humiliated to discover that Bua knew about the pregnancy before her. No, Kaneez had to be spared the knowledge.

The more Bua thought about it, the clearer it became to her that Fareeda was her only possible option. But how was Bua to tell Fareeda without involving herself? She wanted to help, but all her sensitively attuned antennae warned Bua to steer clear of this one.

And, after all, as she reasoned to herself, it wasn't as if Rani had appealed to *her*. Rani had approached Sister Clementine, and it was therefore Sister Clementine's responsibility to see it through. When the nun had refused to take Rani into the clinic, Bua had persuaded her to put a word into Fareeda's ear. In bringing Sister Clementine to the house, Bua believed she had done her bit, but, unfortunately, the nun's timing had been poor, and nothing had come of the visit.

While Bua was hopeful that Rani would be able to solve the problem herself – after all, the father of her unborn child could well be unmarried and happy to have Rani as his wife – she was still anxious. Time was slipping by, and soon everyone would know. She wished she could do something but knew with absolute conviction that she must not.

Happily, not all of Bua's dilemmas were so thorny. That same morning, word had come from Samuel Masih, a distant relative who lived on the other side of the village, that his eyes ached to see Bua, and that his buffalo, too, were pining for her blessings. Having heard that some misfortune had befallen his buffalo, Bua resolved to visit him. A pat of buffalo butter would be a small return for the favour he no doubt wanted to ask of her.

It was in a happy frame of mind that Bua set off to see Samuel. For the moment, her worries about Rani were relegated to the back burner and she was determined to enjoy the afternoon. She was looking forward to throwing her weight around. She was pleased that Laila – who had once again been denied permission to visit Rani – was accompanying her, for the girl's presence served as a physical reminder of Bua's social position. Of course, she would have been outraged had anyone suggested that she was using Laila as a prop.

As they strolled towards Samuel's place, they passed cane fields the villagers had just begun to harvest. The men hacked at the crop with axes and scythes, while the women tore off the leaves and stacked the cane into heaps. All around was the sound of chopping and rustling as the tall plants fell to the ground. Village children milled about shrieking and waving long sticks of sugar cane. Their faces sticky with cane juice, they tore off the stiff bark-like peel with their teeth and attacked the fibrous centre. As Laila went past, two grinning urchins ran up to her. They thrust a cane in her hand and ran back to join their friends. Green-gold in colour, the cane was as long as her leg. Laila tucked the cane under her arm and waved her thanks to the children.

'I'll eat it when I get to your cousin's house,' she told Bua.

'Good. It'll put some strength in you,' said Bua, embarking on her favourite topic of Laila's diet. 'I'm not asking you to eat, eat all day. No, Baba, what good would that do if you are eating factory oil and machine butter? Might as well eat dust and ashes. No, you do like this – you fry your egg in hand-churned buffalo butter in the morning and have a dollop of butter on your chappati in the afternoon and a smear on your toast at tea time and another dollop on your rice at night and then you see. You'll be strong as a rock, cheeks blooming, eyes flashing, teeth sparkling, hair shining. Everywhere you pass, people will stop and say in wonder, "Who is that healthy girl? How her ayah must have fed her! Blessings on her, blessings." Of course, I will be dust in the graveyard by then, and you will have long forgotten me, maybe even got a new ayah.'

'I don't like your butter. It stinks of cows' udders,' Laila grimaced.

Bua poked her in the side. 'Becoming too much of mem-sahib, you are. This stinks of this and that stinks of that. Where do you want milk to come from? The canal?'

'Besides, Dadi told me I mustn't grow any more, so I can't possibly have your butter.'

'No, you mustn't grow any taller. But your grandmother never said anything about growing broader. With pure butter your waist will become like the trunk of a banyan tree, round, strong, solid.'

'I don't want to become a banyan tree.'

'You don't want anything. Funny girl, you are.'

Samuel Masih was a peasant. He was a small, shrivelled man with a face like a walnut, and hands like spades. Samuel lived close to the canal. It was visible from his hut, a gleaming, silent presence in the background. His hut was dwarfed by a peepul tree. Two buffalo were tethered under its shade. At Bua and Laila's approach, a black dog chained to the tree barked hysterically. Frightened by its fury, Laila shrank into Bua's side. The buffalo looked up from their feeding troughs to stare balefully at the visitors.

When Samuel saw that Bua was accompanied by Laila, he hurried to his hut and emerged with a string bed on his head. He set it down under the peepul. The stench of dung was overpowering. Laila wrinkled her nose but did not like to mention the smell. Bua, however, had no such scruples. She had decided that her kinsman was going to have to work hard for this favour.

'Eh, Sami, you want to give us headache, placing this cot in all this dung, haan?' she said, holding her nose. 'Move it this side more.'

Samuel not only moved the bed but also unwound the

once-white cloth from around his head and gave the bed a wipe. Bua made a great show of gathering up the folds of her calf-length kurta before lowering herself on the bed.

'I know this is not what you're used to, but you might as well sit down,' she said to Laila. 'Mind your dress. Your mother brought it all the way from England. And so much it cost.' She looked meaningfully at Samuel, who lowered his eyes in a show of respect. Bua continued in her haughtiest voice, 'You can't imagine what difficulty I had persuading her parents to let *her* come with me. "Take her where, Bua?" they asked. "But we've never let her go so far. And that too to a sharecropper's hovel?" But I begged them, saying you were my cousin and how honoured you'd be if she came. So in the end, they sighed and said, "All right, Bua, but only for you."

'So here we are, but for a few minutes only. Then it will be this baby's lunch time. The Owners are very particular. I have to wear this big watch so I don't forget.' She flashed her wrist, encircled by a man's watch. 'But why's this place like a graveyard?' she enquired, looking around her. 'Where is that no-good wife of yours and your children? How many there are now? Seven, eight?'

'Eight,' Samuel replied sheepishly. 'Youngest – a boy, but – came three weeks ago. They've all gone to cut the cane across the canal.'

'You tell them to cross the canal carefully. That fool, your wife, can she look after the children?'

'It's the canal, Bua, that's undone me,' Samuel moaned. He squatted on the ground beside them. 'Just last week, my second son, Nikka, he's twelve now, took the buffalo out in the afternoon. One of them had calved. A fine heifer he was, strong and beautiful, but as they got to the canal, a car came racing by, blowing hard on its horn. The heifer panicked and galloped straight into the canal.' Samuel covered his eyes.

'It's a hard blow to lose a good animal like that,' said Bua. 'Maybe God has a purpose in this also.'

'That's what I thought, Bua.' Samuel blew his nose into his hand and wiped it on the ground. 'Maybe Nikka wasn't meant to look after the animals. Maybe he was meant to work in a nice house, with kind rich people, as a driver.'

'Just look at you!' Bua's hand flew to her mouth in mock astonishment. 'You think nice rich people let twelve-year-old boys drive their cars? You know how much cars cost? More than you can make in your lifetime, that's how much. Forget drivery. He'd be lucky to get a place as a gardener.'

'Thank you, Bua.' Samuel touched her knees. 'When shall I bring him?'

'You think you are catching a train? These things take time. The Owners listen to me like school children listen for the finish-time bell, but they don't like employing children. I'll have to say Nikka is sixteen. I'll send for you when the time is right. You're not to trouble me before then. Otherwise, I won't lift a finger. How are your buffalo milking?' Bua eyed the animals. 'I was telling this little Bibi, how much of milk they give. And so creamy, it could have come straight from England. Best butter they make.'

Samuel took the hint.

'Oh, Bua, I nearly forgot, I have kept some butter aside for you. Let me fetch it.' He disappeared into his hut. He returned with a bowl filled to the brim. 'There's more whenever you need, Bua.'

'How am I going to take this without the flies getting to it? Your head is also cracked, Sami. Get me a cloth I can cover it with.'

'This is all I have, Bua.' He tugged at his turban.

'No, no, so dirty. Flies are better than this rag. I'll use my own shawl. And remember now, don't trouble me.' She held out a hand to Laila. 'Come, baby, time for your lunch. Your mummy will be waiting at the table.'

Samuel came to see them off as far as the road. Bua walked off without a backward glance. When they were at some distance from the house, Laila pulled free of Bua's clasp and asked her why she had been so nasty to her cousin.

'Nasty? Me? Listen to you! I went all the way, and that also walking, to listen to his problems. How was that nasty?'

'You said his cloth was filthy and that it was smelly under the tree and that our car was too expensive for his son to drive.'

'So? Did I lie?'

'No, but it wasn't nice. You made him feel dirty and poor.'

'You don't have to be polite to be nice. It will be very nice of me to get his Nikka a job.'

Just then, a tonga jolting behind them drew abreast, and the horse slowed to a walking pace.

'Even though I only saw you from the back side, Bua, I knew it was you straight away,' Sister Clementine called out. 'Hello, little Laila. How are you?'

'Fine, thank you.'

'Salaam, Sister,' said Bua. 'Where are you going?'

'Home, only. If you're going my way we can share this tonga.'

'Yes, please, Sister. My old legs are getting tired now with walking very little also.'

Bua clambered up beside Sister Clementine in the back seat, and Laila climbed up by the driver in the front. She laid her sugar cane carefully on the seat by her. She half expected Bua to admonish her for sitting next to a strange man and order her into the back but, for once, Bua did not demur. It suited her to have Laila in the front. Bua waited just long enough for the tonga wallah to prod his horse into a trot before broaching the subject of Rani in a hushed voice.

'Has the girl been to see you again, Sister?'

'Which girl?'

'The one who came to the church that day? Who wanted you to take her to the clinic, for, for – for you know what . . .' She made a face at Laila's back as if to explain her reticence.

'*That* girl.' Sister Clementine nodded vigorously. 'No, she hasn't.'

'Oh! I was quite sure she had.'

'Why?'

'Well, because we went to her place four days ago and she seemed . . .' She peeked at Laila to see if she was listening, but she had her back to them. The tonga driver had handed Laila the reins, and she sat far forward, concentrating on the job. Bua hoped that she wouldn't be able to hear much over the creak of the wheels and thud of the horse's hooves. 'The girl seemed different. Still nervous, but much less frightened than that day at the church. Wanted to know if I'd told anyone.'

'Have you?'

'Haw, Sister! How you can ask? As if I would!' Bua waited two beats before asking: 'Have you?'

'Me? What good would it do me to tell anyone, tell? As it is, your mistress is running after us poor sisters with a knife. I say something, and all the blame will come on our heads. "Yes, yes," she will say. "It is all your doing, spoiling our girls and all. I know you Christians." More I think about it, more I know that silence is golden.'

'Sister jee, my mistress wouldn't say that. She respects you all too much.' Sister Clementine opened her mouth to disagree, but Bua hurried on. 'So, I was saying, Sister, the girl looked different to me. Remember how she was that day, her face all swollen with crying, and she looking over her shoulder all the time? Well, now she looks calm, not so much happy, but calm. So I wondered if she had been to see you and whether you had helped her?'

201

'Of course not,' Sister Clementine snapped. 'As if we would! Shame on you, Bua, for asking. You think we sisters want to burn in hell?'

'Never, never, Sister jee. *I* know you wouldn't, Sister. So good and pious you are. Everyone in the village is always saying, "That Sister Clementine is God's own angel come down into this sinful world to show us the way. When we are all lying in our dark graves, cold and dead, thinking now the devil will come, suddenly a light will shine, and it will be Sister Clementine with an electric torch come to show us the way up to heaven." That's what they say about you, Sister.'

The nun looked mollified.

'So I wondered,' Bua murmured, 'what had happened to make the girl look relieved. I knew she wouldn't go to the midwife in her village. She does these jobs for a price, but ten, ten tongues she has. Telling her anything is like asking the mullah to make announcement on the mosque's loudspeaker after Friday prayers. Rani wouldn't have gone to her.'

'Did you see her stomach?' Sister Clementine spoke into Bua's ear. 'Is anything showing yet?'

'Girl looks very thin, still,' Bua whispered back. 'No bump, no nothing. But she's the type who won't show till ninth month, almost. And then like snake that's swallowed an orange.'

'She couldn't have gone to another midwife in some other village?'

'I don't think so. Midwife from our village is away in Kasoor – her daughter has the big fever. The other village, Dera, which is close to the girl, is where her mother and stepfather live. She'd be too scared to go there.

'So why is she looking happy then?'

The tonga lurched over a rut in the road, and Laila was thrown against the driver's side. Bua swung around, glared at the driver and pulled Laila back to her own corner of the seat. She turned back to Sister Clementine and resumed their conversation.

'Would the child know anything?' Sister Clementine cocked her head at Laila. 'Maybe the girl has confided in her.'

'Even if she were to tell the child, child wouldn't know what was what. She's not grown-up yet,' said Bua, by way of explanation.

'Could it be that her man means to marry her and that's why she's happy?'

'Once men have taken what they want, Sister, why should they marry? Tell? Still, we can only pray.' Bua sighed. 'What a pity that Fareeda Bibi didn't listen to you that day. If only she had.'

'I did my best. Holy Mother was seeing. But your mistress wasn't listening. Too busy with that snake, Jacob.' Sister Clementine folded her hands primly in her lap.

'A pity, a big, big pity.'

'She didn't even offer me a cup of tea.' Sister Clementine sniffed. 'Or water even. I had to pull out a chair for myself. Otherwise, she would have made me stand like a beggar. That's no way to treat a guest, is it? And that, too, a guest who is a stranger in your land. So much she hurt me, Bua, only I know what wounds I carry in my heart.'

'My Bibi is not like that.'

'Are you saying I'm lying?'

'No, no, Sister jee, not at all. All I'm saying is I don't know why Fareeda Bibi was like that that day.'

'Who knows who is like what? Still, I did my best. The girl was unlucky. Here, Bua, you better get off. I'm going on to the convent.'

12

Colonel Khursheed Butt's dislike for Tariq was based not on a personal aversion but on a general antipathy he reserved for people with privileged backgrounds. The colonel liked to think of them as 'slackers and softies', given to extravagant sentiments but lacking in the moral fibre and decisive action that counted on a battlefield. Himself a scholarship boy from a missionary school, the colonel had worked hard for everything in life and rewarded himself for his efforts with unwavering self-respect.

The night of Hester's dinner, the colonel had been in Colewallah for a month. He had hoped for better things by this stage in his career, for Colewallah was a small cantonment about ten miles from Sabzbagh and Bridgebad. But he had manfully swallowed his disappointment and prepared to administer the agricultural district of small market towns and scattered villages with the grace befitting 'the good sport' he considered himself.

Now, driving towards Sabzbagh, he told himself that he had come to call on Tariq at his home in his official capacity – the new colonel acquainting himself with a local grandee. However, if the colonel were to be frank, he would admit that since that evening at Hester's he'd been consumed by a gnawing curiosity to see Tariq's set-up for himself. Tariq had irritated the colonel intensely that evening.

First, there was the leftie garbage spouted with a scornful disregard for the tremendous fight the army was putting up in Bengal. Then, there was all that smug, self-righteous rot about improving the lot of his villagers. But what had incensed the colonel most of all was the way those two white dinosaurs had hung on to his every word. Visionary, indeed! The colonel snorted. Given his own way, the colonel would like nothing better than to shove Tariq into the marshy wilds of Bengal at the point of a bayonet and see how fast his urbane Oxford manner evaporated.

As for his open-necked shirt and old tweed jacket! The colonel's lip curled at the memory of Tariq's clothes. He'd shown Tariq a thing or two about dressing well, he thought, stealing a look at himself in the rear-view mirror of the car. Straightening his peaked cap ever so slightly, the colonel wondered idly how Tariq would receive him. And that uppity wife of his! Had he, Khursheed Butt, been married to her, he would have taught her a thing or two about manners. He was looking forward to this meeting today.

But when the colonel's chauffeur drove up to the bungalow, it was to find that the Azeems were not at home. Fazal informed the colonel that Tariq was at the factory and Fareeda and Laila were in Colewallah town. Undeterred, the colonel alighted from the car and announced that he would wait. Fazal showed him into the sitting room and asked if he would like some tea. The colonel declined, but just as Fazal was about to leave the room, he said, 'On second thoughts, why don't you go and fetch your master? Tell him he has a guest. Hurry, I don't have all day.'

Tariq and Fareeda were not averse to guests arriving unannounced, for it could sometimes get lonely in Sabzbagh. So Tariq did not mind when Fazal came to fetch him. When Tariq entered the sitting room, he found the colonel hunched over a table, peering at a framed cluster of old family photographs. Tariq cleared his throat noisily. The colonel did not turn around. Mildly peeved, Tariq marched up to him and tapped him on the shoulder. The colonel spun around.

'Ah, Tariq Sahib, I was acquainting myself with the pictures of your worthy forbears. A distinguished lot, I must say.'

Tariq gestured to the sofa on which the colonel had placed his swagger stick and cap. Tariq was about to ask after his guest's family but held back. He had a feeling that the colonel would get to the point of his visit in his own time.

'I must congratulate you on arranging your house so elegantly, even in the depths of the provinces,' said the colonel.

'It's Fareeda's doing.' Tariq shrugged. 'You can compliment her yourself when she returns from Colewallah. Would you care for some tea, Colonel?'

'I only take tea at breakfast.'

'Something cold then?'

'Nothing just now. Thank you,' he added, almost as an afterthought. 'I see you are fond of reading.' The colonel nodded at the rows of books.

'Oh, those. They were my father's.'

'Your father was from these parts?'

'Yes, my family has lived here for many years.'

'How many?'

'Am I being interrogated?' Tariq laughed, only half in jest.

'I apologize if it came across that way,' replied the colonel stiffly. 'So! In what direction do your literary tastes run?'

'I'm not sure I have any particular literary tastes,' said Tariq. 'But I suppose I like biography.'

'How surprising!' The corners of the colonel's lips lifted.

'Why?'

'Because I am also fond of biography. I wouldn't have thought that you and I'd have much in common. Don't you agree?'

Tariq shrugged. 'I haven't thought about it.'

'*That's* the difference, you see.' The colonel smacked the arm of his chair for emphasis. 'You don't give much thought to a casual introduction over dinner, but I do. I take very little for granted, whereas I suspect you do. But then, you can afford to.'

'I don't quite follow . . .'

'You and I, Tariq Sahib, we are very different people, our reading preferences notwithstanding. We come from different worlds. We also view it very differently. You pride yourself on being a liberal. You want to smarten up your peasants. You feel sympathy for the poor downtrodden Bengali. You would, were it up to you, advocate talks, rapprochement, compromise.' The colonel laughed. 'All very worthy sentiments, but misplaced, don't you think?'

Tariq digested his guest's outburst in silence. Something had obviously provoked him. Tariq frowned as he tried to recall his comments before the colonel's little rant.

'Come now, don't deny it. You are a bit of a leftie, aren't you?' mocked the colonel.

'I don't think my sympathy for the Bengalis is at all misplaced,' replied Tariq primly. 'But enough about me, Colonel. Where do *you* stand?'

'Politically?' The colonel stretched out his legs and, tilting his head to one side, viewed his shiny boots with approval. 'That's easy. I stand with my country. I'm a simple man. A patriot. A soldier. And I'm proud to say I think like one. When someone threatens the territorial integrity of my country, I regard him as an enemy. An enemy who should be taught a lesson. And, since you ask, Tariq Sahib, let me tell you that I have no faith in the politicians you probably hold dear. They are lying, manipulative and selfish, each and every one of them. The true guardian of this country is the military. But please don't think I'm not appreciative of the efforts you are making here.' The colonel flicked a tiny speck from his khaki trousers. He raised his gaze and smiled blandly at Tariq. 'A man in your position needn't throw himself so wholly into his charitable works.'

'A man in my position?' queried Tariq.

'You know, old landed gentry. Feudal, some people may call you. Your grateful peasants would still tug their forelock, even if you didn't run your factory.'

'My family's association with this place makes it incumbent on me to contribute. And I certainly don't think of it as charity,' Tariq replied angrily. 'The people of my village are as involved in it as I. I can also tell you, they are much keener on their own progress than I could ever be.' His words sounded wooden to his own ears. Why was he bothering to explain himself to this jackass soldier? It riled him that the colonel had managed to put him on the back foot. He had nothing to apologize for. He was proud of his work. And who else could run the project, if not him? If the colonel couldn't see that, then it was *his* problem, not Tariq's.

'My mistake. I admire your efforts wholeheartedly.' The colonel spoke silkily. 'But still, it must be nice to receive all that adulation. When I met you at Mrs Bullock's, I thought to myself, why would a man who has had your opportunities and education bury himself in a village like this? But now,' he said, looking around him once more, 'I understand all too clearly. In the big city, Tariq Sahib, you would be advantaged, certainly, but you'd be one of many. Here, you get to run the show. If I were in your place, I, too, would want to come back to this house, this status, this certainty. Good choice.'

Tariq looked at his visitor's toothbrush moustache, crew-cut hair and stiff starchy uniform and felt a strong urge to throw him out of his house.

'If I can be of any assistance to you in your worthy work, please do not hesitate to get in touch,' said the colonel, steepling his fingers.

'Thank you for your kind offer, but we've stumbled along for almost eight years now, Colonel, without your or anyone else's help. I think we can manage.'

'Not just eight years, Tariq Sahib. I would say for at least three generations, if those photographs are anything to go by.' He nodded at the table.

So that was what had riled him, Tariq realized with a jolt. He'd taken exception to the photographs, to his background. They had made him insecure. Pleased to have found the colonel's Achilles' heel, Tariq smiled.

'I must correct you,' he said, lazily crossing his legs. 'It's eleven generations, not three.'

The colonel flushed a dark, angry red. 'Actually, I came to invite you for dinner,' he said. 'I'm afraid we won't be able to provide as refined a setting as this. But we shall do our humble best.'

Tariq did not extend an invitation in return. He stood up. He was tired of the colonel's insinuations, and there was work to be done at the centre. The colonel took the hint and also rose to his feet.

'I'll ask my wife to give Mrs Azeem a call soon.'

'There's no hurry. Please take your time.' Tariq sauntered into the hallway, opened the front door and stood aside to let him pass.

The colonel's driver leaned against the car bonnet, probing his ear with the car key. As soon as he saw his boss, he leapt to the back door and pulled it open. Ignoring the driver, the colonel placed his cap on his head and gazed about him, in no apparent rush to leave.

'That tree is very big.' He pointed with his swagger stick at the silk cotton tree. 'It rather looms over the house. Are there any bedrooms under it?'

'Yes,' replied Tariq.

'Ever thought of getting it cut?'

'It's weathered its fair share of storms.'

'But storms are not bombs.'

'Aren't you being rather dramatic?'

209

'One cannot overstress the spite of the Indians.' The colonel smacked his palm lightly with the stick. 'We have fought them before, and we know what we are up against. There is nothing to which they will not stoop.'

Tariq looked at the tree. A long-gone Irishwoman had planted it many years ago, and now his daughters' swings hung from its lowest branch. Through the lattice of its yellowing leaves, he could see the dark bulge of a beehive in its upper boughs.

'If the house *were* to be bombed, we'd get blown up, tree or no tree,' said Tariq. 'When do you expect war to be declared?'

'I couldn't say. All I can tell you is that nobody values peace more than a soldier. Now that I am here, could I have a look around your factory, too?'

'No, you couldn't,' said Tariq. 'We're working on a large order, and it holds things up if visitors have to be shown around. Now, I have to get back.'

'On my next visit then.' It was more a statement than a question, but Tariq let it pass, vowing not to let him anywhere near his factory.

The colonel raised his hand in an ironic salute to Tariq and then, with a swish of tyres, he was gone.

Tariq was sitting on the veranda when Fareeda returned from her weekly shopping expedition to Colewallah. She had the satisfied air of a woman who had accomplished much in little time.

'Weren't you going to spend the afternoon at the factory?' Fareeda asked Tariq, pushing her dark glasses up over her forehead.

'I was called back to the house by an unexpected visitor.'

'Who?' Fareeda dropped her handbag to the floor and drew a chair up beside Tariq.

'Colonel Butt.'

'What did he want?'

Tariq turned up his palms. 'I honestly don't know.'

'But, still. He must have said something.'

'He said an awful lot. But I still don't know exactly why he came. Other than to invite us for dinner.'

'He came all this way to personally deliver an invitation?'

'And to check us out. I suspect he came to see the house, the factory, the whole scene, so to speak.'

'So, he was being nosy, was he? Typical! *I* couldn't care less where he lived and how.' Fareeda made a dismissive gesture with her hand. 'Anyway, did we pass muster?'

'*You* did. He approved of your decorating skills. Wanted me to congratulate you on "managing to live elegantly even in the depths of the provinces". ' Tariq mimicked the colonel's stiff manner.

' "In the depths of the provinces"? How deliciously quaint! I wonder where he learnt that phrase?' laughed Fareeda. 'I hope you didn't accept his dinner invitation?'

'God, no,' shuddered Tariq.

'So, what else did he say?'

'Not a lot. I asked him when he thought the war would start, but he gave me some patronizing guff and took off soon after, thank God.' Tariq stood up. 'Jumped-up little toad, swaggering about in his flunkey's uniform! Had the nerve to ask me to show him my factory. I'll have to be gagged and bound before I go anywhere near his cantonment, let alone his house.'

'Seems like it was quite an eventful visit after all. I hope you told him to go to hell.'

Tariq shrugged. 'If I had, he'd have stayed till next year, giving me several pieces of his manic mind.' He paused, before adding, 'I think we should go to Lahore and fetch Sara.'

'Why?' Fareeda sat up. 'He did say something about the war, didn't he?'

'No. I'd just feel happier if she was here.'

Tariq stood with his back to Fareeda, staring out into the garden.

Fareeda picked up her handbag and stood up. 'I also want to bring my mother,' she said. 'I don't like the thought of her being by herself at such a time in that huge, echoing house.'

'Of course. We'll leave tomorrow. My mother is to return from Sargodha in three days. Should anything happen before, I suppose she's as safe with my sister as she is here.'

'You think it could happen as soon as that?' Fareeda tried to keep the panic out of her voice.

'I have the feeling that we are sleepwalking into a war.'

'In that case, I'd better call Lahore now and tell them we're coming. What time shall I say?'

'Some time after lunch. Around three?'

Fareeda told Laila of the proposed trip to Lahore later that evening, while she was brushing her daughter's hair. They were in Fareeda's bedroom. Fareeda sat on a stool, and Laila was on the ground, her back resting against Fareeda's knees.

'We'll go to Lahore tomorrow,' Fareeda said casually, brushing Laila's wavy hair with long firm strokes. 'We'll bring Sara back with us.'

'Is she ill? Has she also got typhoid?' Laila tried to twist around to face her mother.

'No. Hold still. I can't do your plait if you keep jerking your neck.'

'But the holidays don't start till the twentieth of December.'

'Of course, the holidays.' Fareeda smiled. 'I'd forgotten about those. No, darling, we're not bringing her back for the holidays, but for something else.'

'What?'

'Your father and I think that there might be a war.'

'With fighter planes and bombs and tanks and special spies on parachutes?'

'Where did you learn all this?' enquired Fareeda.

'From *Where Eagles Dare*. We saw it twice at the Regal Cinema with Nani.'

'There will probably be tanks and planes, though we're not likely to see them. But I don't think there will be special spies on parachutes.'

'And will the Indians come here on their tanks?' asked Laila.

'To Sabzbagh? I hope not.'

'And if they do? Will we fight them with Aba's partridge gun?'

'They won't come here,' said Fareeda firmly. 'Stop sucking that ribbon and pass it to me so I can tie your plait. There.'

'But if they do come, I'm ready to fight them, you know. Both Rani and I.'

'How?' asked Fareeda.

'I can't tell you. It's top secret.'

'OK then.'

Laila was about to skip off when a thought struck her. 'Does Sara know about the war?'

'I haven't told her, but it is quite possible that she's heard from your grandmother, from Nani.' Fareeda replaced the brush on the dressing table and straightened the stool.

'So will we wait for Sara to come back to the house or will we rush into the school and take her in the middle of the class?'

'We'll get to Lahore in the afternoon,' Fareeda explained, 'long after Sara has returned from school. Next day, we'll keep her back, and I'll write a letter to Sister Maria explaining her absence, which I'll put in the post before we return to Sabzbagh. Satisfied?'

Laila nodded. 'Just as well you're not going to take her in the middle of Mrs Abdullah's class. She teaches my class maths also, so I know how strict she is. She'd scold you and send you out of the class for interrupting. You can smile all you want, but I know Sara will die of shame.'

It would be fun to have Sara back again, particularly if there was going to be a war. They could play nurses together, and collect food and blankets for the soldiers, and Laila could show her Hester's horse. They could also have exploratory expeditions, to check how far the enemy had penetrated into their territory. Sara was good at organizing. She could marshal the hordes of tangle-haired children from the village into an obedient little posse of explorers – something Laila was too shy, too diffident, to attempt on her own. Though a little bossy at times, Sara could be an exciting companion. But she must make sure that Sara did not muscle in on the Terrific Two. She must forewarn Rani not to let her into their secret. Besides, there was still the identity of her bridegroom to be discovered before Laila departed for Lahore.

'What time will we leave tomorrow?' Laila asked.

'In the afternoon,' Fareeda replied absently, as she leafed through her telephone book. 'Will you please pipe down now? I want to make a couple of phone calls.'

'One last question?'

'What?' Fareeda groaned, shutting the book in resignation.

'If we're not leaving till the afternoon, can I go and see Rani in the morning?'

'This is the fifth day in a row that you've asked me that question. Why is it suddenly so crucial for you to see Rani?' asked Fareeda, annoyed.

'I can't tell. I promised.'

'If you can't tell, then you can't go,' Fareeda snapped, flicking open the book.

'Please?'

'Laila!' There was a distinct note of warning in her voice.

Laila slouched towards the door. How could she leave for

Lahore without knowing whom Rani was going to marry? As it was, every night, just before she dropped off to sleep, Rani's face would drift before her closed eyelids, wavy, frond-like, a reflection on water. She would appear just as Laila had last seen her – a finger pressed to her lips, reminding her of the promise. The image would dissolve suddenly, as if a stone had been hurled into water.

What if Rani's wedding took place while they were in Lahore? Hadn't she said that it was going to be very, very soon? Laila hoped that she hadn't got around to buying her clothes and her bridal sandals yet. Without those, she wouldn't marry, would she? But what if she did? And went to live far away, for ever? Sardar Begum had said that girls found it very hard to come back to their old homes after they got married. What if Rani never came back, never visited Kalanpur again? 'Please, Allah,' Laila prayed under her breath, 'don't let Rani go away for ever.'

Tariq and Fareeda received a telephone call while having breakfast the following morning. It was from the engineers of the Oil and Gas Board, requesting Tariq's presence at his land near Kalanpur, where they were going to lay gas pipes.

'They will have to dig up part of my wheat crop, and they've been told to do it in my presence in case I object later,' explained Tariq between mouthfuls of toast. 'Apparently, they've had some complaints in the last two villages they tackled.'

'What time will they lay the pipes?' asked Fareeda.

'They've asked me to get there at four.'

'You won't get back till at least six. I thought we were leaving directly after lunch. I hate travelling on that road in the dark. You know that.'

'I had no idea they were going to spring this on me today. I suggested Jacob oversee the work, but they insist I be there.

I know it's inconvenient but it means that, finally, we'll have a gas connection. Would you mind if we went tomorrow?'

'I suppose not. I'll have to call my mother and tell her. But we *will* leave tomorrow? Promise?'

'We'll leave tomorrow, as early as possible. By the way, where's this butter from?' He examined the fluffy white butter on his knife. 'It's not from my mother's, is it?'

'It's from Bua. No doubt to soften me up for the request which is bound to follow.'

'Trust her to keep her oar in. What does she want?'

'I'm sure I'll be enlightened before long. Any news from the British Development Association yet?'

'Only a short note.' Tariq stroked Fareeda's cheek with the back of his hand. 'They say we'll receive a full reply in a couple of weeks, once they've had time to assess everything.'

'At least we're still in the race. Now leave me to my crossword,' she said, reaching for the coffeepot. But, a moment later, Tariq strode back into the sitting room.

'What is it now?' asked Fareeda.

'It's that damned Mashooq. Fazal has just informed me that he's here and demands to see me this instant. I said he should come back after I return from Lahore, but the wretch refuses to leave. Says he'll camp out in the yard till I see him.'

'Just get it over with,' advised Fareeda. 'I don't want him hanging around.'

Mashooq lounged on a bench by the garage. With his face turned up to the sun, he hummed a ribald Punjabi song. He was of average height and delicate build. His pomaded hair was arranged into a cluster of tight little curls all about his gaunt, strangely hairless face. He had a thick wad of tobacco tucked into one cheek, and a brown trickle of juice dribbled from the corner of his mouth. Hosing the car a few feet away, Barkat was doing his best to ignore him. Every now and again, however, the driver would look up from his task and throw

Mashooq a dirty look. If Mashooq was aware of Barkat's hostility, he seemed unmoved by it.

Mashooq sat up and, hawking deep in his throat, spat an arc of tobacco juice in Barkat's direction. He rubbed the back of his hand across his mouth, smearing brown-stained saliva over his cheek. Flashing Barkat an insolent smile, he shut his heavy-lidded eyes. He settled his head back again and draped himself over the bench with studied nonchalance.

Barkat flung down the rag with which he was polishing the bonnet and was about to stride around the car towards Mashooq when Tariq appeared. Mashooq's manner changed abruptly. He jumped up from the bench. He bowed his head, lowered his eyes and folded his hands before him.

'Salaam, Sahib.' He made to touch Tariq's feet, but Tariq stepped away. 'Your slave prays for your long life and good health and prosperity for you and yours.'

Tariq nodded curtly, trying not to show his revulsion. There was something effeminate about Mashooq's narrow shoulders and the way his pomaded hair curled confidingly into the nape of his neck. Tariq could smell the flowery aroma of his scented tobacco from where he stood. And what was that glistening brown streak across Mashooq's pock-marked face? It looked like pus had oozed out of his cheek.

From the hesitation in his manner, Tariq guessed Mashooq was about to ask a favour. It wasn't the first time that he had approached Tariq with a request. A couple of years previously, he had asked Tariq for help in obtaining his identity card; and then there was that occasion when Tariq had received a pleading call from the jail, where the local inspector had held him for drunk and disorderly behaviour. Tariq had been sorely tempted to let him rot but had capitulated under combined pressure from Sardar Begum and Kaneez.

Personally, Tariq thought that Fatima would be better off without him, but that, he accepted, was not his decision. All he could do was make her life a little easier by entertaining her husband's occasional petitions and, as far as possible, keep him out of trouble.

'What do you want, Mashooq?'

'What do I want, Sahib? I want to spend my life at your feet.'

'Yes, yes, that's all very well, man. But what do you *want*?'

'I didn't want to inconvenience you, Sahib, for I know how busy a man of your position is. Believe me, Sahib, I would rather drag myself on my belly over broken glass than bother you with my petty problems. But what option does a poor, insignificant creature like I have but to appeal to your munificence?'

'Now, Mashooq, I'm leaving for Lahore tomorrow morning, and there's a lot I have to do before then. I can't stand around all day listening to your theatrics, so if you want me to do anything for you, you'd better spit it out,' said Tariq.

'Sahib, my tongue falters at the thought of burdening you with the misfortune that has befallen me.'

'What misfortune?'

'I, the father of four children, have lost my job. But I have not lost it, Sahib.' Mashooq wiped his eyes with his sleeve. 'I was tricked out of it by miscreants, by troublemakers. I am innocent as a newborn. My only fault, Sahib, is that I am too trusting,' he sobbed. 'I am no match for these strange times, for these crafty people.'

'So you've been sacked?'

'No, Sahib, I've been tricked.'

'Oh, for God's sake! I'm asking you a straight question. Have you or have you not been sacked?'

'Sahib, I've been thrown out of the milk factory.'

'Why?'

'This poor, simple villager was the victim of a devious plot. Yesterday afternoon, Sahib, as we went back to work after the lunch break, I told Sarwar, a co-worker, that I was thirsty, and that I'd get a drink from the tap outside and join him in the factory. "There's no need," he said. "Why go all that way when I can quench your thirst right here?" He had a bottle with him, Sahib, a dark-brown glass bottle. He held it out to me and said, "Go ahead. Slake your thirst."

'Now, as you know, Sahib, I have, once or twice, at the insistence of friends, taken a sip or two of alcohol.' He smiled sheepishly at Tariq. 'But I know what that is like. It smells of rotting dates and looks like cloudy water. But this, Sahib, was different. I can't describe it, but it was fragrant. I said to Sarwar, "But this is not water." "No," he said, "it's sandalwood sherbet, from Lahore." Unworldly as I am, I took a few gulps and followed Sarwar into the factory.

'No sooner had I begun work than I felt a strange heaviness in my limbs. Next, I felt dizzy. The factory was spinning around me. I was aware that the owner, Shamshad Sahib, had come in and was asking me something. But try as I might, I could not answer him. My tongue was cleaving to my palate. The last thing I remember was tearing at my collar, which was tight as a hangman's noose. Then I passed out, Sahib.

'When I came to, it was dark, and I was sprawled by the side of a deserted road. My bicycle was lying on its side. The tyres were spinning as if someone had kicked them in passing. Looking about me, I realized I was on the canal road. I staggered to my feet. With every step I took, a shooting pain ran from my head straight to the soles of my feet.

'I wanted to curl up and go to sleep. But because of my duty to my wife and children, I climbed on to my bicycle and went home. Sahib, don't ask with what difficulty I made the journey. Allah must have been watching over me.' He turned his face up to the sky as if in gratitude.

'Go on.'

'The next morning,' continued Mashooq, 'meaning today, still feeling unwell, I went to the factory. As soon as I entered, I noticed people were giving me strange looks and whispering behind my back. At first I thought I might have a bruise on my face, but I checked in a glass and I was fine, or as fine as an ugly fellow like I can ever be. And then, Shamshad Khan Sahib comes striding into the factory, followed by his foreman, and starts screaming at me to get out, never to show my face there again. What things he said, Sahib,' Mashooq blubbed, his shoulders shaking. 'What names he called me. A pig would blush with shame if he heard.

'Pushing and kicking, he flung me out of the door and down the stairs. As I got to my feet, I saw Sarwar. He was watching me from a window. He was smiling, Sahib, *smiling*! Beside him was his brother, whom he'd been trying to find a job in the factory for weeks. Shamshad Sahib had told him he could only take on extra staff when there was a vacancy. Only then did I understand, Sahib, what a cruel joke had been played on me.'

'You certainly know how to spin a dramatic tale,' remarked Tariq dryly.

'It is no tale, Sahib. I swear on my dead mother's grave. I promise you, it is the truth. I am ready to swear on the holy Koran.'

A scornful laugh erupted from Barkat, who had been leaning against the bonnet, listening to Mashooq's narrative.

'As if anyone would allow this dirty dog to touch the Koran,' he muttered.

'That's enough, Barkat!' Tariq glared at the driver.

Mashooq smirked at Barkat and then switched his gaze back to Tariq, quickly replacing the smirk with a wounded look. 'Sahib, you can believe what you want. But I am telling the truth.'

'All right, suppose I accept your story? What do you want me to do?'

'I can never presume to tell you what to do, Sahib. I can merely make the humble suggestion that you write to Shamshad Sahib, telling him that he's made a mistake and he must take me back. Allow me to deliver that note to him. After that, you need bother yourself no further on my account. I've been enough of an imposition on your time and patience.'

'What makes you think that Shamshad Khan will take you back if I ask him?'

'Like all of us here, Sahib, he holds you in the highest esteem. Don't we know how you got rid of that cruel police-man who used to terrorize us in Sabzbagh? Don't we know how you helped us when the floods came? Don't we know how you help our sick, our unemployed? He would do anything for you. Besides . . .' Mashooq left the sentence hanging.

'Besides?' prompted Tariq.

'I happen to know, Sahib,' Mashooq said in a low, conspiratorial voice, 'that he is very keen for you to put in a good word for him with the new colonel at the cantonment. One favour, as they say, begets another.'

'You've done your homework well,' observed Tariq with a wry smile. 'But then, I always knew that, whatever else you may be, you're a thorough sort of man. You'd leave no stone unturned to obtain a favour or settle a score.'

'Settling scores is the privilege of powerful people like you, Sahib. It is not for humble folk like me. I just want my job back so I can feed my children.'

'Before I write any note to Shamshad Khan, I'd like to hear his side of the story.'

'There are no sides, Sahib.' Mashooq cracked his knuckles. 'There is only one, the truth, which I have already told you.'

'Still, I must have all the facts. You wait here while I call Shamshad Khan. If what you say is true, you'll have your note.'

'Sahib, remember who I am,' Mashooq called out after Tariq. 'I am the son-in-law of the woman who has worked for your family for forty years. Would I lie to you?'

But Tariq had already disappeared into the house. Muttering an oath, Mashooq kicked at the bench.

'Afraid of being found out, eh, Mohammed Mashooq?' sniggered Barkat. He leaned against the car, fingers drumming on the bonnet. 'But if you are as "innocent as a newborn" what do you have to fear?'

'Shut your filthy mouth!' Mashooq snarled, and flung himself on the bench. Still chuckling, Barkat went off into the kitchen.

A little while later, Tariq flung open the back door and strode into the yard.

'How dare you come here and feed a pack of lies to me? What do you take me for? A bloody fool?' he shouted.

'Sahib, I don't know what you mean,' Mashooq whimpered.

'I'll tell you what I mean. I just called Shamshad Khan, and he told me how you arrived drunk at work. How you were taking slugs from a bottle you kept hidden under your shirt. How you were yelling obscenities, singing lewd songs and taunting your fellow workers. How, when a fight broke out and the foreman reprimanded you, you smashed the bottle against a table and threatened him with its jagged end. When he fetched Shamshad Khan, you attacked him. When they threw you out, you stood outside the factory, swaying on your feet and screaming that you would abduct Shamshad Khan's daughter. You then went into great detail about what you would do to her. And this in the hearing of all his employees. Now you know what I mean? Now you remember what happened? Or is the fog still clouding your drunken brain?'

'Sahib, sahib.' Mashooq flung himself at Tariq's feet. 'Forgive me,' he wailed. 'I am so ashamed. I didn't know that was what happened. All I can recall is feeling ill and being thrown out and then waking up on the canal road.'

'Get up.' Tariq tried to shake his ankles free of Mashooq's grip. 'You well know this is not the first time you've shown up at work blind drunk,' he shouted. 'Had I been in Shamshad Khan's place, I would have tossed you out the very first time, but he's a decent man, who knew you had four children, so he gave you another chance. This is how you repay his generosity? With drunkenness and violence? And then you have the gall to come here and ask me to write him a letter demanding that he take you back. Instead of apologizing like an honest man, you hide behind lies and bluster. Get up, you snivelling coward. Get up and get out.'

'Where can I go, Sahib?' he moaned.

'Go to hell. And let go of my feet before I kick you off.'

Mashooq released Tariq's ankles. Uncoiling slowly like a cobra, he stood up and looked Tariq in the eye.

'You have made up your mind, then?' he asked softly. 'You have decided that I am lying and he is telling the truth? May I ask why?'

'Because I know Shamshad Khan to be a truthful, decent man,' replied Tariq. 'And I know *you* for the filth you are.'

'You are siding with him because, like you, he is rich, and I am poor,' Mashooq said in a toneless voice. 'You rich men always stick together. The rest of us can drown in the canal, for all you care. Pretending to be great charitable souls with your factories and your speeches. Well, I don't want your charity. I want my rights. *You* try feeding five mouths on a factory worker's wage and then tell me if you don't feel like drowning your misery in drink.'

'Get out of my sight this instant.' Tariq spoke through gritted teeth. 'Before I have you thrown out.'

'Just as you say, Sahib,' sneered Mashooq. 'But remember this also, Sahib, that I don't forget an insult. And today you have insulted me.'

'I've seen thousands like you, Mashooq,' scoffed Tariq. 'And I've found them to be cowards. Do your worst. Your threats don't frighten me. Now get out of my house.'

13

Mashooq left Tariq's house undecided what to do. He had left his bicycle at the gate, thinking he'd cycle straight to the factory from there and, presenting his note with a flourish to Shamshad Khan, saunter in. In fact, he had boasted as much to the other labourers when he had arrived at the factory that morning to find his entry barred.

'See if I'm not back in half an hour,' he had yelled, as they'd filed into the factory. 'I'll march in like a rajah, just wait and see.'

There was no question of going back to the factory now. He stuck his hand in his pocket and found a crumpled piece of paper. Pulling it out, he unrolled it slowly. It was a five-rupee note. Enough for two drinks. He could get the rest on credit. He was about to mount his bicycle when he heard a rustling sound behind him. He stopped and listened. There it was again. It was coming from behind a hedge by the gate.

'Psst! Wait. Listen to me.'

He leaned over the chest-high hedge and saw a girl crouching on the other side. She had a pointed chin and tilted eyes. Her thin sallow face was bracketed by two beribboned bunches of hair.

'You are Mashooq, aren't you?' The girl was forthright. As if it was her God-given right to question him. 'Fatima's husband.'

Mashooq noted her gold earrings and spotless cream cardigan with a pale-blue velvet edging. This must be Tariq's daughter. What was her name? His hands itched to rip off her earrings. But they were too close to the house. If she cried out and he was caught, Tariq wouldn't spare him. He took a deep breath and, clenching his fists at his side, nodded in reply to her question. Then, moving closer to the hedge, he said, 'You know, I'm a foolish, forgetful fellow. What was your name?'

'Laila. I'm Laila,' she replied.

Despite her finery, she looked like a runt. She had skinny legs and a stringy chicken neck, begging to be wrung. She hadn't taken after her mother. Fareeda was a beauty in her remote, disdainful way. He had often amused himself with fantasies about her. He knew how to melt that haughty reserve, how to make her sizzle like butter in a hot pan. The girl was speaking.

'I saw you back at the house. From the pantry door. I couldn't hear what was going on, but I saw you throw yourself at Aba's feet.' She had happened to pass by the door and had seen her father and an unfamiliar man facing each other across the yard. She had been too far away to hear their exchange, but she could sense the tension in their body language. Mashooq had his back to her, but the fury in Tariq's face had shocked her. It was only when Mashooq was limping away that she had suddenly recognized him.

She had seen him before. Barkat had been driving Sara and her through Sabzbagh bazaar one day when Mashooq crossed the road before them. He had limped across at a snail's pace, wheeling along a bike that looked too heavy for him. Barkat had honked impatiently. He had stuck his head out of the window and shouted, 'Oye, Mashooq, you miserable dog, get out of the way before I mow you down.' Mashooq had spun around, his face clenched into a fist.

Watching him limp down the driveway of her home, it had dawned on Laila that perhaps Rani had sent him to Sabzbagh. Unable to reach Laila herself, perhaps she had enlisted her stepfather's help. Laila knew Rani had little to do with Mashooq. She seldom mentioned him. And when she did, it was always with rancour. She loathed him for taking away her mother and then abusing her as he did. He would not have been her first choice as a messenger. But perhaps he'd been her only choice. Why else would he come to their house? He had no connection with them, save through Fatima. Could he have told Tariq Rani's secret? Was that why her father had been so furious? Laila needed to know.

'So why did you throw yourself at Aba's feet?' she enquired again, tilting her head to one side like an inquisitive mynah.

Mashooq bared his tobacco-stained teeth in a grin. Could he charm her into handing over her earrings? They were worth at least a couple of months' wages.

'What a pretty little girl you've grown into.'

'I haven't. I'm just like I was.'

'Well, I think you are very pretty. And so does, so does,' he cast around for a name that would mean something to her, 'so does Rani.'

'Does she?' Laila flushed. 'How do you know?'

'She told me.' Mashooq noted the flags of colour in her cheeks with satisfaction. He was on the right track.

'When?'

'Today.'

'Did you see her today?' she asked.

'Of course. I'm coming straight from Kalanpur. I went to drop off some cane juice that Fatima had sent for her.'

'But you don't go very often to Kalanpur, do you?' The girl looked doubtful.

Mashooq shook his head. 'Not all of us have time and money like your Aba, you know. If I don't go to the factory every day, my children starve. That's why I can't see Rani as much as I'd like.'

'How was she?'

'Fine. Just fine. She sent her love. Asked me to tell you how much she misses you.'

Laila's face clouded over. 'I miss Rani, too. She's my best friend, you know. I wish I could go and see her, but my parents won't let me. Did she tell you anything else?'

'Lots, but I promised her I wouldn't tell,' replied Mashooq, playing for time. He stared at Laila's neck. It wouldn't surprise him if there was an amulet on a gold chain under her cardigan. A rich brat like her. Bound to have one. He looked over her shoulder. He could hear the drone of a lawn mower, but he couldn't see anyone.

'Where's your ayah?'

'Oh, she's tidying my cupboard,' the girl replied haughtily. 'I managed to slip away without her seeing me. I wouldn't have been able to talk to you like this if she'd been with me.'

'And why's that?' He rose on his toes to get a better view of the drive.

'Because she says you're not a nice man. That you beat your wife. And make rude noises in the bazaar.'

'She does, does she?' Mashooq spread out his hands and smiled winningly. 'Do I look the sort?'

'I don't know. Bua doesn't lie.' Then she remembered the story of the baby and the bush. 'Well, only sometimes. Why was my father angry with you just now?'

Mashooq was bored of parrying her questions. A sharp kick on the shin would send her flying. He gave her a small obsequious smile over the hedge.

'Because I'd got into a fight with someone who had bad-mouthed your noble father. But your father was upset, for he believed that it was *I* who had said the bad words. Even though I swore I hadn't.'

'What had the man said?'

'I can't say.' Mashooq looked down at his hands. 'Not to a child. But, rest assured, I made mincemeat out of that scoundrel who said your father was an arrogant, bossy bastard who needed a kick up the arse. I couldn't stand by and hear

him say that without beating him into a pulp. Now could I?'
He looked at her from under lowered lids. 'If your parents
won't take you to Kalanpur, why don't you come with me,
hmm?'

'How?'

Mashooq patted the seat of his bicycle. 'On this.'

Laila shook her head. 'I couldn't. Ammi would be angry.'

'She doesn't have to find out,' he murmured.

'She finds out everything.'

'Tsk. Rani will be disappointed. She wanted to see you so
much. She sent me to fetch you. "Get Laila," she said. "I want
to tell her a secret." But if you won't come, I'd better go.' He
placed a foot on a pedal and made as if to mount his bike.

'Wait!' cried Laila excitedly. 'I *knew* she'd sent you. I also
know what she's going to tell me. She almost told me his
name the last time I went to Kalanpur, but then Bua came in
and she stopped. And now I'm going to Lahore tomorrow,
and by the time I come back, she may even be married, and
I won't know . . .'

'Married? Did you say married?' Mashooq spun around.

Laila paused. 'Didn't she tell you? You said she'd told you
lots of things.' Doubt flickered in her eyes.

'Er, of course.' Mashooq cleared his throat. 'Of course she's
told me about her marriage. But I've forgotten the exact date.
Remind me.'

'Soon. Very soon. Maybe even next month.'

Mashooq started. It was the twenty-eighth of November.

'Her mother, I know, doesn't know about her wedding.
Does her grandmother?' he asked.

'Kaneez?' Laila pursed her lips. 'No. I'm the only one who
knows. And you, I suppose. She made me promise I wouldn't
tell anyone, and I haven't. Not my parents, not Bua, no one.
She trusts me because we're partners. Did she make you
promise too?'

'Oh, yes, she did. And her, um, fiancé? Have you met him?' He watched her through narrowed eyes.

'No. I don't even know his name. Do you?'

'She was going to tell me, but we were interrupted.'

'Same thing happened with me. Suppose he's not from around here, and she goes off to live with him? Then how will I meet her?' asked Laila. 'Now you see why I'm worried?'

'I'm worried too,' Mashooq said. 'Between you and me, I'm worried about whose idea this marriage is. Could it be hers, do you think?'

Laila considered his question. 'I think it is. She said she'd been meeting him secretly, but then something bad happened, because he got angry with her and said she'd spoilt his life. She thought he was going to run away and leave her all alone. He had begun to shout at her and didn't want to meet at their secret meeting-place any more. But it's all different now. He's being nice to her again and has even said he'll bring his parents to ask Kaneez properly to let them marry. Like they do for good girls. But he's told her that if she tells anyone, he won't come. That's why it's such a secret.'

'I see.' Mashooq rubbed his chin thoughtfully.

'Laila? Laila, where are you?' Bua's voice drifted across the garden.

Laila backed away. 'I must go. But will you tell Rani that I'm going to Lahore today and will she please, please, not get married till I come back?'

'Laila?' Bua's voice was closer. Laila could hear the irritation in it.

'Did you hear me?' Laila ran back to the hedge and peered over it, but Mashooq was gone.

It was dark when Mashooq staggered out of the liquor shop. There was something he had to do. It was gnawing at the edges of his mind, but he could not quite remember. Something to do with Tariq. Or was it Shamshad Khan? No, it was a girl. But who? He vaguely remembered a girl with gold earrings standing behind a hedge. Was it her? No, she was too young. It was another girl. And then he remembered. Squaring his shoulders, he limped across the street to his bicycle, mounted it with some difficulty and rode off into the night.

Her embroidered bed-sheet in one hand and a pair of scissors in the other, Rani sat staring at the wall ahead. Then, suddenly, she ripped into the sheet. The cloth was tough and initially resisted the frenzied jabs of her scissors. But she went at it again and again, until the sheet lay in tatters around her. Panting, she looked down at the ribbons of white cotton scattered on the floor. In the gloom of her unlit room they looked like torn love letters. There was a smudge of colour among them. Bending down, she picked up the scrap. It had a purple rose embroidered in neat satin stitch, still intact in its corner.

She thought back to the day when she had embroidered the rose. Laila had come to visit, and Rani had been so happy, so hopeful. The rose blurred before her eyes. Rani pressed the embroidered fragment to her mouth. Great gasping sobs racked her slender frame. She sank to the floor still clutching the scrap of bed sheet. Long after the tears ran dry, long after her hiccups subsided, she lay curled up on the floor, her knees against her chest. She turned on to her back, only to feel nausea well up in her throat. Rani pulled herself off the floor and stumbled across to the privy.

When she emerged, the quarter was dark. She had not switched on any lights earlier, and darkness had fallen, un-noticed. Rani was feeling her way across the yard when a hand descended on her shoulder. She shrieked.

'Hush. Are you mad to scream like that?' rasped Kaneez.

'Oh, Amman, it's only you.' Rani's shoulders slumped in relief.

But Kaneez was not listening. She gripped Rani's arm, dragged her into the room and slammed the door behind them. She flicked on the light and saw the scraps of cloth littering the floor. Rani stood blinking in the light, rubbing her arm absently. Her eyes were swollen and her face still streaked with tears.

'What is this?' Kaneez hissed, gesturing to the floor.

'Nothing,' mumbled Rani, looking away.

'Nothing? This is nothing? And I suppose your vomiting is also nothing? Twice I have heard you now. First you blamed it on guavas, and I, blind, trusting fool, believed you. And the sickness and tiredness? How you've tricked me! How you must have laughed behind my back! Whose is it?'

'Whose is w-what?' stammered Rani.

'Don't lie to me, you bitch.' Kaneez yanked her plait. 'Answer me! Whose is it?'

'Nobody's.' Rani quavered.

'Nobody's? *Nobody's?* You dare to tell me that?' Kaneez stepped back and struck Rani full in the face. Rani fell against the string bed. And then Kaneez was upon her, raining blows on her arms, face, neck, wherever she could reach. Shielding herself with a pillow, Rani cowered in a corner.

'Amman, please stop,' she cried. 'Please, I beg of you. Have mercy, for God's sake.'

'Did you have mercy on me, you whore, when you begot this foul child?' panted Kaneez. 'Did you stop to think of me, of your mother, of yourself? *Did you?*' she screeched.

'I'm sorry, I'm sorry. Forgive me,' Rani sobbed.

'Forgive you?' Kaneez sank on to the string bed. Suddenly all the fight went out of her. She seemed shrunken and beaten, her hands hanging useless between her knees. 'How can I forgive you?' she said bitterly. 'When you have lied to me and made a fool out of me and humiliated me like you wouldn't humiliate your worst enemy? You should have put your hands around my throat and squeezed the life out of me. That would have been kinder, quicker.'

'Don't say these things.' Rani raised stricken eyes to her grandmother. 'I never meant to hurt you. He *promised*. He promised to marry me. This,' she thrust a fragment of the sheet at her grandmother, 'this was my dowry. I worked on it when you were at the haveli. I bought it from the money Tariq Sahib gave me when I passed my exam. I thought I was getting married next week. He said we would. He promised. I'm the one who's been humiliated and lied to. Oh, I wish I could die.' With her head pressed against Kaneez's knee, she wept.

Kaneez's eyes were glazed, her ears deaf to Rani's pleas. 'All my life I've been dogged by misfortune,' she said in a flat voice. 'Allah took away my husband, then he took my daughter's. I bowed my head and accepted His will. He then sent me Mashooq. For these last twelve years, since the day I gave your mother to Mashooq, I have known no peace. The only thing I had left was my dignity. And the hope that it would be different for you. But today you have robbed me of both. I have nothing left.'

'Please don't say that,' Rani begged.

Kaneez continued as if Rani had not spoken. 'Not once since she married has your mother asked me to send you to her, not even for a day. Her eyes starve for the sight of you, but she'd rather endure a hundred beatings than let Mashooq near you. She sends messages whenever she can, asking after you. I never told you because I thought it was best this way. Best that you think that she's forgotten you. If you had known and wanted to go to her, how could I have stopped you? Here, under Sardar Begum's protection, I thought you were safe. What will I tell Fatima now? That I have failed her yet again?' Kaneez's voice cracked.

'I'm sorry, I'm sorry,' Rani wailed. 'You haven't failed her.

I have failed her. I didn't know it could happen like this. I've never known a mother, and you've always been so cold, so distant. I believed him when he said everything would be all right and he would look after me and make sure I wouldn't get into trouble. He bought me a red dupatta, and glass bangles, and apricots and toffees. He said nice things to me. He said I was pretty, he made me feel special, like a lady from a rich house. He made me forget myself.' Rani's voice lowered to a whisper. 'I know it was wrong, but I didn't do it to humiliate you, I did it because . . . because I trusted him and he made me happy. And when I realized what had happened, I tried to get it . . . wasted. I went to the nuns in Sabzbagh,' she mumbled. 'But they turned me away. They said it was against their religion.

'And then . . .' She took a deep, shuddering breath before continuing. 'I begged him to help me. He said he would. He said he'd take care of me. He promised to marry me. So I didn't tell you, thinking that I would be married in a month. You'd have been proud, Amman, to see me married and living in my own home. His people are well off. He said he'd tell his parents and they'd come to you to ask for me, properly, like respectable people do. But I waited and waited and they never came. I went looking for him, to the secret place we used to meet, but I couldn't find him. He'd disappeared. I was going mad with fear and worry. So, today, when I could think of nothing else, I went to ask at his house. I know it was wrong and shameless of me, but what could I do? They wouldn't let me in. They drove me away from the door, saying he had gone away to Lahore. For ever. And they said that if I ever showed my face there again, they'd tell everyone that I was trying to pin my sins with other men on him. That I was bad, brazen, shameless. They drove me away, Amman, they drove me away like a stray cat.'

Kaneez sat in silence, listening to Rani's muffled sobs. When she spoke, her tone was flat, detached, almost as if she was discussing Sardar Begum's register.

'Who else knows?'

'No one. I've told no one,' Rani replied in a thick, nasal voice.

'How far gone are you?'

'I've missed twice, I think,' Rani whispered.

'Who is the father?'

'What does it matter now? He's gone.'

'So you are still protecting him.'

'I'm not,' sighed Rani. 'But I see that it's no use.'

'You're right,' Kaneez agreed. 'It's no use. Nothing is of any use any longer.' Brushing Rani's hands off her knees, she trudged to the door. 'I wish you had never been born,' she whispered in a hoarse voice. Then she stumbled out into the dark yard.

'Where are you going?' Rani called out after her.

Kaneez did not answer. Rani heard the scrape of metal against wood when Kaneez lifted the latch of the yard door. There was a creak as the door swung open. It shut with a bang, and then there was silence. Burying her face in her hands, Rani curled up on the floor again.

By the time Mashooq reached Kalanpur, night had fallen. The five-mile cycle ride in the cold night air had cleared his head. He knew now what he had to do. He would show everyone – all those who jeered at him, insulted him and belittled him – that he was not a man to be taken lightly. The time had come to silence them. The time had come to collect his dues.

Mashooq pulled his thin jacket around him to ward off the creeping cold and parked his bicycle against the outer wall of Sardar Begum's haveli. It was a moonless night made darker still by a thick fog that had descended in the last hour. The path to the servants' quarters was narrow and bordered on one side by the wall and the other by a sluggish stream. He cursed Sardar Begum for not installing a light bulb there. Keeping one hand against the wall, he picked his way carefully. The path was slippery. He didn't remember it being quite so long. Once he slipped on what he suspected was cow dung. Swearing under his breath, he picked himself up and scraped the sole of his shoe against the wall. He looked over his shoulder. There didn't seem to be anyone about. A goat bleated somewhere. He couldn't tell if it was close or far away.

He reached the quarters without encountering anyone. The mist was thinner here. There were lights on in one or two of the windows. He hid behind a tree trunk, undecided what to do. A figure passed within a few feet of him. Even in the darkness and the fog he could tell it was Kaneez. Her stooping back and shuffling gait were unmistakable. She made for one of the unlit quarters. Mashooq waited until she had opened the door and disappeared inside. Then he followed her.

He pressed his ear against her door. He could hear a peculiar noise from the roofless privy, almost as if someone was gargling. He frowned in concentration. No, it wasn't gargling. It was more like vomiting. He was about to try the door when he heard the splash of water and then, a moment later, Kaneez's voice, unusually harsh, asking a question. He didn't hear what she said for, suddenly, quite close by, a dog barked. Mashooq flinched and pressed himself to the door. Someone shouted at the dog and hurled a stone. There was a dull thud as the stone hit the ground and rolled away. The dog barked again, but half-heartedly, as if it couldn't really be bothered. Mashooq couldn't hear very much now. Kaneez had gone into the inner room. He saw a thin slice of light through the crack in the door. He tried pushing at the yard door gently. It opened with a creak. He froze, expecting Kaneez to come out. But no one heard him. He let himself in and shut the door behind him.

He tiptoed across the yard towards the room. Although he knew it was dangerous, he pressed his face against the join of the two doors. He could see a foot, a narrow, shapely foot – which could only be Rani's – on the floor. Good, at least she was here.

He hadn't seen her for over a year, when he had come to drop Fatima on one of the rare visits he allowed her to Kalanpur. Rani had been a pretty little thing then, a little on the skinny side. She must have filled out now. Girls grew fast.

Kaneez appeared to be arguing with Rani. He couldn't make out Rani's mumbled responses, but Kaneez was shrieking. Pressed against the wall, Mashooq listened intently. He didn't know how long he stood there. He was too engrossed to feel cold or tired. Once or twice he was tempted to burst in on them. But he held back, biding his time.

Eventually, the door opened. Once again, Kaneez passed within a couple of feet of him. Mashooq withdrew into the shadows, but Kaneez never looked back. Opening the latch, she let herself out. Mashooq waited a few moments and then slipped into the room. Rani lay on the floor with her back to him. She was still sobbing.

14

The Azeems set off for Lahore soon after breakfast the following day. Dark clouds smudged the sun, but there was no trace of the mist from the night before. Fareeda and Tariq sat in the back of the car with Laila between them. Bua was in the front beside Barkat. The car cruised out of the gates, past the mustard fields, the now bald cane fields, the mango orchard, the guava orchard and the convent. Barkat slowed the car down to a crawl as they came to the bazaar. The shops were open and doing brisk business. The narrow street was clogged with traffic. Peasant women sauntered along with their purchases piled on their heads. Entire families of four or five perched precariously on bicycles – the father in the seat, the mother on the back carrier with a baby in her arms and the older child balanced on the cross bar. The Zephyr was the only car on the street. People stared as they passed by.

The bazaar held a special fascination for Laila, for she seldom came here. Her favourite shop was Decent General Merchants. It sold everything from the portable loos that Hester called thunder boxes to prickly-heat powder. Its owner, Chaudhry Mohammed Sadeeq, FA pass, was a corpulent man who always sat on the small veranda fronting his shop, his hairy feet resting on a plastic stool. Rows of conical brassieres, nylon Y-fronts and the horsehair plaits favoured by elderly ladies with thinning hair hung above him from hooks in the ceiling. Mr Sadeeq waved to Tariq as their car passed his shop.

Next to the general merchant was the barber, who serviced his clients on the pavement. A client in a dhoti and singlet sat in a chair. He raised his arm. The barber slapped foam on to his armpit and, quick as a flash, shaved it off with a long curving blade. Then came Tip-Top Tailor. A rusted metal board above his shop read, 'Top Class Tailors for Top Class Peoples. Come One, Come All.' Last in this row was the traditional healer, who also conducted his business on the pavement. He sat cross-legged on an empty sack, with the tools of his trade laid out in front. There was a placard behind him with a bold sign in Urdu. 'Available here,' it read, 'miraculous cures for bleeding piles and masculine weakness.'

They passed the fly-infested butcher's, the grocer, the cobbler, the police station and donkey carts piled high with oranges and guavas. A spicy, buttery aroma of fried samosas filled the car. They were passing the stall that sold them. There wasn't much point asking Fareeda if they could buy some.

'Have you seen the flies on them?' she'd say to Laila. 'And I'm sure they're fried in Mobil oil.'

Once they were out of the bazaar, the car gathered speed. They were in open country now, with fields all around. The round, smoking towers of brick kilns cropped up here and there. They passed the sugar mill, with a long queue of tractors piled high with cane waiting by the gates. And then they were on Laila's favourite bit of the road. It came after the level crossing, a long stretch over which the shisham trees on either side met in an arch above the road. Save for the shafts of sunlight that pierced the canopy now and then, the light under the trees was pale and dim, as if on a lake bed. Laila shut her eyes and waited for the play of mauve and yellow shadows on her eyelids. When the car emerged from the tunnel, Laila was asleep, her head slumped against her mother's shoulder.

Fareeda tilted Laila's neck to make her more comfortable.

'She's nodded off,' Tariq observed.

'She didn't have much sleep last night,' explained Fareeda. 'Far too excited about going to Lahore and rescuing Sara from school. I meant to ask, why did Mashooq come to see you?'

'He's been sacked,' said Tariq. 'Wanted me to get him reinstated.'

'Did you?'

'No. He deserved the sack.' Briefly, Tariq recounted the events of the day before.

'What *is* his problem?' asked Fareeda in exasperation.

Tariq did not reply. Staring out of the window at the green blur of fields and orchards, he wished, as he had many times in the last decade, that he had done what he could and put a stop to Fatima's second marriage. For the truth was that he had disliked Mashooq at first sight.

But Tariq had met Mashooq only a few days before the wedding, when Sardar Begum had casually broken the news of the proposed nuptials to him. Suspicious of his mother's unusual restraint in not divulging the news sooner, Tariq had insisted on meeting Mashooq. Sardar Begum reluctantly acceded to her son's demand and sent for Mashooq from Dera. A meeting had taken place at her haveli.

Tariq had managed to hide his dismay at Mashooq's un-savoury appearance. He had questioned him about his job, his background and his plans for the future. Mashooq had answered smoothly, almost glibly. But Tariq had been sceptical of Mashooq's fluent humility and, sensing her son's reser-vations, Sardar Begum had called a halt to Tariq's probes. Before Tariq could demur, she had sent Mashooq packing on a made-up errand.

Tariq had voiced his objections, but his mother had told him that both Kaneez and she were satisfied with Mashooq's credentials and that the wedding date had already been fixed for the following week. Sardar Begum vouched that Fatima was happy with the match and had agreed to it readily.

Tariq suspected even then that Mashooq was a canny opera-tor making a calculated move. Fatima was pretty and docile and, between help from Tariq, his mother and the savings that

Kaneez had managed to scrape together, was likely to receive a decent dowry. And he was probably well aware of her vulnerability. After the mother and daughter had been vilified so thoroughly by the villagers for losing their husbands early in their marriages, Fatima was unlikely to dump him and march off home.

As Sardar Begum confided in her son a couple of years after the marriage, when she had questioned Mashooq about his background, he had informed her with a sad smile that he had never known his parents. He had grown up in an orphanage in Karachi. They kept him there till he was a teenager and then kicked him out. He drifted around for some years doing petty jobs – a tea boy in a truck driver's canteen, a labourer on a construction site, a guard at a school.

But he had wanted to see the world, so when a truck driver offered him a lift to Lahore, he leapt at it. He said he hung around Lahore doing the same sort of jobs. But big cities were expensive and pitiless. He said he dreamt of a stable life with the family that he'd never had. When acquaintances advised him to head for a smaller town where his money would go further, he acted on their advice and once again climbed on to a bus.

The bus disgorged him at Colewallah town. He stayed in Colewallah only a month but didn't like the squalor. He yearned for the golden fields and shady trees of a village and eventually found Sabzbagh. One day, he arrived at the milk factory, which had just started up, asking for a job. He got it, worked hard and, after a couple of years, settled in Dera, the village where he hoped to bring Fatima.

When Mashooq had proposed for Fatima, Kaneez and Sardar Begum had checked up on him in the usual way. The local matchmakers had never heard of him. Nor had the mullah, even though he officiated at nearly every marriage and funeral within a radius of three miles.

Despite their best efforts, they drew a blank. No one knew him or anyone related to him. It seemed as if he'd just dropped from the sky. But they were in a hurry, and his story was believable. He had kept all the details vague. Karachi was far away. It was difficult to check orphanage records there. He seemed pleasant, spoke little and kept to himself. That was all anyone knew about him then. But if they were unable to dig up any reassuring facts about him, they hadn't uncovered a shady past either. Still, Kaneez had her doubts. But Sardar Begum talked her out of them.

Initially, the marriage seemed fine. But within a few months, he began, bit by bit, to reveal his true nature. Sardar Begum was appalled at her own error of judgement. Fatima had not been married a year when Sardar Begum was visited by some relatives from Champa, a village near Colewallah town on the other side of the canal. Mashooq happened to be making a rare visit to the haveli that day. Just as they were coming in, he was leaving. Averting his face, he scurried out. But they'd seen him.

That brief encounter unveiled his past. It transpired that Mashooq was from Champa. His mother's people were cobblers, low caste and dirt poor. All they had was the small, grimy shop at which his grandfather plied his trade. His mother was born deaf and mute. Although she had a proper name, no one remembered it. She was simply Boli – the deaf girl.

When Boli was about twenty – she was single, because no one in the village wanted her – her belly began to swell. According to her parents, she had been raped when she went into the fields one night to relieve herself. But her assailant had terrorized her so that the girl would only cower and shiver whenever the parents tried to question her. The villagers dismissed the story as a barefaced lie. The girl had been up to no good and was trying to shift the blame. No one thought to discover the identity of the man involved.

Boli duly gave birth to a boy. He was tiny, with a shrivelled foot. Just as they'd called his mother Boli, the villagers found a name for him – Harami, the bastard. They said his deformity was his punishment for being a bastard. A brand, as it were. He grew up in the village, shunned and ridiculed by everyone, except his mother and grandparents.

Children refused to play with him, grown-ups wouldn't let him into their houses. The lords of the village occasionally sent grain to the boy's family, or perhaps some old clothes once a year, a conciliatory gesture in recognition of the hereafter, but their largesse did not extend further.

As he entered his teens, the boy developed some unsavoury habits – a fondness for alcohol and a propensity for violence. But though unlettered and wild, he was enterprising. He'd go off to Colewallah and work as a loader at the truck depot. But the money was soon drained away at the town's cheap liquor shops. Tariq's relatives could not recall the exact date of his departure. One day, Mashooq left the village, and they didn't see him again. Until that afternoon at the haveli.

Sardar Begum was furious – furious at Mashooq for lying, but more furious with herself for believing him. She felt doubly guilty now for not discovering the truth about Mashooq, and for advising Kaneez to accept his proposal. She consoled herself with the thought that she had done her best to rectify her mistake by offering to have the marriage dissolved and assume full financial responsibility for both Fatima and her unborn child. But as long as Fatima wanted to stay with him, there was little she could do.

'Life was hard enough for Fatima, as it was,' said Tariq, winding up the car window. 'It will be harder still with Mashooq out of a job.'

'You should try and find him something when we get back. For Fatima's sake and their children's.'

'I've had just about enough of him. If I see him on doomsday, it will be too soon.'

It was midday by the time the Zephyr reached the outskirts of the city. They passed all the familiar landmarks – the big orphanage with its concrete walls and small, mean windows; Bata, the shoe factory, which always smelt of burnt rubber; the cacophonous coach station with a jumble of technicolored buses disgorging gaggles of dazed passengers weighed down with bundles of clothes and tired, shrieking children.

The Zephyr stopped at a traffic light, amid a plethora of three-wheeled rickshaws, cars, vans, bullock carts and motorcycles. Beggars with twisted limbs and matted hair wove in and out of the waiting traffic. Barefoot children selling pocket-sized Korans and peeled oranges pushed up against the cars. They tapped insistently on the raised windows of the Zephyr. Fareeda and Tariq stared straight ahead, but Laila shook her head at a skinny girl with a runny nose. 'No, thank you,' she mouthed at her through the closed window. The girl stuck her tongue out at Laila and darted off.

As the car approached Gulberg, the traffic thinned and the road became wider. Jumbled buildings, garlanded with loops of exposed wiring, gave way to large houses set well back from the road. Traffic here was polite, ordered and consisted mainly of gleaming cars. The Zephyr drove parallel to the narrow canal. As always, Laila marvelled at how small, how innocuous, it looked after the Sabzbagh monster. You could practically ford it with a hop, skip and a jump.

The car turned into the quiet, shady road on which Fareeda's mother lived, and Laila counted off the two houses before her grandmother's. First came the residence of the high court judge who had been C. P. Khan's bridge partner, followed by the lavish turreted mansion that had belonged to a prominent Hindu family before Partition. It was now the home of a retired general. And then the car swished through the wrought-iron gates and up the gravel drive of Yasmeen Khan's home.

Set in a big garden with fountains and rose bowers, the house was an art deco edifice built on C. P. Khan's retirement. It had been the talk of the town then, the imposing mansion of C. P. and Yasmeen Khan. To Laila, the white-painted house, with its prow-like façade, looked a little like an ocean liner she had once seen in a film. In her mind's eye, she could see it cutting a regal passage through a calm blue sea, little puffs of white smoke rising from its tall white chimney into a cloudless sky.

The house had vast reception rooms filled with Persian rugs, Chinese porcelain, Japanese lacquerware and English silver – silent testimonials to the tastes and travels of the Khans. The Khans had been a gregarious couple and their house a focus of musical soirées, political debate and influential dinner guests. But six years ago, on C. P.'s death from cancer, a hush had fallen upon the house. Yasmeen, who, until then, had cheerfully made a career of her husband and home, suddenly found herself redundant.

For a while Fareeda had feared that Yasmeen might unravel. She took to shuffling around the house in a crumpled kaftan with yesterday's newspapers clutched in her hand. But with the arrival of her granddaughters, now old enough to attend school in Lahore, she had rallied, and the Yasmeen whom Laila found sitting cross-legged on a silken Bokhara rug, tuning her sitar in the sitting room, was very much the brisk, independent and capable Yasmeen of old.

'Laila!' Yasmeen gave a cry of delight and, pushing the sitar to one side, rose to her feet. She threw her arms around Laila and dropped several kisses on top of her head. The bifocals she wore on a silver chain around her neck brushed Laila's face. Laila hugged her back, pressing her cheek against the soft linen of her grandmother's shirt. Her clothes smelt, as always, of Surf and, more subtly, of the perfume she liked above all others, Floris's Lily of the Valley.

With her arms around her Lahore grandmother's slim middle, Laila couldn't help thinking how different it felt to her Kalanpur grandmother's soft, squashy tummy. Unlike Sardar Begum, who was ponderous both in body and movement, Yasmeen was still slender and energetic. Although, in fact, there was only a year or so between the two women, Laila and Sara always thought of their Lahore grandmother as infinitely younger. And a lot more fun. Whereas Sardar Begum was always reminding them to think of the hereafter ('How will you answer Him on the day of judgement if you don't listen to your grandmother?') and urging decorum ('Always keep your ankles crossed'), Yasmeen encouraged them to be adventurous.

With Yasmeen they would go boating on the river; explore the narrow bazaars in the walled city; and get taken to her artist friends' studios. Yasmeen could also speak fluent English, drive a car and play Monopoly. Sardar Begum saw no reason to speak English when the British had departed long since, drive when she employed a driver, or handle fake money when her purse bulged with the real stuff.

'How are you, little one?' Holding Laila's face by the chin, Yasmeen turned her towards the window. 'Come into the light so I can see clearly. Yes, I see you've improved. No longer the sickly thing your mother whisked off from under my nose. How do you feel?'

'Fine, Nani, honest. Where's Sara?'

'In her room, waiting for you.'

Laila sped to the bedroom she shared with her sister. Sara already knew of her family's expected arrival, so it wasn't quite the surprise Laila had hoped it would be. Her elder sister, in fact, was ready to leave with them. Her suitcase stood packed in a corner and her bulging school bag leaned against it.

'Of course I knew you were coming, dummy,' Sara said witheringly, when Laila blurted out that they'd come to take her.

'To protect you from the Indians,' Laila whispered. 'They're coming any day now.'

'To protect *me*?' Sara scoffed. '*I'm* coming to protect *you*.'

'Me? How?'

'With this.' Sara held out her palm towards Laila. A flat metal object the length of her middle finger lay on it. It was dull silver and looked like the handle of a fork.

Laila knew better than to reach for it. 'What is it?'

'It's a weapon.' Sara pressed a catch in its side, and a tiny blade flicked open.

'Ooh! What's it for?'

'It's for the Indians.' Sara closed the knife with a little click and slipped it back into her pocket.

'Where did you get it from?'

'None of your business,' Sara replied in a superior voice.

'Can I hold it?'

'It's not for babies. It's dangerous.'

Laila thought hard. 'I've also got something. But I'll only show you if you let me hold the knife first.'

Sara considered Laila's suggestion for a moment. 'First I'll see your thing, then I'll decide.'

Laila dug into her skirt pocket and pulled out Hester's ivory horse. In the bright light of the bedroom, it looked small, insignificant.

'Who gave it to you?'

'Mrs Bullock.'

'Why?' Sara scowled.

'Just because.'

Sara snatched it off Laila's palm and sniffed at it. 'Doesn't smell of anything.' She examined it closely, turning it this way and that. 'Nah, it's just a horse, a toy horse.' She shoved it back towards Laila.

'It's not a toy. It's a wishing horse,' Laila claimed rashly. 'You make a wish, rub the horse and your wish comes true.'

'OK then, wish for a big chocolate cake to appear right now.'

'It doesn't work like that.'

'It doesn't work at all.' Sara's tone was scathing. 'It is just a silly toy. Just because you've been with Ammi and Aba alone in Sabzbagh, you think you know everything. Well, you don't. I'm the one who's been going to school and learning things. You're just a baby.'

Laila looked at Sara through smarting eyes. She had changed in the time that Laila had been at the farm. Her hair was done in one plait instead of two. She looked grown-up. Her earrings were also different. Instead of the little gold rings that both sisters had always worn, Sara now had a pair of tiny pearl studs that Laila had never seen before. She'd also learnt to lift one eyebrow. It made her look mean. Nasty.

'It's not a silly horse,' Laila shouted. 'And I'm not a baby. I know lots of secrets that you don't.'

'What secrets?'

'Nothing,' Laila muttered, turning her back on Sara.

'Be like that then.' Sara shrugged and flounced off to the bathroom.

Deflated, and perilously close to tears, Laila sidled up to the alcove that housed their two identical desks and cork noticeboards. At least her blue-painted desk and the BOAC mug that held her coloured pencils still looked the same. She quickly counted the pencils. Yes, they were all there. And so was everything she had put on the board.

The drawing Laila had made last term of a vase with pink roses, which had won her a star at school, was still there, as was the photograph of Sara and her, taken outside the Lahore museum by their grandmother the day she'd taken them to see the Gandhara statues. Yasmeen had been in raptures over the vast, two-thousand-year-old statues, but privately Laila had thought that the men looked funny with their eyes half-closed as if they had thumping headaches. She also did not like the way they wore their hair piled on top of their heads in small frizzy buns.

Laila's British Council Library card was up on the notice-board, as was the postcard of Big Ben her parents had sent when they'd gone to London the year before. It looked a bit faded now, but it was pinned in the right-hand corner, exactly where she'd left it. Good, it didn't seem as if Sara had been messing with her things.

Glancing over her shoulder to ensure that Sara was still in the bathroom, Laila moved over to her desk to see if she had acquired anything new. The display on her noticeboard was reassuringly familiar. There was that photograph of Fareeda looking glamorous in a black-chiffon sari at a party; and the good-luck peacock feather Sara had found on Hester's farm last summer, which Laila had coveted desperately for a whole month. There was a school timetable that Laila hadn't seen before and the ticket stubs of a film showing at the Rex Cinema. Laila straightened the ticket and read, *Thief of Baghdad*. She wished she could have gone too.

Gingerly, she prised open Sara's stationery box and found six new felt-tipped pens. That wasn't fair. She didn't even have one. Laila pulled off the cap of the yellow pen and inhaled its heady petrol scent and made a mental note to badger her grandmother for a set exactly like Sara's. She heard the loo flush in the bathroom. Hastily replacing the pen in the box, she moved back to her own desk. It wouldn't do to be caught snooping, particularly when Sara was in that funny mood. She heard her sister come up behind her. Laila pretended a deep interest in her noticeboard.

'The driver's cat has had kittens. Want to come and see?'

Laila spun around, nodding eagerly. Sara smiled and held out her hand.

That evening, when the girls had gone to bed, the adults retired to C. P.'s library after dinner. It was a comfortable room, still imprinted with C. P.'s personality. A teak roll-top desk with a sheaf of his monogrammed writing paper still in its top drawer dominated the room. The walls were lined with shelves bearing his enormous library of leather-bound books and a phalanx of silver-framed photographs of C. P. with heads of state and sundry dignitaries. Amid the pompous black-and-white photographs of Nasser, De Gaulle and Khrushchev was a smattering of family photos, of Fareeda on her wedding day, of his grandchildren as plump babies and himself and his wife relaxing on the deck of a cruise ship, he sporting a Derby and she, cat-like, dark glasses.

A log fire burnt in the grate, and Fareeda, Tariq and Yasmeen sat on a squashy leather sofa facing it. Fareeda poured herself another cup of green tea and, curling her feet under her, broached the subject uppermost in her mind.

'You know, Mummy, that there's going to be a war, don't you?'

Yasmeen nodded. 'Yes, I can see it coming.'

'You should come and stay with us in Sabzbagh. It will be much safer there.'

'Why should Lahore be more unsafe than anywhere else?' Yasmeen got up to stoke the fire.

'For God's sake, the border is only thirteen miles away,' cried Fareeda. 'I'd die worrying if you were all right.'

'Well, then, you mustn't worry,' her mother replied, replacing the poker.

'You *know* I'll worry.' Fareeda's voice rose in exasperation. Yasmeen held up her hand to bring the discussion to an end.

'It's sweet of you to ask, but, no. I can keep busy here. What would I do at the farm but get in your way? I have my old servants here with me. We'll take care of each other. Now, stop looking so anxious. This is not the first upheaval I've lived through, you know. In fact, we stayed right here in Lahore through Partition. And if I could stay put with murderous mobs prowling the streets, then what are a few skirmishes on the border?'

'How do you know there'll be just skirmishes? Or that they'll be restricted to the border?' questioned Fareeda. 'Anyway, the point is, I wasn't old enough to worry then, but I am now.'

'You were just a girl then,' Yasmeen reminisced with a misty smile. 'Do you remember anything from then?'

'A few disjointed things. I remember our Hindu gardener – Nathoo Ram, wasn't it? – leaving with his family on a bullock cart. I remember their parrot cage hanging from the side of the cart. And Daddy's double-barrelled Holland and Holland propped up by his bed for several days. And all those whispered, worried conversations among the adults. I remember the distant chants of mobs and feeling a sense of danger quite clearly.'

'Hmm, it was a dangerous time,' recalled Yasmeen. 'But also a very exciting time. We were getting freedom. And our own country. Pakistan. We'd fought for it for so long. We'd marched on the streets and protested and gone on strike against the British. And Mr Jinnah, so ill, so emaciated and yet so resolute. He was up against a whole stableful of wily Congress wallahs, aided and abetted by that ghastly Mountbatten. But, in the end, he trumped them all.'

A log fell in the grate, scattering a small shower of sparks. Tariq replaced Yasmeen's empty cup on the tray.

'We had such high hopes of this nation,' Yasmeen sighed, staring unseeingly at the curling flames. 'I never imagined it would unravel so fast.'

'Perhaps we were never a nation,' ventured Tariq.

'But we *were*,' insisted Yasmeen, shifting her gaze to Tariq. 'That was Jinnah's whole point, wasn't it? That we, the Muslims of the subcontinent, were a distinct nation and needed our own homeland. Why did we stop being a nation twenty-five years later? *Why?*'

'The distance was a fault line,' pointed out Fareeda.

'Also, our culture is different. And our language,' said Tariq slowly.

'So why were they not a consideration in '47? No, it wasn't meant to be like this,' Yasmeen whispered in a husky voice. 'We weren't meant to split, to shatter. I was there when this country was made. I remember.'

15

The car was a warm, snug cocoon as it sped through the dark to Sabzbagh. The windows were up against the cold night air, and there was a faint aroma of the chicken patties Yasmeen had stuffed through the open window of the moving car as it pulled out of her driveway.

'In case the girls get hungry,' she'd called out, waving till the car was out of sight. There had been tears in Fareeda's eyes when she'd embraced her mother.

'Now, now, there's no need to weep.' Yasmeen had patted Fareeda's back. 'I'll be perfectly safe here. You take care of yourselves and telephone me every day.'

She had hugged and kissed the girls and held the Koran over their heads muttering prayers of safekeeping as they filed out of the house and into the car. The girls had kept up a constant chatter for the first half of the journey. But now, just a few miles short of Sabzbagh, there was silence in the car, except for the purr of the engine and the soft snuffles of Bua's cat-like snores.

Laila stirred under the folds of her mother's pashmina shawl and blinked in the headlights of an oncoming truck tearing towards them on the dark, narrow road. Barkat flashed his headlights and swerved to avoid the truck.

'Are we there yet?' she asked, rubbing her eyes.

'No, a little while longer,' murmured Fareeda.

There were no lights on the Lahore–Sabzbagh road. Laila could discern some dark smudges beyond the window, which she took to be the trees bordering the road. The car was lit within by the half-light of the dials and switches on Barkat's dashboard. Laila could make out Sara's head slumped against Bua's shoulder on the front seat.

'Barkat, what news of your son?' Tariq asked the driver.

'I haven't had a letter for a while, Sahib,' replied Barkat, changing to a lower gear as they reached Sabzbagh. 'But, in the last one he sent, he seemed . . . strange. He didn't sound like the boy I sent out.'

'Hmm.' Tariq didn't like to ask what 'strange' meant. 'I expect he will be a changed man when he returns. A man can't fight a war and not let it affect him.'

'I pray to Allah that he *does* return,' said the driver in a gruff voice. 'Or I won't know how to face his mother.'

'Of course he'll return,' said Fareeda. 'Soon it will be all over and he'll be home with you.'

'May Allah hear your words,' said Barkat, slowing the car down to drive through Sabzbagh bazaar.

'Are we there yet?' Laila asked again.

'Yes, see, there's the church?' pointed out Fareeda. 'You can make out the cross against the sky.'

'Wake up, Sara, we're home.' Laila reached forward to shake her sister's shoulder. 'Bua, Bua, wake up. We've arrived.'

Golden light spilled out from the windows of their house. Dressed in a thick coat and muffler, Fazal came down the steps. Tariq opened the door, and swirls of cold air curled into the car.

'Oh, Mother Mary, so cold,' muttered Bua, covering her head with her shawl. 'No use pushing me, Saru. I won't open the door until you button up your sweater.'

Tariq stepped out of the car. The two-day break in Lahore had been a nice change. He had caught up with some friends over a long lunch at the Imperial Club and also paid a useful visit to Mr Davies of the British Development Association. Tariq stretched his arms above his head and looked up at the sky. It was a clear frosty night and the sky was the colour of lapis lazuli.

The girls tumbled out of the car, giggling and pushing at each other in their eagerness to get inside.

'Here, here, do up your sweaters.' Bua bustled after the girls.

With her handbag slung over her arm, Fareeda ascended the steps into the house.

'Everything been all right in our absence?' Tariq asked Fazal. The bearer was helping the driver lift their bags out of the boot.

Fazal put the suitcase down deliberately and said, 'Well, Sahib, everything has been fine here with us, but at Kalanpur . . .' His voice trailed off.

'What's happened at Kalanpur?' Tariq's tone was sharp. 'Is my mother all right? Speak!'

'Oh, yes, yes. Your mother's still in Sargodha, Sahib.'

Suddenly, a scream tore through the house. Clustered around the boot of the car, the three men looked up, startled. Tariq bounded up the stairs and into the house. He saw Fareeda kneeling on the floor, facing Kaneez, who was huddled in a chair. Kaneez's face was buried in her hands, and she was sobbing uncontrollably. The girls stood nearby, clutching Bua's hands, looking on in troubled silence. A single drop of sweat trickled down Bua's temple.

Nobody had noticed Tariq enter, but when he shook off his jacket, Bua looked up and saw him. She darted him a frightened look. Tariq motioned her to take the girls away. Bua scurried out, dragging the girls behind her.

'What's happened, Bua? What's the matter with Kaneez? Tell, please.' Their whispered questions were cut off by the click of the door shutting behind them.

Tariq approached the two women. Fareeda had her back to him and was murmuring to Kaneez. He touched Fareeda's shoulder and indicated to her that he wished to speak to Kaneez.

'Kaneez,' said Fareeda, moving aside. 'Tariq Sahib is here and would like to speak to you.' Kaneez lifted her head and raised a ravaged face at Tariq. Her eyes seemed to have receded so far back into her skull that, for a moment, Tariq thought he was looking at empty sockets. Her pink scalp was visible through sparse strands of grey hair. Tariq drew up a chair and took one of Kaneez's work-worn hands in his own.

'What's happened?'

'She's gone,' Kaneez whispered hoarsely. 'I've looked everywhere, but I can't find her. It's my fault. Me and my cursed bad luck. I wish I'd never been born.' Her shoulders started to shake again.

'Shh,' said Tariq. 'Who has gone?'

'My girl.'

'Fatima?'

'No, Rani. Rani's gone. Oh, my little girl. She never hurt anyone. She was so innocent, still a child.'

'Kaneez!' Tariq asked urgently. 'Are you sure it's Rani who is missing?'

Kaneez nodded.

'How long has she been missing?'

'Two days,' she said in a choking voice.

'When was the last time you saw her?'

'Two days ago, I came home after locking up the haveli for the night.' She drew a deep breath. 'It must have been seven. I remember, I said my evening prayers at the haveli and then I checked all the doors and windows like I do every night. Only then I came home. She was there. We talked. Then I went back to the haveli, and when I returned, it must have been an hour later, an hour and a half at most, she was gone.'

'Did you ask if anyone had seen her leave? Any of the neighbours?'

'It was a foggy night. There was no one about. Everyone was indoors. I asked, but no one saw or heard anything.'

'Where could she have gone?' Fareeda wondered aloud. 'Has she ever gone off like this before?'

'Oh, no, never.' Kaneez shook her head emphatically.

'Do you have any idea why she may have disappeared? Could she have gone off with someone willingly? Or was she involved in some fight or something? I need to know, Kaneez, if we are to find her.' Tariq pressed her hand.

Kaneez looked at Tariq and bowed her head. A tear splashed on to Tariq's hand.

'If you want us to help, you must tell us everything you know or even suspect,' Fareeda said. 'Could she have gone to see her mother, for instance?'

'Why should she go there? Anyway, I've checked. I didn't want to worry Fatima, so I asked a neighbour, and she said no one had seen Rani anywhere near there.'

'And you've asked all of Rani's friends?' enquired Tariq.

'I *told* you. No one's seen her since that day. Everybody in Kalanpur knows that she's missing. Allah knows what dirty thoughts they are thinking. The shame, the shame.' Kaneez covered her face with her hands.

'There's no shame,' Fareeda said in a crisp voice. 'Our only concern should be for the girl. She may have had an accident or something.'

'What happened, Kaneez? Tell me the truth,' urged Tariq.

'We argued.' Kaneez spoke in a small numb voice. 'I told her I didn't want to see her. Then I left for the haveli. I had nowhere else to go. I sat in the kitchen. I tried to do some work – Nazeer is away, so I thought I'd clean out the masala box – but my hands were shaking so much that I couldn't do it. So I gave up and sat there by myself. When I went back home, she was gone.'

'Did she take anything with her?' Tariq asked.

'No.'

'What did you quarrel about?' Fareeda wanted to know.

Kaneez stared at her hands lying limp in her lap.

There was a cough behind them. Fazal stood in the doorway with the luggage.

'Sahib, may I bring this in?'

'Yes, take it through to the bedrooms.'

Fazal passed by, his face averted from the group around the chair.

Fareeda called out after the bearer. 'Rehmat has cooked dinner for us, hasn't he? Could you serve it to the girls on a tray in their room? Ask Bua to get them ready for bed as soon as they've eaten. We won't eat just yet. We'll be in the sitting room. Make sure we're not disturbed. Kaneez, have you eaten?'

Kaneez shook her head.

'I thought not,' Fareeda tut-tutted. 'There's no point in starving yourself on top of everything else.'

'I don't want anything,' said Kaneez.

'All right, I won't force it on you. But at least come into the other room.'

After the chill of the hallway, the sitting room was warm. A fire burnt in the hearth, and two table lamps with ivory-coloured shades bathed the room in a mellow light. The heavy damask drapes had been drawn, and the fruit tray sat on the rosewood coffee table. Tariq walked across to the fire and stood with his back to it, his hands tucked deep into his pockets.

Fareeda motioned Kaneez to a chair. But Kaneez sat down on the floor.

'Sit on the chair, Kaneez,' Fareeda ordered.

'No, I'm happier here. I'm not used to chairs.'

Fareeda shrugged. 'You were going to tell us why you and Rani quarrelled. Kaneez?'

'Please don't make me say.' She was weeping again. 'It's too shameful. I can't.'

'You must.' Fareeda insisted. 'We have to know.'

Kaneez wiped her eyes. Then, in a halting voice, she told them about Rani's sickness, her listlessness, her own growing suspicions, and then that evening's terrible scene. She did not spare herself, recounting her shock and fury truthfully. But when she came to the part when Rani had tried telling her of her own disappointment and betrayal, she broke down again.

'I didn't listen to her,' she sobbed. 'I wanted to punish her. But what else could I do? I never dreamed, never ever imagined that such humiliation could ever visit our house. How was I ever going to hold my head up again? And now she's gone. When a young girl goes missing, people believe the worst. Oh, why did I have to see this day? What will I tell Fatima? Why does Allah hate me so?'

'Stop this nonsense at once,' Fareeda scolded.

Kaneez shrank into herself, staring vacantly at the far wall.

'Tariq,' Fareeda asked in English, 'do you believe her story?'

'What do you mean, "story"?' Tariq asked. How could Fareeda ask him that? Why on earth would Kaneez invent an account which she clearly found so humiliating, so distressing? Didn't Fareeda know Kaneez well enough to realize how dearly she cherished her honour? To invent a story to besmirch it would be plain lunacy.

'But the girl was so bright, so alert,' Fareeda continued. 'She couldn't have been so foolish.'

'She was an innocent,' he snapped. 'Girls like her get seduced and deserted every day. How can you have lived here all these years and not known that?' The only thing that surprised him was that Rani had managed to keep it secret. Why, in that village where everyone knew everyone else's business, did no one know?

'If she was in trouble, why she didn't come to us?' asked

Fareeda. 'OK, not you, because you are a man, but me. Every-one knows I'm not judgemental. I would have helped her.'

'Oh, for God's sake, Fareeda, can't you understand?' Tariq shouted, striking his thigh with a balled fist. 'The girl was confused and frightened, and there we were jabbering on about her bright future when she had a time bomb ticking inside her. She didn't come to us because she probably thought she'd let us down. What could she say? "The schooling and job is fine, but could it just wait for a bit, while you arrange an abortion for me?" Have a heart!'

'But she went to the nuns at the convent. If she was afraid of being judged, why go to a convent?' Fareeda's voice rose in exasperation. She was irritated at the thought of Rani throwing herself at the mercy of her adversaries. Why them and not her? It was just the sort of ammunition she did not want the nuns to have. 'If they knew, didn't she think I would find out? Sooner or later Sister Clementine was bound to . . . Oh, God, oh, God.' Fareeda clapped a hand over her mouth.

'What?'

'Sister Clementine *did* come to me,' Fareeda said slowly. 'She came that day when you were away in Colewallah, and Jacob was here, and I was trying to write that wretched report. She said something about looking after – or was it helping? – young girls in trouble, and then sometimes not being able to help them.

'I thought she was babbling, and I was in a hurry, so I sent her packing. I remember telling Hester that I couldn't understand why she had come. She'd come to warn me about Rani, and I didn't listen. Oh, God, what have I done?'

'But why didn't you listen? She came all this way to warn you, and you didn't even give her a hearing?' asked Tariq incredulously. 'How could you be so careless?'

'I *told* you I didn't understand. And I was in a hurry to finish the report, which, incidentally, *you* should have done. So I told her that every woman in the village knew she could come to me. And I would help. Of course I would. *You* know that.'

'So you failed to help the one person who needed your help the most.' Tariq's face was bleak.

'Are you blaming me for her disappearance?' Fareeda stared at her husband in astonishment. 'I made a mistake, but it was an accident. I didn't do it deliberately. You know how fond I was – am – of the girl.'

'I know, I know, I'm sorry,' said Tariq. He made a small, impotent gesture. 'I'm not blaming you. Kaneez?' he asked, switching to Punjabi. 'Who did you say was the father of Rani's child?'

'I don't know,' Kaneez mumbled into her shawl.

'This is no time for prudishness,' said Tariq. 'If we are to find the girl, we must know everything. She may have run away with him.'

'I've *told* you, I don't know who he was,' repeated Kaneez. 'She wouldn't tell me. I asked, but she wouldn't say.'

'But if this cad has already left the village, how would she run away with him?' asked Fareeda. 'Unless he came back to fetch her?'

Tariq shook his head. 'Even if he'd thought of marrying her, I think, once his family found out, they'd ensure it wouldn't happen. Assuming the story is true, he's probably been bundled off somewhere distant. I don't think he'd come back to fetch her. If he'd had that sort of nerve, he would've married her in the first place. I was asking because I thought his family might be able to throw some light on her disappearance.'

'Still, I wonder who it was?' mused Fareeda. 'Kaneez, have you any ideas?'

'I never imagined she could do such a thing,' sobbed Kaneez.

'It could have been anyone,' said Tariq. 'From Rani's account, it sounds as if he's young. I suspect he is also relatively well off. Or so it seems from the way his people drove her off. We could ask around. Her school friends or girls from the village may know something. Maybe she had confided in someone, or perhaps they'd been seen together. Someone's sure to know something. I can't believe she told no one.'

'No, please, please,' Kaneez moaned. 'I don't want it coming out. The girl will be ruined. We will be shamed. Have pity on me.'

'But I thought you'd already asked around?'

'I have, but I haven't told them that Rani's been missing for two days,' mumbled Kaneez. 'All I said was that she was late for some work I wanted her to do and, if they saw her, could they ask her to come home quickly. All of today I've been here, waiting for you. They think she's with me. Her reputation is all she's got. Once that goes, she may as well be dead.'

'How can you say that?' burst out Fareeda. 'The girl may be in danger, and all you can think of is her reputation?'

'Perhaps reputations don't matter to rich people. But that's all poor people think of,' Kaneez muttered.

'I know. I know. We'll be as discreet as we can,' promised Tariq. 'No one need know her condition. But we have to tell the police and start a proper search. With any luck, she may be at a friend's, someone you've overlooked, but we can't take any chances. You say she's been gone for two days. You've had no news of her. None of the people you've asked have seen her. A girl can't evaporate like mist without . . .' Tariq halted.

'Without what?' questioned Kaneez.

'Nothing. Have you informed my mother?'

'I haven't. At first I didn't think it was anything serious. I thought Rani was sulking somewhere. It was only after the next morning, when she hadn't returned, that I started getting worried. Then I did what I could. Asked the neighbours, Fatima . . .'

'But you say she doesn't know.'

'No.' Kaneez's eyes welled up again. 'I don't know what to tell her. Also, I'm afraid of what Mashooq will do if he finds out.'

'You will have to tell Fatima. She has to know.'

'Please, please, find Rani first,' Kaneez beseeched Tariq. 'Find her, help me, help us all. Please, I beg of you. I can't face Fatima.'

'I'll do my best.' He put an arm around the old woman.

Tariq then suggested to Kaneez that she spend the night with them at Sabzbagh. But she insisted on returning home.

'What if my girl comes home tonight and finds it empty? What will she think?' she cried. 'No, I have to go and wait for her. Your mother is also returning tomorrow, and she will wonder what's happened if I'm not there.'

'She'll find out soon enough,' Tariq remarked dryly. 'You shouldn't be alone tonight.'

'I've always been alone.' Kaneez got up and shuffled out into the cold, dark night. But she returned from the front door and, clutching Tariq's arm in a surprisingly firm grip, rasped, 'Find my child. For Allah's sake.'

Fareeda, Laila and Sara walked past the guava orchard to the convent. A brisk breeze swirled copper-coloured acacia leaves around their ankles.

'Look, Sara, the trees are full of sky,' said Laila, pointing to the bare branches of shisham and acacia trees bordering the road.

'You're such a baby,' Sara huffed, hurrying to keep up with their mother, who had quickened her pace now that they were close to the convent. 'They're not full of sky, they're naked, that's what.'

'Don't snap at your little sister,' Fareeda admonished Sara. 'She's right. You can see the sky through them now that the branches are bare.'

'Come on,' urged Sara. 'We have to go and find Rani.'

'Yes, we have to find Rani,' Laila echoed dully.

When Laila had woken that morning, everything had seemed the same – her toys and books were arranged neatly on their shelves, her amber horse was poised on the sill and she could hear Amanat humming while clipping the creeper outside her window. Laila stretched her toes out to the end of her warm bed, luxuriating in the softness of the sheets and the silken weight of her quilt. She'd been contemplating breakfast – fried egg or omelette, toast or paratha? – when suddenly a huge slab-like heaviness had descended on her chest. She had remembered the events of the night before.

Despite Bua's best attempts to put them to sleep, the girls were still awake when Fareeda and Tariq finally retired to their bedroom. Bua pleaded a headache and slipped out. Dressed in their pyjamas, the girls sat on their parents' bed, a satin coverlet over their legs.

'You're not asleep yet?' asked Fareeda.

'Where's Kaneez? Is she dead?' Laila wanted to know.

'Why should she be dead?' Tariq raised his eyebrows.

'She looked so sad, as if she wanted to die,' mumbled Laila.

'I know what you mean, darling.' Tariq took his younger daughter's hand. 'But she'll be fine. Right now, Barkat is dropping her back to Kalanpur.'

Tariq had then told the girls that Rani was missing. No one knew where she had gone, but they were all going to look for her and, before long, find her. Sara had bombarded her parents with questions. Had Rani run away? Had she left a note? Had she taken anything with her? Had she been kidnapped? Then why had she gone? While Fareeda tried to answer, Laila had sat with her head bowed, tracing the coverlet's pattern with a finger.

Tariq had got on to the telephone the next morning, and Fareeda had decided to call on the nuns. Eager to help, the girls had tagged along.

'Do you think Rani will be with Sister Clementine, Ammi?' asked Sara, tugging at her mother's shawl.

'I don't think so, but she may know something that could lead us to Rani.'

'Like what?'

'I don't know. Let's see.'

Now that they were within sight of the convent, Laila's nerve failed her. What if Sister Clementine told her mother that she had been there with Bua when Rani had first come to the church? That would get her into trouble with both Bua and Fareeda. But she couldn't not have come. Suppose they found Rani at the church? Then Sara would've taken all the credit.

'Ammi, I feel like going to the bathroom.' Laila stopped in the middle of the path.

'Can you hold on for a bit?' Fareeda asked. 'You can use the bathroom at the convent. We're almost there.'

'Or else you can walk home and go there,' said Sara. 'I can go on to the convent with Ammi.'

'I'll hold on. I'll wait till I get home with you.' Laila slipped her hand into her cardigan pocket and held Hester's horse, which she had brought along with her for good luck. It fitted neatly in her cupped palm. Clutching it tight, she said a silent prayer for both Bua and Rani.

'Please, Allah, let Bua not be angry with me, and let Rani be safe, and let us – no, me – find her. Thank you.' She debated whether to say 'over and out' like they did in war films, but then she remembered that the war hadn't started yet.

Laila followed her mother and sister through the gate.

There were fewer leaves on the trees since Laila's last visit, and the dahlias had died. A man in a lungi and kurta was sweeping dead leaves off the path. He raised a hand in greeting.

'Is Sister Clementine in?' Fareeda asked.

'Yes, I'll go call her.'

A few moments later, Sister Clementine came hurrying round the hedge that separated the church from the convent. She looked as if she had been disturbed at breakfast. There were breadcrumbs on her habit front.

'Good morning, Sister.' Fareeda smiled, turning on the charm. 'I apologize for dropping in without warning. I hope we didn't disturb you.'

'No, no,' Sister Clementine reassured her. She'd been anxious when she'd heard of Fareeda's unannounced arrival, but her reserve melted away under the warmth of her smile. 'And you've brought the girls also. My, how they've grown up and all.' She beamed at her visitors. 'Just like my dahlias.'

'Thank you, Sister. I hope you are well.'

'Me? Oh, yes. Very much, thank you.' A breeze lifted the edge of the nun's wimple. Laila craned her neck for a glimpse of the shaven head that Bua had told her all nuns had. 'They leave a fringe all around, like reeds around a pond, but shave off the rest. Clean, and holy it becomes then,' she'd said. The nun smoothed down her wimple and, mistaking Fareeda's formal enquiry after her health as genuine interest, broke into a stream of delighted chatter.

'My sister, elder by six years, name of Sharmila, she is having three children and her eldest, you know, Padma, is now eighteen, bless her, and is getting married. Imagine! When I last saw her she was a toddler, only. Such big, big eyes she had. Nice Catholic boy she's marrying. Has a cycle-repair shop. Very respectable and good, my sister writes. Never drinks, never gambles, never does anything,' she gushed. 'But best thing is, they've invited me for the wedding. Sharmila says it won't be same without my blessings. Just before Christmas it will be. And then there will be Christmas at home. Mother Superior is returning next week, and I'm going to ask her if I may go. Haven't been home for fourteen years. Imagine! But I can still smell the banana groves, you know. And taste the sea breezes and the coconut.'

'I do hope you can make it, Sister,' Fareeda said. 'It will be nice for you to go home after such a long time and see your family again.'

'It *has* been a long time, too long.' Sister Clementine blinked. 'Only I am knowing how long. When my mummy and daddy died, the Lord bless their souls, I couldn't go. I was needed here, Mother Superior said. For His work.' She gulped back the tears. 'I'm not complaining, Mrs Azeem. The Lord has been kind to me. But I do so long to go home.' She pressed a handkerchief to her quivering lips.

'I'm sure you will, Sister.' Fareeda patted her arm. 'I wonder if I could have a word with you? Preferably somewhere private.' Fareeda flicked a glance at the sweeper.

'A word? With me? Oh.' Sister Clementine's face fell. There was an edge to Fareeda's voice that made her uneasy. Though Fareeda had couched it as a request, Sister Clementine recognized an order when she heard one. This wasn't a friendly call, after all. Fareeda hadn't come to apologize for her high-handedness. Looking at them properly, she saw that Fareeda's demeanour was grave, and the girls also looked doleful. Sister Clementine dabbed her forehead with her handkerchief. She noticed the crumbs on her front and brushed them away impatiently. She wished she hadn't babbled on about her niece's wedding. Sister Clementine felt disappointed and resentful. Recalling Fareeda's past rudeness, she had a good mind to tell her to come back and discuss whatever she wanted with Mother Cecilia when she returned. It would serve her right to be thrown out of the convent like she'd been thrown out of Fareeda's house.

'Sister?'

'Oh? Yes, all right,' she said wearily. 'Please to follow me.' Sister Clementine led the way into her home. She opened the front door and showed them into a large, spotlessly clean room, bare save for a square table with four canvas chairs set around it. A sheet of plastic patterned with poinsettia and pineapples covered the table. Thin nylon curtains hung in another doorway and there was the clatter of crockery beyond. Someone was clearing away breakfast. There was a strong smell of burnt toast.

Sister Clementine pulled out a chair. It squeaked on the tiled floor.

'Please sit,' she said.

'Now, Sister,' began Fareeda, taking the chair opposite Sister Clementine's. 'You came to visit me not long ago. I'm afraid I was busy at the time and didn't hear you out. I'd very much like to know what it was that you came to tell me.'

Sister Clementine glanced at Fareeda. She looked elegant, assured in her olive-green shalwar kameez and biscuit-coloured shawl embroidered with a green paisley border. Aside from a slender gold watch and a diamond ring, she wore no jewellery. But a vein throbbed at the base of her throat, and Sister Clementine could tell from the rhythmic smack of the plastic tablecloth against her calf that Fareeda was shaking her foot under the table. The older girl chewed on her thumbnail. The younger girl stared at the floor.

Sister Clementine got the feeling that Laila was nervous and did not want to meet her eyes. Sister Clementine was distinctly uneasy as well. What would Mother Cecilia have done in her place? She wouldn't offer an apology, that was for sure. Instead she would force one from Fareeda. After all, it was *she* who had been rude. Pushing her out of her house like that! And in front of Jacob also.

Fareeda moved her hand, and Sister Clementine noticed the sparkle of the solitaire in her ring as it caught the light. Her shawl looked soft in a silky, woolly, expensive kind of way. Sister Clementine was daunted by their differences. Forcing an apology was out of the question. But she could ask a question. Answer her question with one of her own.

'Mrs Azeem . . .' No, that didn't sound right. Too high-pitched, almost like a squeal. Clearing her throat, Sister Clementine began again. 'Mrs Azeem, I will answer your questions, but will you tell me something first? Why do you want to know? Has anything happened?'

Looking Sister Clementine squarely in the face, Fareeda said, 'Although you mentioned no names that day, I suspect, Sister – but do correct me if I'm wrong – that you came to see me about a particular girl. And the girl in question was Rani? My mother-in-law's maid's granddaughter? Am I right?'

Sister Clementine nodded. Fareeda had assumed the role of interrogator again, but there was something steely in her eyes, which the nun found hard to face down.

'Am I also right in believing that the girl came to you a while before your visit to me and asked you to help her?'

'Um, yes.'

'And you didn't?'

'How could I?' Sister Clementine burst out. 'What the girl wanted . . . what she asked . . .' She glanced helplessly at the girls. Why had Fareeda brought her daughters if she wanted to talk shameless talk? 'It is against my faith. Human life is sacred to us. Particularly an innocent baby's.'

'Of course, of course,' Fareeda murmured. 'But you didn't refer her to anyone else? You didn't ask her to come to me, for instance?'

'I tried. But would she listen? Like a mad dog, she was. Howling and shrieking, all sweaty and shivery. Came here in the middle of our service, banging on the door in front of the whole congregation. I told her to go home and tell her mummy, and she'd get her married and then we'd be happy to do her case. Delivery, I mean. But she wouldn't listen. Just kept repeating that they'd kill her.'

'*Who* would kill her?' Fareeda's voice sharpened. 'Did she say?'

'How am I supposed to know the comings and goings in other people's homes? What's it to me? I mind my own business. Besides, why you don't ask *her* who's going to kill whom? Why are you asking me?' Sister Clementine crossed her arms over her chest.

'I can't, Sister. The girl has disappeared. She hasn't been seen for three days, and we are very worried. That's why I've come to you.'

'Disappeared? Blessed Mother!' Sister Clementine clutched her throat. 'Are you sure she hasn't gone visiting or something? Young girls can be careless, no? Once, I remember, as a young girl, no more than your big child here, I went to see my auntie and didn't tell my mummy. So worried she was, when I got back that evening, you should have seen . . .'

'I don't think she's gone visiting, Sister,' Fareeda interrupted. 'In her condition I doubt if she'd go off on a jaunt. Her grandmother's made enquiries. She's not been seen in the neighbouring villages. Which is why I came to you. To see if you could suggest something that we might have missed.'

Sister Clementine pulled out her hanky again.

'With my hand on the Holy Bible, I can swear to you, she hasn't been here after that one time. Later, only, your Bua persuaded me to speak to you. She said it was best if I told you. "Let them deal with Rani," she said to me. "The girl is like family to them. No good for you or I to get mixed up in this. They might be angry at first with us for knowing, but they'll fix it inside, without anyone knowing on outside."

'I was not agreeing at first. Head Mother is not here and too much of responsibility is on me. Also, I don't want to poke my nose in other people's dirty business. So I said no. But Bua said if it comes out you knew and did nothing, think how much headache it will be then. So I said, "All right, Baba. I'll go, for the girl's sake." So I went to tell you to help the girl, but you were not in listening mood.' The nun looked accusingly at Fareeda. 'Instead, you shooed me out without so much as a glass of water. But I did my duty. My conscience is clean.'

'*Bua* told you to speak to me? She knew about Rani?' Fareeda's forehead creased as she tried to digest this information.

'Oh, yes, she was here that Sunday when the girl came.' The nun nodded at Laila. 'Ask her, *she* was here too. She spoke to her.'

Stunned, Fareeda turned to her crimson-faced daughter.

'Laila, is this true?'

With her eyes glued to the table, Laila nodded.

'Why didn't you tell me?'

'Because I promised Bua I wouldn't tell you that she'd brought me to the church,' Laila mumbled. 'I wanted to see the inside of the church and hear the songs on the piano. We didn't know Rani was going to come here.'

'And Bua? Why didn't she tell me?' Fareeda's voice was harsh.

Realizing that she had blundered, Sister Clementine now hastened to limit the damage she had caused.

'Bua was wanting very much to tell, with her whole heart,' she explained. 'But she was afraid – of your shouting. You would ask why girl hadn't come to you. Why she had come to us. "How they will take it coming from me, a children's ayah only?'' Bua said. So I told you in her place. We did our best, but it was *you* who wouldn't listen. God was watching.'

'Since then you've had no contact with Rani?'

'None.'

'And Bua? Has she had any news of her?'

Sister Clementine stared at the plastic tablecloth. 'I am not knowing,' she muttered.

'Sister?' There was a note of warning in Fareeda's voice.

The nun looked up, indignant. 'I told you, Mrs Azeem, she hasn't come here and I haven't been there. So how could I be knowing?'

But Fareeda recalled that Bua had been to Kalanpur since then. She had accompanied Laila there on the day she'd had her last headache. Fareeda asked Laila, 'Has Bua seen Rani again?'

Laila was aware of the nun's discomfiture and Sara's stare. But, most of all, she was conscious of her mother's stern eyes boring into her skull. She daren't look up in case her mother locked eyes with her. She would pull the truth out of her throat then, as easily as reeling in a bucket from a well.

Fareeda reached across the table to lay a hand on Laila's arm. 'Laila, listen to me, darling,' she said in a gentler voice. 'It is very, very important for you to tell me the truth now.' She squeezed Laila's arm lightly. 'If you keep anything from me, anything at all, it might mean we will never see Rani again. Do you understand?'

Laila's eyes flew to Fareeda's face. 'Never see Rani again?'

'Never, never, never,' shouted Sara, resentful of her younger sister's critical role in this gripping drama. While she'd been studying and doing gym and homework in Lahore, Laila had not only kidnapped her friendship with Rani but had also been mixing with grown-ups and attending church. 'And it will be all *your* fault!'

'Sara, stop it!' said Fareeda.

'Is it my fault that Rani has gone?' Laila asked in a small voice. 'I promise I didn't tell anyone our secret.'

'What secret, darling?' Fareeda leaned closer to Laila.

'That she was going to get married,' Laila whispered. 'And that she was embroidering her bed sheets with purple roses and planning to buy gold shoes like a bride's, and a water set, and that he was going to ask Kaneez properly for her . . .'

'*Who* was going to ask Kaneez properly?'

'The man Rani was going to marry.'

'Who was she going to marry? *Who?*'

Laila looked around the table at the three pairs of eyes trained on her. 'I don't know.' She shook her head slowly. 'She didn't tell me. She was about to, but then Bua walked in and so she didn't say. I asked you to let me go to Kalanpur so I could ask her, but you said I was to play in Sabzbagh,' Laila wailed. 'Dadi said when a girl gets married she has to go and live in her husband's house, no matter how far. Has Rani gone to live with her husband in another country?'

'No, darling, I don't think so,' Fareeda said softly. 'But tell me, does Dadi also know about Rani? Her wedding, I mean?'

'No. Rani only told me and made me promise on everyone's life that I wouldn't tell anyone. Not you, not Bua, not Sara, not anyone,' sobbed Laila. 'I crossed my heart and hoped to die. So I couldn't tell. Not ever. But now I've broken my promise and we'll all die.'

'Don't worry. You've only broken it for her safety. Not for anything else, so it doesn't count.' Fareeda patted her hand.

Suddenly, Laila remembered that Mashooq also knew about Rani's wedding. Rani had told him. He didn't know the name of the man either, but he *did* know when she was getting married, except that he'd forgotten the exact date. Laila wondered whether she should mention it to her mother. She peeped at Fareeda from under her lashes. Her mother's lips were set in a straight line, and her jaw was clenched. Perhaps she'd better not mention Mashooq. Besides, Fareeda hadn't asked her if anyone else knew. All she'd asked was whether her grandmother knew – a question she had answered truthfully.

'See, Mrs Azeem? Bua didn't know.' Sister Clementine couldn't keep the triumph out of her voice. 'She wasn't deceiving you. She herself didn't know.'

'But Bua knew,' Laila explained. 'She told me that Rani had been a naughty girl. She said Rani had broken a jug in Dadi's house and told no one. That's why she had come here to Sister Clementine to ask for forgiveness in the church.'

Fareeda and the nun exchanged a look. Fareeda rose from the table. She smoothed down her shirt and beckoned to the girls. 'I'm sorry to have troubled you, Sister. Thank you for all your help.'

'No trouble, Mrs Azeem,' said Sister Clementine, relieved that her interrogation was over. 'Oh, look at me.' She slapped her forehead. 'I haven't even offered you a cup of tea. What a junglee you must think me!'

'Please don't worry,' Fareeda assured her. 'We'll come again. Or better still, you must come and see us, when all this has blown over. I'm sorry I was so short with you that day. You must allow me to make amends.'

'Oh, surely, surely. But let me know what happened to the girl, yes? I'll be waiting and praying.'

'You do that, Sister. Pray for her.' Fareeda touched the nun's shoulder lightly.

'One last thing.' Sister Clementine placed a restraining hand over Fareeda's. 'They are saying there's going to be a war with India. Hundred per cent. Is that true? If so, how will I go home?'

'I don't know, Sister. All I can say is, pray. Pray for our countries, pray for yourself and pray for Rani. Pray for everyone's safe homecoming.'

'*Especially* Rani's,' added Sara meaningfully.

'Yes, but you are rich and important.' Sister Clementine clutched at Fareeda's hand. 'Please help me get home. If anyone can do it, you can.'

A refusal was on the tip of Fareeda's tongue, but when she saw the longing in Sister Clementine's face, she averted her eyes.

'Er, we'll see, Sister. We'll see.'

'That means, yes. No?' Sister Clementine's eyes sought Fareeda's.

'As I said, Sister, we'll see.' Fareeda removed her hand from the nun's grasp.

Fareeda was preoccupied on the way home. She seemed unaware that the girls were finding it difficult to match her pace. Trotting by her side, Laila asked, 'It wasn't the jug, was it?'

'What?' Fareeda asked absently.

'Rani didn't come to the church for the broken jug, did she? She wouldn't have been so upset just over a jug. She came for something else. What was it?'

'Hmm?'

'Why did she come?' Laila was running now, as she increased her pace to match her mother's.

'I'll tell you later.' Fareeda did not look at her daughter.

'Please, Ammi.'

'I said "later".' Fareeda sounded annoyed.

'Nobody tells me anything.' Laila gave up trying to keep up with her mother and fell back with Sara. Her head was flooded with images from the past few days – Rani bedraggled and desperate, banging at the church door; Bua's frigid disapproval in Kaneez's quarter; Sister Clementine following Fazal into the house, looking back at Bua over her shoulder; Rani embroidering purple roses; Mashooq peering over the hedge; Kaneez howling in the night; Rani framed in a doorway with her finger pressed to her lips.

She knew there was a mystery there. If she were a good detective, she would be able to solve it. George had gone missing once in *Five Fall into Adventure*, and Dick, Anne and Julian had found her. But there were three of them and she was only one. With Rani gone, she wasn't even the Terrific Two, but just Laila Azeem, eight and a half, Class 4B, Convent of the Blessed Virgin, Lahore, Pakistan.

Sara saw that her sister's shoulders were hunched and that her neck drooped as if it were too fragile for the weight of her head. Sara knew what it felt like to be on the receiving end of Fareeda's frigid disapproval. Their mother seldom raised her voice at them, but she had a way of looking disappointed, let down even, that was designed to make the girls feel rotten about themselves. Given the choice, they'd much rather have a scolding than this silent censure. But they were never given the choice. Sara put an arm round Laila and squeezed her shoulder.

'Don't worry. It wasn't your fault,' she whispered. 'I know what it feels like to have Ammi cross with you. But Rani will turn up.'

Laila gave her a grateful look.

'Thanks. Do *you* know why Rani came to Sister Clementine?'

Sara shrugged. 'Nope. Something shameful to do with marriage, maybe. But one thing I *do* know, Aba will find her, no matter what.'

Laila was less confident of Tariq's ability to locate Rani. So far, he seemed as clueless as anyone else. She hoped Sara was right.

16

Tariq was about to climb into the car when his daughters and wife reached home. The girls dashed to their father, demanding to know where he was going.

'To Kalanpur.'

'To look for Rani?' they chorused. 'Can we come too?'

'Not today.'

'But I haven't even seen Dadi yet,' Sara complained.

'I'll take you tomorrow. I promise. Now run along. I'm getting late.'

'Any news? Any luck with the police?' asked Fareeda, once the girls were out of earshot.

'None. They haven't heard of a girl who answers Rani's description. But I've reported it to all three police stations – here, Colewallah, as well as Hisar. The local inspector – decent chap by the name of Feroze – said he'd check personally in Sawan, Bridgebad and other villages across the canal. And I called the colonel in Colewallah. Since he has all those soldiers at his disposal, I thought he might turn up something that the police may well miss.'

'I hope he was civil?'

'Oh, yes.' Tariq grimaced. 'Very businesslike and to the point. Thankfully, he didn't probe too much. What about you? Learnt anything useful?'

'Nothing about Rani's whereabouts. Anything specific you want to chase up in Kalanpur?'

'A couple of things. One is to see my mother and talk it over with her. Then to check whether Kaneez has really alerted anyone or if she's still trying to keep it quiet. I also want to make enquiries in the neighbouring villages. Run some basic checks and start a proper search. I'll see if I can lay my hands on a photograph of Rani for a newspaper or television ad – should things come to that.' Tariq lowered himself into the seat beside Barkat. 'What's your plan for the afternoon?'

'I have some unfinished business with Bua, and then I'm going to question all the servants and also call a couple of busybodies from the village – perhaps that awful mullah as well – and see if anyone knows anything.'

'Do remember Kaneez's sensitivities, won't you?'

'I won't broadcast Rani's condition, if that's what you mean,' said Fareeda stiffly.

After lunch, Fareeda spent a long time closeted in the dining room with Bua. The girls were sent out into the garden, where they pondered on what was transpiring indoors.

'I hope Bua won't be cross with me,' said Laila. She sat cross-legged on the grass, watching Sara stand shakily on her swing.

'Don't worry, she won't. I'll tell her that it was Sister Clementine and not you who ratted on her,' Sara replied in her best elder sister voice.

'Thanks, but still . . . I hope Ammi's not going to scold her too much.'

'Bua will be OK.'

But Bua did not feel OK as she stood on wobbly legs facing her enraged employer. Fareeda sat at the head of the polished dining table, her reflection in it clear as a mirror. It seemed to Bua as if she was under attack from two Fareedas.

'You work for me. Do you understand?' Fareeda had not raised her voice, but it was sharp as a scythe. Her words came hissing and whistling at Bua across the length of the table like flung plates. 'Your first loyalty is to *me*. Anything like this happens, you come to *me*. You *don't* plot and plan behind my back.'

'I didn't plot . . .' Bua's words were cut off by another barrage from Fareeda.

'Is this how you repay my trust?' The veins in Fareeda's neck were taut. 'By taking matters in your inept hands, by keeping secrets from me, by sending emissaries to me? Who do you think you are?'

'I was afraid you would be angry,' Bua wailed. 'I wasn't to know the girl was going to disappear. If I'd known, I would have told you, I would have told her grandmother, I would even have told the Sahib. But how was I to know?'

'You've made me look like a fool in front of my mother-in-law,' said Fareeda. 'She'll find out the girl came here, pregnant, frightened and desperate for help, and we let her slip away. And why? Because a stupid ayah decided to play stupid games.'

'Sister Clementine tried to tell you, but you wouldn't . . .'

'What is Sister Clementine to me? Why should I listen to her? If you'd had the sense to come to me yourself, the girl would be sitting safely at home. No one would have known a thing. Now, thanks to *you*, the news is all over the district, and we don't know what's happened to her – where she is, who's got her, whether she's alive or dead even. Who will take the blame if we can't find her, Bua?'

'Oh, no, no, don't say that,' Bua snivelled. 'Sahib will find her. She'll be all right. You'll see.'

'I've always trusted you. It hurts and angers me to think that you did not trust me.'

'I did, I do, I promise. Forgive me. I made a mistake.' Bua held out her hands to Fareeda, palms pressed together, begging forgiveness. 'You can't doubt my loyalty. I've loved the girls like my own. One is my heart, the other my liver. Please don't say you don't trust me.'

'Go. Go to the girls.' Fareeda made a weary gesture dismissing Bua. 'If you hear anything about Rani now, you are to come to me *immediately*. Is that clear?'

When Bua reached the girls in the garden, her eyes were swollen and puffy. In mute sympathy, the girls went up to her and put their arms around her.

'Laila didn't tell Ammi about Rani coming to the church, Bua,' said Sara. 'Sister Clementine did.'

Bua received the news in silence.

'I told Ammi that it was *I* who wanted to go to the church, to see the inside and hear the piano. That it wasn't your fault that I was there that Sunday,' added Laila. 'I'm sorry if Ammi was cross with you. She was cross with me too.'

'Very cross,' confirmed Sara. 'But it is Ammi's fault too that Rani's missing. If she'd listened to Sister Clementine, none of this would have happened.' Though Sara did not know exactly what Sister Clementine had come to tell Fareeda, she had pieced together enough to guess that her mother's refusal to listen to the nun had made things worse.

Bua pulled the girls to her and kissed their foreheads. 'May Jesus bless you. You are good girls. Feeling for your old, wronged ayah. Come, let's go to the kitchen. Your mother is busy in the house. Doesn't want any noise.'

In the kitchen, Rehmat sat cross-legged in his swivel chair, pulling on a cigarette. Fazal was on the bench. When the girls entered with Bua, Fazal vacated the bench for them and pulled up another chair for himself. Both men noticed Bua's puffy face but did not comment. The kitchen smelt of warm milk. Placing the hookah before Bua, Rehmat went over to the hearth. He returned with three thick pottery mugs full of steaming tea.

'Here, have it with biscuits.' He proffered an old Ovaltine tin to the girls. 'Dip them in and nibble the soft bits.'

'Aren't you going to have some tea also?' asked Laila.

'We've had.' Fazal held up his empty mug. 'Strange business this, the girl disappearing like a wisp of smoke, no, Rehmat?'

Rehmat nodded. 'But funny things happen to young girls.'

'What funny things?' asked Sara.

'Some get possessed by jinns, others by evil spirits. Maybe she's run off with a jinn. When Bibi asked me today if I knew anything, I told her as much.'

'What did she say?' asked Fazal.

'She told me not to talk rot.' The cook sniffed. 'But the Others don't know about jinns. Just because they don't see them, they think they don't exist.'

Fazal chuckled. 'Be thankful she didn't say worse. When she questioned me, I said even my guardian angels had no idea. That's the truth. How should we know what's happened to her? We're not responsible for the girl's safety. Ask Kaneez, she ought to know. This Kaneez, though, what a wretch she is. The minute I saw her face yesterday, I knew it was bad news. First her damned son-in-law comes and makes trouble, and then she howls the place down like a cat whose kittens have drowned. Do you know,' he said, addressing himself to Bua, 'until the Others' arrival, she just sat on the front doorstep weeping for three hours? Not one word could we get out of her, except, "Hai, my kismet, my kismet."

'We asked her to come in, but she wouldn't budge. Did she want water? No reply. Stubborn as a mule she is. We had to call Amanat and lift her bodily and bring her in, otherwise she would have frozen by the time all of you came. And the Others would have blamed us. Missing girl is missing girl, but we would have been in jail for Kaneez's murder. So proud she is, as if she were an ambassador's secretary. Won't talk to you straight. Serves her right if the girl's run off with someone.' Fazal snorted.

'Touch your ears, Fazal, and beg God's forgiveness,' shouted Bua, slamming down her mug. 'May no evil enter a house with young girls. You have daughters of your own.'

'And you shouldn't make fun of Kaneez either.' Sara rose to the maid's defence.

'Nor of Rani,' added Laila.

'He's not making fun of them,' placated Rehmat. 'We are simply trying to understand what happened. Bua, do you know? When Bibi asked, I blamed the jinns because I didn't know what else to say. It's not nice to talk about unmarried girls, but I wonder if there was a young man involved?' Rehmat gave Bua a sidelong look.

'Shame on you for even suggesting!' Bua glared at the cook. 'Have you ever heard any such thing about Kaneez or, for that matter, Fatima, that you feel you can talk such dirty talk about Rani? And she living in the shadow of Sardar Begum's house! You think young men can come and go as they like there? You think it's a hotel, or, or . . . worse?'

'Allah forbid, Bua. Whoever suggested such a thing?' Rehmat backtracked hastily.

'No one, no one,' added Fazal. 'No question, Kaneez is stubborn and standoffish, but no one can doubt her character. Fatima also is same. Still, I wonder what happened to Rani? Three whole days she's been gone now.'

'Why should you wonder?' barked Bua. 'People fall down wells all the time. They get abducted, lose their memories and drift off somewhere, have accidents. But none of this will happen to her. You'll see. Tariq Sahib will find her. He knows everything and everybody in the whole district, no, the whole country. He has the police, the babus, the whole army in his pocket. When Bibi asked me, that's what I said. "Just you wait and see," I said.'

'No doubt he's a man of influence and courage,' agreed Rehmat. 'He should have been a general in Dhaka. Then we would have seen the Indians run like frightened girls.'

'I don't think he likes wars,' said Sara. 'He says he doesn't believe in killing men.'

Fazal spoke. 'That's true. That's his one problem. Too weak to kill. Not like General Latif, in whose house I worked in Rawalpindi. Now he was a soldier all right. Slayed ten fully armed Hindus – bristling with machine-guns, grenades, knives, pistols, even an atom bomb – in the '65 war, with his bare hands. He used to say to me, "Fazal, you should have been a soldier. With your bearing and physique, you are wasted waiting at tables." But I replied, "General Sahib, I go straight to heaven for waiting on a man such as you."' Fazal looked around for approbation, but when none came, he sighed and asked, 'How's Barkat's son doing? I don't like to ask him.'

'His wife says there's been no news,' volunteered Sara, who had already made a quick trip to the servants' quarters to announce her return. 'She's very anxious.'

'Must be,' said Rehmat. 'I heard on the radio that even Yahya Khan can't get through to General Niazi. The Hindus, blast them, have cut all lines of communication.'

'Does that mean we've lost?' breathed Laila.

'The war hasn't even started yet, Lailu,' said Rehmat. 'But General Niazi says if the Indians want Dhaka, they will have to drive their tanks over his chest. He will never surrender.'

'Spoken like a true soldier, and a true Muslim,' declared Fazal.

The sky was still streaked with pink when the camouflaged army truck came to a halt on the canal road at six-thirty the next morning. A posse of soldiers sprang out of the tarpaulin-covered back, blowing on their hands and stamping their feet against the biting cold. At the sergeant's whistle, they quickly fell into a neat column on the road. At his second command, they were off, jogging as one.

The sun's rays struck the canal, turning the water to a metallic shimmer. Frost spiked its grassy banks. The bare branches of acacia and shisham trees trailed in the muddy water, trapping the odd discarded plastic bag and fallen leaves floating on its surface.

In the branches of one such tree, a soldier in the front saw a patch of sky blue. It was entangled in one of the bigger boughs, quite close to the bank. What was it? Intrigued, the soldier looked again. It was definitely cloth. Only cloth would balloon up like that. He had jogged abreast of the tree now and had a better view. He peered through the tangle of branches and saw a slim bare arm, only half covered by the blue cloth caught in a branch.

'There's someone in the canal!' the soldier cried. Breaking ranks with his company, he raced to the bank. He could see not only an arm now but also a torso, face down, just below the surface of the water. It looked as if it was a woman's. Her hair was long and loose, and fanned out in the water like the fronds of an underwater plant. He shouted over his shoulder for help.

The soldiers freed the girl from the branch's rough embrace and lifted her out of the canal. Gently, they laid her down on the grass. They checked her pulse, then smoothed her wet hair off her face and saw that she was young. A soldier shrugged off his khaki sweater and wrapped it around her. At the sergeant's instruction, they laid her in the back of the truck. The soldiers then jumped in and drove away.

The call came late that evening. Sprawled on the sitting-room floor, Sara and Laila were playing Ludo. Tariq and Fareeda sat listening to the radio. The telephone jangled in the bedroom. A moment later, Fazal was at the door.

'Sahib, it's Colonel Butt's orderly calling from the cantonment. The colonel wishes to speak to you.'

Tariq flung down his magazine and left the room. After a second's hesitation, Fareeda followed. The girls looked up from their game.

'You stay here.' Fareeda shut the door firmly behind her.

Tariq sat on the edge of the bed with the receiver to his ear. Fareeda sat down beside him.

'Yes, Colonel, I understand. Where was she found?'

The line crackled with static and, though Fareeda strained to listen, she could not catch the colonel's words.

'Right. No, no, I can come right away,' said Tariq. He paused, then said, 'Sorry, I didn't catch that?'

Tariq's knuckles gleamed white as his grip tightened on the telephone.

'Are you sure?' he asked. 'I'll be with you in forty-five minutes.' He replaced the receiver on the cradle.

'Have they found her?'

'Yes. Yes, they've found her. They fished her out of the canal this morning.'

'Is she . . . ? I mean, she isn't . . . dead, is she?' whispered Fareeda.

'She is.' Tariq stared at the floor. His voice was flat, tone-less. 'Rani is dead. They found her body. The colonel thinks it's Rani. It's a young girl, about sixteen or so with hazel eyes and dark brown hair. They want me to identify the . . . the body.'

'It may not be her. I mean, she's not the only girl of that age with light eyes. And why on earth should she be in the canal? It could be anyone, anyone at all. Couldn't it? I mean, just because a teenage girl has been found . . .' babbled Fareeda.

Tariq turned his face slowly to Fareeda's. The resignation she saw there silenced her.

'When are you going?' she whispered.

'Now.'

The girls looked up as Fareeda re-entered the sitting room.

'Where's Aba gone?' questioned Sara with a searching stare.

'To Colewallah. For some work.'

'So late?'

'Yes, so late,' Fareeda snapped. She swallowed and began again. 'It was something urgent to do with, er, the factory. Oh, look, you're playing Ludo. Can I join in?'

17

Colewallah cantonment was the size of an estate. Despite the lateness of the hour, the sentries on duty were alert and saluted smartly as Tariq's car drove through the tall, spiked gates. The Zephyr glided past the officers' mess, which was fronted by a wide veranda. The walls were hung with an array of silver military plaques glinting in fluorescent light. Potted plants as keen and alert as the sentries stood in orderly lines on the veranda.

On they drove, past playing fields, parade grounds and residential bungalows, behind spacious gardens to the small military hospital at the other end of the cantonment. At the sight of this well-ordered affluence, Tariq could never check the disparaging comments which flew out of his mouth.

'Look at it! Just look at this obscene spread. This bloody army's sucked the country dry.'

This time, he said nothing.

He was shown into the hospital's reception. It was a small room with photographs of past military doctors on the walls. They looked identical, all with neatly clipped moustaches and short spiky hair. An orderly informed him that the colonel was on his way. Tariq looked at his watch. It was ten-fifteen. Perhaps his journey had been in vain. Perhaps it was not Rani, as Fareeda had suggested, but some other girl lying somewhere in this hospital. He hoped it was. But he knew in the pit of his stomach that it wasn't.

The door swung open and Colonel Butt entered, followed by a white-coated young man. The colonel was still in uniform. He wore a thick khaki sweater over his shirt. He shook Tariq's hand and introduced him to his companion.

'This is Captain Mushtaq. He is our doctor here. Mr Tariq Azeem of Sabzbagh. Shall we, Captain?'

The doctor led the way down a short corridor to a double door at the end. He slid back the bolt. A strong smell of formaldehyde wafted out. There were four empty hospital beds lined up against a wall and what looked like an operating table mounted on wheels in one corner. A shrouded form lay on the table.

Now that he was actually here, Tariq faltered. He stopped in the doorway while the doctor and colonel went over to the table. When Tariq did not join them, the colonel looked up enquiringly. Tariq approached them slowly, forcing himself to place one foot in front of the other. The captain lowered the sheet, and Tariq gazed down on Rani's still, bruised face. Her nose looked broken and her blue shirt was torn at the neck. Tariq noticed a blade of grass in her loose chestnut hair. He removed it gently. Her hair was silky to the touch.

He shut his eyes and saw another Rani. A one-year-old Rani, astraddle her father's shoulders at Kalanpur. With cheeks like pink grapefruit, and two tiny teeth. Her dimpled hands gripped fistfuls of her father's hair. Rani as a wailing toddler on the day of her mother's second marriage, her arms wrapped tight around Fatima's neck, refusing to be pried away. A six-year-old Rani with a scrubbed face and pigtails, on her first day at school. Solemn and excited in her new uniform, she was carrying a large satchel, which was empty save for a pencil and a banana. Rani, weeping over a stray kitten run over by a motorcycle. She had buried it beneath the neem tree, and for weeks afterwards, whenever he visited his mother, Tariq had noticed a marigold lying on the spot. A beaming Rani, as she was three months ago, showing him her report card and delightedly accepting a gift from Fareeda for passing her exam.

'Is this the girl, Tariq Sahib?' asked the colonel.

Not trusting himself to speak, Tariq nodded.

The colonel motioned to the doctor, and he covered Rani's face again.

'Will you come with me to my office, please?' the colonel asked Tariq. 'I have something to tell you.'

Colonel Butt's office was a square room. Looking up, Tariq noticed that the ceiling was exceptionally high. He felt as if he was sitting at the bottom of an immersion tank, waiting for the flood. Shaking his head, he made himself focus on concrete things, to tether himself to the physical world. A glass display cabinet in the right-hand corner with seven shiny sporting trophies on its top shelf and five on the bottom. A grey metal filing cabinet in the other corner. A framed map of Pakistan behind the desk. The desk clear, except for a pad of lined paper, two pens, a pencil and a ruler, all in a plastic tray. An electric bar heater. A still ceiling fan. Two tube lights.

'Tariq Sahib, this must have been hard for you.'

Tariq couldn't tell from the colonel's expressionless face whether he was genuinely sympathetic, or hostile. Either way, he told himself, he didn't care.

'I believe the girl's family has been in your service for many years.'

'Her grandmother's worked for my mother since before I was born. Where exactly along the canal did your soldiers find her?'

'Half a mile downstream of a village called Champa. I'm told it's near here.'

'I know the place.'

The colonel told him how the soldiers had found Rani's body and brought it to the cantonment. They could have taken her to Champa, which was the nearest settlement, to check if anyone could identify her. But since the suspicious death of a young girl was a sensitive matter, the sergeant on duty decided it would be safer to bring her to the cantonment and await instructions from the colonel. The colonel had been away in Lahore on official business and so he had not been informed till his return, well into the evening. Afterwards, he had spent an hour or so with Captain Mushtaq, who showed him the body, before calling Tariq.

'I regret the delay in informing you. It was most unfortunate,' said the colonel.

'It doesn't matter.' Tariq sighed wearily. 'She was already dead.'

'That much we can be certain of. However, what we *don't* know for sure is how she died. The captain doesn't think she drowned.'

'I'm sorry?'

'Drowning, he thinks, was not the cause of the girl's death,' said the colonel.

'Why?' Tariq sat up in his chair. 'I mean, how can he know?'

'The captain is a very keen doctor. He was one of the best medical students of his year. Most doctors would not have conducted a post mortem. But he did. The captain will gladly go over his findings with you. I have, in fact, requested him to wait at the hospital. As I understand it, there was no water in the girl's lungs.'

'So how did she die?'

'She has many injuries. Her jaw is broken, as is her arm, and you no doubt saw her smashed nose. But the captain puts the probable cause of death down to a blow to the head. There is considerable damage to her skull.'

Tariq stared at the trophies unseeingly. How could Rani have suffered so? Three days ago she was safe in his mother's back yard.

'Could her injuries have been caused by an accident? Say, a hit-and-run by a bus or a truck?' Tariq asked.

'Possibly. But no trucks or buses ply the canal road.'

'The accident may have taken place on the main road, which, after all, is only a quarter of a mile away, and the driver or whoever, could have brought her body to the canal and dumped it in there.' Even as Tariq voiced his theory, he realized it sounded far-fetched.

'Not very likely. If a truck driver wasn't seen running over the girl, why would he take the trouble to carry her body all the way to the canal and dump it there? And if he was seen, he'd be hell bent on getting away. She could have been knocked down by a passing car on the canal road. Rare though they are, cars do occasionally use that road. But again, why bother to throw her in the canal? In most hit-and-run cases, drivers don't even pause long enough to check whether the victim is dead, let alone move the body.'

'Could it have been suicide?' Tariq wondered aloud. 'But even if she threw herself off a height, or in front of a car, how do we explain the canal bit? And she couldn't have jumped into the canal, because, as you say, there's no water in her lungs.'

'Precisely,' said the colonel crisply. 'In any case, the girl's injuries are more consistent with an attack. Someone killed the girl and threw her body into the canal, hoping, probably, she'd be carried far downstream.'

'But why would anyone do that to Rani? She had no enemies. She was a child, barely a few years older than my daughters. Why would anyone break her jaw, her skull . . . ?' Tariq shook his head in disbelief.

'There's one other thing.' The colonel picked up a pencil from the tray and examined it closely. 'Captain Mushtaq suspects the girl had also suffered a miscarriage very recently.'

'A miscarriage?' Tariq echoed. His mind began to race. Could the father of Rani's unborn child have done this? If she had threatened to reveal his identity, he could have turned nasty. He could have come to her house, taken her off under some pretext, killed her and then dumped her body in the canal. 'Er, does the doctor know if it was a spontaneous miscarriage before her injuries, or was it brought on by them?'

The colonel seemed puzzled by the question. Then, his brow clearing, he asked, 'I take it the girl was not married?'

Tariq shook his head.

'Ah, I see. Hence your mention of suicide.' The colonel dropped the pencil back in the tray. 'Unfortunate, most unfortunate. But then these things happen. Particularly when you expose young village girls to radical influences for which they are unequipped. It confuses them. They lose their way, take wrong decisions. Fatal decisions, in some cases. And when they do, Tariq Sahib, there's no one to help them. All those who encouraged them before are nowhere when these girls most need them.'

Tariq winced. But he was too exhausted to argue or even bother to explain that Rani had never worked at his factory.

The colonel continued with a twisted smile: 'But, thankfully, reviled though we are by some, we are here to mop up the mess. She may have had a brutal death, but at least her dead body has been treated with respect.'

'My thanks to your brave boys for rescuing Rani's corpse,' retorted Tariq. 'And to you for treating it with respect. But crimes of passion like this one are common here. Have been for centuries. I don't know as yet who killed her and why, but I am ready to bet that she was a victim of her own naivety. Some ruthless, ignorant bastard took advantage of her innocence and killed her.'

The colonel received Tariq's outburst with a snort of derision. 'That's convenient! Blame the girl for her own death. "What did she die of?" "Oh, she died of innocence!" It certainly lets you off the hook, Tariq Sahib, for bringing her murderer to justice. I suppose now you will drive back to your lovely home with its leather-bound books and have a good night's sleep in your soft, warm bed for, as far as you are concerned, this girl died of natural causes.'

'I don't have to listen to this rubbish from an ignoramus like you!' spluttered Tariq, rising to his feet. 'How dare you pass judgement when you know nothing of this girl, her . . . her history or family? And, for that matter, you know still less of me . . .'

'Oh, I have your measure.' The colonel lounged back in his chair. 'You make all the correct noises about human rights, but when push comes to shove, you are too fastidious to get your hands dirty. Now, if you'll excuse me, I've had a long day. Captain Mushtaq will give you whatever information you need.'

The colonel stood up. Signalling to Tariq to precede him, he flicked the light off in his office. Outside, under the inky December sky, he turned to Tariq and said, 'The captain will be at your disposal, but if you need me, you have only to call. And I *am* sorry about the girl, Tariq Sahib.'

Tariq peered at the colonel's face to see if he could detect any traces of mockery. But it was too dark to tell. He turned on his heel and headed for the hospital.

It took an hour of Ludo to allay the girls' suspicions. Pacing the room after they'd gone to bed, Fareeda wasn't sure if she'd been entirely successful. Laila had looked anxious, while Sara had eyed her sceptically. It had been difficult to keep up the act of enforced jollity under that scrutiny. But with the girls packed off to bed, at least she could drop the pretence.

Whom had Tariq found at Colewallah cantonment? Was it Rani? But her mind refused to venture further down that bleak path. No, no, it must be someone else. A case of mistaken identity. Yes, that's what it would be. After all, the colonel had never seen Rani. How could he be so sure it was she?

Typical of him to be so presumptuous, so sure of everything.

Was that Tariq she'd heard in the driveway? She ran to the window, lifted the curtain and, cupping her hands around her eyes, stared out into the still, dark night. No, no car. She let the curtain drop and looked again at her watch. It was ten to twelve, almost two hours since he'd left. Should she call? Find out if he'd got there safely? The road could be so dark and misty at this time of night. No, of course he'd got there safely, otherwise the colonel would have called. He didn't look the type to wait patiently. Just like Sardar Begum. Oh, God, what would they tell Sardar Begum? And Kaneez? How would they break the news to Kaneez? And Fatima?

Tariq did not return for another hour. Exhausted, Fareeda had fallen asleep. But the minute she heard the creak of the bedroom door, she woke with a start.

'Tariq, is that you?' She switched on her bedside lamp.

Tariq blinked. 'I'm sorry, I didn't mean to wake you up.'

'Wake me up? I've been waiting for you all evening.' Fareeda sat up. 'What happened? Was it Rani?'

'Yes.' He sat on the bed and pulled off his shoes.

Fareeda looked down at her hands clutching the quilt. She felt as if she was choking. She leaned her head on her drawn knees and gave vent to the guilt, anxiety and grief she had been holding in check. From across the bed, Tariq watched her cry. Tired and numb, he let her weep. He dropped his shoes to the floor and turned his back on his wife. At last, Fareeda's tears subsided. Pushing her hair off her face, she reached for a tissue from her bedside table.

'Where was she found?' she asked in a nasal voice.

'About half a mile downstream of Champa. Some soldiers found her body caught in the branches of a tree overhanging the canal. They brought her to the cantonment and told the colonel. The rest you know.'

'No, I don't,' shouted Fareeda. 'How did she end up in the

canal? How long had she been dead when they found her? How did she die? I know nothing.'

'Keep your voice down. The colonel thinks she was murdered.'

'Murdered?' Her face paled. 'What do you mean, murdered?'

'She had been beaten savagely. The military doctor had done a brief inspection, but he thinks she didn't die of drowning. There was no water in her lungs.'

'Who could have killed her? And why? For God's sake, why?'

'I don't know.'

'Is that all you can say? That you don't know?' she hissed.

'Yes, that's all I can say.' Turning to face her, Tariq said carefully, 'For the last two hours, I've been looking at the broken, abused body of a girl scarcely older than my own daughter. The whole time I was there, I was thinking of what to tell her mother and her grandmother. I've been thinking of what I could have done to prevent her death. So excuse me if I can't supply the name of her murderer or his motive at your command.' Picking up his shoes, he marched into the dressing room.

When he emerged a few minutes later in his pyjamas, Fareeda was still sitting up in bed. Tariq walked over to his side of the bed, got under the covers and turned his back on Fareeda. Fareeda switched off the lamp and lay back on the pillows, staring up at the ceiling. After a few moments, she spoke out.

'I'm sorry. It must have been harrowing for you to see her like that.' Her voice was husky. 'I don't understand what's going on. When the colonel called, I couldn't believe it was Rani. When you confirmed it, I thought she must have committed suicide. And then you told me she was murdered. I . . . I don't understand. I could have saved her,' she continued, her voice breaking. 'More than you, I am to blame. Had I listened, Rani would have been alive today. It's my fault that she's dead.'

Tariq was silent for a long while, but when at last he spoke, his voice was flat. 'It's not your fault. You didn't even know she was pregnant. Had she wanted you to know, she would have come to you herself. No one knows what actually happened. Until we find out, it's pointless to speculate. Try and get some sleep. Tomorrow is going to be a long day.'

Fareeda asked, 'Where is Rani spending the night?'

'At the cantonment. Luckily it's the winter, but still they can't keep her for long. We'll have to get her body over here tomorrow.'

Before the girls awoke the next morning, Tariq and Fareeda drove over to Kalanpur to tell Kaneez and Sardar Begum. They decided to tell them the truth, because Kaneez would probably want to bathe the body herself. And if she enlisted the services of the woman who normally performed the ritual funeral bath in the village, rumours were bound to seep out like blood from a wound.

The two old ladies were in the haveli courtyard when Tariq and Fareeda arrived at Kalanpur. Sardar Begum took one look at her son's grim face and, grasping her maid by the arm, drew her down gently on the divan beside her. In halting, disjointed phrases, Tariq told them what had happened. Kaneez appeared not to have understood. She looked in confusion from husband to wife. Unable to meet her eyes, Fareeda looked away.

'Quick, someone get some water,' Tariq was shouting over his shoulder in the direction of the kitchen. He was down on his knees, beside the daybed on which Kaneez had crumpled. She looked lifeless, her face the colour of chalky dust. Sardar Begum had her head in her lap, and stroked her grooved brow.

'Kaneez,' she called softly. 'Kaneez, my dear, open your eyes.'

Even through the mist of tears and the red haze of pain that seemed to tinge the world, Fareeda was struck by the gentleness of Sardar Begum's manner. This was a side to her that Fareeda had never seen before. She watched her martinet of a mother-in-law comfort Kaneez while choking back her own tears.

'Shall I call a doctor?' Tariq asked his mother.

'No doctor, shoctor,' muttered Sardar Begum, dashing off her own tears. 'Let her at least grieve in private.'

Fareeda fetched a glass of water. Sardar Begum wet her fingers and dabbed them over Kaneez's temples and lips.

'Can you hear me, Kaneez?' The maid's eyelids flickered. She rubbed her tongue over her cracked lips and her eyes opened. For an interminable moment, she stared unseeingly at Sardar Begum's face bent over hers. And then a tidal wave of pain seemed to wash over her face. A scream rose from the pit of her stomach and echoed round and round the courtyard. Arms flailing, Kaneez tried to rise from the bed, but Sardar Begum held her down.

'Forbearance, fortitude,' she murmured over and over to the maid. 'It is Allah's will.'

Kaneez was beside herself. She tried to fight off Sardar Begum, but her mistress's grip was too strong. She had Kaneez's arms pinned to her sides. Arching her body, Kaneez threw back her head and howled, but still Sardar Begum held on. Finally, the maid's head slumped against Sardar Begum's shoulder and deep, quaking sobs wrenched her frame. Sardar Begum stroked her head and rocked her in her arms like a baby. Looking at Fareeda and Tariq over Kaneez's shoulder, she mouthed at them to fetch Fatima.

The road to Dera was a pot-holed, bumpy track bordered on either side by a thick growth of thorny bushes. The village was a cluster of mud huts around a stagnant pool. Fatima's hut was much like the rest, except for the mulberry tree in its front yard. She was draping the washing on some bushes outside her house when the Azeems drove up. Fatima had been beautiful once, with large lustrous eyes and finely etched features, but years of hardship had extinguished her beauty. Now, her cheekbones elbowed out of a gaunt, weary face. Her welcoming smile faltered when she saw their faces.

'What has happened? Is my mother all right?' she asked, wiping her damp hands on her shawl.

'Yes, she's fine, but can you come with us for a little while to Kalanpur?' asked Tariq.

A crowd of curious onlookers, consisting mainly of Fatima's neighbours and their many children, had gathered around them. A small boy of no more than five years detached himself from the crowd and came to stand close to Fatima, slinging an arm around her leg.

'Yes, but can I bring this little one with me?' she gestured to the child half hidden behind her. 'The older ones will be all right till I come back. I won't have to stay long, will I?' She looked nervously at Tariq.

'Of course you can bring him,' said Tariq. 'You can take along the older ones too if you want. There's plenty of room in the car.'

'No, they'll be fine here. Sakeena here will keep an eye on them till I come back. Won't you?' Sakeena, who had a baby balanced on one hip, nodded.

'What about Mashooq? Where is he?' asked Fareeda, looking around.

'He's not here,' replied Fatima quietly.

'Shall we go?' asked Tariq.

They spoke little on the way to Kalanpur. From his perch on his mother's lap, Fatima's child gazed solemnly at Fareeda. His elongated amber eyes reminded her of Rani.

Staring fixedly out of the window, Tariq seemed to be unwilling or unable to talk. Fatima tried to speak a couple of times but checked herself. Fareeda was thankful for that. She reached across the seat and grasped Fatima's thin, brittle hand, holding it tight till they reached Kalanpur. They escorted the mother and child into the haveli.

Tariq and Fareeda emerged ten minutes later, dismissed by Sardar Begum.

'You go home to your children,' she ordered. 'I will look after these two.' She flicked her chin at the mother and daughter, howling in each other's arms. 'You've done your bit. Now they are my responsibility.'

As soon as they reached home, Fareeda and Tariq called the girls and Bua to the sitting room and broke the news to them. They told them only that Rani's body had been found the day before in the canal. She seemed to have drowned. Even as Tariq spoke, Fareeda knew that Bua and the entire village would learn the whole story soon enough. Fareeda thought she might tell the ayah herself, but not just yet. She was too exhausted. Bua wept into her shawl, but the girls took the news in stunned silence. Laila's mouth trembled, and Sara stared down at her shoes, fiercely blinking back her tears. Fareeda tried to gather them to her, but while Sara stiffened, Laila broke away and ran out of the room. Bua made to follow her, but Fareeda called her back.

'Leave her be, Bua. She probably wants to be alone for a bit. I will go to her in a little while.'

Laila ran into her bedroom and slammed the door behind her. Dragging a stool to the door, she reached for the bolt and shot it home. She did not want anyone to find her, to comfort her with lies about how everything would be all right. She knew that nothing would be right any more. She slumped down on the bed. Her eye fell on the carom board propped up against the wall. Something was missing. The poplar switch that Rani had made for her and which usually stood by the board was gone. Suddenly it became imperative to find it.

She leapt to her feet and, throwing open her toy chest, began to toss out teddy bears, a skipping rope, dolls, a globe, a tattered kite, plastic dolls' crockery. She got to the bottom and still didn't find the switch. She flung open her wardrobe and pulled out all the clothes. It wasn't there either. She looked under the bed and behind the curtains. She swept all her precious Enid Blytons off the shelves, but still no switch. Furious, she lifted the carom board above her head and hurled it to the floor with a deafening crash. But there was no slender little poplar switch behind it either. She had lost it. She had lost that beautiful switch that Rani had made for her that day at the picnic.

Walking slowly, Rani had followed her back from the stream. Laila had been sitting on the car bonnet, lifted up there by Barkat. On seeing Rani approach, Laila had turned her face away in a deliberate snub. From the corner of her eyes, she had seen Rani's tremulous smile flicker and die on her face. Bua and the two chauffeurs had looked reproachfully at Laila, but she had told herself that she didn't care. They didn't know how horrid Rani had been to her. Wordlessly, Rani had held out the switch to Laila. But Laila had sat on her hands and tossed her head. Rani had handed the stick to Bua.

'I made it for Laila,' she'd said in a husky voice. 'But I don't think she likes it.'

'Of course she likes it,' Bua had assured Rani. 'She likes anything you make for her. And this is such a pretty stick. So nice and smooth and light.' Noticing the elder girl's quivering chin, Bua had told Laila off.

'When someone gives you a gift, you take it nicely. You don't turn up your nose like a memsahib.'

Though Laila knew she was in the wrong, she had been too

proud to apologize. Later, at home, Bua had stood the switch by the carom board. Turning her back on Bua, Laila had pretended indifference. The minute Bua had left the room, however, Laila had leapt out of bed and picked up the switch. Bua was right. Like all the things Rani made, it was beautiful, light and silky to the touch. When Laila had gone to bed that night, the switch had been clutched in her hand.

Now, surveying the devastation in her room – mounds of toys, clothes strewn all over the floor, scattered books, the gaping doors of her empty wardrobe – Laila sank to her knees. Pressing her face into the side of her bed, she wept for her lost friend.

Rani was gone. Never again would Laila hear her throaty chuckle or see those arrow-straight brows shoot across her forehead. Laila would not wear bracelets fashioned from jasmine or splash her bare feet in a cold stream. No one would tell her stories of warrior princesses or mend the broken wings of fallen birds. The lame chick would die under its upturned crate, and the single surviving bed sheet would moulder in its tin trunk, unseen, unused. Rani would never visit Lahore, never taste a tutti-frutti or see the royal mosque with the golden domes. She would not go anywhere or see anything again. Her curiosity had been extinguished, her laughter silenced. Rani was gone.

Laila's tears were salty, splashing down her face and on to her lips. Her chest ached and her eyes burned. She felt hot and hateful. Rubbing her arm across her nose, she reached into her pocket for a hanky. She found the wishing horse instead. Sara was right. The horse was just a toy after all. It was as powerless, as ignorant, as she was. It had let her down. As had her parents. They hadn't found Rani. She felt the tears rise again, like bile, in her throat. The amber horse slipped from her fingers and fell to the floor.

She had failed Rani. She had not been a good partner. Partners looked out for each other. They never let the other get lost. Or die. She had betrayed Rani. Broken her promise. Told her secrets to Fareeda. And instead of herself dying, as she had hoped – cross my heart and hope to die, she'd said – *Rani* had died. Rani had paid the price for Laila's perfidy. She wished her mother hadn't forced those confessions out of her at the convent. She wished Bua hadn't lied to her. She wished Fareeda would tell her why Rani had been so upset, why she had died. She hated her parents, she hated Bua. She wished someone would explain.

But Laila knew she would get no explanations in her home that day. They were all too fraught, too raw, to offer consolation, let alone clarification. And then she remembered. There was one person who was outside her home, who knew what had ailed Rani. She would go to her. She would demand an explanation from Sister Clementine.

Laila climbed up on to the stool once more and undid the bolt. She tiptoed along the corridor. She heard Fareeda's soft murmuring voice and Sara's sobs from behind the closed door of the drawing room. Hurrying through the dining room, she let herself into the pantry. She encountered no one. Opening the pantry door that led into the yard, Laila stepped out into the afternoon. Her heart thumping and eyes cast down, she crossed the empty yard. She walked unobserved past the vacant bench where Mashooq had lounged, past the open garage where the now dusty car was parked, past the clothes line, heavy with washing, past the vegetable patch, with its rows of lettuces, carrots and cauliflower.

Once she got to the bend in the drive, she broke into a run. She raced by the hedge where she had encountered Mashooq, past the guava orchard and up the steep incline on to the canal road. She didn't spare a look at the canal, didn't stop to toss a stone into its murky depth, or marvel at the swirls and eddies near the banks. She sped down the road, the thud of her feet and the rasp of her ragged breath loud in her ears. She encountered just a single goatherd along the way, chewing on a long stick of sugar cane. He took one look at her and hurriedly shooed his alarmed goats out of her way. She ran past him without a backward glance.

By the time Laila got to the church, her temples were pounding. At the church gate, she stopped. Doubling over, she clutched her aching sides and took huge gulps of air. She unbuttoned her damp cardigan and looked down at her socks wrinkling around her ankles. She heard Bua's voice echo in her head, 'What will the sisters think, eh, Lailu?' Defiantly, she ignored the voice and, pushing open the gate, went through. The church door was ajar, and she could hear the murmur of voices within. She wondered if it was prayer time.

Now that she was here, she had no idea how to find Sister Clementine. Nor did she know how to approach her. Could she ask directly like Fareeda had, or must she sidle up to the question, like Bua usually did? Would she have to wait till they were alone, or could she ask in front of anyone who might be there? How would Sister Clementine take it? Now at the door, she was tempted to turn back, but then she thought of the Terrific Two and stepped in.

It was dim within. She could see a couple standing at the far end by the altar – a nun and a man. The man was speaking in a low voice. The nun was silent but, every now and then, she would toss her head and snort. Just as Laila was screwing up the courage to call out, the nun turned and saw her. It was Sister Clementine. She had a pile of books in her arms.

'Ah, Laila, come in, come in. Has your mummy sent you with news for me?' She placed the books on a table and beckoned her over.

Laila walked up the aisle. The man, she saw now, was Mr Jacob.

'Hello, Miss Laila.' He was snug in a woollen scarf and checked jacket, which Laila recognized as once having belonged to Tariq. 'What brings you here today? And no Bua?' He looked over her shoulder. 'Is she following?'

'Er, y-yes,' stammered Laila. 'I raced her and got here first.' Uncomfortable with the lie, Laila looked away. Without the congregation, the church was just a big empty room. She was standing by the blue-painted niche that housed Mary's statue. Up close, Mary had blank, shallow eyes and thin, blood-red lips.

'Babu Jacob found me here, sorting out the hymnbooks.' Sister Clementine put an arm around Laila's shoulder and drew her into her side. Laila got a whiff of stale sweat smothered under talcum powder. Sister Clementine was addressing Laila, but she was actually watching Mr Jacob, who stood in front of her with his hands folded and eyes cast down.

'Babu has come to me with a special request today. And you know what that is?' She lowered her voice to a conspiratorial whisper. 'He wants me to ask Sister Clara to teach his daughters to play the piano, so they can be proper English memsahibs. Isn't that right, Babu?'

Mr Jacob cleared his throat. 'Not memsahibs, Sister,' he mumbled.

Sister Clementine ignored him.

'First, I was thinking I'd say no because Babu wasn't very nice to Sister Clementine the last time we met. Now were you, Babu? Ignoring Sister and taking side of others. Sitting comfortably when Sister was made to stand. Hmm?' Babu Jacob shuffled his size eleven feet. 'But how can I refuse anyone anything these days, with me being so happy about going home and all? So I thought, even if others are unkind,' she jerked Laila's shoulder, 'and disloyal,' another tug, 'I would forgive and forget, like a good Christian. No, Lailu?' Now she looked at Laila and laughed. 'So I'm saying yes.'

Mr Jacob thanked the nun. Reaching behind him, he produced a box of sweets. It was wrapped in 7-Up-green crepe paper and tied with a tinsel bow. He hurriedly removed the wrapping, flipped it open and offered it to Sister Clementine.

Eagerly the nun craned her neck to examine the riches nestling within – glistening pink balls of chamcham frosted with shavings of coconut; big yellow globes of luddoo studded with pumpkin seeds; sticky orange coils of jalebi; and creamy, silvered bricks of barfi. She hummed as her thick fingers hovered with exquisite indecision over the box. She swooped down on a chamcham and popped the egg-sized delicacy whole into her mouth. Biting down into its juicy, syrupy centre, she shut her eyes to savour the moment. Babu Jacob watched with satisfaction. He offered the box to Laila, but she shook her head and tugged hard on the nun's hand, as if it was a bell chord.

'Sister, I want you to tell me about Rani.'

'Rani? What about her?' Sister Clementine licked the syrup from her fingers and looked about keenly for the box. Babu Jacob opened it quickly and offered it to the nun again.

'Hmm, now let me see. What do you think I should have, Babu? Barfi or luddoo? I'm thinking barfi is being better after chamcham. Oh, only top ones have silver paper? Shame. Never mind, I'll have one from top then.' She pinched a cube of barfi delicately between thumb and forefinger. She tilted her head back and, lifting the sweet aloft, lowered it leisurely into her mouth.

'Why did Rani come here that day?' repeated Laila, now irritated with the nun. Her voice was loud, peremptory. 'I want an answer.'

Sister Clementine glared at Laila. She continued to chew, deliberately, ponderously, all the while watching Laila through slitted eyes.

'You want to know, huh?' she asked. 'And I am, what, your

servant, that I have to answer? Everybody wanting, wanting from me all the time. Sister, teach my daughter.' She looked pointedly at Mr Jacob, who flushed. 'Sister, answer my question. Sister, tell me this, tell me that. Well, what is anyone going to do for Sister, huh?' But then she paused, recollecting her last encounter with Fareeda. Her manner mellowed.

'Rani, that girl who came here?' She patted Laila on the head. 'Oh, she'll turn up soon enough. These sorts always do after they've had their fun and games, you know, and brought shame on everyone. She'll slink back home like a kicked cat, just wait and see. But when she comes, I won't be here to tell you that I told you, because I'll be far away home in Kerala having Christmas and wedding with my family.'

'When are you going, Sister?' enquired Jacob.

'As soon as Mother Superior returns,' the nun chirped. 'Next Friday she's coming back.'

'But, Sister, I'm hearing borders are closed, and guarded night and day. No one's coming and going over them.' Jacob buttoned his jacket, as if preparing to leave.

'No one, except those who are knowing big, big people in high-up posts. For them, borders are unsealing, gates are swinging wide, cars are being waved through, soldiers are saluting, everything is happening,' the nun twinkled. 'Now this nice little girl here, her mother has promised me that she will make sure, personally, that I get through the border in time for Christmas with my family.'

'She hasn't promised,' corrected Laila dully, stepping away from Sister Clementine's side. 'She just said, "We'll see." Which usually means no. Except that she can't be bothered to say it right then.

'And Rani hasn't brought shame on anyone,' Laila continued. 'It's mean of you to say that. Mean and nasty.' She stamped her foot, and the noise, though small, echoed in the empty church. 'She's *not* a kicked cat. She's my friend, she's good, and kind, and we're p-p-partners. You don't even know that she's not coming back. And it's all my f-fault.' Tears slid down her cheeks.

A loud silence greeted Laila's outburst. Mr Jacob cleared his throat and took a hesitant step towards Laila. He had heard about Rani's disappearance but did not know yet that she was dead.

'Laila. Come here, child,' he said.

But Sister Clementine pushed him aside. She pulled the girl to her and, pinching her chin between a thumb and forefinger, forced her to look up.

'What do you mean, your mother hasn't promised?' she hissed.

Laila gaped at the nun. Sister Clementine's eyes bulged like hard-boiled eggs. Her lips were curled back over her beige teeth. Laila had never seen her so enraged.

'Well?' she barked. Her fingers bit into Laila's chin.

Laila flinched. Her eyes wide with alarm, she mumbled, 'Ammi does it with us too. She says, "We'll see," when she doesn't want to say no.'

'But she promised right here in this convent,' Sister Clementine muttered thickly. 'She said she'd send me. Home. To my family. After fourteen years. Fourteen! You know how long that is? Longer than you've been alive.' Sister Clementine flung Laila away from her and, tottering blindly to a bench, sank down on it.

'So it was all a joke, was it?' she muttered to herself. She replayed the scene of Fareeda's last visit to the church in her mind's eye. She saw Fareeda's pale hand resting lightly on her own plump arm. She heard again her murmured request for prayers, her gracious invitation to tea. It had never crossed her mind to question Fareeda's sincerity. How they must have chuckled on their way back, the girls and their mother. The gullible nun had taken them seriously. They'd probably gone home and told the father also. She could picture them sitting around their polished table, in front of that funny painting in the coffee-scented room, having a good laugh at her expense.

That room in which Fareeda hadn't even asked her to sit down. And Jacob had refused to meet her eye. And Fazal had smirked pityingly as she had slunk out, dismissed. And Bua, who had thrust her in knowing, fully, how much her mistress loathed the nuns. They were all in it together. Had been from the start. They'd plotted to humiliate and belittle her. As had her family, really. Cowpat, to whom they hadn't written more than half a dozen times in fourteen years. Cowpat, who was now being summoned home with a little request 'of whatever, be it big, be it little, you can spare for the new couple'. Sister Clementine pressed a hand to her aching, bloated stomach. Now there was going to be no respite from chappatis and the pain.

'Sister,' Laila approached the nun nervously. 'Sister, please don't be angry, but I must know. Why did Rani come here?'

Sister Clementine's head swivelled around. She stared at Laila as if seeing her for the first time. Then she laughed – a high, brittle, unfunny laugh.

'Rani? You want to know about Rani?' She lumbered to her feet and shuffled up to Laila. 'Let me tell you about your friend then. She is no rani. She's a shameless, dirty, lying little bitch. That's your friend.' She prodded Laila's chest with her stubby finger. 'She's unclean. Unclean and defiled and disgraced, and she'll burn in hell for her sins. She came here wailing, begging me to waste the rotten fruit of her shameless doings.'

Confused and frightened, Laila shrank away, but Sister Clementine bore down on her, swaying like a top-heavy cupboard. Laila took another step backwards and came up against Mr Jacob. Turning her head, Laila looked up at him. He seemed troubled. His brow was creased and his lips were pressed together. He placed his hands protectively on her shoulders.

'Sister,' he protested quietly. 'Sister, please! Take care . . .'

Sister Clementine ignored him. Her eyes were fixed on Laila. 'You think she's pretty, no?' she panted. Her face was inches from Laila's. Beads of sweat glistened on her upper lip. 'Pretty with her big, big eyes, long hair and delicate body. Well, let me tell you, she's a slut.' Laila flinched as tiny specks of Sister Clementine's spittle landed on her cheeks. 'Yes, she's a slut. That's what she is, your precious friend.'

Mr Jacob's grip tightened on Laila's shoulders. 'Sister,' he warned, drawing himself erect. 'Sister, I've told you to be careful.'

Sister Clementine glowered at Mr Jacob. 'I'm sick of being careful,' she spat. 'I'll say what I want.'

'No you will not, Sister.' Speaking softly, he addressed himself to a spot above the nun's head. 'Laila is a child. You must not speak to her like this.' He paused and swallowed, as if summoning up the courage to whisper, 'I won't let you.'

'*You* won't let me?' she sniggered. 'Well, stop me then. Try. Go on. Because *I* will have my say. Rani is a whore,' she announced, her contemptuous gaze on Mr Jacob now. 'Rani is a whore, a whore, a whore,' she repeated in a voice loud enough to be heard outside the church.

'*Enough!*' thundered Babu Jacob. Laila jumped. His shouted command bounced off the floor, crashed into the walls, ricocheted off the ceiling fans and skittered round and round the benches, till its echo faded gradually into silence. Sister Clementine froze. She stared, fish-mouthed, at Mr Jacob. The huge swaying cupboard that had been about to crush Laila a moment ago shrank in an instant to a tiny, rickety bureau.

'That's enough,' Mr Jacob whispered. He took Laila's limp hand in his. 'Come, child. I'd better take you home.'

He nodded at Sister Clementine, who stood moist-eyed and

shaking, stranded in the middle of the church. Babu Jacob led Laila out into the sunshine to where his bicycle was parked under the mango tree. Laila felt as if she had leapt off a manic merry-go-round. She was dizzy and queasy.

'Go on, child.' Mr Jacob's lips lifted in the ghost of a smile. 'Climb up.' But when Laila continued to stand there, motionless, he lifted her up and carefully placed her side-saddle on the crossbar. Then, reaching down to pin bicycle clips on to his trouser cuffs, he climbed up behind her and sailed out on to the canal road.

'You came alone, didn't you?' When she didn't reply, he asked, 'Did you tell anyone where you were going?' Again, Laila was silent. 'I thought as much,' he muttered to himself.

Mr Jacob pedalled his ancient black Raleigh at a stately pace. They glided past the thick clumps of elephant grass growing low on the canal bank. A milky chocolate colour today, the canal glittered beguilingly in the sun's oblique rays. Laila imagined Rani floating on her back in the canal. Feet together, hands clasped over her bosom and loose hair rippling out in a dark halo around her head, her sightless eyes were open, reflecting the deep, disturbing blue of the sky. Laila squeezed her eyes shut to banish the image.

She opened her eyes and saw Mr Jacob's hands gripping the handlebars. His tobacco-brown skin reminded Laila of her father's battered old wallet. Mr Jacob cycled smoothly, avoiding the ruts in the road. She had never imagined him capable of the fury he had shown in the church.

'Babu Jacob, may I ask you a question?' she whispered.

'Surely, Lailu,' he murmured, above her head.

'What is a whore?'

The bicycle wobbled for a moment and then righted itself. Suddenly nervous, Laila clutched at Mr Jacob's forearms in mute appeal.

'It's all right, I won't get angry.' He was silent for a long while, and then he drew a deep breath and said, 'A whore, Lailu, is a person who is forced to do difficult things.'

'What difficult things?'

'Things a person wouldn't normally want to do.'

'What was Rani forced to do that she didn't want to?' Laila frowned. She was confused by all these oblique comments. Why wouldn't anyone speak to her plainly? What had Sister Clementine meant when she'd shouted about Rani's filth that she had come to get wasted? Rani wasn't filthy. She was one of the cleanest people Laila knew. She bathed every day, even though she didn't have a nice bathroom with tiles and a tub. Her hair was always glossy, and she never, ever got nits. And her breath was fragrant, scented with aniseed, unlike Sister Clementine's own sour exhalations. Sister Clementine had a nerve to call Rani dirty.

'I'm not saying Rani is a, er, you know a, er, whore,' denied Mr Jacob, clearing his throat. 'It is not a nice word, and I don't think we should use it for Rani. In fact, it's not a word we should use at all.'

'Then why did Sister Clementine use it?'

'Because she was angry. I don't think she meant it either. She must be regretting it even now.'

Laila wasn't about to grant Sister Clementine the tiniest shred of concession after her performance at the church. Unlike her mother, Laila had always had a soft spot for Sister Clementine. Bua had told her often how holy the nun was, how much she prayed, how closely God listened to her. Charmed by the appurtenances of the church, Laila had not only accepted but endorsed her ayah's opinion whole-heartedly. Laila had defended her to Fareeda. ('She's *not* a busybody, she's kind and good and . . . and she plays the piano and admires my dresses.')

But Sister Clementine had squandered that goodwill today. Never again would Laila plead the nuns' cause with her mother, never would she visit them at Christmas with flowers and cakes, never ever would she step inside that horrid church. Poor Rani, who'd had to throw herself at the nun's mercy.

She sat bolt upright on the crossbar, the unexpected movement causing Babu Jacob to swerve. That was it! That was why Rani had come to the church. She wanted a particular kind of help only the nuns could give. The nuns had refused her. But why?

'What did Rani want from Sister Clementine when she came to the church? She wanted something that Sister Clementine wouldn't give? What was it?'

Mr Jacob shifted uncomfortably on his bicycle seat. 'That is something you should ask Rani when you next see her.'

'No, *you* must tell me,' insisted Laila.

'I can't.'

'Why not?'

'Because it's not something I can talk to you about. Ask Rani, she'd be able to explain to you much better than I.'

'But I *can't*,' wailed Laila.

'And why not?'

'Because she's dead, you see,' mumbled Laila. 'They found her yesterday. In the c-c-canal. The soldiers called Aba and he went to see her in Colewalla c-cantt.'

Mr Jacob pressed hard on the brakes. He planted a big sandalled, socked foot on the ground on either side of the bike and gathered Laila to him. At first she stiffened, but then she let go of the cycle bars and turned her face into the scratchy wool of his jacket.

'Oh, my poor child,' he murmured, stroking her head. 'I am sorry, so, so sorry. May God have mercy on the soul of that poor deceased child.'

Laila clutched his lapels and sobbed into his chest. Mr Jacob held her gently.

'She is not lost,' he said softly. 'She is still with you. Those we love never leave us. They stay with us in our hearts. They become part of us. They never die.'

Laila lifted a tear-stained face to his.

'Does that mean Rani is a shaheed?' she hicupped.

Mr Jacob smiled a sad, wise smile and tucked a damp lock of her hair behind her ear. 'It means that as long as you hold on to her memory, she will not die.'

'Rehmat said that shaheeds go straight to heaven. No questions asked. Is Rani in heaven now?'

'Of course she is.' Mr Jacob wiped her tears with a large handkerchief. 'Now, remember this,' he said in a low, serious voice. 'I know Rani was older than you, but she was still a child, and when children die they go straight to heaven, because children's souls are like puffy white clouds. They are not stained with any sins, nor are they black with dark deeds. They are light, pure and clean. God receives them with open arms and a tender heart. "Come, my child," He says, "come to me."'

'But you don't *understand*,' cried Laila. 'I was supposed to look after her.' And then she told him all about their secret partnership, her role as Rani's spy, Rani's strange pendulum moods, the tantalizing mystery of her fiancé's identity, her own desperation to solve it, Mashooq's surprise visit to Sabzbagh, Kaneez's terrifying grief and then that last trip to the convent with Fareeda and Sara when she had broken her promise and betrayed Rani. Once she had started she couldn't stop. Laila rambled on about the delicious excitement of forming the Terrific Two, her desire to please Rani, her fear of annoying Fareeda and exposing Bua, her frustrated rage at her own impotence and confusion about what lay at the core of the mystery and, finally, her awful guilt at betraying Rani.

Mr Jacob listened in attentive silence, starting only once when she mentioned Mashooq and their chat over the hedge. But swept away on the tide of her own narrative, Laila did not notice Mr Jacob's reaction. When she lapsed into silence, Mr Jacob tilted back her chin with a crooked forefinger and looked her full in the face.

'Now listen to me. *It was not your fault.* You have not betrayed Rani. You are *not* to blame. Sad, awful things happen in life. They happen to everyone. But remember what I said about children. They are pure. *You* are pure. You are innocent, and so was Rani. No matter what people say, God knows that, and He is the only true judge.'

'Are you sure? Are you sure it's not my fault?'

Mr Jacob grasped her by the upper arms and said, 'Look at me as I say this. You. Are. Blameless. Of that I am sure. As sure as I am of night being night and day being day.'

Despite Laila's protestations, Mr Jacob insisted on cycling Laila all the way home. He wanted to come in and have a word with Fareeda, but Laila begged him not to. She didn't want to get into trouble for going to the church again. And she wasn't sure whether she wanted to talk to Fareeda just yet. By dissolving into another flood of tears, she prevailed upon Mr Jacob to drop her off in the back yard. That way, with some luck, she could sneak into the house without being seen, although she did not tell him that.

As she crossed the yard, she saw a stranger on the bench. He was dressed in a grey shirt and khaki trousers, and a narrow black belt was slung diagonally across his chest. He twirled a black beret in his hands and looked restless, as if waiting for someone.

'It's Feroze,' Tariq said. 'The police inspector.' He had come to the sitting room to tell Fareeda about his brief conversation with the visitor in the yard. 'I'm going with him to the station.'

'What's happened?'

'He says he found a man lying face down in the bazaar this morning. He was dead drunk, but when he tried to lift him, he came to. When Feroze heard him mutter "Rani", he threw him into the lock-up and came over.'

'Does he recognize the man?' Fareeda's voice faltered. 'Is he from this village?'

'He says he is lame.'

'Oh, God, no. Not Mashooq?' Fareeda gasped.

'That's what I intend to find out.' Tariq's voice was grim.

18

Inspector Feroze was a rarity in Colewallah district – a popular policeman. He was a peaceable, good-natured widower who took off for a couple of hours each afternoon to collect his children from school, give them lunch and drop them off with his sister before returning to work.

Fortunately, the duties of a policeman in Sabzbagh were not onerous. There had been a big case a few years back, a murder in a land dispute, but his predecessor had dealt with that. These days, the only cases requiring his attention were sporadic instances of cattle-rustling and the occasional brawl. Had his presence been requested in cases of domestic violence, he would not have shirked his duty, for he was a conscientious man. But much to Inspector Feroze's relief, the police were seldom alerted in domestic situations. Hence, his life in Sabzbagh was peaceful, even uneventful, just as he liked it.

Inspector Feroze's predecessor had been widely feared and hated. With a visceral contempt for what he called 'devious peasant bastards', Inspector Takdeer had used the smallest excuse – an argument in a shop, an insolent stare, a snicker behind his back – to wield his thick bamboo cane. Often, people were kept overnight in the solitary lock-up in the station and given the dreaded police phenti, a brutal beating, after which blood had to be hosed off the floor. Unable to curb the inspector's excesses, Tariq had manoeuvred hard behind the scenes to have him transferred. When his efforts were rewarded after a couple of years, people from three villages came to thank Tariq with gifts of live chickens and baskets of freshly picked mangoes.

Thus it was Mashooq's great good fortune to be found by Inspector Feroze that morning. Having thrown Mashooq into a cell, Feroze took off on his motorbike to inform Tariq. When Tariq arrived at the station, Feroze took him directly to Mashooq's cell. It was a small room with a skylight, from which a bright beam of sunlight poured in and spot-lit the brick floor.

Mashooq sat in the shadows, on a string bed in the corner. His eyes were bloodshot, and his shirt was torn and splattered with reddish-brown stains. There was a bad bruise on his forearm and what looked like a crescent of bloody tooth-marks. Despite his ragged appearance, he looked calm and self-possessed, leaning back against the wall with his hands clasped in his lap.

He greeted Tariq with a hesitant smile and even raised his hand to salaam. Mashooq appeared sober, with not a trace of his old mocking insolence.

A constable arrived with a chair and placed it behind Tariq.

'Please sit down, sir,' said Feroze, hovering by the door. 'Would you mind, sir, if I went to collect my children from school? I'll drop them off at my sister's and come straight back.'

'No, you go ahead, Inspector.'

'Should you need any assistance in my absence, sir,' he said, glancing at Mashooq, 'Constable Charagh will be waiting outside the cell. All you have to do is call out.'

'I don't think it will be necessary.'

Tariq pulled the chair up to Mashooq's bed. He sat down, crossing his legs.

'I want you to tell me, Mashooq, where you've been since that afternoon when you came to my house four days ago.' Tariq strove to keep his voice even and low. 'I want you to tell me the truth, because I'll find out if you don't. So don't waste my time with lies.'

Mashooq looked down at his hands. 'I have nothing to hide. I shall tell you the truth.'

He told Tariq that, after he left his house, he went to the bazaar in Sabzbagh and, finding some money in his pocket, decided to have a drink. He stayed in the bazaar longer than he had planned, drinking steadily. He couldn't recall much about what happened when he came out. All he remembered was that it was cold, dark and foggy. It was definitely very foggy, he said, nodding his head, because it took him a long time to cycle to Kalanpur.

'Why did you go to Kalanpur?'

A motorcycle beeped on the road outside, and a pigeon flapped past the skylight.

'I went to get Rani.'

'To get Rani?' Tariq was puzzled. Then a horrifying thought occurred to him. 'Had you been seeing Rani? Had you had relations with her?'

'How could I? I was never allowed within touching distance of her.'

'Then why did you go to Rani?'

'Shortly after you and I parted that day, I discovered – don't ask how, for I shan't tell you – that she was getting married secretly with great haste. My suspicions were aroused. I was already seething with rage. I wanted to get even with you but didn't know how. And then I was told this of Rani. It was as if Allah had shown me the way. He had set this task for me. I knew then what I had to do. I had to sort out Rani. And through her, you.'

Gripping the arms of his chair, Tariq nodded at Mashooq to continue.

Mashooq recounted the details of that night. He told Tariq how he had arrived at Kalanpur undetected, followed Kaneez to her quarter in the thick mist and overheard Rani's confession of pregnancy. His suspicion confirmed, he had wanted to rush in and strangle her, but had held back. It seemed as if Kaneez had just found out. She demanded to know who was responsible, but Rani wouldn't say. Rani cried and begged Kaneez to forgive her, but she wouldn't listen. She walked out, leaving Rani alone in the quarter.

Mashooq had waited for a while to see if Kaneez would return. And then, when she didn't, he went in. Rani was lying on the floor, sobbing. She didn't hear him enter. When he called her name, she sat up with a start. She quickly wiped her face and pulled her dupatta up to cover her head. That gesture annoyed him. Why pretend to be modest after what she'd gone and done? It was hypocritical, deceitful. He didn't like it.

She asked him what he was doing there. He told her that he had come to fetch her. Her mother was ill and had asked for her. 'What about my grandmother?' she asked. He said Fatima didn't want to worry her old mother. She just wanted Rani. 'But she's never asked for me before. Is she very ill?' she persisted. He could tell she was suspicious. He said she was ill enough to send him cycling three miles on a freezing, foggy night just to fetch her. She thought for a minute and then said, 'All right, I'll come with you. But I want to leave word with the neighbours, or my grandmother will worry.' Pretending nonchalance, he shrugged and said she was being silly. Fatima had told him specifically not to worry Kaneez, and here she was, wanting to cause her needless anxiety by alerting the neighbours. They would exaggerate her illness tenfold when they reported it to Kaneez. And, anyway, she would be back in a couple of hours, before anyone even found out that she'd gone. She nodded, took her shawl and followed him out into the night. No one saw them leave.

Now that he had her with him, he didn't know what to do. He had thought briefly of punishing her then and there in the quarter but had been inhibited by the proximity of the neighbours, who would no doubt have come swarming in at the slightest noise. They might not have even let him finish his business. Besides, his brain was in turmoil. He had never expected Rani to be so sinful, so devious, so shameless. It was as if a kitten had suddenly bitten off his hand. And the worst of it was, she seemed to have no idea of the enormity of her sin.

'Oh yes,' he scoffed, 'she cried and said she was sorry to Kaneez, but only because she had been found out. She had no idea of what she had actually done. She gave herself willingly before marriage to a man and conceived a bastard – a *bastard*.' He spat out the last word in a voice soaked in loathing. He shook his head and said, 'There can be no greater sin. There *is* no greater sin. And, for that unborn child, no greater injustice.'

He left Kalanpur with no firm plan in mind, with her sitting on the back of the cycle. He tried to think of the places he could take her. Obviously, his own village was not an option. Nor was Sabzbagh. But then he remembered there was a disused brick kiln about a mile away from Kalanpur. He could take her there.

As he cycled into the night, he pondered feverishly on the possible identity of the father of Rani's child. The girl, fortunately, was silent. The brick kiln that he had in mind was a little way off the main road. They would have to cut across some fields to get to it. When they reached the bit where they had to get off and walk, she made a fuss. This was not the road to her mother's house. Where had he brought her? She wanted to go home. He told her the proper road was all dug up because the gas wallahs were laying new pipes, and this was a short cut. She seemed to accept his explanation, for she said no more.

It was dark and the ground was soggy. They were treading on a narrow path between two cane fields. The cane grew higher than their heads on either side, and they could hear jackals calling and moving through the crop. She was nervous and kept stumbling but didn't complain again. Presently Mashooq saw the kiln stack outlined against the dark sky. There was a small hut to one side that the overseer once used. He took her there. He told her that they'd take a little rest because he was tired after the long ride to Kalanpur. She said she'd rather press on. But he insisted. He brought the cycle in, lest a passer-by spot it outside. There was nothing in the hut, not even a stool. It was as dark and cold as a grave. He leaned the cycle against a wall. She stood in the doorway with her back to him, looking out towards the fields.

He went up and stood behind her, so close that he could smell the grassy scent of her hair. He thought fleetingly of how nice it would have been were she not soiled, but then he remembered how sly she was and he felt himself tremble with anger.

'Whose child is it?' he hissed in her ear.

'What do you mean?' She spun around.

He told her he had overheard everything and wanted to know which son of a bitch she had been lying with. She started to whimper. Backing away from him, she tried to make a run for it. He grabbed her arm and dragged her back into the hut. He kicked the door shut and stood with his back to it. He asked her again whose child she was carrying. She backed away.

So he lunged at her and shoved her to the ground. She clawed his face and bit and kicked and pulled his hair. But she was no match for his fury and his strength. Afterwards, he asked her again who had fathered her bastard. She had been crying softly into her hands, but at his question, she brushed off her tears and placed her hands proudly over her stomach.

'This,' she said, 'is no bastard. This is the child of the man I love.'

'The one who fled like a rat and left you to face the world alone? Fine man he is!' he scorned.

'He was *made* to run away.' In that tiny hut her voice rang out with as much dignity as she could muster. 'But even if he's gone, he's left me with my happiest memories. And those, neither you nor anyone can take away from me. I am proud that I went with him. Proud that I'm having his child. He's my Ranjha. And I'm his Heer.'

'You're his slut, that's what you are.' He sprang at her in the dark and, with his face inches from hers, demanded, 'Tell me his name. What's the motherfucker's *name*?'

'No!' she screamed. 'I'll never tell you. Your filthy mouth would soil his name. But one thing I *will* tell you, he's worth a thousand of you, you lame, pockmarked *bastard*. You repulse me.' She spat at him then, catching him full in the face.

Not even pausing to wipe his face, he hit her across hers. Once he had done so, he found he couldn't stop. He punched her with his fists and kicked her with his heavy leather sandal. Then he got the chain and padlock he used to lock his bicycle and smashed it on her back. He hit her with all the rage pent up within him against Tariq and her. He avenged himself for the slights he had suffered at the hands of Sardar Begum, Shamshad Khan, Barkat, the villagers of Champa and anyone else who had ever done him wrong. He kicked her for begetting a bastard. It was bad enough to commit the sin she had, but then to try and protect the evil-doer? No, that was intolerable. It showed that she wasn't penitent. It proved she was a liar. She might even now be intending to go back and meet him again. She deserved no quarter from him.

Rani tried to shield herself. She kneeled on the floor, her arms curled around her head, her knees drawn up against her chest to protect her belly. Infuriated by her desire to shield her bastard child from his righteous wrath, Mashooq caught her by the forearm and pulled her to her feet with a ferocity that almost dislocated her arm. He raised his hand to hit her again but, with a swiftness which caught him by surprise, she grabbed his arm and sunk her teeth into it, not letting go even after the blood ran down her chin. Shocked and in pain, Mashooq kicked her hard in the stomach. She screamed as she fell, hitting her head, he thought, on the brick floor, because he heard a loud crack. And then silence. He kicked her twice in the side as she lay there on the floor, but she made no effort to move out of his reach. Mashooq realized Rani had passed out. He, too, was exhausted, so, with his back against a wall, he slumped to the floor.

He was woken at dawn by a shaft of sunlight slicing through the crack in the door. Mashooq blinked and rubbed his sore head. He felt disoriented and parched. His arm throbbed. He gazed around him and remembered where he was. He looked around for Rani. She lay in a heap in the middle of the hut. Her clothes were splattered with blood. Her nose was a squashed, bloody mess. She didn't seem to be breathing. But when he put his head to her chest, he saw that it was rising and falling ever so slightly. He touched the side of her head. Her hair felt sticky and matted. His hand came away bloodstained.

Mashooq didn't know what to do with her. He could have left her there, but he didn't want her body to be found. He wanted to remove her, and her bastard child, from the face of the earth. He thought of digging a grave and burying her alive, right there in the fields. But he knew he didn't have enough time. Already the sun was up. Soon, farmers would be heading that way.

Mashooq's account was interrupted by the sound of approaching footsteps and voices in the corridor outside the cell. Feroze stuck his head around the door.

'I'm back, sir,' he said to Tariq. 'Shall I sit here with you now?'

'Yes, why don't you do that, Inspector? Because I think this man is about to make a confession of murder, and I'd like you to be here when he does that.'

'Sir?' Inspector Feroze's jaw dropped. Recovering his composure, he said, 'I'll just get a stool and some paper and a pencil.'

When Feroze was ready, Tariq quickly recapitulated for the inspector all that Mashooq had said so far.

'Have I got the facts right?' Tariq asked Mashooq when he'd finished.

'Yes.'

Feroze wrote it all down.

'Mashooq,' said Tariq. 'Continue.'

Mashooq straightened his back and continued. Reviewing his options, he realized his best choice would be to throw her into the canal. He'd let the fish feast on her. He knew that, battered and broken as she was, she had no hope of surviving the water. Even if her body were fished out twenty miles downstream, no one would know who she was. So he slung her over his shoulder and emerged from the hut. He had to leave the cycle behind, because he couldn't manage the two. It couldn't have been more than six in the morning when he set off. As the sun rose higher, Rani grew heavy on his shoulder and, despite the early morning chill, he began to sweat. His chest burned and his legs ached.

Luckily, the cane beyond Kalanpur hadn't been harvested yet, and it provided good cover. Avoiding the road, he stayed in the fields, stopping for a brief rest now and again. Finally, he saw the canal up ahead. Only then did he break cover and make a run for it, or as close to a run as he could manage with the unconscious girl weighing him down like a sack of rocks.

The inspector asked if she was still alive then.

Yes, replied Mashooq, she moaned when he threw her

down on the bank. She opened her eyes and looked at him, but with an unfocused, glassy gaze. Her face was flushed and damp with sweat. Her lips were cracked.

Mashooq tilted back his head and shut his eyes.

'I knew she had lost the baby. I told myself it had had a lucky escape. It would never know how bastards are treated. It would be spared the torment, the jeers. It occurred to me then that I was the instrument of its deliverance. I had been appointed by Allah to put both the sinful mother and her bastard child out of the misery and shame awaiting them in later life.'

Mashooq swung his legs to the floor and, resting his elbows on his knees, leaned towards his interrogators.

'Don't you see? I liberated them both. I removed the dishonour from Rani. As for the baby, I rescued it from living hell. It was all planned up above. Allah wanted me to redeem myself. First He informed me of Rani's perfidy. Then He sent me to Kalanpur that night. It was nothing short of a miracle that I got there through that fog in the state I was in. I was meant to overhear that conversation between Rani and Kaneez. I know I have not led a perfect life, but this was my opportunity to wipe my sins away. And I did. I did not shirk my responsibility.'

The door was pushed ajar on hinges that needed oiling. Tariq and the inspector both turned towards it. It was the constable with a steel tray bearing three bottles of 7-Up. He looked hesitantly at his boss.

'Hurry up and pass them around,' whispered the inspector, nodding at Tariq to remind the constable whom to serve first.

As soon as the constable had left, Tariq barked out at Mashooq, 'When did Rani die?'

Mashooq took a big slug from the bottle and swallowed it with a loud gulp. 'Ah, perfect,' he murmured.

'Sahib asked you a question,' Feroze reminded Mashooq.

'I'm coming to that. I was about to roll her over the edge, into the canal, when she suddenly opened her eyes. She looked straight up at me but didn't seem to see me. And then she sighed and died. I know, because I checked her pulse, both in her wrist and her neck. I also listened to her chest. There was nothing. So I rolled her over with my foot, and she fell with a splash. Within minutes she was gone.'

Squatting on the bank, Mashooq said he scooped up a handful of muddy water and slaked his thirst. He then washed his face and neck and lay down to rest with his back against a tree. He must have been more tired than he realized, for it was almost midday when he woke. His body was stiff and chilled to the bone. He looked around for his cycle and remembered that he had left it behind in the hut by the brick kiln. When he reached the kiln, farmers were already harvesting the cane in the surrounding fields. Fortunately, he did not recognize any of them. And nor they him. Watched silently by the farmers, he entered the hut. He found his discarded jacket on the floor. He saw that the ground was bloodstained. But he did not dwell on it. He retrieved his bike and cycled down to Champa, his old village.

He didn't know why he felt a compulsion to go there. It was a good couple of hours' ride away, but he didn't think twice about it. He stood his bicycle under a tree and walked over to a well where he had played as a child. There was a group of children playing there, none of whom he recognized.

An incident from the past came vividly to him. When he was about seven, boys from the village tried to put him in a bucket and lower him into the well. It had been their idea of a prank. Terrified, he had fought them with all his puny strength. He'd scratched and kicked and swore till he'd fought free. He had run as fast as he could, but his limp slowed him down. His tormentors had soon caught up with him and clobbered him until he felt as if his whole body was one throbbing wound. At last, when he thought he was going to pass out, they had stopped, but only on condition that he would repeat after them five times, 'I'm a dirty, lame bastard and I am the lowest of the low.' But that afternoon, he realized that those old memories no longer had the power to hurt him. He had cast off that burden. He had finally escaped his past, his history. He was free.

Having relayed the events of that day, Mashooq sighed and closed his eyes. He did not seem at all distressed by his confession. Nor did he seem remorseful. On the contrary, Feroze was startled to notice, he was smiling serenely.

'Inspector, you have heard and recorded this man's admission of murder?' asked Tariq.

'But I haven't admitted murder,' protested Mashooq, looking from Tariq to the inspector. 'I did not *murder* her. Murder is a sin. I did not murder her. I cleansed her. I carried out Allah's will.'

'You terrorized a child and beat the life out of her, you bloody coward,' shouted Tariq. 'And you dare tell me that you didn't murder her?'

'But I didn't. I'm not just saying it to walk free. I was going to give myself up anyway. I'm not ashamed of what I did. I'm proud of it. After I returned from Champa, I came to Sabzbagh to give myself up voluntarily. I knew there would be a search on for Rani, and I wanted to tell you what had happened to her. To put your minds at rest, as mine was.'

'Then how did you come to be face down in the gutter this morning?' asked Feroze.

'Old habits die hard, I suppose,' murmured Mashooq, rubbing the back of his neck. 'I got into Sabzbagh at about seven that evening. In the bazaar, I bumped into an old friend, who was returning from a cockfight in which he'd won some money. "Come, let's celebrate," he said. I declined, but he insisted. I hadn't eaten for two days. The drink affected me more than I thought it would. What happened after that,' he shrugged, 'you know.'

Tariq took a step towards the bed and thrust his face into Mashooq's. 'I shall make sure that you pay for this, Mashooq,' he ground out. 'You shall stand trial for the murder of an innocent girl, and you shall hang for it.'

'Hang? For protecting the honour of a sinful girl? For saving her bastard child from a miserable life? For removing the stain of dishonour?' Mashooq frowned in puzzlement. Then he shrugged and said, 'Do what you have to. I know I did my duty. My conscience is clear.'

Tariq drove straight to Kalanpur from the police station. It was dusk by the time he reached the haveli. Sardar Begum had withdrawn into her bedroom with the two women. A brazier of coals stood in the middle of the room, and mother and daughter sat huddled by it. Fatima's son was in her lap, wrapped in her shawl. Only his face peeped out from its folds. Sardar Begum sat on a sofa, cross-legged, rocking back and forth as she read aloud from the Koran that lay propped open before her.

Tariq slumped down beside his mother and stretched his legs out in front of him. He was soothed by the rising and falling cadences of Sardar Begum's Arabic recitation. He was a child again, in bed with fever. His mother, dark-haired and smooth-skinned, bent over him, reciting this very same verse from the Koran. Her cool, attar-scented hand stroked his burning forehead.

Tariq looked at Fatima. She seemed as if she had aged ten years in a single afternoon. She gazed at the fire, hollow-eyed, defeated. Sardar Begum read to the end of a passage, then closed the book. She kissed it and touched it to her eyes. Rising to her feet, she trudged to the mantelpiece, where she laid it down. Only then did she speak to Tariq.

'What news have you brought now?' she asked.

Editing the more sordid details, Tariq recounted Mashooq's story. When Tariq finished, there was a muffled cry from Fatima. Her fist was in her mouth, and tears cascaded down her face. Kaneez had her arm around her daughter but gazed dry-eyed at the brazier, her hawk-like face bleak. Fatima's son nodded against his mother's bosom.

'Where is he now?' asked Sardar Begum.

'At the police station. Tomorrow we are going to register a case against him and, once that happens, he will probably be moved to Colewallah jail to await trial.'

'Trial? What trial?' Kaneez raised a puzzled face.

'Mashooq's trial for Rani's murder,' Tariq repeated.

'Did you say the trial will be held in a court at Colewallah?' Kaneez had put aside Fatima and was now facing Tariq.

'Yes, at least in Colewallah. Perhaps even in Lahore, if the case goes up to the High Court.'

'High Court? Lahore? What do you mean?'

'Mashooq has admitted to killing Rani. His statement has been taken down by Inspector Feroze at Sabzbagh station,' Tariq explained. 'Mashooq will have to stand trial for murder and explain to a court why he did it. If they find him guilty, which I am sure they will, since he has already confessed voluntarily, he will either be hanged or imprisoned for life.'

'Hanged? Oh, no, we can't let that happen,' said Kaneez.

'Why ever not?'

'Think of the scandal, the shame, if it comes out that Rani was killed by her own stepfather. No, no, it must never come out.' Kaneez shook her head. 'There is to be no trial.'

'You can't mean that. You are overcome right now. We can talk about this tomorrow,' said Tariq.

'No!' Kaneez repeated. 'I know what I am saying. There is to be no trial.'

Tariq stared in disbelief from his mother to Fatima and Kaneez. Sardar Begum met his gaze impassively. Fatima stared into the fire, as if hypnotized by it. But there was a challenge on Kaneez's lined old face.

'Why is there to be no trial?' asked Tariq at last.

'Because we have suffered enough,' replied Kaneez. 'I never thought that in my old age my face would be blackened like this. It's bad enough that the whole world should know my girl ran away and was then pulled out of the canal three days later by passers-by. Still, it was Allah's will. But for Mashooq to stand up in court in front of strangers and tell them how she had begotten a child in sin and how he had to kill her to protect our honour – no, I can't endure that humiliation. You will not speak of a trial again and you will have Mashooq released.'

'And if I don't?'

'I am not strong and powerful like you. I cannot make you do it. But I am begging you, Tariq Sahib. I have lost everything. Now allow me this one comfort: that the world does not find out about my child's fall. Leave her memory untarnished. I implore you. Let me live out the few days I have left with some scraps of dignity.'

'Listen, Kaneez, I *know* what your fears are,' said Tariq. 'I know the honourable life you have lived and at what cost to yourself. I also understand the huge sacrifice that Fatima has made. Believe me, I *understand*. But there is more than just your honour or Fatima's suffering at stake here. What about Rani's right to justice? And what about Mashooq? He gets off free? Does that seem right to you?'

'I don't have answers for everything.' Kaneez bowed her head. 'It was Allah's will. On the day of judgement, He will decide Mashooq's fate.'

Tariq was quiet for several minutes. Then he shook his head.

'I'm sorry, but I can't do it. I won't be able to live with my conscience. I owe it to Rani to give her justice in death, even if I didn't give her protection in life.'

'Tariq Sahib, I beg of you. Don't rip the sky off my head,' cried Kaneez, clutching his feet.

'Sit up,' Sardar Begum ordered Kaneez. 'You don't have to throw yourself at his feet.' To Tariq she said, 'It is not for you to give justice. That is for Him. And this is not about *your* conscience, either. It is about *their* honour, *their* loss.' She jerked her chin at the group by the fire. 'There is a limit to everyone's endurance. Kaneez has reached hers. First she finds out Rani is pregnant. Then she discovers she is missing, then dead. And now she's learnt she has been murdered by her own stepfather. Kaneez's face has been blackened, her nose has been cut. What do you want now, to parade her naked through the streets?'

'Mashooq is a murderer. What do you want me to do? Embrace him, garland him, congratulate him like a war hero?'

'Don't be foolish,' snapped Sardar Begum. 'I'm merely asking for his release. This matter should die here and now. I won't let you put these women through more humiliation. What has Kaneez ever had but her good name? In the last days of her life, you will not take that away from her.'

'All right! All right!' Tariq held up his hands. 'But just tell me one thing. Were Rani not related to Kaneez but was some other girl in the village, would you allow Mashooq to be let off? Whichever way you look at it, he's murdered an innocent girl, hasn't he?'

'Rani committed a sin. She paid for it with her life. She had stained her family's honour. Mashooq, rightly or wrongly, removed the stain.' Sardar Begum shrugged and asked, 'And have you thought how you will appear to the world, Tariq Azeem, publicly fighting for the rights of a girl who has brought shame and dishonour on her people?'

'I can't believe you said that.' Tariq stared at his mother. 'Rani was a child, only a little older than your granddaughters. At least tell me you didn't mean it.'

'It doesn't matter what you think I believe,' she muttered.

'What about Fatima? I suppose she will go back to live with Mashooq as if nothing has happened?'

Fatima's head jerked up in panic.

'That is for Fatima to decide. It's not for you to worry about.'

'It *is* for me to worry about. How do you know his honour won't be roused again and again?'

'He won't do it again,' stated Sardar Begum. 'He is at peace now. He feels he has acted honourably and can stand alongside respectable men. He is no longer the bastard.'

'But the soldiers at the cantonment know that Rani died a violent death. They pulled her out of the canal, remember?' pleaded Tariq. 'All those who saw her know she didn't die of natural causes. The doctor even did a post mortem. He knows, so does the colonel. How are you going to silence them all?'

'We won't need to.' Sardar Begum's tone was brusque. 'They have better things to do than to gossip about Rani's murder. Also, if a war breaks out tomorrow, do you think they will have time to think of anything at all?'

'But Rani's body is still at the cantonment,' Tariq pointed out. 'When I go to have it released, the colonel is bound to ask me what progress we have made in finding her murderer.'

'You can tell him the truth: none! You have made no progress, and Rani's family want their child's body back. That's the end of it.'

Knowing the colonel as Tariq did, he doubted whether that would be the end of it. The colonel would be a relentless hound on the scent of his quarry. He would lose no opportunity to taunt Tariq. How would Tariq look him in the face, knowing what he did and yet powerless to act on it? So far, Tariq had only dealt with grief and guilt. Now he knew he was about to taste humiliation.

'Since there doesn't seem to be anything for me to worry about,' Tariq said bitterly, 'I'll go home and let you decide everything.' He rose from the sofa and went to the door.

'No, wait,' Sardar Begum called out. 'There are still a couple of things I need to ask of you.'

Tariq turned around stiffly. He looked beaten.

'I want you to tell your inspector that Rani's grandmother, who was her guardian, has decided to forgive Mashooq. She can ask for blood money in exchange for his freedom. But she is forgoing that, too, for his release tomorrow.'

'Anything else?' Tariq asked, raising his eyebrows.

'Yes, make sure the inspector doesn't speak of it to anyone. After all, he owes his job to you. He can do that much to repay the favour. Take the report from him, if necessary. It must be hushed up. As far as the rest of the world is concerned, Rani had an accident. She slipped and fell into the canal and was drowned. Is that clear?'

Tariq gave his mother a salute. 'Of course, as my personal, loyal servant, the inspector will not breathe a word to a soul.'

'This is no joking matter,' retorted Sardar Begum.

'I've never felt less like laughing,' replied Tariq . 'May I ask how you are going to ensure Mashooq the drunkard's silence?'

'Leave that to me.' Sardar Begum looked grim. 'I've been soft on that man, but now he will understand what I am made of. His house is my property. You didn't know that, did you?' Sardar Begum's mouth twisted into a grimace. 'A few months back, he came to me for a loan. The fourth time since his marriage to Fatima. When I refused, he threatened to sell the house, to throw his family out. I bought the house from him so at least Fatima could be sure of a roof over her head.

He will not be able to return to it now. Nor will he find a job in this district.

'The district commissioner owes me. His father was our carpenter, who lost his hand in an accident. Your father looked after him and his family and gave money especially for this boy to be educated. You don't remember because it happened when you were a baby. The DC came by to pay his respects when he was first appointed to Colewallah. I asked him not to tell you about the connection because your father never wanted his charity publicized. Since then, the DC's asked several times if there is anything he can do for me. I can get Mashooq hounded from this district, if I want.'

'My congratulations, on arranging everything so neatly.' Tariq inclined his head with an ironic smile. 'Anything else, or may I take my leave?'

'There is one other thing.' Fatima spoke in a trembling voice. 'Can I have my girl's body?'

'Of course. I'll fetch her tomorrow from Colewallah. And Fatima? My heartfelt sympathy.' His voice broke. Composing himself with a visible effort, he let himself out.

19

Rani was buried the next day, on 3 December 1971. It was a small funeral, attended only by her family and the Azeems. Sardar Begum, Laila, Sara and Fareeda waited at some distance in the car while Tariq and Barkat lowered her slight, shrouded body into her grave. Mashooq had been released but had not attended her funeral. At Dera, he told his neighbours that he had said her funeral prayers already. It was bitterly cold, and the air was thick with the threat of rain. As the Azeems drove home from Kalanpur, Barkat switched on the radio, with Tariq's permission, to catch the news. A flat, impersonal voice informed them that Pakistani armed forces had bombed Indian airfields earlier that day and the two countries were at war.

The next day, Fareeda checked all her food stores with Fazal. Then she had extra candles, kerosene, battery cells and torches brought in and moved the girls' beds to the guest room on the other side of the house, far from the spreading branches of the silk cotton tree. Bua carried her mattress into the girls' room and laid it across the door. The Indians, she declared, would have to riddle her with bullets before she let a single one across the threshold. Nevertheless, Sara slipped her penknife under her pillow for extra protection. Once the girls had gone to bed, Tariq unlocked his gun cabinet. Carefully, he lifted out his shotgun and cleaned it. He counted up thirty-six cartridges, then, returning them to the cabinet, locked it again. He went around to Kalanpur to ask Sardar Begum to move in with him. She refused. She had her Allah to protect her, she said.

In the kitchen, Rehmat sharpened his knives. Fazal put duct

tape on all the glass windows and packed away Fareeda's cut-glass tumblers and fine china. Barkat camouflaged the gleaming car with mud paste and helped Amanat dig an L-shaped trench in the back garden for shelter during air raids. The old Laila would have been electrified by these preparations, but now she watched them from a distance, as if they were for a stranger's party. She wondered whether anyone had moved the red chillies Rani had stashed behind her door.

Over the next few days, the radio was only switched off at night in the Azeem household. They learnt that, though vastly outnumbered, Pakistani soldiers fought like cornered tigers on the eastern front. They were not only containing the Bengalis but also throwing back wave after wave of Indian soldiers. Heroic though the troops were, they were surpassed in bravery by the air force, which brought down dozens of Indian fighters in the space of a few days. When the radio was not reporting on the war, it was playing rousing military songs. Laila and Sara soon grew familiar with Noor Jehan's patriotic anthems.

Despite the media's best efforts to rouse nationalistic fervour, those were anxious days for almost everyone. They were particularly worrying for the people whose relatives were fighting in East Pakistan. Barkat grew quiet and apprehensive as the casualty reports trickled in. But the days slipped by with no news of Shareef.

They grew used to the black-outs at night and, once, when an air-raid siren sounded at midday, Fareeda rushed the girls into the trench. But after half an hour's uneventful wait, they emerged feeling cramped, cold and bored and went back to their business with a mild sense of deflation.

And then a week later, while the girls were at breakfast with their parents, Fazal bustled into the dining room with a pot of tea. As a rule, Fazal never bustled. He considered it beneath his dignity to do so. If he was in a hurry, he glided a little faster than normal. But, today, he was definitely bustling and, had the family been at all attentive, they would no doubt have noticed his flushed face.

But Tariq was helping himself to some toast and did not register. Nor did Sara, who was busy twisting long gloopy threads of honey around her spoon. As for Fareeda, her attention was focused on her younger daughter, who was listlessly pushing an uneaten fried egg around her plate. The girl had not eaten a single proper meal since Rani's death, Fareeda reckoned.

So no one reacted when Fazal took a step back, pulled himself erect and, clasping his hands behind his back, cleared his throat portentously. Miffed, he announced in a loud voice:

'Sahib, last night a bomb fell on the farm.'

'A bomb?' squealed Sara. 'Where, when? Oh, please, can I see it?'

'What are you talking about, Fazal?' asked Tariq.

'A bomb, Sahib. It fell on the farm last night. Midway between here and the milk factory. The Indians dropped it.'

'A *bomb*? Surely we would have heard a bomb?'

'It was a bomb all right, Sahib. This big it was.' Fazal stretched out his arms. 'But it didn't make a sound. Or do any damage. All it gave off was light, bright as noon.'

Now that Fazal mentioned it, Tariq recalled that he had woken up suddenly in the night. He thought he'd heard a humming sound, but by the time he'd sat up in bed, he couldn't hear it any more. His bedside clock said five-thirty. Too early to get up. So he'd pulled the covers up again and gone back to sleep.

'Who told you?' he asked Fazal.

'Samuel Masih, Sahib. He's Bua's cousin. The bomb fell thirty yards from his hut.'

'By the big peepul tree?' piped up Laila. 'I know the place. Bua took me there.'

Sara shot her an envious look across the table.

'Exactly!' Fazal nodded.

'And the bomb, what's happened to it?' asked Tariq.

'It's lying where it fell, Sahib.'

'Isn't that dangerous? Suppose it goes off?' Fareeda wondered aloud.

'Oh, no, Bibi,' laughed Fazal cheerfully. 'It won't. Samuel's children have been rolling it around all morning and nothing's happened.'

'Oh, for heaven's sake . . .'

'From Fazal's description, I guess what they dropped was a light bomb,' explained Tariq. 'It acts like a giant flare, illuminating the terrain down below and allowing pilots to assess whether there is any target worth engaging. They probably saw open country and realized it wasn't worth their trouble. The bomb's already done its work, so it won't explode, if that's what you are worried about, Fareeda.' Addressing Fazal, Tariq asked, 'Are you sure that was the only bomb that was dropped?'

'Yes, Sahib. Samuel had a good look around as soon as the sun came up. He says there's nothing else. The cane's been cut now, so it's easy to see. But if you want, you can ask him yourself.'

'Is he here?'

'He's having tea in the pantry.'

There was a crescent of servants gathered around Bua's cousin as he sipped tea from a glass and regaled them with colourful details about the bombing. He was relishing this rare attention and embroidering the story for his rapt audience.

'Then I shook my fist at the pilot and shouted, "Begone! Get out of here, you coward!"' he said. 'Far up in his plane he heard me. Small chap he was, with a bald head and goggle eyes, and you should have seen how his teeth chattered with fear! I heard them all the way down in my field. Then I hollered at him again, and he scooted off like a pigeon in front of a cat.'

Samuel snapped his fingers, to indicate the speed with which the Indian fled, and laughed raucously, displaying his rotten teeth to his admiring audience. Basking in his reflected glory, Bua placed a possessive hand on Samuel's shoulder and smirked. Just then, Tariq, tailed by his family and Fazal, entered the pantry. Immediately the crescent dispersed.

'Now what's this I hear about a bomb near your hut?' asked Tariq.

Samuel Masih got to his feet and salaamed. Cracking his knuckles, he began his story.

'Well, Sahib, the day before I'd gone to sleep with a pain in my neck. Ever since my heifer drowned in the canal three weeks ago, I've had this nagging pain . . .'

'Tell me from the point when the bombers came,' Tariq cut in. He was familiar with the peasant habit of prefacing a story with the events of the month before.

Samuel began again. He woke before dawn and came out of his hut to milk his buffalo. He heard a humming sound, with a sort of rumbling throb to it. He looked up and saw two dark shapes in the sky. The planes were flying low. The one at the front released a big white bubble. As it floated down slowly, there was a soundless explosion of light. It was so bright that he could see the hairs on the backs of his hands. The light, he realized, was coming from the cylindrical object hanging from the bubble. The planes did a couple of turns and flew off. Gradually, the light dimmed and went out altogether. When the sun came up, he examined the cylinder that had landed just a few paces from his house. It was like an iron log and, though easy to roll, it was heavy to lift. The bubble, he saw, was actually like a soft, silky umbrella, attached to the cylinder with ropes.

'I thought you should know, Sahib, you owning all the land around, I mean.' He lowered his eyes respectfully.

'You did right, Sami,' murmured Bua from the sidelines. 'I'm sure Tariq Sahib will remember your loyalty.'

'Has anyone other than your family seen the bomb yet?' asked Tariq.

Samuel Masih shook his head.

'I suppose I'd better let the colonel know.'

'What can he do?' asked Fareeda.

'I'm surmising it's a light bomb, but it would make sense to get his chaps to check it.'

'Oh, please can we check it too?' Sara pulled on her father's sleeve. 'Please? I've never seen a bomb before.'

'I suppose there's no harm in having a look.'

Fareeda looked unsure. 'Is that a good idea?'

'I'm pretty certain it's harmless. But just to be on the safe side, we'll park far away and wait for the colonel's men to give the all clear before going anywhere near. OK?'

'Yes!' Sara punched the air.

'Now, Samuel, you go home and wait for us,' Tariq instructed. 'We'll follow in the car as soon as I've spoken to the colonel.'

The colonel sounded harried on the phone.

'Yes, what is it?' he barked, after the most minimal of greetings.

Tariq informed him about the bomb.

'I think,' he continued mildly, 'that it poses no immediate danger. It's most likely just a light bomb . . .'

'Let *us* be the judge of that, Tariq Sahib,' the colonel cut in. 'You stay put in your house and leave the bomb to us. We'll be there directly.' The line went dead.

'Rude bastard!' muttered Tariq. If there had been any doubt

in his mind about going out to the bombsite before, it was erased by their exchange. He would *not* take orders from some prat in uniform. Piling his family into the car, he told Barkat to drive out there immediately.

'And put your foot on it! I want to get there before he does!'

In the event, the Zephyr got there well before the colonel's jeep. Barkat parked the car a couple of hundred yards from Samuel's hut. A crowd of villagers had gathered around the site. Despite Fareeda's protestations, Tariq strode off with an eager Barkat to see the bomb. Ignoring Sara's pleas to be allowed to accompany Tariq, Fareeda permitted the girls to come out of the car. Sara immediately trained Laila's binoculars on the crowd near the hut.

'Yes, I can see Aba bending towards the ground,' she commented. 'I think he's touching the bomb. Ooh, lucky him. Now he's walking off into the fields. Bua's cousin's with him.'

'Yes, it's a light bomb,' Tariq confirmed on his return. 'There doesn't seem to be any other bomb. Still, you'd better wait here till the soldiers come.'

A few minutes later, a cavalcade of military vehicles swept past them in a blur of khaki tarpaulin and camouflage paint and came to a halt beside the hut. Amid thudding of car doors and loud shouted commands, a dozen troops jumped out of the jeeps and sprinted towards the gathered villagers and shooed them aside. Some soldiers bent down to examine the bomb while others fanned out into the adjacent fields for a recce. From his vantage point by the car, Tariq could make out the colonel in the knot by the bomb.

Half an hour later, all the soldiers reassembled by the hut. They conferred briefly and then dispersed. Once more, doors were slammed, engines gunned and then, reversing smartly, they drew up back towards the Zephyr. Tariq leaned against its bonnet, his arms crossed nonchalantly across his chest. The colonel alighted from the passenger seat of the first jeep.

'My men have performed a thorough check.' The colonel flicked his head back in the direction of Samuel's hut. 'Aside from the one bomb near the hut, they've found nothing.'

'Did you know about this raid?' asked Fareeda.

'Of course!' insisted the colonel. 'The planes flew over the cantonment at precisely five-thirteen. The light bomb was no doubt meant for us, but the pilot misjudged his target.'

'So then it *is* a light bomb?' asked Tariq.

The colonel reddened.

'It would seem so,' he muttered.

'Only *seem* so?' Tariq raised his eyebrows in simulated surprise. 'I thought your men had performed a thorough check? But, if there is still some doubt, then I'd better not let my daughters go near. If your men are not competent to give us an all clear, then we'd better . . .'

'*Of course*, they are competent,' barked the colonel. 'It's just a shell of a light bomb, nothing more. For all I care, you can cart it back home and display it in your sitting room.'

'But being simple-minded civilians, we were not to know that, now were we?' said Tariq silkily. He noted with great satisfaction that a pulse was beating in the colonel's temple. 'We were told – *ordered* – to stay well back, and that is what we did.'

The colonel glared at Tariq and marched back to the jeep. At his terse order, the cavalcade roared off in a cloud of dust. Tariq grinned as he watched it bounce across the empty fields.

At Sara's insistence, Barkat dragged the bombshell back to the car and heaved it into the boot. It was about the size of an umbrella stand. On the way home, Sara was full of suggestions as to its proper display. They could hoist it above the mantelpiece perhaps or build a plinth for it in the yard or, better still, on the front lawn. They could put a plaque on the plinth noting the date it fell.

At Sabzbagh, the entire population of the Azeems' staff

342

quarters turned out to see the bomb. Displayed like a trophy in the backyard by Barkat and Sara, it was the object of much wonder and comment.

'Imagine, such a small thing lighting up the whole world!' whispered Barkat's wife.

'Did you hear Bua's cousin chased off two whole planes bristling with Indian soldiers single-handedly?' said Amanat's son.

'It was going to explode, oh, yes, that's what the Indians wanted, but the minute the bomb touched this country's sacred soil, it lay down like a lamb,' commented Rehmat's son-in-law.

There were no further air raids and no more bombs in Sabzbagh. But the fighting, they heard, was fierce in Sulei-mankee, thirty miles away at the border. Still, the radio bulletins were resolutely upbeat and spoke of the courageous advance of Pakistani forces. Then, one afternoon, a programme of stirring songs was interrupted by an urgent announcement: Dhaka had fallen. The Pakistani army had surrendered. That day, the girls saw their father cry for the second time in their lives. The first had been when he had buried Rani.

Over the next couple of days, Barkat learnt that Shareef's unit had also surrendered. Since they did not receive word of his death, Barkat concluded that his son must be one of the 93,000 Pakistani troops taken prisoners-of-war.

'I never expected this, Sahib,' he said to Tariq, as he drove him towards Colewallah. 'I come from a village of soldiers and, though we all know that martyrdom is an honour, I dreaded receiving that telegram telling me that my boy had died fighting. That was my worst fear. I never for a moment thought he would lay down his arms meekly like a girl. Death, I think, would have been preferable to this disgrace,' he said in a voice thick with emotion. 'How will I ever live down this shame, this stain on our honour?'

Tariq looked out at the countryside flashing by. The fields which until recently had been tall with cane were now freshly ploughed to receive the new seed. The ploughed furrows were a deep rich brown.

'Oh, I don't think death is preferable to disgrace, Barkat,' said Tariq, recalling Rani's face on the operating table. 'If it was my child, I'd take disgrace over death any day. People make too much of disgrace.'

Later that afternoon, Laila wandered in the garden by herself. Sara had gone with their father to Bridgebad to choose the long-promised foal. Tariq had planned the trip by way of a treat to cheer up the girls. But, claiming a headache, Laila had begged off. She had no enthusiasm left for foals or even dogs. Bua was at the church and Fareeda was on the veranda dealing with a villager's request for some winter clothes.

Laila went to watch the gardeners fill in the trench that Barkat had helped dig. On the day of the surrender, Barkat had picked up the bombshell and, with tears streaming down his face, had hurled it into the trench. It had lain there for three days, taunting them all with its dark metallic gleam, until Fareeda had wearily instructed Amanat to fill the trench.

There was a new boy working alongside Amanat. He seemed unsure of what to do and from time to time darted a quick glance at Amanat to follow his movements. Each time he caught Laila's eye, he blushed and looked down. Watching them smooth over the soft brown earth, Laila was reminded of Rani's grave.

She was about to walk away when a hand touched her lightly on the shoulder. Looking up, she saw Fareeda. Just a short while ago, Laila would have smiled and even slung an arm around her mother's waist, but today she took a small step sideways, deliberately putting some distance between them. Fareeda noticed the gesture, and an iron fist closed around her heart. She wanted to scoop Laila into her arms

344

and hold her close, but she knew the girl would not allow it. Although Laila had not said as much, Fareeda was aware that she blamed her for Rani's death. She could see it in her averted gaze and hear it in her loud silence. Over the long, sleepless nights that had followed Rani's murder, that same sense of culpability had also gnawed at Fareeda. No matter how much she tried to reason with herself, she could not absolve herself of the guilt. She knew, rationally, that the rawness of grief would abate with time, but would she ever be rid of the corrosive knowledge that she could have prevented Rani's death?

But, more than her own guilt, it was Laila's misery that really tore at Fareeda. She could not bear the sight of that pensive little face, the dull eyes, the pinched mouth. She couldn't remember when she had last heard Laila laugh. Whereas Sara had wept and mourned and recovered, Laila had retreated behind an invisible wall of grief. She could be seen but not touched. Fareeda was at a loss as to how to pierce that armour of pain. She had never imagined she could feel so helpless with her own child. Now, as she observed Laila watching the gardeners, she wondered what was going through her mind.

'Laila? Darling? Shall we go for a walk?'

Laila shrugged. Fareeda held out her hand, but Laila immediately plunged her own hands into her pockets. Fareeda let her hand drop to her side and began walking. She was relieved to note that at least the girl was following, albeit slowly. Slackening her pace, Fareeda walked through the back-yard, past the vegetable garden and, coming around to the front of the house, she went down the drive. In a light voice, she talked of the change that winter had wrought on the garden. She pointed out the tight green buds on the kachnar tree that would burst into mauve flowers come spring. She commented on the smell of wood smoke, the arrival of the year's first calf in the village, the call of the black partridge, the lengthened shadows, frost on the grass. She wondered aloud what colour foal Sara would choose, what they would name it, whether Tariq's mare would take to it. Laila did not take the bait. Wordless, she slouched behind Fareeda.

Eventually, Fareeda, too, fell quiet. In silence, they walked past the guava orchard, recently picked clean of all its fruit.

'Can we go up on to the canal?'

Startled by Laila's unexpected request, Fareeda nodded.

The canal road was tranquil, as usual. On the far bank, a man drove along a donkey cart. The donkey had a bell around its neck. The soft, tinkling sound carried over the lazy, silken sheet of water. A kingfisher swooped over the canal in a vivid flash of blue. Leaving the tamped earth road, Laila went across to the grassy bank, where bulrushes grew in thick clumps. For a moment, Fareeda thought Laila was about to leap over the edge. She wanted to lunge after her, grab her by the arm and pull her back to safety, but she fought down the urge and, gripping her elbows, stayed where she was. Laila stood motionless, looking out on to the water. After what seemed like an eternity to Fareeda, Laila spoke.

'Did . . . did the soldiers find her here?' she asked, with her back to her mother.

Fareeda shook her head. Then, realizing that Laila couldn't see her, she said, 'No. Not here. Further down the canal, well past Sabzbagh.'

Laila nodded. In a low voice, she said, 'Good.'

Despite her inner voice advising caution, Fareeda blurted out, 'Why "good"?'

As if explaining something elementary to a child, Laila replied, 'Because I would never again be able to come here if they had.'

'I miss her too, you know. I wish she were alive.'

Laila spun around. 'Then why *didn't* you save her?' she spat. Her hands were balled into fists by her sides. 'Why didn't you *find* her?'

'I *couldn't*,' Fareeda cried. 'By the time I found out she was missing, she was already dead.' Then, taking a deep breath, she added in a lower voice, 'It wasn't as if she was hiding somewhere, waiting to be found. The night she left Kaneez's house, that very same night Rani was beat . . .' Fareeda bit her lip and looked away. 'Rani had a terrible accident, and died the next day. It happened while we were *still in Lahore*. By the time we got back, she was already dead.'

'She had an accident?' Laila echoed. 'She didn't kill herself?'

'No, she didn't kill herself,' replied Fareeda, meeting her gaze squarely, relieved that at least in this she didn't have to lie. 'Why did you think she'd killed herself?'

'Because of Heer,' whispered Laila. 'Heer from *Heer Ranjha*. She wanted to be like Heer, you see, and she even told me that as long as she had fun beforehand, she wouldn't mind dying. Everybody, she said, had to die some time. And then, then I thought.' She stopped and continued with some effort. 'I thought that perhaps she'd found out that I'd told her secret to you and to punish me she ran away and killed herself,' she said, staring at her feet. 'That's why I was hoping you'd find her, so I could tell her, so I c-could ex-explain . . . and say s-sorry.' Two fat tears rolled down her cheeks.

Fareeda gathered Laila up in her arms. Laila did not pull away. They stood locked together on the canal bank. A cool breeze rippled over the water and sighed through the bulrushes. A lone parrot watched them from a thorny branch above. Eventually, Laila stirred against her mother, and Fareeda reluctantly released her. Laila rubbed the back of her hand across her nose, and Fareeda realized that her own face was also wet.

'Here.' Carefully she tore a tissue in half, and offered one piece to Laila. Mother and daughter both blew their noses together.

'Laila?' Fareeda's ragged voice had a hint of entreaty to it. 'Laila, there's something I want to tell you. Will you listen to me, please? Because I think it's important that you should know this. Here, sit down next to me.' Fareeda drew Laila away from the water's edge and on to a slight, grass-covered rise on the bank. Laila drew her legs up and placed her chin on her raised knees. She sat apart, her face in profile to Fareeda.

'As you know, better than anyone else, Rani was a very special person,' Fareeda began. 'She was talented and pretty and loving and funny but, most important of all, she was spirited. She wanted to see the world, try new things, have adventures, explore, be free.'

'She longed to go to Lahore, to see all the shops, wear golden shoes . . .' Laila recalled. 'Even Rubina Cinema she liked so much, Ammi. She had a shirt made especially like Heer's.'

'Did she?' Fareeda smiled. 'Rani was different to her mother. She wasn't meek and submissive like Fatima. And she certainly didn't want a life like hers. I think,' Fareeda's voice dropped to a murmur as she reflected aloud, 'Had Rani ever been in Fatima's place, she would have left him the first time he struck her. She wouldn't have stayed. No,' Fareeda shook her head decisively, 'I can't see her submitting month after month, year upon year . . .' Conscious of her daughter's puzzled gaze, Fareeda collected herself. 'Rani was different,' she said. 'She wanted to lead a life of her own choosing. And she wanted to be free to make that choice.'

'What choice?' queried Laila.

'In this case, the choice of a friend. She told you about her secret friend, didn't she?'

'She did. She said he was handsome and kind and good. I

348

think he made her happy, because every time she spoke about him, she'd get a big sunny smile on her face.'

'But you know, don't you, that she took a big risk in making that friend and in meeting him in secret? She knew that if she were found out, she'd be in trouble. Kaneez would never have forgiven her. Even your grandmother would have been furious. She could have been removed from her school, beaten, even forcibly married off. But Rani thought it was a risk worth taking, because if she hadn't, she would never have known the pleasure of that friendship. Your friend was brave, Lailu. Although she had no protector, no support, she went ahead and did what she had to. I want you to remember this one thing.' Fareeda reached out and, taking Laila gently by the chin, turned her face towards her. 'Rani's life may have been short – and, at the very end, brutal – but in that short life, she managed, in very difficult circumstances, to snatch some real happiness. So we may grieve for her and miss her, but we must also be very proud of her.'

As Fareeda's voice lapsed into silence, she felt a sudden sense of lightness, as if an immense vulture perched on her shoulder had suddenly flapped its black wings and flown off. Up until that moment she had thought of Rani's life as a tragic waste. Fareeda was accustomed to measuring success and failure of any one life by its concrete accomplishment. Tariq's success was his factory, Sardar Begum's her bumper crops, Yasmeen's her model home. But now she realized with a jolt that, for some, the audacity to dream was a feat in itself. Rani's struggle was her achievement.

Laila touched Fareeda's arm. 'Sister Clementine said that Rani was dirty and that she'd go to hell, but Babu Jacob told me that Rani's soul was pure. He said she was innocent and good and God would welcome her. She was a good person, wasn't she, Ammi?'

'The best. The very best,' whispered Fareeda, covering

Laila's small hand with her own. She did not ask Laila when Babu Jacob or indeed Sister Clementine had spoken to her. There would be time enough for that. As there would be for the many questions that her daughters would no doubt ask her about Rani as they grew older and understood more.

They sat there in companionable silence, listening to the lap of water and the buzz of a solitary dragonfly. Their reverie was disturbed by the loud toot of a car. Across the canal, the Zephyr was jolting along the dirt road. Half hanging out of the back-seat window was Sara, waving madly at them.

'Look! It's them. They're on their way back.'

'So it is,' said Fareeda, rising to her feet and brushing dust off her clothes. 'Shall we go back to the house and find out how they got on?'

Thrusting her hands in her pockets, Laila also stood up and took a step towards her mother. But, as if suddenly recalling something, she stopped.

'Wait,' she said. 'There's something I have to do first.'

She turned back to the bank, where there was a small gap between two stands of elephant grass. Edging in between them, she reached into her pocket and pulled out the amber horse. Just yesterday Bua had found it lying under her bed. Now, Laila gazed at it one last time, memorizing the taut neck, the flicked-back ears, the delicate, outstretched legs. Gingerly, she stepped out on to the lip of land where the rushing water was just inches from her feet, raised her arm and flung the horse into its brown, swirling depths. The horse rose in a graceful arc, landed with a tiny splash and disappeared.

She watched the canal for a while. Then, sighing, she slid her hands into her empty pockets and walked back to where Fareeda awaited her.

'It's over,' she said simply. 'We can go home now.'

Epilogue

So, you see, I remember. I remember it all. The war, the defeat. Rani. How can I ever forget Rani? My friend, my mentor, my *partner*. I've tried to make myself forget. God knows I've tried. But I can't.

I was fifteen when I learnt the truth – exactly the same age Rani had been when she died. It was the anniversary of Rani's death. 29 November. A weekend. I was in Sabzbagh with my parents. From my mother's garden, I picked some of Rani's favourite flowers – slender narcissi, blood-red roses, black-eyed gerbera – and got Barkat to drive me out to her grave.

The graveyard was deserted. Instructing Barkat to wait for me by the car, I picked my way past the humbler section of the cemetery where the poor buried their dead in anonymous mounds of earth, to the richer, more prosperous part where, as Babu Jacob would have said, the 'affording types' were interred. My father had of course bucked the system by burying Rani among the wealthy corpses. My mother had had a jacaranda tree planted near by so that she could lie in its shade.

I brushed dead leaves off her grave and placed the flowers at her feet. As I straightened, I saw a man watching me. Small and emaciated, he was dressed in a torn sweater and grimy shalwar kameez. He looked vaguely familiar, but I couldn't place him. Accustomed to a respectful lowering of the eyes from the men of my village, I was annoyed by his unflinching gaze. I raised my chin and stared down my nose at him. His lip curled, and he took a few steps towards me.

Then I placed him. That rolling gait was unmistakable. He

halted by the headstone of Rani's grave. The colour must have drained from my face, because he laughed his old hyena laugh. The cackle turned to a phlegmy, consumptive cough that left him clutching his middle. When the cough subsided, he drew his hand across his mouth and rasped, 'I'm dying. I cough up blood. See?' He held up his palm. I recoiled from the sight of his bloodstained spittle. He rubbed his hand on his shirtfront, leaving a faint trail of blood on his chest. 'So I came to say goodbye.' He gestured to the ground, where Rani lay between us.

I had always imagined that if I ever came face to face with Mashooq, I would gouge his eyes out. And yet here I was, transfixed by a horrible fascination.

'I haven't been quite myself since your grandmother had me exiled. Then I fell ill. With no money . . .' He shrugged. 'Money or no money, at least I have the comfort of an easy conscience.'

'An easy conscience?' I gasped, finding my voice. 'You killed an innocent girl!'

'She wasn't innocent. She was carrying a child. A bastard.'

'So? What was it to *you*?'

He shook his head. 'I don't expect you English-speakers to understand our ways. Your father couldn't. Why should you?'

A thought occurred to me.

'How did you know she was pregnant? Who told you?'

He grinned, revealing several missing teeth in his pan-stained mouth.

'Can't you guess? Think!' He tapped his temple. 'With your expensive education, it should be easy for you.'

And then, suddenly, I knew.

It was at that moment that my life changed.

I told no one of my encounter with Mashooq. Not my sister, not my parents. This was my doing, my burden. As I withdrew into myself and later my work, they tried to reach me, to understand, to help. But I would not let them. Over the years, I saw their concern turn to anxiety, then anger and finally to helpless resignation. But they still try and reel me in whenever they can. This New Year bash is one such attempt.

Sometimes I suspect my father knows. Where I sense bewilderment, and, yes, impatience, in my sister and mother when they consider me, I see a particular compassion in my father that he shows no one else. I smile at him now and slip my hand into his. He squeezes my fingers.

'Can't you forgive yourself?' he asks. 'Whatever it is for which you are punishing yourself, can't you let it go?'

'Some things are beyond forgiveness.'

'Nothing is beyond forgiveness. There is no sin great enough. You have to let the past go. You *must* engage again, if only to ensure the same mistakes are not repeated.'

'And yet here we are, going to war with India again.' Even as I say it, I know it's a cheap shot.

'Are we?' He turns to me in the dark. 'Are we going to war? It may look like that but, believe me, it won't happen. We will not go to war again. If nothing else, we've learnt how ruinously expensive it can be.'

The sound of counting reaches us from the marquee. 'Ten, nine, eight . . .' The countdown to the New Year has begun.

'Shall we go and see in the New Year?' he asks.

'Can we stay here instead?'

'We can do whatever we want.'

We stand side by side in the dark.

Acknowledgements

In the five years it took to write this book, I was helped by many people. I am grateful to Aamer Hussein, Richard Murphy, Jugnu Mohsin and Najam Sethi for their encouragement. Thank you to Pankaj Mishra for his astute advice at critical junctures. I owe a debt of gratitude to Shomit Mitter, who stayed the course and gave generously of his time and insight throughout. To my brother, Mehdi, I owe thanks for refreshing my memory. I am indebted, too, to my enthusiastic agent, David Godwin, and to my editor, Juliet Annan, for her wisdom and keen judgement. My thanks, also, to the fantastic team at Penguin, who made the last lap of this journey such a pleasure. And, finally, to Shazad, my husband, my friend, my lodestar – thank you.